I0536489

HUNTER'S HONOR
A Novel of Suspense

BRENDA POTTS

Brenda Potts

TITLES BY BRENDA POTTS

Adult Fiction Suspense

HUNTER'S HONOR

Adult Non-fiction

ILLINOIS WHITETAILS

HUNTING DREAM JOBS

Youth Fiction Mystery

SECRETS OF TURKEY RIDGE

Children's Fiction Rhymes

THIS DEER

Coloring Books

ALL WHITETAILS

HUNT FISH COLOR

JOURNEYS AFIELD HUNTING & FISHING

MY HUNTRESS

WILDERNESS PRINCESS

WILDLIFE & NATURE

WONDERFUL WHITETAILS

www.BooksByPotts.com

HUNTER'S HONOR is a work of fiction. Names, characters, places and incidents are the product of the author's imagination or are used in a fictional manner. Any resemblance to actual events, locales, persons (living or dead) is coincidental and not intended.

This book contains adult situations and language that may not be suitable for young readers.

Copyright 2019. All rights reserved.

ISBN 13: 978-0-9991003-2-5

Published by Midwest Legacy Marketing

www.BooksByPotts.com

Cover Design by Brenda Potts

Front Cover Art by Brenda Potts

Back Cover Photo – Whitetail Buck in a Frosty Field by rogertrentham from iStock 178525089

**DEDICATED TO
STAN POTTS**

**SPECIAL THANKS TO
SHIRLEY SIMMERING**

Brenda Potts

KING JAMES VERSION
NUMBERS 30:2

"If a man vow a vow unto the LORD,

or swear an oath to bind his soul with a bond;

he shall not break his word,

he shall do according to all that

proceedeth out of his mouth."

ONE

Shiloh Lawson shut off the engine and watched in the beam of her headlights as billowy clouds of dust from the dead end, gravel road began to settle around her truck.

When the lights went out it took time for her eyes to adjust to the darkness around her. The cuticle shaped moon provided little light.

She hesitated, struggling with an irrational fear, not of the dark, but of the family whose land bordered hers. Too stubborn to give up her favorite hunting area, she turned the dial to prevent the truck's internal lights from coming on before opening the door of her white, crew cab Chevy Silverado. The cool air rushed in to caress her face.

She paused, listening to the silence. "Winter is a long time going," she whispered to herself.

Legal shooting time was still several minutes away. She shivered and zipped up her jacket before sliding out of the truck.

A great horned owl hooted in the distance. Another one

9

answered it. The familiar sound eased her mind.

She pushed away negative thoughts and let the calling fill her heart. That same calling had pulled her from a warm bed. It had reached into her soul and pulled her to the woods. It was something ethereal that words failed to explain. Only another hunter would understand.

She twisted her shoulder length, auburn hair into a pony tail, readjusted her cap and slowly closed the door, careful not to make too much noise.

Although she had roosted turkeys along the distant field edge the night before, there could be others within hearing distance. A life-long hunter, being quiet in the woods came natural to her.

Already dressed in full camouflage, she retrieved her camo turkey vest from the back seat and slipped it on over her jacket. She unzipped the brown canvas and leather gun case and pulled out her twenty gauge shotgun. The weight of the gun felt natural, hanging by its sling, over her left shoulder. The single shot TC Encore had been a gift from her father on her thirteenth birthday. It patterned well out to fifty yards and she had confidence in it.

Birds were not yet chirping, but it wouldn't be long before daylight brought new life. Spring was winning; slowly easing winter back into its proper place as the seasons fought over control of the land.

Hardwood timber on either side of the road hid her approach to the field. She kept to the middle of the gravel road as she walked. The damp, dew covered weeds softened her footsteps, making her approach to the field edge as quiet as possible. She wore knee-high rubber boots whether deer, squirrel or turkey hunting, just like her dad had always done.

She didn't need a flashlight. The trek was familiar. Shiloh had hunted on their western Kentucky farm with her family most of her life. Sadly, she lost her father to cancer at an early age. Her older brother Syder, moved west not long after he shot and killed one of the Dugan brothers. It was a long story. One that Shiloh played over in her mind all too often.

When she reached the metal gate she stood in silence to listen and survey the grassy meadow. A marshy area filled the center of the bowl-shaped field. The sun was beginning to glow on the eastern horizon. There was barely enough light to make out the dark, black, shapes of her uncle's cows scattered throughout the two hundred acre pasture surrounded by barbed wire. Shiloh unlocked the gate and opened it just enough to step through, careful not to show herself in the open. She closed the gate, thankful she had taken time the night before to spray lubricant on the hinges to stop them from squeaking.

She stood quietly next to a big, white oak tree. Her uncle once told her the great hardwood was estimated to be more than two hundred years old. It had been a sapling when her ancestors arrived on the farm. It was the matriarch of a giant stand of oak, hickory, walnut and elm trees surrounding the pasture. A diverse mixture of vegetation traversed ridges and creek bottoms for miles around her.

The Lawson family moved to Kentucky not long after the United States Congress made it the fifteenth state in 1792. The state's official symbol, a gray squirrel, was stirring in its nest of leaves above her. She sighed in disgust at herself for not looking up into the oak's mighty branches as she approached the field. She hoped the turkeys were not roosted directly over her head.

She loved being in the woods just before sunrise. The inability to see well in the early moments of the day somehow heightened her other senses. The scent of fresh earth and floral bouquets mixed with the odors of wild things, some pleasant, some not. A skunk had passed through the undergrowth some time during the night not far from where she stood.

Shiloh waited for the turkeys to begin their morning conversations from the treetops. From the first moment a big gobbler answered her call she had been hooked on turkey hunting. She loved hunting with her family as a child. Now, years later, wisdom learned from her father and uncle, along with experience garnered through hours in the woodlands, told her to wait. She had learned long ago patience was a powerful yet difficult component of turkey hunting.

As she listened for the first calls of her quarry, Shiloh felt a twinge of sadness. She missed her father and older brother Syder. They had hunted this field together many times.

When Shiloh had been born, in a bold gesture her parents let Syder pick her name. He was seven years old at the time and his big dream was to go out west to work on the Shiloh ranch with his TV hero. Syder was obsessed with the television series, *The Virginian*. After careful consideration Syder announced that his new baby sister would be named Shiloh. She was just glad the boy hadn't named her Trampas, after the top cowboy hand in the TV series.

Shiloh's mind wandered back to the night Al Dugan was killed. She was seventeen at the time, visiting her older brother at his apartment in town. Syder was living alone and working odd jobs to save money to move out West. He had been reluctant to leave once their father had been diagnosed with cancer. He delayed his move away from Kentucky when the doctors told them they didn't have many years left with their father.

Shiloh and Syder had been up late that fateful night watching yet another western movie re-run.

Syder brought popcorn to Shiloh. Her older brother was six feet tall, physically fit with reddish blonde hair, freckles and green eyes. He took after their mom's side of the family. Shiloh looked more like her dad, tall and slender, with auburn hair and brown eyes. No freckles.

At midnight a desperate pounding started on Syder's front door. He told Shiloh to stay put and went to look through the side window to discover a young woman crying and clutching her arms around herself.

Shiloh thought she looked terrified, and cold.

Syder recognized her and opened the door. He asked, "Becky, what are you doing here? What's wrong? Why are you crying?"

Becky Woodsen scrambled through the open doorway. She slammed the door shut and fumbled to lock it. She turned to Syder and sobbed out the words, "I can't get it locked, here, lock this, hurry! It's Al. He's gone crazy. He's been drinking all day. He thinks I'm having an affair. He says he's gonna kill me!"

She ran into the living room as if looking for a place to hide. Her bleached, blonde hair needed a touch up because

13

her true hair color, black, was visible at the roots. She wore a low cut, tight fitting, pink tank top that left little to the imagination, and a black skirt covered with pink sequins. The skirt was short, which left plenty of leg showing between the hem and the top of her black and pink cowboy boots.

Syder locked the door and followed her into the room. He grabbed her arm and forced her to look at him before he gruffly said, "Becky, you and Al are always fighting. I doubt he is going to kill you over this argument."

All three of them were startled when Al Dugan beat on the door. He shouted, "Becky! I know yer in there! Is this who you been running around with behind my back? Syder, I'm gonna shoot both of you fuckers!"

Becky wrenched her arm away from Syder and looked wildly around the room.

Al started kicking the wooden door. He fell over twice, but was able to get back on his feet and resume assaulting the door. He was balancing a beer in one hand and a gun in the other. Al was an intimidating figure, six feet tall and stout with a bushy brown beard and thick neck. He wore six-pocket camo pants and a black T-shirt with a white skull and crossbones on the front. His black ball cap was turned backward.

Syder whispered to Shiloh, "Get behind the couch and take her with you. And be quiet, both of you!" Syder grabbed his phone from the desk and dialed 911. While he waited for an answer he retrieved his Glock forty-five caliber handgun from the safe.

Becky started screaming obscenities at Al, which only fueled his rage. The door started to break a little more with each kick. If not for his drunken state Al would already be

14

inside, but he kept losing his balance with each try. Becky pleaded with Syder, "Please don't let him get inside. He's out of his head. He has a gun. I know he is gonna shoot me, I know it!"

Syder yelled, "Al, just calm down. Stop kicking the door. The police are on their way!" He looked at Shiloh and said, "Just stay behind the couch. I have the police on the line now they will be here any minute."

Al was oblivious in his drunkenness and more determined than ever to kick in the door. He kept at it, making progress with each strike of his heavy steel-toed boot. The door was giving way. Syder moved away from the entrance, and away from Shiloh, to the opposite side of the room. He intended to draw Al's attention away from the girls hiding behind the couch if Al succeeded in breaking through before the police arrived. Syder put the phone on speaker, placed it on the countertop and gripped his pistol with both hands and shouted, "Al, stop it! I have a gun and I will have to shoot you if you come through that door!"

"Officers are less than five minutes away," said the dispatcher.

To Shiloh, the whole experience seemed to play out in slow motion. Even though hidden behind the couch, she had a clear view of everything that was taking place.

Becky was face down on the floor, with her hands over her ears, crying and babbling, "Don't let him in! He's going to kill us all! He's crazy!" She kept repeating the words between sobs.

Suddenly the door gave way and Al burst through in a stumbling lunge that carried him into the foyer. He stood with legs apart, swinging the gun all over as if looking for a target. Al was holding a Smith & Wesson Governor revolver capable of carrying six rounds of ammunition. His finger was on the trigger. When his eyes focused on Syder he froze. "Where is she? Where is that bitch hiding? I know she has been coming here!"

Syder tried to keep his voice calm as he said, "Al, you're drunk. Becky and I are not having an affair. Now put the gun down." When Al didn't comply, Syder pointed his gun at him. "Al, we can talk this out. Al, listen to me." Syder sensed his words were making no difference so he raised his voice and warned, "Put the gun down Al, don't make me shoot you!"

What happened next was burned into Shiloh's memory with strange clarity. It seemed to play out in slow motion.

Al stood still, staring at Syder. He took a drink from the long-neck bottle of Budweiser and lowered his gun hand. He blinked a few times as if reasoning out the situation. Then Becky screamed and all hell broke loose.

Al threw his head back and took another long drink from his beer, while rolling his eyes in Becky's direction. He threw the bottle at Syder and pointed the gun at Becky. With a drunken punch of the finger he pulled the trigger. A bullet shattered the glass lamp on the table next to the couch, and buried into the drywall, missing Shiloh by less than an inch. At the same moment the airborne beer bottle spun past Syder's head, but he didn't flinch. Al swung the gun up in the air and shot at the ceiling. Then his eyes focused on Syder with a look that would have terrified a rabid dog. He started to slowly lower the gun in Syder's direction, about to take careful aim.

Syder shot three times. He didn't miss. His bullets hit their mark and Al went down as if he had been dropped lifeless from the sky.

The silence lasted two seconds, and then Becky began to shriek. "You shot him! Oh my God, you shot him! Al! Al, baby! Are you alright! Oh my God!" She crawled across the floor on her hands and knees toward Al's body. "You bastard!" she screamed at Syder. "You idiot! You killed him!" Becky threw herself across Al's lifeless body and sobbed.

Shiloh and Syder stared at each other for a moment. They were dumbfounded and in shock over what had just happened. Syder came to his senses and quickly kicked the gun away from Al's lifeless hands. He wasn't sure if Becky would grab it in her state of mind, which seemed oddly irrational after all she had said upon arrival at his door just minutes before.

Shiloh ran into Syder's arms. "You saved our lives. You had no choice."

Syder put his gun down on the table behind him and held Shiloh close. They stood together, trembling, as the police arrived and took over.

Syder was cleared of any wrongdoing. Becky told the Dugan family a wild tale that was nowhere near the truth. They never forgave Syder for killing Al and proceeded to make life miserable for him. The oldest Dugan, Henry, and his dad Hank, kept up a string of harassments. Syder's tires were punctured more than once; his dog was poisoned and various other aggravating misdemeanors finally drove Syder to go ahead and move west to pursue his dream of working on a ranch, just two months after their father died.

Although no one could prove the Dugans were responsible for the harassment, Shiloh and Syder were certain those two were guilty.

Fortunately not long after Syder left, someone called in an anonymous tip and the two Dugan men were eventually convicted of selling marijuana and several other drug related offenses. They each got hefty fines and prison terms. Hank's sentence was greater since he had a long history of run-ins with the law. He also had a storage locker filled with stolen property. He became violent when they came to arrest him, striking out at the police officers, which added years to his sentence.

The oldest son, Henry would be out not long after Shiloh's college graduation. His release could rekindle problems for her and Syder.

TWO

Shiloh was lost in thought when the first gobble sounded. It was a welcome diversion from old memories. By now she could see clearly across the meadow. A black-capped chickadee landed on a small tree branch next to her head, abruptly taking flight when she moved her arm.

With binoculars she could make out the shapes of a few turkeys roosted in the trees about two hundred yards away on the opposite side of the pasture. She lowered herself to the ground and used a rise in the terrain to sneak around the corner of the fence to set up her decoys. She pulled the decoys and stakes from the pouch in the back of her vest. She shoved the stake of her hen decoy into the ground and slid the rubbery hen in place. The decoy had several pellet wounds but still looked realistic. After placing the half-strut jake decoy near the hen, she crawled backwards out of sight.

She quickly unclipped the padded seat cushion on the back of her vest and tucked herself into the brush of a honey suckle bush with a large elm stump to her back. They had found many mushrooms over the years at the base of the elm,

19

but Dutch Elm Disease had finally toppled it. She hoped it was still too cool for ticks. Even though she had taken the precaution of spraying her clothes and boots with permethrin the night before, the devilish blood suckers were still a source of worry. She pulled her mesh facemask over her nose to cover most of her face. Luckily it was not yet warm enough for bothersome gnats and mosquitoes.

Stowed securely inside the big pocket on the left side of her vest was her favorite box call. The handmade, walnut, beauty was a gift from her uncle Jete, whose skills could transform wood into heirlooms, cabinets, tables, picture frames, or most anything. His signature and the date were expertly burned into the bottom panel.

Another turkey gobbled. This bird was to her left and much closer. Shiloh smiled. It sounded like a big tom. The ones on the other side of the field gobbled in return. Shiloh thought they sounded like jakes and let them repeat their symphony a few more times. She wanted to coax the closest tom from his perch so she began using her mouth call to simulate a hen.

The lone gobbler on her left was fired up by her soft yelps, clucks and purrs. He gobbled three times in succession before going silent. She heard him fly down. The thump-thump-thump sound of his wings sent Shiloh's heart racing when he launched from the tree limb to the ground. She could not see him, but a few moments later she saw the other turkeys fly down. There were six. Cautiously she used her binoculars to get a better look at them. She could see their tiny beards, none more than two or three inches long. "All jakes," Shiloh whispered under her breath as if to affirm her previous guess.

She had seen a small flock of jakes run off a big gobbler more than once, apparently emboldened by their numbers. She hoped these would not come her way.

Ten minutes passed. The woods and field were alive with the sounds of nearby song birds and a few crows off in the distance. Shiloh kept the shotgun ready, balanced expertly on her bent left knee. None of the birds gobbled on the ground. She could see the jakes. They were slowly walking her way. Shiloh grinned under her face mask as she watched them move about, remembering Jete's tale about the discovery of fossils of giant flying turkeys as tall as kangaroos that once roamed Australia. She wondered about the prehistoric origins of these Eastern wild turkeys.

Another five minutes passed with no sight or sound from the lone gobbler. She cautiously turned her head to the left to look for him. Nothing. Then she heard it. The sweet guttural sound of spitting and drumming came from directly behind her. The sharp spit "pfft" followed by the low, soft drum was unmistakable. This old tom was smart enough not to step into the open with those jakes nearby. He was trying to invite the hen to him just as Mother Nature intended. The gobbler's footsteps were noisy in the dry woods. She could hear him drag his primary wing feathers through the dirt and debris of the forest floor.

A pair of Canada geese flew overhead and disappeared. Shiloh began to worry the jakes would get to her decoys before the gobbler worked his way out into the open where she could get a shot.

Off in the distance she thought she heard a hen call. It sounded as if it was across the fence on the Dugan farm.

Shiloh wondered if another hunter had made the call.

The predicament quickly took another turn. From her right came a lone black coyote. Shiloh could see his bright yellow eyes as he trotted along. The jakes noticed the coyote too.

Their heads came up and within moments they were all running back the way they had come. Shiloh could still hear the gobbler behind her. Luckily he could not see the coyote from his position in the timber behind the stump. The coyote stopped as if deciding its next course of action. Shiloh hoped it did not know chasing the jakes would be a waste of time and energy. She hoped it would follow the flock of turkeys in the opposite direction. Suddenly, it noticed her decoys.

"Come on over here Wiley," Shiloh whispered under her breath. "This could easily turn into a coyote hunt."

The coyote stared at the decoys for several moments. It was one hundred yards away. It sat down, as if needing to think about this situation. Shiloh could still hear the gobbler behind her. It was strutting back and forth less than thirty yards away and slightly downhill. She wondered if it could see her decoys. And if not, would it lose interest and walk away? Luckily the gobbler could not see the coyote because of a slight rise in the terrain.

After what seemed an eternity, but was only about three minutes, the coyote decided something wasn't quite right about the decoys and trotted after the jakes. The gobbler was still strutting back and forth behind Shiloh.

The suspense of the hunt was whittling away at Shiloh's patience. She thought briefly about trying to get on her knees and turn around enough to get her gun against the stump and shoot the gobbler. She knew moving was a foolish idea; she would need to move slower than humanely possible and be completely silent. Shiloh argued with herself over what to do. Stay put or move? She decided if the gobbler started to walk off she would make a quick move and try to shoot him before he got out of range. Otherwise she would stay put. Thankfully, her wait was about to pay off.

The jakes had not run very far and gobbled from across the field. The big tom gobbled in return; abruptly folded his wings and walked past her less than fifteen yards away, right toward the decoys. She was afraid to blink. The bird was at eye level and close.

She had to let him get all the way to the decoys and begin strutting again before she could raise her shotgun. Sunlight hit the iridescent feathers highlighting shades of bronze and gold. His tail was fully spread and his head was bright red, mixed with hints of white and blue. The gobbler put on a magnificent display for the hen decoy. Shiloh gently eased the hammer back, willing it not to make an audible click.

When he cleared the hen decoy Shiloh took aim at the base of the gobbler's head and gently squeezed the trigger. The specialized blend of turkey load, with number five, six and seven shot could put an average of two hundred and ninety pellets in a pie plate at forty yards. Traveling at twelve hundred feet per second the pattern of shot struck the turkey in the head and neck, knocking him off his feet. The turkey started flapping its wings and digging at the dirt with his feet and spurs, but could not regain its footing after the lethal impact. Shiloh grabbed the spent shotgun shell from where it lay, smoking by the bush, and shoved it in her vest pocket.

Within seconds she was up and running to the gobbler.

She put her foot on its head until the turkey took its last breath and was finally motionless. She bent down to examine her prize. A quick estimate told her she had a mature tom with sharp, curved, two inch spurs and three beards; the longest was nearly twelve inches. Feelings of reverence, gratitude, sadness and exaltation swirled through her as the ancient ritual of the hunter-prey relationship played out in her heart and mind.

Shiloh arranged the bird on the ground with the beards clearly visible and spread the wings to display their beautiful pattern. She took out her cell phone and took a close-up shot of the spurs, then a full frame picture of the entire turkey lying in the green grass and texted a picture of the turkey to Syder. Even though he was several hundred miles away she knew he would be pleased with her success.

Shiloh filled out her harvest log, called in her turkey and recorded the confirmation number. She took off her vest and carefully stuffed the turkey into the large back pouch and smashed the foldable hen decoy in with it. The jake decoy would not fit. She tugged a mesh orange bag from the pocket and slipped the decoy and stakes into it. She stood up, lifted the vest and labored for a second to put it back on under the weight of the bird. When it was in place, she snapped the front clasp, adjusted the weight, shouldered her gun and headed for the gate.

When Shiloh arrived at her truck with the gobbler she tossed the orange mesh bag containing the jake decoy into the bed of the truck, put the tailgate down and gently placed her shotgun on the tailgate. Then she shrugged out of the heavy vest and placed it beside the gun. She worked to get the decoys out then shoved the gobbler forward into the bed of the truck. While she was busy putting her gun into the case on the driver's side back seat, the youngest Dugan brother stepped out of the woods, crossed the dry creek and walked up to her truck. Shiloh returned to the tailgate to rearrange the decoys and stakes into her vest pouch before closing the tailgate. She didn't notice him until he spoke.

"Looks like you got a good one Shiloh," said Klu as he came closer. Shiloh instantly went on guard knowing full well her unloaded shotgun was inside its case in the truck and useless at this point. She had her own Glock forty-three caliber handgun in her turkey vest pocket but did not relish the idea of another Lawson-Dugan firearm incident. She cussed herself for not taking the handgun out of the vest pocket immediately and moving it to her waist. She had a concealed carry permit in her wallet. She picked up the vest and slipped her hand inside the pocket and turned to face Klu. She didn't care that she might be overreacting by carrying the handgun. Lots of things could happen to a woman alone in the woods.

"Yes, I did. He is a good one too. Check him out." She stepped away from the truck as if to give Klu room to look at the bird, when in fact, she just wanted more distance between them.

Klu Dugan was the same age as Shiloh. At five feet, ten inches, he was an inch taller than her, clean shaven, handsome and muscular like a bull-rider. His powerful physique was not honed in a gym; rather it came from hours with a chainsaw and ax, cutting wood on his family farm, to supply the local campers and others in search of a cord of firewood.

Shiloh suspected Klu of stalking her but couldn't prove it.

Edges of their properties were separated by an unnamed dry creek bed that only flowed into Lost Baby Creek during heavy rains. It could be just a coincidence that he was out turkey hunting nearby, but Shiloh doubted it. She wondered what the chances were that she was hunting her east pasture while Klu Dugan was hunting the west side of his land at the exact same moment. His truck was nowhere in sight.

"Wow! Three beards! And look at those spurs, he's a real limb-hanger. That's awesome, congratulations." Klu said it so genuinely that Shiloh wondered if she was over-reacting to his attentions. Klu had never really done anything to threaten her, but she was biased toward the whole Dugan clan. Rumors of their suspicious activities toward Syder and their illegal escapades were common gossip. She heard they kept half-wild pit bulls around to warn off trespassers. She had seen a couple of the dogs running deer last fall but they had not noticed her in the treestand. Thankfully she hadn't encountered them on the ground.

"Are you hunting turkeys?" Shiloh blushed with the absurdity of the question. "Of course you are, why else would you be out here now carrying a shotgun?" she mumbled to herself.

"Oh yeah. I'm just doing a little runnin' and gunnin," Klu said lifting his shotgun as evidence. Shiloh doubted he had a turkey permit in his pocket.

"Well, I have to go. Nice seeing you. Good luck." Shiloh used one hand to close the tailgate and the other to hold the vest. She carried her vest to the front driver's side door, opened it and jumped into the front seat with the vest in her hands. She closed the truck door and pulled the handgun from the pocket and stuck it under her thigh. Then she placed the vest on the floor in front of the passenger seat and started the truck. She locked the doors, then waved as she backed up, turned the truck around and drove a little too quickly down the gravel road.

Klu watched her leave without saying a word or waving goodbye. He watched the dust boil up from behind her truck for a few moments as she drove away, then crossed the dry creek bed and walked back onto his property.

There was some disagreement over whether the dead end, gravel road was private or public. There was no street sign. It had not been maintained very well in the last few years and only lead to the spot near the dry creek bed and Lawson's east pasture. They had just always called it the dead end, gravel road. It had always been considered the dividing line between the east edge of the Lawson farm and the west side of the Dugan land. Both families used the road.

She shivered as she wondered where Klu's truck was parked and how long he had been out there. Had he been nearby when she got out of the truck in the dark? Shiloh's Bluetooth picked up her cell phone as a call from her brother rang over the truck speakers. She punched the button on the steering wheel to answer the call.

"Hey girl, looks like you learned a thing or two from your big brother about turkey hunting. Now what are you going to do with it?" Syder teased.

Shiloh laughed, "Yes I did learn what not to do by watching my big brother. I'm going to pluck him and save him for the next time you come to supper."

"The last time you cooked me a turkey it tasted like old

shoe leather that you boiled in a dirty bucket of rain water over a campfire for three days," Syder exaggerated.

"Oh you know that is not even close to the truth!" Shiloh said with a laugh. "It was a little tough I will admit. But I have a new recipe."

She didn't want to mention the brief interaction with Klu Dugan but had always confided in her brother so the words just came out. "I ran into Klu Dugan a few minutes ago. He walked up to my truck as I was putting my gun away." Instantly she regretted mentioning it, knowing it would cause her brother to worry. And she could take care of herself. "I don't want you to worry. I had my Glock in my pocket and he seemed quite nice. He never really bothers me, but he just shows up at odd times out of nowhere, which is weird."

"Weird, is an understatement. There is something weird about that whole family. And their girlfriends." Syder added the last part in reference to Becky and her wildly inaccurate version of what happened the night Al Dugan died. "You just keep your eyes open. Better yet, why don't you come live with me and Mary? We could use some extra help with the ranch and the outfitting business. We are getting several female clients and Mary can't always guide them. Our business is growing. You graduate from college soon. What are you going to do?"

Shiloh was so surprised by the offer she couldn't think straight. "What? Are you sure? Wait a minute, let me pull over." Shiloh stopped the truck and put it in park. The doors unlocked automatically and she quickly locked them back. She hated that feature on her truck. "So what does Mary have to say about this?"

"Hold on a minute you can ask her yourself." Syder put the phone on speaker.

"Hi, honey! Nice job on the longbeard. Now quit playing around in the woods and go pack your stuff. We finally finished the house and now that trailer is sitting empty right there in the back yard. You can live there and have your own place with lots of privacy but also be right next door. Syder is right. We need some extra help now and you would fit in perfectly. We would love to have you!"

"Uh, I am so happy to hear you say that," Shiloh chose her words carefully. "Actually I am really glad you think I would make a good guide and ranch hand. Really happy. Yes, really," she stammered. "I, uh, have been meaning to talk to you all about just that. Well, not exactly that but sort of that."

Syder took the phone off speaker and said directly to Shiloh, "What's going on? You are almost stuttering. Is that Dugan kid bothering you?"

"No, no, it's not that. I actually drove down the road a bit. He is nowhere around." Shiloh looked to make sure her statement was true. "It's just that I have some plans I have been meaning to talk to you about."

Syder waited a moment. "Well, are you going to tell me what the plans are or do I have to guess?"

Shiloh took a deep breath. "Ok, so, here's what I have in mind, or I mean, here's what I am going to do." She took another deep breath. "I'm going to start an outfitting business on our farms, guiding deer and turkey hunters. Mom is going to cook and help organize. And Uncle Jete is in. He agrees it is a good idea. The Lawson farms are well known for big bucks and plenty of turkeys. And we have Gram and Gramps' old ranch house now that the tenant farmer is going to retire and move to town. So, I've already been to the bank with the business plan and they approved a small loan for supplies, treestands, ground blinds, and a tractor for food plots." Shiloh paused. "Syder, are you still there? Did I lose our connection?"

"Yes, I am still here. You were talking so fast I couldn't get a word in edge wise. First off, I reckon you have thought about this for a while. You don't usually do anything without making a list and researching every possible angle. But I don't know many outfitting businesses run by a woman. Except for that one female elk outfitter in New Mexico, she does a dang good job. You are going to have your work cut out for you. Not that I don't think you can actually do the work. I just know guys aren't gonna accept this too easily. How will you get clients?" Syder asked with genuine concern.

"I have a booth reserved at the big sport show in Pennsylvania. Uncle Jete is going with me. We are working on the booth design now. I'm taking some of my deer head mounts. Mom put a photo album together. Between you, me, Dad and Uncle Jete we have killed some giant bucks on our farms over the past twenty plus years. And need I mention who currently holds the record for biggest and most bucks killed?" Even though Syder could not see her, Shiloh pointed at herself with a smile.

"No need to remind me, it's you." Syder said. "Well, I think it's a pretty cool idea. Dad always wanted the entire family to make a living off the farm. It has been in the Lawson family for three hundred years. I know he would want me there too, but we all know Mary needs me out here," Syder said with a laugh. "Go for it Shiloh. I think it is a great idea. Besides, what the heck were you going to do with a double major in Art & History?"

"Well there was no need to major in biology like you did since we both know that Uncle Jete knows more about nature and biology than all of those college teachers combined and he only has a high school education. It's as if I have been at the University of Jete my whole life, because every trip to the woods with him is a lesson. You should know that as well as anyone."

"Little sister you make an excellent case. I just wish you could draw then an art degree would make more sense," Syder teased. "At least you aren't running off to Paris to study painting or something crazy like that."

"You have a lot of room to talk, you ran off to Montana to work on a horse ranch."

"Well of course I did, this beautiful woman needed me. I married into the biggest horse ranch in Montana and now I get to hunt and guide for mule deer, elk, and mountain lion. Oh hey I almost forgot, we got two new hounds and we are going to offer lion hunts this winter. The population is getting really good here on the ranch."

"That is awesome. I've always wanted to hunt mountain lion. Maybe I will come for a visit and you can show me what you think you know about mountain lions," Shiloh jabbed.

Syder teased back, "Just remember if your deer hunting operation doesn't work out, we will always have a spot for you here in Montana." Then he changed his tone, "Seriously. I really mean that."

"Thanks Syder. I love you and Mary too. I will call you

later with more details. Right now I need to get this bird home and get it taken care of."

"See ya kid. Be careful." Syder hung up.

THREE

Shiloh daydreamed as she drove, imagining what it would be like to work on the Montana ranch with Syder and Mary. It was a short trip to the Lawson family farmhouse where her mother still lived. She took the turkey into the barn to process it for the freezer. Her mother came out to greet her.

"Hi Sweetheart. Looks like you had a good morning." Dorothy Lawson was three inches shorter than her daughter with curly red hair, green eyes and a quick smile.

"I did. This gobbler had me nervous for a while because he kept strutting behind me and wouldn't come into the open. He finally made a mistake and as a result, got to ride home with me in the pickup truck."

"Here, let me help with that."

Dorothy and Shiloh worked on the turkey and got as much meat from it as they could. Shiloh saved the beards, spurs and tail. She spread the tail and poured salt on the base of it and left it to dry on the top shelf of the work bench. She dipped the ends of the beard in salt and put them with the tail. Later she would set the beards into the shotgun shell and hang them from the leather cord she had in her old bedroom. She had been saving the mementos every year since she started turkey hunting. There were fourteen so far. Shiloh put the carcass in the back of her truck and washed her hands.

"I'm just going to run this over to the bone pile. Then I'm going home to shower, maybe do some errands. Hazard and I will be back later. Thanks for the help, Mom." Shiloh hugged her mom and got into the truck.

Dorothy waved goodbye. "See you later," she called as Shiloh closed the door. She took the turkey meat into the house. After cleaning it she put half of the breast in a large baggie and put it into the refrigerator. The rest she put into packages for the freezer.

Shiloh's grandparent's ranch house was just across the street. Shiloh drove her truck behind the ranch house and down one of the dirt roads to a large ravine in the middle of the farm. Her Uncle Jete called it the bone pile ravine. They had killed more than one coyote cruising for an easy meal of bone and scraps left from meat processing that had been tossed into the bone pile. She tossed the turkey carcass into the ravine near a cow skull. Buzzards and other woodland creatures would be feasting soon.

It was about a thirty minute drive to her apartment, which gave her time to daydream again. Someday she would find the time to go elk hunting. It was on her bucket list along with visiting the Terry Redlin gallery; shooting a trophy-class, non-typical whitetail with a drop tine with her bow; hunting a mountain lion and creating an oil painting someone actually wanted to pay money for.

When she pulled into the driveway of her college

apartment she quickly snapped back to reality. Her dog Hazard met her at the gate. Hazard could jump the fence but never did. She kept him inside the fenced in yard when she was gone for his own protection from other dogs that might roam the neighborhood. So far, there hadn't been a problem.

After living in the country and attending Cedarwood High School, Shiloh wanted to try life in the big city, which is what they called Findlay, Kentucky. Family friends had renovated the attic of their garage and rented it to Shiloh for next to nothing. She could walk to Findlay University and had a place for her dog.

Hazard was a mutt with an amazing nose and uncanny intelligence. He could track anything. They were often called in the fall to locate wounded deer. Hazard had been a gift from Syder. Not long after his dog had been poisoned and died, two puppies were abandoned at the shelter so he decided they should adopt the dogs.

Once again Syder got to choose names. He named his dog Duke and christened Shiloh's dog Hazard. Another favorite TV show. Shiloh was certain Syder watched too much TV as a child. Their best estimate of Hazard's bloodline gave him coonhound, bloodhound, lab and Australian shepherd heritage. He was long-legged like the hounds, with fur like the shepherd and a lab disposition. He didn't know a stranger.

Hazard let himself in through the doggie door, grabbed a couple bites of food and settled into his blanket on the couch. Shiloh took a shower and sat down next to him. It wasn't long before they were both asleep.

Klu Dugan finished taking care of the gobbler he shot after talking with Shiloh at the dead end road. He cut the breasts into pieces and placed the meat into a crockpot in his motor home to slow cook for the next twenty four hours.

Technically it was Al's motor home. After Al was killed, Becky moved into the Dugan family home with him, his mom, dad and older brother. She said it was too lonely in the motor home. Klu had asked Becky if she cared, and she had not, so he moved his meager belongings to the twenty-five foot motor home parked less than twenty yards from the main house. It was fully contained with wood interior, beige carpet and could sleep four people. The master bedroom was in the rear. It had a small kitchen with microwave, stove, refrigerator and sink. He hooked up to the electric service and water from the house. Every few weeks he drove to the local campground, spent the night and dumped the sewage into the septic system set up for campers.

Other than going in for meals, Klu seldom entered the main house.

After her nap, Shiloh and Hazard jumped into her truck and headed east toward her mom's house. Shiloh's college apartment was thirty-three miles from the family farm where she was raised. She took advantage of every opportunity to go home. The two story, white farmhouse had been in the family for one hundred years. Before her dad died, she had helped him and her uncle set up the scaffolding to scrape and repaint the wood siding, redo the roof and install new windows. She painted the shutters black. They added a huge wrap around front porch and a big deck on the back. Every Saturday evening she went home for supper with her mom and her uncle, Jete. When she arrived just before supper time the house smelled wonderful from the aromas emerging from the kitchen. She let Hazard out to run freely around the yard and outbuildings.

A few minutes after Shiloh arrived, Jete pulled up in his dark green, Chevy Silverado HD, crew cab truck. The Duramax diesel engine had its own unique sound. He entered the kitchen with great fanfare, removed his ball cap and said, "This morning I pooped out a pile of turds so tall a circus dog couldn't jump over it!" He then took a bow, stood straight, placed his cap on the back of a chair and sat down. "Hello ladies, did you miss me?"

Shiloh and her mom looked at each other and burst into laughter.

Jete's brown eyes sparkled. He grinned and said, "What? Don't you remember how great-grandmother Lawson used to give us a bowel movement report each day when she got to be ninety years old? Well, today I feel about ninety so I thought I would start informing you early."

Dorothy said, "You have been playing cards with that crusty old bunch of guys at the taxidermy shop again, haven't you?" It was more statement than question. They were quite used to Jete's bizarre sense of humor.

Jete was six feet, three inches tall and slender. He had a moustache and thick head of dark brown hair with hints of grey. His skin was leathered and tanned from many hours in the sun working the farm, taking care of the cattle and carving wood. His woodworking abilities were well known and much sought after. Whenever she encountered a stuck jar lid Shiloh always handed it to Jete. She delighted in giving him the pickle jar because he would always drink the juice and make funny faces when she was a little kid.

Her dad's fraternal twin brother looked nothing like her father, but sounded just like him. For Shiloh, it was comforting and heartbreaking at times to hear him talk. Jete knew this and often came up with outrageous comments just to break the spell.

Sensing the good mood, Jete decided to keep the entertainment going, "Yes, I did stop by the shop but did not stay long. I believe Mulch may have been working on a skunk, which reminds me of a story. Did I tell you about the time I almost woke up dead at the Cat Piss Motel?" Jete grinned.

"Oh my gosh, yes! Many times!" Dorothy protested. "You and Jack got into more trouble than I care to remember. Shiloh, never go to Kansas with your uncle. There is probably still a warrant out for his arrest after all these years."

Jete winked and looked directly at Shiloh. "I want you to know your dad and I did nothing illegal. In Kansas."

"How about Pennsylvania? Is it safe to take you to the east coast? We have that big sport show in about a month remember?"

Jete paused and stroked his mustache as if deep in thought. Finally he said, "I don't recall causing any problems in that part of the country."

"Good, relieved to hear it. Oh, I talked to Syder today. I told him and Mary all about our plans. He said it sounded like a great idea and wished us luck."

Dorothy sighed, "I wish your brother was here to be part of this new venture."

"Yeah, me too," Shiloh agreed quietly.

Jete cleared his throat and said, "We all know if it weren't for the king of the deuterostomes Syder would still be here."

Dorothy stopped stirring the batter and looked at Jete. "What on earth is a deuter-thing-a-some?" she asked.

Jete leaned back and looked at Shiloh. "Tell her honey."

Shiloh shook her head and laughed then replied, "Oh no, this one's all yours."

"If I must." Jete looked at Dorothy, leaned forward and slowly explained his theory. "My dear, when humans develop in the womb the anus forms first. This means that at one point in our lives we were all just ass-holes. Some people never fully develop beyond that stage of life. And old man Hank Dugan is certainly the king of the bung holes."

Dorothy grinned at Jete. "Well my, my, we learn something new every day don't we? I was blessed that your twin brother never developed your unique sense of humor Jete." She pointed the batter covered spoon at him and laughed.

"It's not surprising since we are from different zygotes," Jete said bluntly, as if no other explanation would be needed.

"Of course you were." Dorothy looked at Shiloh and shrugged.

Shiloh added, "I think Syder would have headed west someday regardless of what happened. It was always his dream. But I wish he was here too."

"Well now, are you sure?" Jete teased. "He might try to name our company something ridiculous like, Shiloh, for a baby girl, or Hazard, for a dog." Everyone laughed.

"So it's not like you have a lot of room to talk. Who names their kid Jete? What's up with that?" Shiloh's eyes twinkled.

"I will have you know my mother, your blessed grandmother, told me she could feel me kicking in the womb. She knew it was me and not Jack. So she named me after a dance move. Look it up."

Shiloh grabbed her cell phone and quickly looked up the definition of jete. "Wait a minute. How could she tell the difference in which one of you twins was doing the kicking?"

Before Jete could answer Dorothy chimed in, "Jack always told me 'jete' was your first sentence."

"But jete is one word not a sentence," Shiloh said, holding her phone up with the evidence showing on the screen.

"Oh that's where you are wrong my daughter. In Jete-baby-talk his words ran together so when he asked, 'Did you eat?'... it came out slurred together as jete."

Shiloh and Jete groaned in unison and laughed.

"True story, Jack told me, rest his soul."

Jete added, "Young Jack told a lot of tales. I remember the time he told me the reason it was raining was because all of the angels were crying over the fact that I had been born so ugly." Jete grinned as Shiloh and Dorothy burst into laughter.

"That's so mean!" Shiloh said.

"It certainly was. I'm glad you agree. Your father, my beloved brother was just jealous of my handsomeness." Jete rubbed his chin. "So what are we going to call ourselves? We need business cards and a sign and brochures and a web site and, what else?"

"Everyone has called this place Lawson Farms as long as I can remember. What's wrong with that?" Shiloh asked.

"I'm not sure farm," he held up fingers in aerial quotation marks, "is the right word to describe prime whitetail hunting. People might think we are a deer farm, or a high fence place."

"Maybe so." Shiloh shook her head in agreement.

Dorothy put her hands on her hips and faced the others. "What about Lawson's Hunting Adventures? It sounds exciting." She was wearing an apron over her jeans and T-shirt that read, '*My cooking is so good even the smoke detector cheers me on.*'

"Oh, I like that," Shiloh said with a smile.

"Sounds darn good to me too," Jete agreed.

"Well, that's settled, now we can eat." Dorothy smiled as she turned toward the kitchen counter. "Come get your plates before supper gets cold. If I'm going to be head cook for Lawson's Hunting Adventures I'm going to need your opinions on a few new recipes."

"We should make a rule that Shiloh not be allowed to cook during hunting season, or fishing season. All those in favor say heeeeyouch!" Jete scrambled to get away as Shiloh tried to pinch his ear.

"Very funny. I can cook."

"Just not very well!" Jete jumped back out of range of Shiloh's punch.

"All right you two, cut it out," Dorothy insisted. "Let me know whether you like this venison stew. And try not to get in a food fight."

Klu Dugan sat down at his table and opened his lap top. He started writing. For the past two years he had worked hard to monetize his blog. He wrote two stories about the turkey hunt; one for the blog and the other for his syndicated column in one of the few hard copy newspapers still distributed across the Midwest.

He didn't want his father or brother to know about the writing. Only his mother knew and she was sworn to secrecy. He wrote under the pen name of K. D. Oakley. With the money from his column and blog, along with delivering pizzas at night, Klu had been able to pay for online courses from the community college in Canyon, Kentucky. Just a few more credits and he would have an associate's degree in journalism.

When he finished the blog and the newspaper column he wrote a query letter to a popular hunting magazine to pitch the idea for a story about deer hunting in Kentucky.

He tried to send one query a week. The magazines paid much better than the newspaper column.

FOUR

Becky peered through the curtains in time to see Klu go into the motor home. She didn't think much more about him as she lit up a joint. Klu's mother, Charlene was not home, having gone to town to visit a sick friend and take her supper. Becky took a long toke, letting the marijuana smoke fill her lungs. She held her breath as long as possible and exhaled, blowing smoke on Chito.

Charlene's long-haired, miniature dachshund sneezed in protest and barked. This brought Queenie, Al and Becky's female pit bull, from out of her cardboard box. Queenie had three puppies and was always hungry.

"You hungry girlfriend?" Becky cooed at Queenie. Queenie walked in to the kitchen and stood near her dog bowl. "Okay girl, hang on a minute, I will get ya something to eat." Becky got up from the couch and kicked at Chito. The little dog jumped back then followed her into the kitchen. Becky opened the big plastic tub filled with dog food and poured a scoop into Queenie's bowl. Queenie stared at the dry dog food. She watched as Becky went to the cupboard and opened two cans of moist dog food. She spooned one into Queenie's bowl and the other into Chito's. Queenie gulped the soft food in two bites and walked over to Chito's bowl. Chito growled. Queenie lunged and grabbed the dog by the back of its head. With three violent shakes she snapped Chito's neck and killed the little dog.

Becky gasped then slapped her hand over her mouth to suppress a scream.

Queenie dropped Chito and gulped down the pile of moist food in Chito's bowl. She walked back over to her own dry dog food and started eating as if nothing unusual had happened.

Becky moaned. "Oh no, Queenie what have you done?"

Chito's lifeless body was in the middle of the kitchen floor. Pearls from her handmade collar were scattered around the room, many covered in blood. Blood was pouring from her head wounds onto the floor. "Oh crap, Queenie, you dumb ass. Look what you've done."

Queenie farted and walked back to her cardboard box to feed her pups. Becky stared at Chito trying to figure out how she was going to explain this to Charlene. The two dogs had been living together for a year with no problems. This sudden act of violence left Becky stunned. The joint was keeping her calmer than she might otherwise have been.

"Think!" Becky said aloud to herself. After a few minutes of staring at the lifeless dog she came up with a plan. Becky took a plastic shopping bag from the bottom shelf of the pantry and put it over her hand. She picked up Chito's warm, limp body and rolled it fully into the bag. She pulled a big bunch of paper towels off the roller and cleaned up the blood then shoved the paper towels into the bag with Chito. She gathered all the pearls she could find scattered throughout the kitchen floor and started to put them into the bag too. She hesitated, wondering if they were real pearls. If so, she could pawn them or trade them for some weed. Becky shoved the pearls into the back pocket of her jeans. Then she looked out the window to see what Klu was doing. The lights were on in the motor home but the curtains were closed and she saw no sign of Al's younger brother.

Becky hoped he would not look out the window as she opened the back door. She took the plastic bag containing Chito to the shed. Inside she found a garden shovel. She peered around the shed to check for Klu. Then she slipped into the woods, using the shed to stay out of sight. She went about twenty five yards and stopped. A few scoops with the shovel and she had a shallow hole dug. She dropped the plastic bag into the hole and filled it back up with dirt. She pushed a few leaves and sticks over the hole. After dragging a small log on top of the burial spot she walked back to the shed, replaced the shovel and walked into the house.

Becky surveyed the kitchen, pleased to find no sign of the violent interaction between the two dogs. She washed her hands in the sink. From the pantry she retrieved a bag of chips and went into the living room to check on Queenie. Together they finished the chips.

Thirty minutes later Charlene returned. She honked to let Klu know she was back and to come over for a late supper. It was almost dark and she could see lights on in the motor home.

Klu opened the door and jumped over the broken step of

the motor home. "I need to fix that," he said to himself. Then he walked to her car, opened the door and helped his mother carry groceries into the kitchen.

Becky heard them come in and rubbed her eyes. She met them in the kitchen with smeared mascara. "Oh mother, something bad has happened."

Charlene stopped taking cans out of the grocery bags and looked at Becky. "What's wrong Becky? Have you been crying?"

Klu watched Becky move to the opposite side of the kitchen table.

"Well, I let Chito out to pee a few minutes ago and she was out there doing her business. I watched her from the door. She was done and I called her back in. She started to come." Becky sobbed fake tears. She started waving her arms and hands to add to the story. "A big owl came out of nowhere. It swooped down and took Chito. It just flew off with Chito hanging. It disappeared into the night. I ran out and yelled at it, but it just flew off so quickly. It happened so fast. I'm really sorry."

Charlene stood with her mouth open not able to grasp the story she had just heard. Suddenly she turned and ran out the back door and screamed for Chito. She ran all over the back yard and into the woods looking for her dog.

Klu could hear her calling the dog's name over and over. He looked at Becky, who refused to meet his gaze and pretended to cry more. "Becky, you are full of shit. What really happened? I never heard you yelling out back and I have been home all evening."

"It happened just like I said. I can't help it if you didn't hear anything. It happened so fast there was nothing you could do anyway."

"Bullshit!" Klu took two steps toward Becky planning to shake the truth out of her but stopped short. Queenie had placed herself between him and Becky and was growling. "That dog needs to go Becky. You know it and I know it. She is mean now that she has those pups."

Becky reached down and stroked Queenie's head. "Good girl," she whispered in her ear. "This dog loves me and I love her. She is not going anywhere and neither am I."

Klu stood his ground, keeping an eye on the dog. "Al has been gone quite a while now Becky. You need to move on."

"Have you talked this over with your big brother?" Becky sneered. She pushed her bleached blonde hair back and thrust out her chest. She adjusted her tank top, pushing the strap back up on her left shoulder. "I think he might have something else to say about that."

"Why in the hell would Henry care about whether you were here? He's in prison. He couldn't care less."

"You sure about that?" Becky stood up. "Your mom never visits your dad, but I have been visiting Henry."

"What?" Klu was dumbfounded.

"Yeah. I go visit him. I write him. He writes back. He wants me here when he gets out. He told me so." Becky leaned forward so her ample cleavage showed fully and crooned at Klu, "Maybe you wouldn't mind me staying here either if you let me come visit you later."

"You are disgusting," Klu said, taking a step back.

They both stopped talking when Charlene came back into the kitchen. "I can't find Chito anywhere. I looked everywhere." Her eyes were wide with shock and filled with grief. Charlene was only five feet tall and somewhat frail in appearance. She looked older than her years, thanks in part to the stress of living with Hank Dugan and bearing four kids. Her youngest, a girl, had died in child birth. Charlene hadn't been the same since. Klu and her dog were the lights of her life. With the exception of always being short of cash, the last few years had actually been easier with Hank and Henry in prison.

"Sit down Mom." Klu pulled a kitchen chair out and helped his mother sit down.

Charlene slumped over with her head on her arm and cried. "Poor Chito," she repeated over and over between sobs. "My poor little puppy wasn't much more than a year old."

Becky guided Queenie silently out of the kitchen and into the living room. Both curled up on the couch as if nothing was wrong. Becky turned on the television so as not to hear Charlene crying. She stroked Queenie's fur and lit the joint again. She needed to calm down. The dog was devoted to Becky for some unexplainable reason and Becky loved that everyone else seemed uneasy around the pit bull. It gave her a feeling of power. She had never liked the dachshund. She didn't really like dogs in general, with the exception of Queenie. She wondered how old the pups needed to be before she could sell them or trade them for weed.

After supper Klu drove his late model, silver, Dodge Ram half-ton, pickup truck to his job in town to work a few hours delivering pizzas to the Saturday night college crowd. Klu didn't like the work, but the tips were good. They needed the money. His mom took in plenty of sewing but it did not pay much. He wasn't sure where Becky got her spending money but she contributed very little cash to the household budget.

FIVE

After supper Dorothy called Shiloh into the kitchen. "I was wondering if you had given any thought to moving back home after you graduate." Dorothy put on a new yellow apron covered in blue flowers. Shiloh marveled that her mom always wore lipstick and makeup and looked well dressed for any occasion, even covered with an apron. She had a collection of aprons and always wore them while cooking. She said it made her feel close to her mother.

Shiloh hugged her mom. "I sure have thought about it a lot, especially driving out to the east pasture this morning to turkey hunt. That extra thirty minutes in the wee hours of the morning was a pain. I loved living in town and walking to the University but I think I would much rather be here at home when we start working on the outfitting business full time. I could pay for room and board out of my wages too."

"That would be nice. We have good income from the cash rent of the agricultural land. Your dad left us in pretty good shape with the life insurance money but that won't last forever." Dorothy began washing dishes. "Even with your uncle Jete just a mile down the road it still gets pretty lonely around here so I am more interested in the company than the money. This big old farmhouse needs a few repairs too, so maybe we can work out a barter of chores for room and board, at least for the summer. We will talk money after we get Lawson's Hunting Adventures up and running."

"Sounds like we have a deal," Shiloh said, then hugged her mom again. "I think I will spend the night so I can be here in the morning when the food plot seed is delivered. Uncle Jete and I can go over the farm map one more time before planting begins. Plus I need to go over to Gram and Gramp's place and get that scaffolding out of the barn. I forgot to tell you my professor helped me get hired by the town council to paint murals on two of the county buildings on the old town square in Findlay. It's through some kind of historical preservation beautification grant. Isn't that cool?"

"That is very cool. Congratulations. I'm proud of you."

"I'm a little nervous. It's one thing to paint on a canvas but another thing all together to paint on the side of a building. The perspectives are going to be totally different."

"I see what you mean. I'm sure you will figure it out though, you always do. You are like your dad, always up for a challenge."

"Thanks Mom. I can always count on you for encouragement."

It was nearly midnight when Shiloh settled into bed in her old room in the two story family farmhouse. Posters from her high school days still hung on the walls. Hazard curled up in his dog bed on the floor at the foot of her bed. She had trouble shutting her mind off. She grabbed her phone and logged in to the town social media account for buy-sell-trade posts. She wrote a quick post about the furniture for sale from her grandparent's ranch house and promised photos in the next post. In the morning she would go get pictures of the living room furniture, china cabinets, beds, dining room table and chairs and a few miscellaneous items. The furniture had belonged to her grandparents but had no sentimental value. The family had long ago distributed heirlooms amongst themselves when her grandparents died.

For years the house had been rented to a tenant farmer but he had recently given them notice of his plan to retire and move to town. They had a new arrangement with someone else to farm their ground and pay cash rent for the acreage.

The remaining furniture didn't suit their needs for housing and feeding six hunters so it had to go. The carpets needed ripped up and replaced with tile, and a fresh coat of paint for the interior was on the to-do list. Her mom would handle that. The red brick, ranch house also needed a third bathroom but Jete had the builder scheduled for later in the month.

Shiloh drifted off to sleep content in knowing she was blessed with the support of a wonderful family. She was grateful that her uncle had stepped in to make such a positive influence in her life after her dad passed away.

Klu returned from delivering pizzas well after midnight. He lay awake in his bed staring at the ceiling. He was going over Becky's story in his mind. Although it was quite possible for an owl to take off with a dog as small as Chito, something about Becky's demeanor told him she was lying. He also had trouble falling asleep thinking about his deceased brother's girlfriend becoming his older brother's girlfriend. Henry would be getting out of prison soon. He wasn't sure if he had to go to a half-way house or would be coming directly home. It was his first experience with a family member in prison. His dad had been in jail more than once, but prison was a different situation.

Klu decided to work on an idea for an article about chronic wasting disease in the Midwestern whitetail population. He sat up and reached for his laptop. He could do some research and maybe get sleepy. Within minutes a knock sounded on his door. Klu looked out the window and saw Becky standing outside the door in a thin, white T-shirt.

Klu spoke through the glass, "What do you want Becky?"

"Klu I need to talk to you about something. I'm coming in." Becky opened the door and stepped into the motor home. "Gee, I like what you've done with the place. You keep it real clean in here." She flipped on a light and sat down at the table.

"It's late. What do you want? Are you here to tell me what really happened to Chito?"

"Look, the damn dog got ate by an owl. I can't help what happened. We've got bigger problems than that."

"What do you mean?" Klu closed the laptop and took a seat at the table opposite Becky.

"I was down at the tavern last night and Eddy was there. He wants the motor home back."

"What are you talking about? This belongs to Al. Or technically to us now that he is gone."

"That's what I told him. But he said that Al won the motor

home in a poker game, but that Al cheated and the thing belongs to him. Al never did anything about changing the title and now that he is gone, it's Eddy's word against ours."

"No way. Somebody else was in the poker game and knows what happened."

"Good luck with that. Most everybody is afraid of Eddy. You won't get anybody to say otherwise. He came right up and told me he wanted to talk to me. Said he could help me out now that Al was gone. I told him I wasn't going to need any help because I was Henry's girl now. But he insisted I find a way to get his motor home back. He also said that Ivan, his accountant, wanted to date me but I didn't want to play that game." Becky was hoping to see a hint of jealousy in Klu's eyes when she told him that.

"Well go play. That shouldn't be too hard for you. Why don't you just go pack your stuff and head on over to Ivan's place right now."

"You can kiss my ass Klu Dugan. I wouldn't go out with that creep if he was the last man on the planet."

"I'm so glad to hear you have integrity," Klu laid on the sarcasm as thick as he could.

"Whatever." Becky looked around. "What are we going to do?"

Klu got up and moved to the front of the motor home. He opened the glove box and dug through the papers inside. "There's nothing in here that proves Eddy might be telling the truth about this once belonging to him. Whether he lost it in a bet in a poker game with Al is going to be impossible to prove."

Becky stood up and moved closer to Klu. "Are you

willing to bet your life on that? If Eddy wants this motor home back he damn sure will take it, by whatever means necessary. So are you gonna move back into the house after you give Eddy his motor home back?"

Klu sat down and rubbed his head. "I don't know."

"Here, let me take your mind off your troubles. I'm not wearing any underpants." She started to lift the T-shirt.

"Oh my God Becky, you freaking nymphomaniac. Get out!" Klu stood up and pointed at the door. "Out!"

"Well fine. I can see you are upset. I don't know why you won't spend a little time having fun with me. It really would do us both some good."

"Out!" Klu flung the door open.

Becky walked slowly while lifting the T-shirt higher and higher. When she got through the door she stumbled on the broken fold-out steps and fell to the grass below. She landed on her hands and knees then started laughing. "I know you're looking at my ass."

Klu slammed the door, locked it and turned off the light. He crawled back in to bed and decided not to do any course work. Instead he closed his eyes and thought about Shiloh Lawson until he fell asleep.

Becky crawled into the bed in Al's old room. She thought back over her conversation with Klu. He didn't know the motor home was really hers. In reality it wasn't honestly hers since it was stolen, but Eddy had given it to her. She thought Klu spent too much time alone out in the motor home so she concocted the story about Eddy wanting it back. She wanted Klu to move back into the house so she could see more of him like it used to be when Al was alive. Now that Al was gone she desperately wanted his little brother. She had always had a crush on him. So far, he was the only man who had turned down everything she had to offer.

Growing up, as she began to look more like a woman it seemed to Becky that all the men she had ever known only wanted one thing from her, including her great uncle. Her grandfather's younger brother had stepped in to raise her when her father was killed. She had been thirteen. He always told her what he was doing was not wrong because he loved her. Becky was confused about love. She wondered why Klu was so different from the other men she knew.

It made her want his attentions even more.

SIX

The Lawson trio arrived at church a few minutes early Sunday morning. Shiloh excused herself to go to the restroom. Inside, she almost ran directly into Charlene Dugan.

"Oh my goodness, Shiloh, I'm sorry I just about stepped on your foot," Charlene said, placing a hand over her heart. "Let me take a look at you young lady. You have grown up tall and slender just like your father. I was sorry to hear of his passing. How long has it been since I have seen you?"

"It has been a quite a while Mrs. Dugan. How have you been? How long have you been coming to this church?" Shiloh asked politely.

"A couple of years now. I usually go to the second service but today I have other plans so I came to the early one." Charlene looked down at her shoes, then raised her head and continued the conversation. "I had to make a change, too many gossips at the other church. Prayer chains work well when everyone involved actually cares and prays. But I think it was getting to be more of a gossip chain. Anyway, you look wonderful my dear, God bless you and tell your mother hello."

57

Charlene made a quick exit and left Shiloh standing alone wondering about the whole gossip chain story. She quickly finished her business and went into the sanctuary. She slipped into the pew next to Jete as the music and singing began.

Shiloh had trouble concentrating on the sermon. Seeing Charlene brought back memories of the night Syder shot and killed Al Dugan. When the preacher finished his message and the final hymn of invitation was sung Shiloh could hardly wait to talk to her mom. She shook hands with the preacher and exchanged pleasantries with a few friends, then headed for the door to wait outside.

Her friend Maxine was already waiting for her on the sidewalk. Maxine was dressed in a beautiful two-piece, pale blue jacket and skirt that accentuated her curvy figure. Her dark curly hair was blowing in the wind and she kept pushing it out of her face.

Maxine waved at Shiloh. "Shiloh! Hey girlfriend, how have you been?"

"Maxine! Wow. Gosh. I haven't seen you in a while. How are you?"

Maxine took Shiloh's hand and looked her in the eye. "Shiloh I have something to say to you. I know we have been friends our whole lives and the last three years we kind of lost touch. Well, regardless of that, I still want to ask you something very important." Maxine paused and took a breath before continuing. "I'm just going to come out and say it. Will you be the maid of honor at my wedding this summer?" Maxine squeezed Shiloh's hand and squealed with excitement.

Shiloh's mouth dropped open. "What? You're getting married? You and Delmar have been living together for three or four years now, right?"

"Yes. He finally popped the question last month. We were going to elope, but I talked him into having a wedding here. His online car auction business has really taken off. He's doing really well. No more gambling and alcohol, he's been clean for three years. I know you two got off to a bad start during our freshman year, but he's changed." Maxine let go of Shiloh's hand. "If you need to think about it, I understand." She pretended to pout by poking out her bottom lip.

Shiloh knew, in spite of the theatrics, if she said no to Maxine's request it would break her heart. "Of course I will be your maid of honor, thanks so much for asking me." She tried to cover her lack of enthusiasm by hugging Maxine. "We have been friends since kindergarten and I am sorry we haven't been in touch the last three years. I stayed in college and, uh, you dropped out. We just sort of went our separate ways."

"I know, I know, we went to Las Vegas for a couple years. Delmar finally realized he wasn't going to make it as a professional gambler. Some stuff happened and we moved back home. It's a long story. We will have to get together and I will tell you all about it. Anyway, it will be a very small wedding with just family and some close friends. And of course our daughter will be flower girl. Wait until you see her, she looks just like a mini-me, it's hilarious."

"Good grief Maxine, this is a lot to take in, we definitely need to catch up." Shiloh waved to Dorothy and Jete who joined them and listened as Maxine told them the good news.

Shiloh was beginning to feel good about getting her friend back. They had not spoken since her big disagreement with Delmar. For years they had told each other everything. It was easy to slip back into old ways. When Maxine stopped talking for a moment Shiloh changed the subject and said, "You will never guess who I ran into in the bathroom." Without waiting for them to guess she said, "Charlene Dugan!"

"Really? I didn't know she attended this church," Dorothy answered with surprise. "I thought she went to the one across town."

"She used to but she told me she had to leave because the gossip was so bad. Probably about her, why else would she care? She looked really old and worn out too."

Dorothy gasped and pointed a finger at Shiloh. "Shiloh Lawson, you sound just like a mean-spirited school girl, what's gotten into you?"

Maxine chimed in to defend Shiloh, "Probably from worrying about Henry getting out of prison pretty soon. Rumor has it Charlene is the one who made the anonymous phone call that got Hank and Henry put into prison." Maxine nodded her head to emphasize the bit of gossip.

"Girls! Did you not hear one word of the sermon this morning?" Dorothy scolded. "Straight from the Bible, all about spreading rumors and gossip. James chapter three, verse five, instructs us to control our words, considering how a huge forest fire can be set off by a small spark. Remember any of that?"

Shiloh looked sheepish. "Yes Mother. I guess I was daydreaming. Seeing Charlene got me to thinking back on that night Al Dugan was killed."

"Well, I can understand that, but you still have no excuse for spreading gossip. Now, enough of this, let's go home and cook up a big brunch."

"Oh thanks Mrs. Lawson, can I take a rain check? I have to go get my daughter out of Sunday school class then we are going to my sister's for lunch."

Dorothy hugged her. "Of course, let's make sure we set something up."

Maxine waved goodbye and left, smiling happily.

To avoid Becky, and because conditions were prime for it, Klu decided to go mushroom hunting all morning. He planned on taking the slow-cooked turkey breast in for Sunday lunch with his mom, secretly wishing Becky would fall off the face of the earth. If he found mushrooms he knew his mom would cook them.

He walked straight north into the woods behind his house. New growth was everywhere on the forest floor. Redbud trees were starting to bloom. Mayapples growing in colonies with lobed umbrella-like leaves were spread throughout the timber. Klu knew that morels would not grow if the soil was too warm or too cold. It had to be just right. Old timers had told him when the oak leaves are the size of a mouse's ear it's time to look for morels. He knew to look for certain trees; sycamore, hickory, ash and elm were the ones he focused on most. If an elm tree had started to slip its bark and turn a yellowish green he would check it out.

Within an hour of searching his usual spots he found two hundred morels. He carried them home in a mesh bag and went into the kitchen of the main house. His mom was not yet back from church and Becky was getting a dog treat for Queenie from the box in the pantry. She was wearing a tank top and underwear and quickly adjusted the top when she noticed Klu.

"Well good morning. Looks like you made quite the haul." Becky waited for Klu to respond. "What's the matter?" she asked when he ignored her.

"Nothing." Klu dumped some of the mushrooms into the sink and ran water until the mushrooms were covered. He sloshed them around and used the sprayer to clean off most of the dirt and debris. "Just let these sit a minute. I'll be back to finish cleaning them when Mom gets home."

"I'll be looking forward to your return," Becky crooned as she moved to block the door. "Unless you want me to help you get showered up for lunch."

Klu rolled his eyes. "Not in a million years. Can't you get it through your head that nothing is ever going to happen between you and me?"

"Well I don't see why not. It's gonna be a long time before Henry gets out of prison. You don't have a girlfriend right now. So why are you being so standoffish? Nobody would know if we slipped over to your place, or rather, Al's old place, and spent some time getting to know each other better, if you know what I mean."

"Not gonna happen." Klu noticed his Mom's car coming up the driveway. "Mom's home. Now go feed that damn dog and put some clothes on."

Becky stomped out of the kitchen. Klu turned back to the mushrooms in the sink to finish getting them cleaned and sliced in half. He greeted his mom when she came through the door. "Hey Mom, how was church?"

"Well son, it would have been much nicer if you had been with me, but I won't hold my breath waiting on that to happen. I saw that Lawson girl, spoke to her for a few minutes. She sure has grown up to be a pretty thing."

"You saw Shiloh?" He stopped cleaning the mushrooms and faced his mom.

"Why yes, and why are you blushing? You sweet on her?"

Klu turned back to the sink. "Of course not Mom, don't be silly. There is too much bad blood between our families."

"Well, she spoke to me nice enough. I hope forgiveness is in everyone's hearts over that entire matter. Your brother was a drunken fool that night. I don't think Syder should have killed him, but we weren't there. We have Syder's version of the story and we have Becky's version."

"Yeah, we have Becky's version." He thought to himself about Becky's version. The more he got to know Becky, the more he was starting to believe Syder's version. He was certain there was no hope that his dad and older brother would ever accept Syder's story.

Becky eavesdropped on Charlene and Klu's conversation from around the corner in the living room. When they changed the subject to mushroom recipes she walked over to Queenie's card board box. "Hey pretty girl, mama just found out something," she whispered to the dog. "Our boy Klu has a serious crush on missy Shiloh Lawson. This is why he won't pay me a bit of attention. That bitch needs to go."

Queenie growled in agreement and gulped the dog treat.

Shiloh opened the door to her grandparent's ranch house. It was directly across the hard road from her parent's two story farmhouse. They lived on White Pigeon Road which ran east and west between Findlay and Cedarwood. She opened the curtains and turned on some lights, then proceeded to photograph items for sale. When finished she sat down to post them on the town social media page. It surprised her how quickly she started getting responses. Potential buyers made arrangements to come out that afternoon to look over the furniture.

While waiting for them to arrive, Shiloh walked out to the big barn behind the house and went in to look for the scaffolding she would need to do the mural on the town square. It didn't take long to find what she was looking for.

From behind the scaffolding a multicolored farm cat yawned and stretched. "Hello Ruby. You must be a pretty good mouser because you are fat as, oh now wait a minute, looks like you are quite pregnant. Come here kitty." Shiloh sat down on the barn floor and the cat walked over and began rubbing her side along Shiloh's leg. Shiloh snuggled the cat until it decided to go look for food.

As she walked back to the ranch house, Shiloh's phone rang. "Hey Uncle Jete, I found the scaffolding just where you said it would be. Are you on your way to the ranch house? I already have potential buyers coming out to look at the furniture."

"That's why I called. I'm running late because I found so many morels after church. It's going to be a huge crop this year. I went to the spot behind my house where I always dump the water that I wash the morels in. I bet there were fifty right there. I found another fifty along that ridge where the old elms are and a mother lode under that big sycamore tree. Anyway, I haven't counted them all but it's going to be a little while before I get there. I just want to wash them and cut them in half before I soak them in salt water overnight."

"No problem. People will be coming out all afternoon so I will be busy. Take your time."

"Okay, I might work on a few wood carving projects before I come over. See ya later."

Shiloh went back into the ranch house. She selected a book from the bookshelf in the den and sat down on the couch. Hazard followed her in and flopped down at her feet. "Hazard, do you know how long it has been since I read a book of fiction just for fun? Four years of college textbooks sort of took the desire right out of me to do any leisure time reading. I'm going to have to remedy that." Hazard snuffed as if he understood. Shiloh started reading to pass the time until someone arrived to look at the sale items.

Becky sat on her bed wondering why Klu would be interested in Shiloh over her. She ran a comb through her hair and added another layer of mascara to her eyelashes. She looked through her closet, unhappy with the choices, finally settling on a lacy black bra under a sheer white blouse and a pair of tight black yoga pants. After looking in the full length mirror she decided to tie the blouse up under her bra so Klu could see her figure more easily. "I don't know what he sees in that tall skinny tomboy when he can have this," she said to her reflection.

Charlene called to Becky from the living room. "Lunch is ready!" She served potato salad, beets and green beans with the turkey Klu cooked. It was shredded and slathered in barbeque sauce. Klu piled turkey on a bun and added some onion and more sauce. He filled his plate with food and sat down at the table. Charlene added a small pile of turkey to her plate and joined Klu.

They looked at each other, mentally communicating whether or not to wait for Becky. Klu scooped up his sandwich and took a bite. He raised his eyebrows up and down and grinned at his mom with a mouth full of food. She giggled and shook her head and started eating too.

Becky came into the room and looked at the food. She made a big show of looking for something else in the refrigerator, bending over and searching in the back for longer than necessary. As she closed the door she looked at Klu to see if he had noticed, pleased to find out that he had. A glimmer of hope swirled through her mind as she said, "I'm not really that hungry. I think I will just eat this yogurt." She stood with her back to the counter behind Charlene, looking at Klu. When she started licking the spoon seductively Klu looked down at his plate and chewed quietly.

Klu was mad at himself. Becky did have a voluptuous figure and she was showing it off just for him. He had fallen for her act for all of three seconds, but it was enough to give Becky the upper hand in that moment. He cleared his throat and asked Charlene about Shiloh. "So, Mom, how long has it been since you saw Shiloh?"

"Oh, gosh, years. Maybe at the funeral for her dad. She looks a lot like him, tall and slender with that full head of auburn hair. No freckles though."

Becky threw the spoon in the sink and dropped the yogurt in the trash as she stormed out of the room. Klu smiled.

"What's wrong with her?" Charlene asked.

"I think she has a case of the red ass about Shiloh. Shiloh knows what really happened that night between Al and Syder. The food is really good Mom."

"Thanks to my son, the great hunter," Charlene raised her water glass and whispered, "And soon to be award winning outdoor writer."

Klu grinned and blushed. He raised his glass and whispered in response, "Let's hope so."

By late afternoon Shiloh had sold almost every item posted for sale. People came and walked through the ranch house, chose what they wanted, paid for it in cash, loaded it up and hauled it away. The whole process took less than four hours. Now that the house was nearly empty of furniture it would be easier to paint. Dorothy loved to paint and was excited to get started.

Jete pulled in to the blacktop driveway and stopped his

truck near the back door. He entered the house and looked around. "Wow! Young lady you did well. I never dreamed you could get rid of most of the furniture because of a social media post, but you did it. I can get started ripping up the carpet this week."

"Here's all the money. Can you take it to the bank? I have to go back to school for one more week and then pack up my stuff from the apartment. Mom said I could move back home so I want to get that done as soon as possible. Oh, and they delivered the food plot seed this afternoon too. Said they were late getting it here because of some problem with the delivery truck. I had them put it in the barn. Hopefully the weather will hold and we can get it in early."

"I'm glad to hear you are moving back home. I'm sure your mom will be happy to have someone sharing that big old farmhouse again."

"It will certainly make things easier once we get started full-time. Did you bring any of those morels with you for supper?"

"Indeed I did. Let's go see if your mother will cook them up for us. I brought extra butter and flour just in case she doesn't have enough, because I plan on eating nothing but morels until I cannot move." Jete rubbed his stomach and they both laughed.

SEVEN

Dorothy was hanging a new hummingbird feeder on the porch when Shiloh and Jete pulled up to the house. When they joined her Shiloh asked, "Mom, are you seeing hummingbirds already?"

"Yes, this morning before church I noticed them flying around the empty feeder. So I mixed up some sugar water and am filling it now."

Jete poked Shiloh in the shoulder. "You know hummingbirds migrate on the backs of geese. They hitch a ride all the way south in the fall and come back with them in the spring." Jete removed his hat and walked into the house.

"No way!" Shiloh followed him inside.

"Think about it. Makes sense since their wings are just too small to make the whole trip."

"You are totally making this up."

"I killed a goose last fall and it had six hummingbirds clinging to its back. True story."

"Okay, I'm calling it! *Hunter's Honor?*" Shiloh challenged her uncle with the old family tradition.

"Alright I confess, it was total bull crap, a myth. Why did my mother have to invent that? I can't get away with any wild tales anymore," Jete said with a laugh.

Dorothy explained, "Well Jete, your mother was a wise woman. She had no choice than to come up with something. You and your brother Jack were telling so many wild stories by the time you were six years old she told you all about *Hunter's Honor*. From that day forward if you or Jack told a fib she would challenge you by calling out *Hunter's Honor*. And both of you knew what that meant - if you did not come clean with the truth you would never kill a big buck as long as you lived. To you kids it was a stronger vow than saying I cross my heart or I swear on my mother's grave, almost as strong as saying as God as my witness. I'm quite certain you still believe it."

Jete agreed. "Indeed we did, and do. And from all the big bucks we have killed you can see we never, ever tell a lie if challenged with *Hunter's Honor*. It's been that way our entire lives." Jete looked at Shiloh. "We passed that tradition on to you and your brother. He needed it more than you did. Syder could tell a wild tale in his day."

Shiloh tipped her head and raised her eyebrows at Jete. "Oh, really? I wonder where that talent came from." It was more of a statement than a question.

Jete's eyes were twinkling with mischief when he shrugged. "I think it was from Grandma Lawson."

Dorothy smiled and motioned toward the office, "Come take a look at these paint samples I brought home from the hardware store. Let's see if we can decide on colors for the ranch house. Afterwards I will get cooking on those mushrooms."

As the days passed, Becky fell in to a new routine. She slept until noon, got up to feed Queenie, showered, dressed and left in Al's old jeep. Becky's week was a profitable one. She drove a cargo van for Eddy. She didn't know what was in the back of the van and didn't ask. She just knew that at the end of each trip she was handed a back pack full of cash.

It was an easy job and left her evenings free to spend time at the tavern. Eddy had a big private booth in the back. She enjoyed the free drinks and extra joints he gave her. Eddy's other girls left the booth when she showed up. Becky liked that. It made her feel special.

Klu had no idea where Becky spent most of her time and didn't care. He resented that his mother was left to feed Queenie and her pups later in the day. The pups were getting bigger and could crawl out of the dilapidated old cardboard box. Klu made a mental note to fix up the old dog house behind the shed and move Queenie and her pups outside. The spring weather was warm enough now.

Before the week was out he killed two more turkeys and put them in the freezer.

Shiloh's week flew by. She spent time researching the town history and making sketches for the murals. She didn't have much school work because she had opted to do term papers instead of final exams. The papers were turned in early. For the past four years Shiloh had been taking summer classes and a heavy course load so her final semester was a light one.

She packed her meager belongings in boxes and moved a few at a time to the farm house. She didn't want a graduation party but knew she couldn't avoid some form of celebration.

Her mom was planning a big Saturday night feast and had invited several people. Shiloh was anxious to get started on the work needed for the outfitting business.

EIGHT

Klu made good on his promise to renovate the dog house and move Queenie outside. The dogs seemed to like it. Queenie stayed close to the house as long as Klu kept her dog bowl full. The pups snuggled in old blankets inside the box. Queenie went in and out of the dog house checking on the pups often.

Becky took one look at the dog house and shrugged. She was glad to be free of the burden of looking after the dog. Eddy told her he could sell the pups for her when they were ten weeks old. She wished Queenie had a bigger litter.

Klu decided to ask Becky something he had been wondering about all week. "I was wondering if you have seen Eddy. Have you heard any more about him wanting the motor home back? Maybe he would be willing to sell it to me, would you ask him that if you see him?"

Becky turned to face Klu. "I might be willing to talk to him if you do something for me."

"What's that?" Klu asked with dread.

"Let's go inside and I will show you."

73

"Becky, when are you going to stop this? I don't want to hurt your feelings but I'm just not interested."

"Why not?" Becky stepped closer to Klu. She stuck her bottom lip out in a pout.

"I'm just not, that's all." Klu took a step back, but Becky followed.

"What's the matter, are you afraid of me? I know I'm older than you but I could teach you a few things."

"No, Becky, that's not it. I don't think it's right for you to be carrying on with Henry while he is in prison and be waiting here for him to get out while you keep coming on to me at the same time. It's not right."

"But Klu, honey, Henry never has to know. If you don't tell him and I don't tell him, then what's the problem?"

"Well, it's a thing called morals Becky." Klu was getting fed up with her advances. "And you apparently don't have any."

"Since when did you get so high and mighty Mr. Morals?" Becky started to unbutton her shirt. "I bet I can make you forget all about your fancy morals if you just give me a chance." She closed the distance between them and reached for his belt buckle.

Klu jerked away from her grasp. "Becky, stop it."

"What's your problem?" Becky responded angrily. "It's that Lawson bitch isn't it? You got a big idea about her don't you? Well let me tell you something. She and the rest of the Lawsons don't give a shit about you or anybody from the Dugan family. They killed one of yours don't you remember? I was there. I saw it all. Poor Al just wanted to talk and Syder shot him in cold blood. And that Lawson bitch was there too."

Becky paused, but quickly continued when Klu didn't argue. "She laughed when Syder shot Al. Thought it was funny. Told her brother she was glad he did it. I heard her say it. Said he didn't have any other choice. Well, bullshit. He had a choice. Al would have calmed down if they had just let me talk to him. He couldn't hardly stand up he was so drunk. Yeah he fired his gun but he didn't mean to break that lamp. It was just a stupid lamp and Syder shot him over it."

"Becky, your story doesn't add up. Where were you before Al came looking for you? How did you end up at Syder's apartment? Are you sure Al wasn't following you and somebody else and that's what got him so pissed off that night?" Klu grabbed Becky's arm. "Tell me what really happened that night?"

Becky wrenched her arm away from Klu. "You think you know everything. Well you don't know shit." She stormed off, jumped in Al's old jeep and sped away.

Klu yelled after her, "Good riddance!"

With college behind her Shiloh turned her attention to the outfitting business and doing odd jobs around the house for her mom. While Jete was out planting food plots Shiloh designed the web site and other promotional materials needed for their upcoming sport show. She included general descriptions of their property and other information a prospective hunter might discover by reviewing their web site.

LAWSON'S HUNTING ADVENTURES

Cedarwood, Kentucky

Lawson's Hunting Adventures offers hunters a chance to pursue their dream hunt in the hardwood ridges and valleys of western Kentucky. We have 2200 contiguous acres filled with many trophy-class white-tailed deer and Eastern turkeys. We are located 30 miles east of Findlay, Kentucky in Helix County. Findlay's population is 150,500. The town has a university, community college, two hospitals, a mall and airport. We are also located 10 miles west of Cedarwood, Kentucky, population 1700. The town has a large antique mall, gas station/grocery store, mechanic shop, library, post office, community fishing pond and grain elevators.

*We will provide one guide per two hunters

*We offer bow and gun hunts

*You may choose to hunt from treestands or ground blinds

*Our ranch house is accessible to handicapped hunters

*Five day hunts run from early September through December

*Walk-in freezer available on site

*Meat processing available nearby

*Taxidermist nearby

*Experienced guides with lifelong experience on the property

*Maximum of six hunters per five day hunt

Shiloh added a photo album to the web site filled with pictures of the bigger bucks she, Syder, Jete and her dad had taken over the years. She included a page for pricing and contact information. One section was devoted just to turkey hunting. She added links to the game and fish regulations. She designated a page for directions and location information.

It took most of one day to finish the web site and once completed she turned her attention to designing business cards and brochures. When she finished those she went downstairs to grab a bite to eat before walking across the street to the ranch house. She found Dorothy inside painting the master bedroom.

"Hi Mom, this is looking really nice. I like the colors too. Can you take a break for a minute? I want to show you something." Shiloh sat down on the floor with a couple magazines.

Dorothy placed her brush on the edge of the paint can and joined her daughter. "What do you have there?"

"There are some really cool bedspreads and home décor items in these catalogs. I'm sure we can fix up all the rooms and stay under our budget if we order from these." Shiloh held a catalog out to her mom. Within an hour they had chosen everything they needed to decorate the house. Shiloh opened her laptop to get online and order the items. Then she went back to the farmhouse to finish her chores.

Just as she finished changing batteries in the smoke detector her cellphone rang. It was Jete. "Hello," Shiloh listened but didn't hear an answer to her greeting. "Hello. Uncle Jete are you there?" She could hear the tractor running in the back ground. Finally she heard her name whispered.

"Shiloh, go to my house and get my rifle and bring it out to the east pasture. Hurry!"

"Why, what's wrong?"

"There's a damn pit bull out here and it is chasing my calves. Now go, hurry up!" Jete hung up.

Shiloh ran downstairs, burst through the kitchen door and ran for her truck. She slid to a halt, turned around and ran back into the house. She ran across the room to the safe and opened it as quickly as she could spin the dial. From the left side of the safe she grabbed her single shot TC rifle and some ammunition, jerked a scoped rifle case down from the closet shelf and shoved the gun inside. She struggled to get the zipper closed as she ran back to her truck. Shiloh hurriedly placed the gun case into the front passenger seat, started her truck and punched the gas. Her tires spun in the gravel as she took off for the east pasture. She drove down the dead end gravel road and stopped at the gate. Jete was waiting. She pulled the rifle from its case and ran to him, handed him the box of shells and the gun and slipped through the gate to stand beside him.

"What took you so long? Hey this isn't my gun." Jete loaded the rifle as quickly as if it was his own. "Well, hopefully one shot will do the trick."

"I thought it would be faster if I just brought you my gun instead of going to your house," Shiloh whispered. "I don't see the dog, where is it?"

"I haven't seen it since I hung up the phone with you. It was running my herd around like a sheep dog runs sheep. Bring your truck through the gate, let's go drive around the pasture and check things out. You drive, I'll ride shotgun."

Shiloh did as Jete asked, pulling her truck through the gate while he closed it behind them and jumped into the passenger side. Half way across the pasture they saw a cow with a dead calf nearby. As they pulled closer they could see parts of the calf's hind quarters were eaten. They didn't see the black coyote with yellow eyes as he slipped away through the timber just beyond the fence.

"My gosh, it looks like a wolf has been after this calf!" Shiloh whistled.

Jete ripped off a string of cuss words not suitable to repeat as he walked over to examine the calf. "Son-of-a-bitch!" Jete took off his cap and rubbed his forehead. "If I would have seen that dog sooner I maybe could have saved her. I was using the backhoe and opening up that ditch so we could drive our trucks through to the next field during the hunting season. When I turned around to come back to this gate I saw the dog."

"I wonder who it belongs to."

"Well my guess is it comes directly from the Dugan place. That's the direction it ran. The main house is less than three miles from this pasture. Folks say they have been seeing pit bulls run loose around their property for quite a while now."

"What are you going to do?"

"I'm going to bring the backhoe over here and dig a hole right here and bury that calf. I can't stand the thought of buzzards and coyotes feasting on it. Then I'm going to the Dugan place to have a talk with them."

"I'm going with you!" Shiloh jumped into the truck before Jete could change his mind. "Get in. I'll drive you over to the backhoe."

When they finished burying the calf Jete parked the backhoe near the gate and got into Shiloh's truck. "Drive on over to the Dugan's. Let's see what they have to say."

"Okay," Shiloh agreed, and drove back up the dead end gravel road to the main road, pulled out onto the hard road and turned left toward the Dugan farm. A few minutes later they were driving up the long gravel road to the house. The house was small and needed a new coat of white paint. A gray and black motor home was parked close to the house. A detached garage and shed were in the back yard and several cars were parked in grass that hadn't been mowed for a while.

"It looks like a junk yard here," Jete said as they got closer. "I count four clunker cars and a motor home. Why do they need so many vehicles?"

Shiloh shrugged. She stopped the truck in front of the motor home and watched as Klu Dugan stepped out of it. "Be careful Uncle Jete," Shiloh said when he opened the door. She didn't move.

Jete walked to within a few feet of Klu and stopped. He looked around and spotted the dog house in the back yard.

"What's this about?" Klu asked looking confused.

Jete pointed at the dog house. "I see you have a dog. What kind?"

"Well, we used to have a dachshund. Now we have four pit bulls."

Jete's eyes widened. "Four? Four pit bulls?" He scanned the yard for any sign of the dogs.

Shiloh couldn't hear what they were talking about so she opened the door and started to get out of the truck. Jete yelled at her. "Stay in there." Shiloh closed the door. Something in his voice told her not to argue.

"Relax." Klu chuckled at Jete's reaction. "Three of them are little bitty puppies. The other one, Queenie, belongs to my brother Al. Or used to."

There was an awkward silence before Jete spoke. "So where is the pit bull now, the mother dog?"

"Well, I don't know I haven't been out here." Klu walked to the dog house and looked inside. He could see the puppies but there was no sign of Queenie. "I only see the pups. What's this all about Jete?"

"Your dog killed one of my calves a little while ago."

"How do you know it was our dog?"

"I got a look at it. I'll know it if I see it. What does your dog look like?"

"She's blonde, with a white eye patch, medium build."

"The dog I saw was blonde, but I didn't get close enough to see the white eye patch."

"What was she doing when you first saw her?"

"It was running circles around my cow. She must have been defending the calf."

Klu thought for a moment before speaking again. "But you didn't actually see the dog kill the calf, right?"

"No. But it seems mighty suspicious. The calf wasn't over a few hours old. One bite and it is history. She's a young cow, probably her first calf."

Klu didn't want to fight with Jete but he wasn't backing down. "It's kind of late for a calf to be born isn't it? Most of them are a couple months old now. Something could have been wrong with it and it died on its own. Especially if it was her first calf. Don't you agree?"

Jete thought about the points Klu was making. "There's a slim chance I suppose. You ever had any trouble with that pit bull before?"

Klu looked away and cleared his throat. "Nothing like this."

"Hmm. I get the feeling you aren't telling me the truth. If I asked your mother would she have the same story?"

Klu's jaw tensed as he gritted his teeth. "I reckon we are done here."

"I suppose so." Jete took one last look around and walked back to the truck. He got in and slammed the door. "Let's get out of here."

"What did he say? I couldn't hear a thing you guys were talking about? Do they have a pit bull?" Shiloh quizzed Jete as she drove away from the Dugan house.

"Yeah they have one. Same color as the one I saw. Dickhead says they haven't had any trouble with it, but I know he is lying. I could tell. Wouldn't look me in the eye."

"Did you see their dog? Is it the same one?"

"No. I didn't see it. He also did not know where it was. Next time I see it I'm gonna shoot it on sight."

NINE

It had been an unusually busy night for pizza deliveries. Klu left the last house at one o'clock in the morning. As he pulled out of their driveway he noticed a wooden gun cabinet sitting on the curb next to a two-drawer metal filing cabinet. A *FREE* sign had been taped to the gun cabinet. The items spurred an idea.

Klu stopped his truck and put it in park. He looked around and got out. Upon examination he noticed the jagged, foot long scratch on the side of the gun cabinet and a small break in the glass. A key was in the lock so he tried it and found that it worked. The filing cabinet also had a key that worked. He noticed both items were covered in scribble marks, as if an unsupervised toddler had been left alone too long with a black magic marker. Klu lifted the gun cabinet into the bed of his truck. He decided to take the file cabinet too.

When he got home, Klu pulled his truck close to the shed and got out. No lights were on in the main house. He opened the shed door, turned on a light and quickly noticed the shovel out of place. Klu was puzzled by this since he kept the shed organized and clean. He replaced the shovel and moved a few things to make room for the gun cabinet and filing cabinet. When he was satisfied with the arrangement he carried both items into the shed. He moved his truck closer to the motor home and parked.

As quietly as possible, Klu moved several of his personal items into the shed. He put his rifle, shotgun and handgun into the gun cabinet along with several rounds of ammunition, a rangefinder and binoculars. He left the key hanging in the lock, knowing if someone really wanted to steal his firearms they simply needed to finish breaking the glass. Within minutes he transferred a few more of his possessions to the filing cabinet. Some were valuable, some sentimental. He locked the drawers just to make it more difficult for snooping eyes to see their contents.

With the exception of his laptop, all that remained in the motor home were some boots, clothing and toiletries. He could stand to lose any or all of them without much trouble if Becky was right about Eddy wanting his motor home back. Klu worried they would come for it in his absence, or worse, while he slept. He contemplated going back to the shed to get his handgun, but decided against it. They could have the motor home without a fight. Klu would just have to move back into his old room in the main house as much as he dreaded the thought, knowing Becky would be lurking too close for comfort.

Klu slept well that night and woke up after a full seven hours of uninterrupted sleep, which seldom occurred. He was surprised at the time and quickly got showered and dressed. He had an important errand to do.

Charlene greeted him in the kitchen. "I was just about to knock on your door. Do you want some breakfast?"

"No thanks, coffee is fine. Is it still hot?"

"I can heat a cupful in the microwave if it isn't. Just let me know." Klu filled a mug and took a sip. "It's fine, thanks Mom."

"Big day today. I'm nervous and happy but mostly nervous. What woman gets nervous about a child returning home?" Dorothy walked over to Klu and gave him a big hug. "Thanks for doing this."

"No problem. I wouldn't have it any other way. Henry's bus gets to the station at eleven o-clock right?"

"Yes. He is finally getting out of that terrible prison. I'm glad about the new reform program that lets him come directly home. He says he even has a job lined up at the mechanic shop in town."

"Hopefully that will work out. Henry is really good at fixing cars and stuff."

"I always thought he might open his own business someday. He was always influenced by your father, who never could pass up the opportunity to make a quick and easy buck. I swear that man was on his best behavior when we were dating but once we got married he turned in to a drinker, a gambler and worse." Charlene glanced at Klu. "I'm sorry to talk about your father that way."

Klu hugged his mom. He remembered his father's temper and the many times he took it out on his mom as she tried to protect her sons from his wrath. "He still has a long time to go in his sentence. Let's not think about him now."

"You're right. Well, you better get going. It's almost an

hour drive to the bus station. Don't eat anything on your way back. I want to have a nice lunch of home cooked food ready for your brother when he walks in the door, now get going."

"I'll be back soon."

Shiloh instructed the city workers where to put the scaffolding she brought from home for working on the mural. They placed it on the sidewalk next to the building and adjusted it to make it as level as possible. When they finished, Shiloh took out her sketches and walked across the street to get a different perspective on the project. Her plan was to work on the outfitting business in the mornings and the mural in the afternoon when it was shaded from the sun.

She estimated the mural would take the entire month of June to complete. She wanted it off her list before the summer show season began. In the last two weeks she had booked another sport show in Florida and one in Maine. They could go directly from the big Pennsylvania sport show to the one in Maine. Two weeks later they would head to Florida. July promised to be a busy month. With any luck they could book most of their hunters from those three shows and use social media to fill the rest.

Before leaving Shiloh placed bright yellow caution tape around a perimeter of the scaffolding. She had a few errands to run before stopping at the C and R Hardware store for supplies on her way home.

Klu checked the big clock on the wall of the bus station. His brother would arrive in the next five minutes. He sat down to wait, but quickly stood up when he saw a bus turning the corner and heading toward the station. Klu stuck his hands in his pockets and leaned back against the building to watch passengers emerge from the bus. Henry was the last one off.

He had the physique of a professional football player and was intimidating at first sight.

Henry stretched and looked around. He noticed Klu still standing with his hands in his pockets against the bus station wall. He broke into a grin and walked toward his younger brother. "Hey buddy!" Henry knocked Klu's hat off and pretended to tackle him. Klu quickly responded and punched his brother in the stomach with his fist. Henry pretended the soft blow had done some damage and groaned in fake distress. They both started laughing and embraced. By now people were watching, so they recovered their composure and headed to the truck without saying another word. Klu could feel eyes watching them and turned red in awkward embarrassment mixed with pent up anger over his brother's life of poor choices.

When they got inside the truck Henry asked general questions about Klu's life, his mother's health and the condition of the house and property. Klu answered all his questions but began to wonder why he never once mentioned Becky. "So, you haven't asked about Becky." Klu said in a half question, half statement kind of way.

"Why would I?"

"Well, aren't you two together or I mean gonna be together now that you are home?"

"Hell no. I don't know what Al ever saw in her other than big boobs and an easy lay."

Klu was shocked at Henry's answer. "But, Becky says she is your girl now. That she has been visiting you in prison. And writing to you. And you told her to wait for you, that's why she is living in our house in Al's old room."

"Little brother, that's all one big stinking lie. I haven't talked to her since Al was killed. I know she was screwing around with somebody else while she was dating Al. Al wouldn't believe me so I followed her trying to get proof. I saw her with some old guy, looked old enough to be her grandpa. He had his hands all over her out behind Eddy's Tavern. She got in a car with him and left. I told Al. He punched me in the face and stormed out. He started drinking and driving around looking for Becky. That's the night he got killed."

"I didn't know all that. But it doesn't surprise me."

"Has she been coming on to you? You tappin' that?" Henry looked closely at his brother to gauge his response.

"Yes. No. I mean yes she comes on to me and no I am not having sex with her. She runs around half dressed and tries to get into the motor home with me at night sometimes but I keep telling her to back off."

"I haven't seen a half dressed woman in a long time. Might be hard to turn down that offer, even if it is Becky." Henry leaned back.

Klu relaxed and decided to get answers to more questions about Becky and Al's relationship. "So, do you know anything about Al winning the motor home from Eddy in a poker game? Becky said that is how he got it."

"As far as I know she is telling the truth on that part. Eddy and Al had been playing in a high stakes game downtown. Eddy was losing badly. Al was on a hot streak. Tempers were getting worse as the night went on. Becky was making eyes at Al all night. She likes hanging with the most important man in the room. Eddy and Becky had a conversation off to the side, then Eddy came back and made one big last move and bet the motor home. Al won. Eddy stood up from the table, shook Al's hand and told him to enjoy the motor home. Becky had the keys to it and whispered something in Al's ear that made him toss me the truck keys and go with Becky. They took off in the motor home and the rest is history."

"So the motor home really does legally belong to Eddy, because Al never changed the title or even put license plates on it. The plates have been expired ever since he drove the thing home. Becky moved in to the house after Al was killed. After a while she was driving me nuts. I moved my stuff to the motor home just to get away from her and to have some privacy. But now she says Eddy is saying he wants the motor home back."

"I can't say the motor home legally belongs to Eddy, it could be stolen. But it was in his possession. I wouldn't believe too much of what Becky tells you. She's living at the house still huh?"

Klu sighed with disgust. "Yes."

"Well, we'll see about that."

"I need to stop at the hardware store and get a couple things before we go home."

"No problem little brother. I will just sit in the truck and watch clouds go by. I will sure be glad to see the sky again whenever I want."

Klu wondered if his brother had actually been changed for the better because of prison. It was a confusing thought and hard to believe. He parked outside the hardware store on the square and went inside to purchase a padlock for the shed. He would need to ask Henry about the rules of a parolee having firearms nearby, but until then decided to keep them locked in the shed.

Shiloh was in the office of the hardware store talking with the owner, Carter Winslow, when Klu came inside. She didn't see Klu enter the store. Carter was in his late fifties and wore thick glasses on his hawkish nose. His hands were worn and callused. His salt and pepper mustache matched the color of his hair, which was cut short as in his youth.

Shiloh said, "Carter, I was at the town council meeting last week getting my plans for the mural approved and I was surprised to hear that you are going to close your hardware store. After all these years. It's one of the last remaining retail businesses on the square. My family has been coming here for twenty five years,"

"Thank you for your concerns Shiloh, but we are ready to retire. Well, not fully retire, but it is time. With the new supercenter just two miles up the road it has been harder and harder to keep our doors open. I hadn't planned on getting out until I got to full retirement age. But we ran the numbers and decided it was time to sell out. We have been living in the apartment above the store for thirty years. Rose and I decided to buy the old Hammond place and move to the country. We will have a home and yard all our own for the first time in a long time. Of course I'm going to need to find some part-time employment to help make ends meet since I won't get social security retirement benefits for another five years, or more. But we will find something."

Shiloh suddenly had an idea. "Carter why don't you come to work for us? We could use an extra hand this fall when we start our outfitting business. You're a hunter. Everyone can tell that by the mounts you have on the walls of the hardware store. And Rose could help my mom with the cooking and cleaning. The Hammond place is just two miles from my Uncle Jete's cabin. It would work out perfectly."

"Miss Shiloh, this could be an answer to our prayers. Rose keeps telling me to put things in God's hands, but you know me, worry, worry, worry. I'm going to have to tell her she might be on to something."

"Mom is always telling me the same thing. Let's all get together on Sunday. You're closed that day, so how about I talk to Mom and Jete and I'll get back to you with a time. We can meet and go over all the details and see if we can make this work."

"That is fine with me. I'm sure Rose will be excited to work with your Mom on any project. They have been good friends since grade school."

"Okay, thanks Carter, I'll be in touch." Shiloh closed the door to the office and pulled out her cell phone to call Jete. She wasn't paying attention as she walked to the front of the store. Klu stepped away from the counter at the same moment and Shiloh bumped into him.

"Excuse me Shiloh, I'm sorry I didn't see you." Klu touched his hat brim.

"Hi Klu. No, it was my fault, I wasn't watching where I

was going. Dang cell phones, you know how it is."

They walked to the front of the store and Klu held the door open for Shiloh. She thanked him and walked through, avoiding his gaze.

Klu stood watching her as she walked away. Shiloh could sense Klu's eyes on her. She looked back and waved awkwardly. Henry honked the horn, breaking Klu's concentration. He turned red in the face and got into the truck.

"Little brother who was that? Was that the Lawson girl? She's grown up real nice. Dude why are you blushing? You sweet on her? You are! My God her freaking brother killed Al! Dude! You can't be drooling over a Lawson, I don't care how hot she looks. And don't forget, talk is she made the anonymous phone call that got me and Dad busted."

"I don't believe that any more than you do. Nobody knows who made that call." Klu rolled up the plastic bag containing the padlock and tucked it under the seat.

"Well, let's just say that if I ever find out who did it, I'm gonna kill them."

"Geez Henry, you can't be talking like that!" Klu started to drive home. He made a mental note not to mention the location of his guns to Henry.

"Let's get something to eat. I'm starved," Henry said, rubbing his stomach.

"Mom's got a big feast planned for us to celebrate your homecoming. Wild turkey, morel mushrooms and some other stuff."

"Thank God for my little brother the hunter, keeping the freezer full and providing meat for the family," Henry said as he playfully flipped Klu's hat off his head with a swipe of his bear paw sized left hand.

Fearing that Henry would transition into the subject of hunting gear and guns, Klu quickly changed the subject. "So, I wonder how Becky is going to react to you coming home. Mom and I didn't talk to her about it. We just figured she knew considering she told us she was your girl now. This is going to be real interesting."

Shiloh fought to keep memories of Al Dugan's death out of her mind. Every time she saw a Dugan family member it triggered anxiety. She struggled to keep her mind on the future and feel blessed for possibly finding a solution to their need for extra help in the upcoming hunting season.

As if on cue her cell phone buzzed with a daily devotional text message. She decided to read it before starting the truck. *"King James Version. Philippians 4:6-7 Be careful for nothing; but in everything by prayer and supplication with thanksgiving let your requests be made known unto God. And the peace of God, which passeth all understanding shall keep your hearts and minds through Christ Jesus."*

She felt a peace come over her as she started the engine and headed for home. She couldn't wait to tell her mother and uncle what had just transpired.

Klu drove slowly down the long gravel road to their house letting Henry absorb the views of home. They didn't notice the peeling paint or junk cars or anything else out of place. It was home and they were both glad to live in the country.

Henry entered the kitchen through the back door and lifted his mother off her feet in a big hug. "Hi Mom," he said, holding her close. "It smells awesome in here. And look at this feast of food. Good grief woman, they did feed me in prison, although not as well as this!" He swung Charlene around a couple times and placed her gently back on her feet, making sure she wasn't dizzy. She seemed smaller and more fragile than he remembered.

Becky's voice shattered the happy homecoming. "Henry! Oh man, am I glad to see you. Come over here and give me one of those hugs." She held out her arms.

Henry stared at Becky. As usual, her clothing left little to the imagination. He felt things stirring inside.

Klu's voice pulled his mind back out of the gutter. "Yeah, Becky I'm sure you are glad Henry is home and you won't have to go visit him up at the prison anymore." Klu glared at Becky.

"Well of course honey. I'm sure Henry and I can get reacquainted real fast, isn't that right baby?" She looked at Henry and blew him a kiss. Then she walked across the kitchen, hugged him and gave him a kiss on the lips.

Henry responded by putting his arms around her and squeezing her butt. "Sure Becky."

Charlene coughed. "Okay now, how about we eat some of this food I prepared. Thank your brother and God for providing it for us. Sit down Henry. Becky, stop clinging to him, good grief."

They sat down and passed food around the table. Klu

steamed over the thought his brother might let Becky stay in their house. "So Becky, did you get a chance to talk to Eddy about me buying the motor home from him and making things legal?"

Becky glared at Klu angrily for a split second before catching herself. "Why Klu honey, I haven't seen Eddy. Why would you think I have had a chance to talk with him?"

Klu smiled slyly. "Because I saw you in his big booth at the back of the tavern a couple nights ago. I delivered pizzas to a bachelor party in the private room they have next to the front bar and I saw you. You were dancing with some old guy. He had his hands all over your butt and you weren't exactly objecting. Then the two of you went into the back room. When I left I drove around back just in time to see you get in a car with the old guy. Who was he?"

Becky stood up, clenching her fists. "You spying little bastard. Henry, I was just there because I was gonna talk to Eddy about Klu keeping the motor home. I thought I could convince him. I was just thinking of you and Klu."

"Well Becky, I haven't been home ten minutes and you lied about seeing Eddy and you lied about giving a shit about me and you lied about trying to fix it so Klu can keep that motor home. I suggest you get your shit and get out of this house."

"But Henry, I don't have any place to live. Where am I supposed to go? I don't have a car." Becky's mind was scrambling. She hadn't anticipated this. "Al wanted me to have his jeep. He left it to me when he died. I deserve it after taking care of his dog and this house."

Charlene's mouth dropped open. She started to say

something, but Klu beat her to it. "You are so full of shit Becky. You haven't contributed one dime to this place. And I have been taking care of Al's dog for weeks now. You have been sleeping until noon and been gone every afternoon and night until the wee hours of the morning. I see you stagger in with your clothes all messed up. Just what exactly have you been doing while you are away from here?"

Becky took a step back. She screamed, "Fuck you Klu! Are you gonna let him talk to me like that?" She put her hands on her hips, looked directly at Henry and waited for an answer.

Henry threw his hands up in the air. "I think you better leave Becky. This whole arrangement isn't working anymore. I'm sure you can think of a place to put your head at night."

"Fine! But I'm not leaving my stuff here with you pricks," she shouted as she jerked two large plastic garbage bags from a box in the pantry. She stomped down the hall to her room and started jamming clothes into the plastic bags. She stood on a chair and reached to the back of the shelf, high in the closet. From there she pulled down three heavy backpacks. Only Becky knew their contents. She stood surveying the room and trying to think. She carried the backpacks out the front door and jerked open the door of the motor home and threw them inside. She went back for the two plastic bags which she had to drag to the motor home. Then she stormed back inside to the kitchen.

Klu and Henry were eating. Charlene hadn't touched her food yet. Becky screamed at Klu, "Give me the keys to the motor home! Eddy wants it back and I will see that he gets it. You don't want him sending his goons in here to get it do you?"

"Not until I get my stuff out of there."

"Fine, hurry up. I want to go."

"Becky we are in the middle of lunch can't this wait?" Charlene asked innocently.

"Don't worry Mom, this won't take long. I don't have much left in there except my laptop and some clothes." Klu went out the kitchen door and walked toward the motor home. He unplugged the electric cord and disconnected the water hose before going inside to retrieve his belongings. Becky entered the motor home and tossed two of the back packs into the passenger seat. She was holding the third when Klu asked, "Becky, are you sure you can drive this thing?" By now Henry and Charlene had come out to watch.

"Of course I can. It's not much bigger than Eddy's cargo van and I can drive that."

Henry and Klu exchanged glances.

"What cargo van? I thought you weren't having anything to do with Eddy and now you say you are driving his cargo van? Just exactly what kind of cargo are you hauling Becky?" Klu asked.

Henry stepped closer to the door to hear her answer.

"I don't know what's in the van. I just drive it. It's none of your business anyway. Get your stuff and let me get out of here." Becky stomped her foot in frustration like a spoiled child.

Henry moved closer, until he was blocking the door but hadn't yet climbed up into the motor home. "Becky, what's in the back pack?"

Becky's eyes widened and she held the pack closer. "My

stuff. It's my stuff." She threw the back pack into the passenger seat with the others.

Henry climbed the steps into the motor home. "Becky, you wouldn't be trying to steal some of our valuable family heirlooms would you? Maybe the family jewels are in that back pack." Henry reached for the backpack on top of the pile. Becky shoved his arm away and Henry pushed Becky against the wall.

Klu slipped past them and quickly handed his laptop to Charlene, then grabbed several clothes from the closet and threw them out the door. Charlene hurried to pick them up. Klu grabbed another load of clothes and threw them out too. He quickly pulled open a few drawers and gathered a few final items before stepping past Henry to the outside. He turned and looked back. Henry still had Becky shoved up against the wall. She wasn't resisting.

"Klu, get your stuff and take Mom back inside the house. Becky and I are gonna have a little talk about what's in the back pack."

"Sure thing Henry. Here," he said while tossing the keys to the motor home on the floor at Henry's feet. He bent down to retrieve some clothes.

Charlene turned and hurried to the kitchen door with an armload of Klu's clothing. She took them into his old bedroom and began putting things away. She didn't like the way Henry was treating Becky. It reminded her too much of the way her husband Hank had behaved. She felt powerless to interfere.

Klu gathered his possessions while Henry closed the door. He almost felt sorry for Becky until he realized she was making no effort to protest Henry's advances. He just hoped his brother would be done with Becky quickly and she would move out of their lives for good.

Half an hour later part of Klu's wish came true. Becky drove the motor home away from the house and Henry walked in with one of her back packs. He wasn't wearing a shirt. Klu watched him carry the pack to his room and return to the kitchen to finish eating lunch. Charlene was in her sewing room having lost her appetite. Klu was putting food away and cleaning up. "I left you a plate in the microwave, you can warm it up. Is she gone for good?" Klu asked holding his breath.

"She's not coming back here," Henry replied. "You might say we came to an agreement."

"Well, that's good. We didn't need that motor home parked here if it was stolen. What was in the back pack?"

"Little brother, you're better off not knowing. Thanks for saving me lunch. I worked up an appetite." He smiled and flexed his muscles. "It's good to be home."

"Looks like you kind of bulked up in prison."

"I did. Not much to do. They had a lot of gym equipment, weights and stuff. Better to be the big dog than the lap dog if you know what I mean. So I kept up appearances. May have to go shopping for new clothes later. I put on about twenty pounds of pure muscle." He flexed again to emphasize the fact.

"Well, I'm just glad to be rid of her and that motor home. I was losing sleep at night wondering when Eddy and his goons were gonna show up and take it back."

"I doubt Eddy gave a shit about that thing until recently. My guess is Becky is driving the van to make drug deliveries.

He probably thinks the motor home would be a good cover and hold a lot more contraband. It could be hidden in all those cabinets. Word on the street is that back section of the campground is all under Eddy's control. He keeps bad things out of town and the cops leave him alone. Becky is probably headed there now."

Becky drove the motor home to the campground. She gave the campground host a hundred dollar tip and drove to the back section where she knew some of Eddy's friends were camped. Somebody would help her park the motor home and set things up so she could stay in it.

She was still angry about Henry taking one of her back packs after she had given him a good time. Her anger was somewhat softened by the knowledge she had three more back packs filled with cash stored in a rental locker at the airport. Driving the cargo van for Eddy was lucrative business.

Tomorrow she would take one of the backpacks into town and buy a sports car.

TEN

Shiloh, Jete and Dorothy agreed to meet Carter and Rose on Sunday afternoon at the old Hammond place. Carter wanted to show them the house and talk about plans they had for remodeling it. It was two miles west of Jete's cabin on the south side of the county highway. The house was old and needed several repairs. It had been empty for two years.

Jete kept the yard mowed in an arrangement with the Hammonds who had moved to California without selling the place. When they finished the tour of the house and grounds Rose invited them inside for tea. As they sat down someone mentioned the history of the Hammond place and surrounding county.

Shiloh talked about some of what she had learned in her research for the mural. "Hammonds were some of the first families to settle in this area. Their family migrated from Virginia on the Yellow Wolf River. They were tobacco farmers and may have even known the infamous Daniel Boone."

Carter said, "They must have used that big old barn

101

behind the house to dry the tobacco leaves. It must have been a grand structure in its day. Now it is on the verge of collapse."

Shiloh nodded and continued with her story. "I also ran across that old story about the lost baby. Legend says the first settlers to camp here on their way out west were traveling in a wagon pulled by two mules. It was a family with two babies just barely able to walk. One baby was blonde, the other red headed. Two wolves kept following the party at a distance, well out of gun range. One wolf was blonde, the other coal black. They could hear them howling at night. One night while they were sleeping around the campfire the blonde wolf slipped in to camp and stole the blonde haired baby. Legend says the wolf took the blonde baby because it looked like her pup, which had been killed by a bear. When the settlers awoke in the morning, the blonde haired baby was gone. They searched and searched for it but could find no trace. Every night they could hear the baby crying in the dark timber. One of their party was killed by a bear at night so the others were too afraid to look for the baby for fear of a similar fate. They named the creek that goes through our property from Canyon to the Yellow Wolf River after this legend. To this very day if you go sit next to the Lost Baby Creek on a quiet night you can hear that baby's cries."

Jete grinned. "Your brother believed that story. Jack took him out to Lost Baby Creek when he was little and told him the story. They went catfishing on the river at night and Syder swore he heard the baby cry. It was a couple years before he realized the cries he heard at night were made by a screech owl."

Dorothy smiled and said, "I remember. Jack used that story to keep Syder from wandering off at night when they were fishing the river or camping. It worked too. Syder stayed close at night. I cannot say the same thing for his habits in the daytime though. He was quite the wanderer. I don't think there is one inch of this farm he has not seen. Over twenty two hundred acres and his boot tracks are on every inch of it. He always wanted to know what was over the next ridge. Both my kids are like that, they sure do love the outdoors."

Jete said, "It's a good thing he stopped exploring at the north boundary of our property. Once you get to the top of the bluffs it is flat for a short distance, then it drops off into some mighty steep cliffs into Swale Hollow. Old man Swale and his wife have lived in there for years. We don't see them very often. When it floods I have had to meet them at the road and take them to town. They keep a john boat in the front yard just to float out to the road when it floods. Nice people but pretty reclusive."

Shiloh said, "I guess we better get down to business and discuss our big outdoor adventure. I left my laptop and sample brochures and maps in the truck. I will go grab them and we can talk about Lawson's Hunting Adventures."

Jete jumped up and offered to help. Once outside he teased, "You did not finish the rest of the legend of Lost Baby Creek. They say the stolen blonde baby was raised by wolves and the Dugan family is a direct descendent of that baby."

"Jete! That's terrible, but funny," she said with a laugh. "Here, carry the maps and brochures, I'll get the rest."

They spent the next several minutes going over the maps, discussing current and future treestand and box blind locations.

Shiloh explained to Carter, "We already have about thirty stands and box blinds up, mostly for southwest, west and northwest winds. We should put a few pop-up blinds along the alfalfa fields for early season and the occasional east wind. We plan to take six hunters per hunt, with two hunters per guide. Your job Carter, would include helping us set up new stands later this summer after your store closes. We need to put lifelines in every treestand. We have a side-by-side UTV on site for you to use to drive your hunters to and from stands and help recover deer."

Carter nodded his head. "No problem, I can do all that."

Shiloh continued, "We need to figure out the hunt schedule. Our early season starts on the first Saturday of September. We want to run through the end of December, working around Thanksgiving and Christmas of course."

Jete added, "If we offer five and a half day hunts we could have them arrive Sunday after noon, start hunting on Monday, and let them hunt all the way to noon on Saturday. They would need to leave Saturday afternoon. That gives us Saturday afternoon and evening plus most of Sunday to clean up before the next group arrives."

Dorothy spoke up, "That gives us the ability to attend church Sunday morning. I know Sunday is a day of rest but for this short period of time I think we can make it work. Rose, are you okay with that?"

"Yes, that sounds reasonable enough," Rose agreed.

By suppertime the Lawsons worked out the remaining details with Carter and Rose to help with the new outfitting business.

Klu decided to search Al's old room to make sure Becky did not leave any drugs behind that could get Henry in trouble. Charlene went with him to begin cleaning. She pulled the sheets from the bed and went to the laundry room. Klu looked through all the drawers and closet. He searched between the mattress and box springs finding a small plastic baggy with a hint of marijuana inside. Satisfied there was nothing else in the room he went back to the kitchen to throw away the baggy. When he passed the laundry room he heard his mother cry out.

"What's wrong Mom?" Klu asked, reaching for the jeans she was holding. Henry joined them.

Charlene looked at her sons and unclenched her fist. She showed Klu and Henry what she had found. "I came in to do the laundry and found a basket of Becky's clothes. She must have forgotten about them. I decided to wash them up for her. Before I put any clothes in the washer I always check the pockets. This is what I found in the back pocket of her jeans." She started crying harder.

"Oh Mom, I'm sorry," Klu said as he took the pearls from her hand.

"What's all the fuss over a handful of pearls?" Henry asked.

"Come on, let's all go into the living room. Just leave that laundry here, I'll take care of Becky's stuff." Klu gently guided Charlene into the living room and handed her a box of tissues. "Henry, I guess I forgot to tell you about Chito. Mom had a little, long haired, miniature dachshund. Becky told us she let Chito out to pee after dark one night when Mom was gone to town. Her story was that a great big owl swooped out of nowhere, grabbed Chito and flew off. We never found the dog."

"So what's that got to do with these pearls?" Henry asked.

"Mom made Chito a little collar, decorated it with some pearls she had. The dog wore that collar every day. Mom never took it off of Chito. If an owl took Chito, how did Becky come to have Chito's pearls in her back pocket?"

Before Henry turned to walk back to his room he said, "Somebody needs to ask Becky that question."

Klu left Charlene resting on the couch. She had stopped crying but seemed despondent. He went into the laundry room and took the basket of Becky's clothes to the back yard. He threw her clothes into the burn barrel, poured lighter fluid on the clothes and lit them on fire. He stood back and watched the flames climb higher. Before long the smoke was thick, but thankfully drifting away from the house. He pulled the baggy from his pocket and tossed it in the barrel and walked to the shed to gather some fishing gear. It was time to start refilling the freezer with fish. Klu grabbed his tackle box and a light pan fishing rig and carried them to his truck. He placed them in the bed and went back to the shed for mosquito repellent, a cooler, some old rags and a container of worms.

Henry saw him and walked across the yard. "Want some company?"

"Sure. Do you have a fishing license?" Klu jabbed his finger into Henry's arm.

Henry raised his hands as if surrendering. "How about I supervise and drink beer?"

"That would be a good idea, if we actually had some beer."

Henry looked surprised. "You don't have any beer?"

"No Henry, I quit drinking when Al got killed. Kind of lost my taste for alcohol."

This gave Henry pause. He stood thinking for a few moments before speaking again. "Well, I can see how you would make that decision."

"So do you still want to go fishing?"

"No, I think I will go work on one of our cars. I'm gonna be needing one if I am to be all respectable again with a job and all."

"Sounds like a good idea. Al's jeep is in pretty good shape, probably just needs a tune up and a new muffler. All your tools are still in the garage with the coupe. I'll see ya later." Klu tried not to sound too relieved. His brother was a happy drunk, unlike his dad and brother Al. They got meaner by the ounce. Klu wondered how children from the same parents could be so different. His older brother Henry was pretty even-tempered, drank too much but seldom got out of control. He had a work ethic problem, always drifting toward the easy dollar. Al on the other hand, had inherited all of his father's temper.

Klu decided he was most like his mother, easy going, quiet, shy and responsible. Right now, he needed to get food. Much of what they ate came from the land, not the grocery store. Fishing was fun, but it also provided much needed protein. Although he was the youngest, Klu was the provider, a job he easily accepted. He started the truck and headed for the community pond in Cedarwood.

Becky was putting gas in her new, white, BMW convertible when she saw Klu's truck drive past. She hurried to finish the task and took off to follow Klu. She saw him turn into the community park with the fishing pond. She pulled over to watch him for a few minutes. Klu took off his shirt. Becky wished he would keep going. When she was certain he was alone she drove the remainder of the distance and parked next to his truck. Klu noticed the convertible then realized Becky was the driver. He groaned.

Becky adjusted her clothing and got out of the car. She was wearing high heels and short cut-off jeans. She unbuttoned another button on her shirt and walked over to Klu and said, "I saw you pull in here. How have you been? Doing a little fishing huh?" Klu didn't answer as he gathered his fishing tackle from the bed of his truck, so she continued, "Why don't you come out to the campground, the fishing is much better there, since it is a private lake and all."

"No thanks Becky, this pond is fine. I'm just going to catch a limit of Bluegills. I won't be here long." Klu carried his gear to the pond edge and sat on a bench provided for anglers. Becky watched him, admiring his physique. She took out her cell phone and snapped a few pictures before Klu noticed what she was doing. "Why the hell are you taking pictures of me?" he asked angrily.

"Relax. I was just admiring your tattoo. What is that? A deer?" Becky pointed to Klu's right arm.

"Yeah, it's a deer. It's my biggest buck so far. I got a likeness of it tattooed on my arm last year." Klu realized he was actually conversing with Becky and cursed himself. He didn't want to encourage her in any way.

"Well, it's really magnificent." She raised her cell phone and took a closer picture before Klu could turn away.

"Stop it Becky." He walked back to his truck to get his shirt.

Becky followed. "Do you want to come out to the motor home after you get done fishing? It's pretty nice and really private. Nobody would bother us in the back section."

Klu was getting angrier with her every word. He turned and grabbed her arm. "Maybe we could go discuss how you ended up with Chito's pearls in the back pocket of your jeans."

"What are you talking about?" Becky feigned ignorance as her mind scrambled to explain the pearls.

"My Mom's dog. Chito. Remember? The owl supposedly flew off with the dog? Does that ring a bell? We both know that's bullshit. What really happened?"

Becky stammered, "I, uh, that is what happened just like I said. I ran out after the owl and it had Chito in its claws. And I grabbed something, a stick, and threw it and hit the owl and the necklace must have broken because I could see some of them white pearls fall so I gathered up what I could find and put them in the pocket of my jeans. I forgot all about them. It was so horrible." She tried to cling to him as if needing comfort.

Klu shoved Becky away. "Get off of me."

"But Klu, honey, don't you believe me? I didn't mean to keep the pearls, I was gonna give them back to your Mom, she was just so upset. We all were."

"No, I don't believe you at all. Something else happened to that dog, I'm sure of it."

"Well, if you are gonna be like this I'm leaving." Becky turned and walked back to her convertible. She drove too quickly out of the park, fuming over the thought that Klu turned her down again. She rationalized the rejection by believing it was because of his fascination with Shiloh Lawson. She wondered what she could do to get rid of her competition.

Klu caught a limit of Bluegill in about thirty minutes. He carried them to the fish cleaning station and quickly fileted them; placed them in the cooler and left for home.

Henry was in the garage working on the coupe when Klu arrived. He waved at his younger brother and kept on working. Klu walked in and asked if he needed any help.

"No thanks, I'm about done here. Did you catch us some fish for supper?"

"I did. I need to take them in the house and then I'm gonna cut some firewood to sell at the gas station in Cedarwood."

"You work too hard little brother."

"I ran into Becky today. You were right. She took the motor home to the campground. I asked her about the pearls. She made up some stupid story right there on the spot. Said she threw something at the owl and the collar broke and pearls fell and she gathered them up out of the yard. All bullshit."

"How did you run into her? Did you go out to the campground to see her?" Henry teased.

"No. She followed me to the park. She's driving some new convertible. No idea how she can afford that," he added sarcastically.

Henry snorted. "No idea at all."

"I'll talk to you later." Klu took the filets inside and put them in a bowl of salt water in the refrigerator. He tossed his shirt on the back of a chair and went outside to cut wood.

When Henry got the coupe running he smiled to himself. He decided to run the cobwebs out of the engine with a trip to the campground.

ELEVEN

Shiloh worked on the mural in Findlay. She tried to
include images that represented the history of Kentucky. Each
afternoon she would stop by the hardware store and carry
something back to the old Hammond place for Carter and
Rose. It was on her way home and no trouble. When she
completed the project she worked on checking trail cameras,
and updating the web site and social media pages with pictures
of prospective bucks. It was fun tracking the progress of antler
development. She was beginning to pattern a few shooter
bucks on their farm.

To save on shipping, and give Shiloh a little break on cost,
Carter offered to purchase the lifelines, ground blinds,
treestands and other equipment through the hardware store and
sell them to Shiloh at a price that undercut the supercenter. He
wasn't supposed to do this, but it gave him great pleasure to
know he could pull one over on the retail giant. He was going
out of business anyway so it wasn't like he was worried about
losing the account. He delivered them to Shiloh on the last
Sunday in June.

Shiloh helped unload the boxes and thanked Carter. "Jete and I will be leaving this week for the big show in Pennsylvania. In fact the next three weeks we will have one show after another. Will you stop in and check on Mom whenever you are out working on the remodel of the Hammond house? I guess I should stop calling it that now that it has new owners."

"Sure thing. Rose and Dorothy will be like two peas in a pod out there decorating away. I will do my best to stay in the barn."

Jete joined them as they unloaded the last box. Shiloh chided him. "Well, that was perfect timing. How did you manage to not be here to unload a single box?"

"Just as soon as I think all my ducks are in a row one of the fuzzy little suckers waddles off," Jete offered as an explanation. "I was about to come help but a dude stopped me at the front door asking for a donation to the town swimming pool." Jete winked at Carter. Shiloh did not notice.

"So, did you give him anything?" Shiloh asked.

"I gave him a glass of water." Jete grinned as he slapped his leg.

"Oh man, I cannot believe I fell for that. We don't even have a town swimming pool. Shows you how preoccupied I am."

Carter laughed. "You reeled her in like a carp on a dough ball."

"Hook, line and sinker," Jete agreed. "Too easy. Actually I just had to make a quick fence repair before I got here."

"Did you get the trailer today?" Shiloh asked.

"Yes, I picked it up from the rental place this afternoon.

You want to start loading now?"

"Might as well. Carter, can you stay and help?"

"Sure thing. Just tell me what to do."

"I wish I knew. We built a display and need to take some deer heads so maybe the three of us can put our heads together and get it loaded without much trouble."

Suddenly the sound of a dog shrieking in pain ended their conversation. Before anyone could react, Hazard came running into the barn with a copperhead snake in his teeth. The snake's jaws were sunk into the side of Hazard's face. Shiloh yelled, "Oh my God, Hazard drop it!"

Jete grabbed a shovel and chopped the snake in half. It writhed in agony but did not release its hold on Hazard's face. Blood spattered all over Shiloh and Carter. Jete grabbed a pair of gloves from his back pocket, quickly slipped them on, and grabbed the snake by the back of its head. He took pliers from his other pocket and pried the snake's fangs from their hold on Hazard. Then he carried that half of the snake to the door and threw it as far as he could into the weeds. Carter followed with a shovel holding the other half of the snake and repeated Jete's move.

Shiloh held Hazard in her arms trying not to cry. Carter helped her get Hazard in the back seat. She crawled in beside her dog and cradled his head to keep him calm.

Jete jumped in the front and started the engine. "Carter, give Doc a call and tell him we are coming!" Gravel spun from the tires as they took off for the main road and headed for town. Shiloh held Hazard close as Jete sped toward Findlay. They made the thirty minute trip in record time. Staff met them at the door and carried Hazard into an examining room. They would not let Shiloh or Jete follow them past the front waiting room. A receptionist asked them if they wanted coffee. They declined.

Neither spoke as they waited for the veterinarian to come back with a report. Both were surprised and relieved when an assistant came to get them after just ten minutes. She asked them to follow her to the exam room.

Hazard was being given intravenous fluids and seemed to be fine. He was enjoying the attention from the assistants. Shiloh went to stand near the table to rub Hazards ears. "Is he going to be okay?" she asked.

The vet answered, "We will know in the next twenty four hours. IV fluids will help him recover but we have no real way of knowing how much venom went into his bloodstream. I will give him some antivenin if he starts to exhibit any symptoms. All we can do is keep him here for observation and fluids. We will call you hourly with updates until we close tonight at eight. Be here first thing in the morning. We open at seven."

Before Shiloh could ask a single question an assistant ran into the room and whispered to the vet. "Excuse me, we have an emergency." She pointed across the hall when she had the vet's attention.

The vet nodded at Shiloh. "I will talk to you first thing in the morning." With that, he turned and left the room.

The vet did not get the door completely closed when he left. Shiloh could see across the hall into the other exam room. A beautiful reddish brown Irish Setter was laying on its side on the examining table. The dog's owner, a man Shiloh did not recognize, was holding the dog's head and stroking its fur.

The vet was working on the dog's right front paw. She heard him say, "It looks like someone wrapped a rubber band around this dog's paw." The vet looked at the owner waiting for some kind of explanation.

The owner said, "She has been missing for three days. We just found her this morning. She was limping badly so we just loaded her up and brought her straight in."

"It looks like she has a few bite marks. She may have been in a dog fight. But that doesn't explain the rubber band. I'm going to cut the rubber band off and see if she needs stitches before I work on the bites. I gave her a shot to calm her. She will be semi-conscious while we do this. Just hold her head. This won't take long."

The vet cut the rubber band and blood spurted from the wound. "It must have been compressing an artery. She is bleeding quite a bit."

The owner mumbled, "Uh hmmm." He began to sway, then fainted and fell straight backward, slamming the back of his head against the bottom of the door. As he went down he pulled the heavily sedated dog off of the table and onto himself. Blood spurted from the wound. The momentum of the dog's fall splashed blood across the wall. It reminded Shiloh of a horror movie she had turned off.

The vet told his assistant to take care of the man while he lifted the dog off of the owner and put it back on the table and began working on the bleeding wound. The assistant helped the man stand up and guided him out of the examining room.

As the assistant walked by with the man she noticed the door to Hazard's exam room was partially open and she locked eyes with Shiloh. "Well now that's not something you will see every day," she admitted. "He's fine. I'll be right back." Then she reached over and closed Hazard's door.

"Holy cow did you see all that?" Shiloh asked Jete.

"I did. That was crazy. I know some people faint when they see blood, but that dude went out stone cold. He experienced a severe vasovagal response for sure."

Shiloh and Jete tried not to laugh, but they were both nervous about Hazard and couldn't control their response. They were trying hard not to giggle uncontrollably when the assistant opened their door and came in.

"If you would like to stay with Hazard for a while longer before we take him into the back kennel area just let me know," she said.

Shiloh's eyes widened. "He's never been in a kennel. He doesn't even like going in the dog house in cold weather. He always just stays with me. I don't understand why he got in a fight with a snake. He has been trained to leave them alone since he was a puppy. Nothing like this has ever happened before."

"It's okay. We treat several snake bites a year. The kennel is very nice. Hazard will have a space all to himself. We will treat him like a king, don't worry," the assistant assured.

Jete stood up. "Come on honey, let's go. Give Hazard a big hug and let them take him back to get some rest. He waited as Shiloh hugged Hazard, then guided her out of the exam room. He could tell she was still partially in shock and quite traumatized by the possibility of losing her dog. On the ride home, neither spoke. All they could do, was wait.

TWELVE

Henry began to make regular trips to visit Becky when he wasn't working at the mechanic shop. She always had beer and was up for a romp in the motor home. She seemed quite fascinated with the tattoo on his right arm, taking pictures and admiring it. He didn't see the big deal. It was a good rendering of a non-typical whitetail buck. Unlike his brother's, Henry's buck was not drawn from a deer he killed; instead it was a figment of his imagination with smoke coming out of its nostrils. On his left arm Henry tattooed the high school symbol of an angry copperhead.

Cedarwood Canyon High School was a large school, combining students from the small town of Cedarwood and the southern half of the bigger city of Canyon just a few miles north. Henry's graduating class was just shy of five hundred students. In high school Henry had been a star football player. Built like a linebacker, and taller than his brothers, talk of scholarships surrounded him in his senior year. Then he blew out his knee. His downward spiral began after surgery did not return him to the field.

Becky enjoyed Henry's visits because they gave her a chance to ask about Klu. Whenever she knew he was coming out to see her, to get in the mood, she gazed at the photo of Klu with his shirt off. She occasionally reminded Henry that Shiloh may have been the one who made the anonymous phone call that put him and his father in prison. Henry kept saying he would kill the person who made the anonymous call. She kept Henry full of beer and satisfied. When he left the campground each time his alcohol limit was well out of legal range.

Becky's collection of back packs was growing. She hid them in every cabinet of the motor home and the small trunk of the convertible. When Henry asked for a loan, she gave it to him, knowing she would never be repaid, in money. Eddy's two man goon squad stayed in a camper next to her motor home. They met with people who came to make a deal and kept an eye out for the law. They tolerated Henry and didn't give her any trouble. Eddy had not been to the campground since she first moved in. He hated camping. He hated the insects and campfire smoke.

Tonight however, was different. Eddy was coming to the campground for the second time. Goon one had told her to get rid of Henry so she pretended to have a headache and sent him home early. She was glad to see him go. He was boring and clumsy in bed. She tried to imagine Klu each time Henry was on top of her but it was difficult to compare them. She thought Henry was a hulk and Klu was perfect.

When darkness fell, Eddy's black limo pulled up to her campsite. He got out and stretched. Eddy wore a gray suit and tie. He kept his black hair combed back slick and never wore a hat. He had a pencil thin mustache and pale skin. His face was pock marked from acne in his younger days. She ran to him and gave him a kiss and a hug. He patted her butt and walked over to shake hands with his goons. "Hey boys. How's it hanging? I want you to meet my realtor. This is Ivan. Ivan meet the boys."

Ivan shook hands with the goons. Ivan was also dressed in a suit and tie. He was overweight and had trouble moving around because of arthritis in his knees. He carried a brief case into Becky's motor home and sat down at the table.

An electric golf cart pulled up to the camp site. Eddy's nephew got out of the cart and helped the elderly campground owners climb into the motor home. They sat across from the realtor. Eddy joined them. They shut the door.

Becky sat by the fire and listened to Eddy's nephew talk about football with the goons. He was the campground host, living in a trailer at the entrance to the campground. It was his job to monitor who came and went and notify the goons if a problem was headed their way. There were no cell signals in the back section of the campground so he drove back and forth in the electric golf cart to give them messages from Eddy.

Within twenty minutes Eddy opened the door of the motor home and helped the former campground owners get out of the motor home. They climbed on the back of the golf cart and waited. Eddy instructed his nephew to come to the limo. He and Ivan took back packs out of the trunk. Eddy gave them to his nephew who proceeded to give the couple several back packs. They smiled from ear to ear as he piled their arms full.

Eddy pulled his nephew aside. "Make sure they leave tonight."

"Don't worry Uncle Eddy. Their rental truck is packed and they know to leave tonight. Soon they will be walking on the beach in Florida happy as clams, never to be heard from again."

"Good boy." Eddy patted his nephew's face. "Now get them out of here." He turned to Becky and said, "Come here baby. I want to celebrate my new real estate purchase. You are looking at the new owner of this very profitable campground. Bring me a beer."

Becky jumped up to get a beer for Eddy from the fridge in the motor home. She opened it and hurried back to hand it to him before giving him a hug. "Congratulations, I guess. I thought you hated this place. Why would you buy it?" She sat down across from Eddy on the opposite side of the campfire.

Eddy took a drink. "That's an easy answer. Money. This is a good place to hide funds. There's a hundred acres of timber and a box canyon a mile behind this section that goes with it. It's real private too. No access in and out. Nothing but forest for miles around that." Eddy gazed off into the woods.

Ivan stared at Becky over the campfire. She didn't mind his leering gaze. She was used to it. Most men looked at her with lust in their eyes and she liked it that way. It made her feel a sense of control and self-worth.

Eddy guzzled the last of his beer and tossed the can on the ground near the fire ring. "Let's go Ivan. We have better things to do than hang around this ring of fire." Ivan held the limo door open for Eddy then closed it when Eddy was inside the back seat. Then he lumbered to the driver's side and lurched into the seat. He started the limo, backed it out of the camp site and drove away.

The next morning, Shiloh, Jete and Dorothy were waiting in the parking lot when the veterinary office opened. They exchanged pleasantries with the receptionist inside. The vet came into the lobby to greet them. "Good morning. Good news. Hazard is a bundle of energy this morning. It's like nothing bad happened. Come on back, I'll have one of my assistants bring him to the examining room." Shiloh broke down in tears when they got into the exam room.

"Oh honey, I assume those are happy tears?" Dorothy hugged her daughter. Jete wiped his eyes and cleared his throat. "Not you too," Dorothy said. They all hugged and waited for Hazard.

Five minutes went by. "Did they have to go to the dog park to get him?" Jete whispered.

Shiloh shrugged. She was trembling with relief and weak from little sleep and no food. The door opened and Hazard burst into the room, wagging his tail and wiggling his entire body as he jumped in Shiloh's lap. "Oh my gosh Hazard you are too big to be a lap dog." She laughed and hugged him tight. "I don't know what I would do if you had been killed by that snake."

The vet said, "You need to keep him quiet for the rest of the day, good luck with that by the way, and give us a call if you see any change in his behavior that alarms you. But I don't anticipate any problems. He has been fine all night. A small percentage of snake bites are considered dry bites, where no venom is injected. We cleaned the bite. Here's some antibiotic cream to put on it as it heals. Try not to let him rub it off. You can take care of your bill on the way out." The vet disappeared down the hall.

"I guess he's off to save another dumb creature that is not smart enough to stay away from bad things," Jete joked as he rubbed Hazard's head. "Buddy you sure gave us a scare."

Hazard whined an apology then barked.

Shiloh interpreted, "He says, let's get out of here." They paid the bill and climbed into Jete's truck.

"Where to ladies?"

"Home!" they shouted in unison.

Hazard barked in agreement.

THIRTEEN

Becky slept until noon. When she emerged from the motor home the goons were gone. She thought about what Eddy said about the hundred acres of woods and a box canyon that belonged to the campground. More than once she had seen the goons walk off into the woods, not returning until dark.

She wandered over to the big multi-flora rose bush where they often seemed to disappear. She peered around the bush and could see a faint trail through the woods. She wondered where it went. Becky stood looking into the woods, reluctant to leave the safety of the campsite for fear of snakes and other woodland creatures. She thought she saw movement and quickly walked back to the campfire ring and started to build a fire. She liked staring at the flames.

The goons emerged from the woods. They didn't say much. Becky watched them going in and out of their camper, getting food and drink. They seemed nervous.

Becky asked, "What have you two been doing? What's back there in the woods?" They looked at her without answering. Becky felt like two coyotes were looking at their next meal. "What the fuck are you looking at?" she yelled at them. The goons looked at each other and laughed, then went into their camper. "Fine. Don't tell me, you creeps," Becky muttered. "I'll bet Eddy's nephew will tell me."

Becky walked through the campground looking at the other campsites. There were people all over the grounds regardless of whether it was a weekend or weekday. Becky noticed campers of all shapes and sizes with vehicles parked all about. Smoke from several campfires drifted throughout the site. She fixed the crooked campground host sign outside Eddy's nephew's camper and knocked on his door.

Eddy's nephew opened the door. "Hi Becky," he said, straightening his long, mousey brown hair. He grabbed a rubber band from inside the camper and pulled his hair back into a pony tail. Becky estimated him to be nineteen. He was thin, almost anorexic and smelled like weed. "I guess we have never been formally introduced," he said enthusiastically as he stuck out his hand, delighted with Becky's visit. "My name is Ricky." He stepped out of the camper and stood still.

"Hi Ricky." Becky shook his hand. "Nice to meet you. All this time I never knew you were Eddy's nephew until you came to the campsite the night Eddy bought this place."

Ricky motioned to the picnic table. "Would you like to sit down?"

"Yes, thanks. So, Ricky, how do you like being the campground host?"

"It rocks! I don't have to do much except check people in and out. I can play video games all day and night with no one giving me any grief about making something out of my life." He blushed.

"Oh, I get it. I hate people telling me what to do." Becky continued to engage him in conversation, asking about his gaming and other things, making him feel special. They sat on the picnic table and talked quite a while. She tried to present the impression she was Eddy's girl and knew all about what was going on in his life. Finally she asked about the hundred acres and the trail to the box canyon.

"That's gonna be for Eddy's dog fighting. There's an old corral back there. The guys are fixing it up. It's a big business but you gotta keep moving locations so the cops don't bust up the whole thing."

"Oh yeah, that sounds like a good place for it. No wonder Eddy wanted to buy this place." Becky asked Ricky several questions about dogfighting as she thought about Queenie and the pups. "Do you know when they are going to be ready?"

"The guys said they are ready to do some training pretty soon. They have to go pick up a couple of Eddy's dogs today. They won't be back for two or three hours. Do you want to come in and have a drink?"

"Oh no, thanks. I have plans. I'll see you later." Becky jumped up and walked back to her motor home to think. She checked the time and decided to walk down the trail.

The goons were gone, presumably picking up two fighting dogs for Eddy. She didn't know how long that might take. Once she got twenty yards past the big multi-flora rose bush it was easy to see the path.

After a twenty minute walk she entered a field with an old wooden corral. Beyond the corral was a box canyon. She walked through the corral into the canyon. It was about fifty yards wide at the entrance and almost one hundred and fifty yards long with high rock walls a person could not climb without ropes and climbing gear.

At the back of the canyon Becky found two white canvas tents similar to those she had seen in Klu's magazines about hunting out west. She went inside each one. They were empty. A heavy sledge hammer and several big metal stakes, some with rings on top and some without, lay on the ground outside one of the tents along with several lengths of chain. She opened the lid of a plastic tub next to the chains and was surprised to see several pairs of hand cuffs. Without thinking she took one pair and hid it in her pants before walking quickly back to her campsite.

Ricky arrived in the electric golf cart just as she was putting more wood on the fire. "Eddy called. He wants you to make another run in the cargo van tonight." He handed her a piece of paper with writing on it. "He also said he doesn't want Henry Dugan coming around here anymore. With the dogfighting stuff getting up and running he doesn't want him finding out about it. You gotta be on a special list to get invited to these things."

"Okay. No problem. I'll go change my clothes and get going. Would you put out that fire? Thanks."

Ricky doused the fire and left. Becky emerged dressed for a night on the road. Eddy had told her to dress inconspicuously in jeans, T-shirt and ball cap.

She started the van and drove to a busy truck stop on the interstate going north out of Canyon, Kentucky. She parked the van where she always did and went inside to wait. Just as instructed she didn't look around. In the restaurant she ordered coffee and a piece of pie as always. She waited thirty minutes exactly, payed the bill with cash and left.

A flimsy curtain separated the driving compartment from the back of the van. She did not look in the back. Eddy had explained all about plausible deniability, which she thought sounded like a good thing.

She drove the van out of the truck stop parking lot and pulled back on to the interstate to continue north. She crossed the Ohio River into Indiana, making sure to stay under the speed limit and not attract attention. She followed the directions Ricky had given her, stopping at another busy truck stop several hours later. She parked, went inside the all-night café, ordered more coffee and waited thirty minutes.

She checked her watch. Becky walked to the van, opened the driver side door and got in. She looked to make sure a backpack was hidden on the floor in front of the passenger seat. It was. Becky smiled. Easy money.

Jete negotiated with Shiloh. "If you let me drive I promise not to tell stupid jokes all the way to Pennsylvania."

Shiloh responded, "You mean like, uh, where does the one legged man go for pancakes? Duh. I-Hop."

"Exactly. I have many more just like that one. For instance, do you know why you seldom see elephants hiding in the treetops?"

Shiloh laughed. "No why?"

"Because they are really good at it. Get it? Why don't blind people skydive?"

"I don't know. Why don't they?"

"Because it scares the hell out of their seeing eye dogs."

"Okay you win, I cannot take any more terrible jokes, you can drive!" Shiloh tossed him the keys. "Only eleven hours to the expo center. I booked us a room just west of there. We can be up early the next day to set up. The show opens at five."

"Sounds good. Is Hazard coming on this trip?"

"He's going to stay with Mom. I was going to bring him, since he is the friendliest dog ever I figured he would be a real asset in the booth. But with both of us gone Mom wanted his company."

"She has been living alone in that big house for several years now. What's the difference?"

"I know, but for the next few days you are not one mile down the road like usual. And the tenant farmer is gone from across the street. And the Hammond place is empty. Carter and Rose won't be moved in for a few more weeks."

"I see what you mean. Did you tell her to keep the loaded shotgun by the bed?"

Shiloh nodded and laughed. "She already does!"

"Have you given much thought to expenses and how many hunters we need to book to make this whole thing work?" Jete asked as he closed the driver's side door and put the key in the ignition.

"I have. We are lucky to already have a lot of what we need to get started. We own all our own ground so there are no leases. We have twenty-two hundred acres of timber, creek bottom, ag and food plots on the north side of the road. There isn't much hunting on the eight hundred acres of crop fields south of the farmhouse. I know we see bucks tending does out there during the rut, but it would be really hard to hunt it. We have hunted the whole place for all our lives and already have stands in place. We only needed to buy a few more. It didn't cost much to fix up the ranch house. Insurance was a big new expense. And the walk-in cooler cost a pretty penny. Mom already got the second installment of the cash rent from the new farmer who will plant the crops. The booth fees and travel expenses will add up. But otherwise we are in really good shape to get this business started. If we fill half the available spots for this first year I will be quite pleased. If not, I guess I will have to get a real job."

"I'm sure anxious to see what folks have to say about hunting deer and turkeys in Kentucky. The state doesn't have the big reputation some other states do."

"Oh, that reminds me. Did you see the article by K. D. Oakley about sleeper states? I brought it with me. Thought we could put that on our counter for people to see. I was thinking. Maybe we could invite him to hunt with us, and do a story about us. That would get us some exposure."

"Sounds like a good idea."

"Do you know if K. D. Oakley is a man or a woman?" Shiloh put the magazine back in her briefcase near her feet. "I tried doing an online search and couldn't figure it out. There are no pictures of him or her with any articles. I looked at the blog. No pictures of the writer are there. No social media pictures. There are tons of photos to illustrate the subject of the articles but no photos of the author. It's kind of weird."

Jete raised his eyebrows. "That is strange. How are you going to contact him or her to come hunt with us?"

"There is a contact field on the blog. I could write a message that way."

"Do it. What have you got to lose? But wait. There are a lot of horror stories about girls who meet strange guys with shady online profiles and then he turns out to be a serial killer or something."

"Uncle Jete you have seen too many crime shows. K. D. Oakley is a major columnist. His, or her, hunting articles are all over the Midwest. I highly doubt he is a closet serial killer."

"And yet there are no pictures of the guy." Jete grinned, raised a hand and made a zero with his fingers to emphasize the point. "None. Anywhere."

Shiloh held up her phone. "I'm on the blog site now. Writing the invitation now. Sending it now." Shiloh put her phone down. "He probably won't even respond."

After a minute passed she asked, "How much farther?" They both laughed.

Klu spent the day chopping more wood. He delivered another load to the gas station in Cedarwood. Business was good. Camping season was in full swing. He wondered if Becky was still living in the motor home and if his wood was in her campfire. He couldn't imagine her making a campfire.

When he got home he opened his laptop to work on some stories. An icon popped up telling him about incoming mail. He opened the message from Lawson's Hunting Adventures. When he got to the end of the message and saw Shiloh's name he was shocked. Klu looked up from the laptop and smiled. Imagine Shiloh's surprise if she only knew. The K. D. Oakley pen name had served him well. No one but his mother knew he wrote under an assumed name. Klu was surprised to learn that an outfitting business was starting next door to his family farm. He wondered what Henry and his father would think.

Klu stared at his laptop. Accepting the invitation would be a risk. Could he trust Shiloh and Jete not to expose him? The more he thought about it, the madder he got. Why did it matter if everyone knew the true identity of K. D. Oakley? He had started writing under a pen name years ago to keep it a secret from his father. He couldn't forget the laughter and ridicule his father had bestowed upon him when he first mentioned his desire to become a writer. Klu stood up and paced the floor. He went down the hall to talk to his mother.

Klu found her in the sewing room. "Hey Mom. Got a minute?"

"Of course. What's on your mind sweetheart?" Dorothy put her sewing down and gave Klu her full attention.

"Remember when I told Dad I wanted to be a writer?"

"Yes dear. That was unfortunate. His response was not appropriate. I'm glad you did not let it stop you from pursuing that career."

"Thanks Mom, but I guess maybe I let him get to me too much. That's why I started writing under a pen name instead of my own. Now I have an invitation to go hunting with an outfitter and do a story on them. But they think they are inviting K. D. Oakley and not Klu Dugan."

"What does that matter son? Lots of writers write under different names than their own. You can go regardless of the name on the article. I know you will do a wonderful job no matter which byline is on the story."

"The invitation is from Shiloh Lawson. Apparently she is starting an outfitting business on the family farm right next door to us. She wrote to the blog not knowing it is really me."

"I see." Charlene stood up and embraced her son. "I'm sorry Klu, but your father was not, and is not, a kind man. He was not kind to you boys. He got Henry in terrible trouble. Al would have been just like him I'm afraid. If the only reason you are writing under an assumed name is because of your father's influence, I think you have your answer."

Klu hugged his mom. "Thanks, I feel much better. I'm going to accept that invitation. And to heck with the consequences."

"That's the spirit. Now tell me all about this outfitter thing. They plan to do it on the land adjacent to us?"

Klu could tell she was thinking the same thing he had. "Yes. I doubt Dad or Henry will be happy to hear it."

"Well your dad won't have to worry about it for a few more years, thank heavens. And Henry will come around. He isn't in to hunting as much as you are. He did it, but I think he was always more interested in cars."

"Fast cars, and wild women. That's my brother Henry."

"Oh now, stop," Charlene turned and went back to her sewing. Klu went to his room, opened the laptop and looked at Shiloh's web site. Then he replied to Shiloh, informing her that K. D. Oakley would be happy to accept her invitation to bowhunt the opening weekend for velvet bucks. He asked her to provide additional information. Klu chuckled to himself when he asked her for directions. He knew he wouldn't have far to go to return home if she kicked him out.

Shiloh and Jete pulled into the hotel parking lot. They surveyed possible locations to park the truck with an enclosed trailer in tow, settling on a spot at the back of the establishment. After supper Shiloh checked her emails. "Hey! We got a response from K. D. Oakley! It's a yes for opening weekend. Awesome!" Shiloh fist pumped.

"That's good. Did Oakley say if he is a she or a he?" Jete joked. "Cause if he is a she we are going to need to talk about room arrangements. We are set up for two hunters per room, remember?"

"We'll cross that bridge when we come to it. Let's just worry about actually selling some hunts for opening weekend. Then we will worry about who rooms with whom."

The next morning Jete maneuvered the truck and trailer to the expo loading doors and they busied themselves setting up the booth. Shiloh heard a number of cuss words emanate from under the display board as Jete tried to screw through the wood to secure the deer mounts. After some wrangling they had the display set up and stood back admiring their work.

"Looks darn good to me. We deserve a pat on the back; you for building this fine wooden display and me for tagging these fine Kentucky whitetails." Shiloh grinned at Jete.

Before Jete could come back with a retort a man walked up to stand beside Shiloh and look at the deer heads. "Mighty impressive. Where are you from?"

"Western Kentucky," Shiloh replied. "I'm Shiloh Lawson, this is my Uncle Jete." The stranger tipped his cowboy hat to Shiloh and shook hands with her, then with Jete.

"Pleased to meet you. I'm Tucker Wynne. From New Mexico. My booth is right next to yours."

Tucker wore black jeans, cowboy boots and a silver belt buckle engraved with a bugling bull elk head. His white shirt had silver buttons and looked professionally pressed and tailored. His ensemble was topped with a black Stetson cowboy hat that spent most of its time in a hat box, being donned only for special occasions. Tucker stroked his handle bar mustache and asked if either of them had ever been elk hunting.

Shiloh answered for both of them, "No. But it's on my bucket list. She looked at the two massive six-by-six bull elk he had in his booth. "Wow. Talk about impressive. Those bulls are amazing."

"Thank you. So, have you done this show before?"

"No, it's actually our first show. We just got our outfitting business started. We'll be offering deer and turkey hunts on our family farm. Four of these bucks are mine." Shiloh pointed to the four largest bucks. "The one in the center is Jete's. We brought it because it is so unusual, with the drop tine and non-typical points. With just a fourteen inch inside spread, it doesn't score high, but it is impressive nonetheless."

"Indeed it is. I've been coming to this show for ten years. It's always been a good one. There have been a few times that I filled all of my openings with just this show. Guys would come with the deposit money in their pockets. Of course, the economy isn't quite so good nowadays but the show is still good for plenty of paying customers. Although I've had more than my share of greenhorns come from this part of the country. They read about hunting in the mountains and put that on their bucket list without knowing exactly what they are getting into. I could tell you a few stories, make your hair curl." He laughed and shook his head. "But, I guess it's all part of being an outfitter. Well, I'm going to get something to eat before the circus starts. Let me know if I can help with anything."

"Okay thanks, see you later." Within a few minutes Shiloh had met most of the people in booths all around theirs. "Uncle Jete, I feel like I am part of a family of hunting-show people already. Let's go eat before this circus starts."

"And you're already talking like them too," he teased. "We have an hour to kill, let's get something at the food court and then walk around and look at the rest of the expo. I have a feeling once this thing starts we won't get to see what else is here."

"You are probably right. At least I hope we are that busy."

Becky drove the van to the airport to get her backpacks out of the locker. She stuffed them onto the floor on the front passenger side and covered them with a blanket. Ricky had told her to drive the van because he had a delivery for the campground. She was dressed for a night at Eddy's Tavern. She wore a black strapless dress and had to keep pulling it up over her large breasts. She liked to show her cleavage but not so much as to get arrested for indecent exposure. She hadn't been to town in quite a while. The tight sequined dress showed her figure well. There were no panty lines; she wasn't wearing any.

When she got to the tavern Eddy was seated in his usual booth at the back of the bar. Ivan the realtor was sitting nearby. She was surprised and annoyed when Eddy's other two girls did not get up to leave. They seemed younger than the others she was used to seeing. Becky suddenly began to feel unsure of her looks. She looked around the table. Ivan was leering at her as usual, which made her feel oddly secure that she hadn't lost her appeal. "I need to talk to you Eddy." She stood waiting for an answer.

Eddy whispered something in one of the girl's ears. She got up and left the table. He turned to the other girl and whispered in her ear. She also left the table. Eddy then gave Becky his full attention by looking her up and down. He took a few moments to admire her figure before meeting her gaze. "Nice dress. What do you want Becky?"

"I want to talk to you about getting a new motor home. The one I have now is old. I want a new place, like one of these." She handed Eddy brochures from the RV place in Canyon. "I have enough money to buy it."

"Sure thing baby." He turned and motioned to Ivan. "Ivan, Becky wants a new motor home. Can you take care of that?"

"Sure boss." Ivan looked at Becky. "I can help you with that, no problem. I know a guy. He likes to get paid in cash."

"I can pay cash," Becky answered.

"Ivan, come here." Eddy motioned for him to come closer. Ivan bent down to hear what Eddy wanted to tell him in private. He listened carefully, stood straight and adjusted his suit jacket before turning toward Becky.

Eddy waved his hand to dismiss them, "Ivan, you and Becky go to my private office and take care of the details." Eddy got up from the table and left to follow the two young girls.

Ivan showed Becky the way to the back room. "Sit down. Can I get you a drink?" He pointed toward a small private bar.

"A beer is fine, thanks."

Ivan opened a beer bottle. "Would you like an iced mug for this beer?"

"Sure."

Ivan retrieved a mug from the freezer and poured Becky's beer into it before handing it to her.

Becky took the mug of beer and sipped slowly, keeping her eyes on Ivan. "What did Eddy say to you?"

Ivan sat next to her at the poker table. She could smell garlic on his breath from the pizza he had eaten a few minutes earlier. His fingers were still greasy. "Let me see the brochures. I need to know exactly what you want. I can see that it is delivered. Eddy told me he would take care of the down payment, but you would be required to pay the rest in cash when the motor home is delivered."

Becky liked the idea that Eddy was offering to pay some of the cost and make sure she was taken care of. It made the sting of the other two girls at his booth a little less sharp. Over the next hour Ivan and Becky talked about the things she wanted to buy and how to buy them. She wanted a new luxury car with plenty of trunk room. They discussed make, model, price, and delivery methods for the items on her list.

By the time Becky was on her third beer she began to feel odd. She couldn't keep her thoughts straight. The room became blurry.

When Ivan was sure Becky was completely under the influence of the drug he had slipped into her beer he made a phone call then guided her out the back door. She laughed and giggled and hung on him, babbling incoherently. Ivan helped her crawl into the back of the cargo van. Two bouncers Ivan had summoned carried three large plastic tubs sealed with duct tape into the back of the van and returned to the tavern. Ivan looked around to be sure no one was watching before he crawled in to the back of the van with Becky and shut the doors.

Hours later Becky woke up. Her clothes were disheveled and she had a severe headache. She didn't remember getting into the back of the van. She could recall the meeting with Ivan but nothing after that. Her purse was on the floor next to her. Becky stumbled out of the van and looked around. The parking lot was empty and the tavern was closed. She felt bruised and sore as she crawled into the driver's seat. The keys were in the ignition. Her backpacks were still safely tucked under the blanket on the passenger side floor. It didn't seem odd to Becky. Everyone knew not to mess with Eddy's vans.

She went back to the campground and hid the backpacks in the motor home, then took a nap. The goons unloaded the tubs from the van and took them out of sight.

Ricky had told her the things she ordered would be taken care of, and true to his word, three days later the goons pulled into the campground with Becky's new thirty-one foot motor home. It featured a luxury package with two pull out wings and plenty of storage. They eased it in place next to her old one and made sure everything was in order. Becky transferred her belongings to the new home, making sure the goons did not see her carry the back packs from one to the other.

Ricky delivered a new, full-sized black Cadillac SUV later

that day. Becky was on cloud nine. She wanted to do something to show her appreciation to Eddy. Plus she wanted to make sure he wasn't mad at her for Henry's occasional visits. Once she found out that Ricky was Eddy's nephew she figured he snitched on her. She decided to get on Ricky's good side.

As the week went by, Becky visited Ricky often to get updates on the dog fighting ring. She learned that dogs were bred and trained to fight each other, with some fights lasting one to two hours, ending only when one of the dogs could not go on. The losers were severely injured and usually died. The blood sport was profitable with wagers running into the thousands of dollars. Because dogfighting was a felony Ricky said Eddy didn't want any of them talking about it and that she should stay away from the box canyon for her own safety.

She didn't want to risk going back to the box canyon again. She wasn't sure what the goons were doing back there but didn't want to get caught snooping. She remembered Eddy telling her he could sell the pit bull puppies for her. Now she understood why. She didn't need the money, but figured getting four pit bulls for Eddy would get her some brownie points.

Driving for Eddy was an easy, well-paying job with lots of fringe benefits and she aimed to keep it.

FOURTEEN

Over the next three weeks Shiloh and Jete worked the sport shows and filled forty percent of their openings for the upcoming season along with about twenty percent for the following year. They rolled in to home as the sun set. Hazard ran to greet them, jumping up and down and racing around the truck and trailer.

"Good grief that dog is going to get run over right here in the driveway," Jete said with amusement. Shiloh bailed out of the truck and yelled for Hazard. She was knocked backward by the excited dog. A second dog came running from the barn. Hazard ran circles around them all. The second dog was a young greyhound. Soon it started running in even wider circles. Shiloh stood up and laughed at the antics of the two dogs.

Dorothy came out to greet them. "I see you've met Dixie. She just showed up the day after you left. I have tried to find her owners but no one has claimed her. I think she got dumped. It happens to puppies all the time out here in the country. She and Hazard have become good buddies. I don't have the heart to take her to the pound. She's such a good dog. She does love to chase cars that go by. I hope she doesn't get hit."

"Gosh mom, we have plenty of room out here for a second dog. I think it will be good for Hazard to have someone to play with while we are working. Things are going to get busier with every week. Did I tell you I invited K. D. Oakley to hunt the first week? He accepted. Or she. We don't know which. I guess I better find out."

Jete yawned and stretched. "If you ladies will excuse me I am going home. I'll come back in the morning to unload the display and help you rehang the mounts."

"Okay, thanks Jete. No hurry. I'll see you tomorrow. I'm tired too. After supper I'm going straight to bed."

"I'm just glad you two made it home before the storm hits. It's been moving across Missouri and southern Illinois headed straight to us." Dorothy showed them the radar on her phone. "I was watching the news just before you pulled in. There have already been tornadoes all across southern Illinois. They are predicting it will get here before morning. All we can do is pray that the storm loses some of its power over the next few hours."

"This is really unusual for tornados to hit this time of year. I'm sure it will fizzle out long before it gets to us," Shiloh responded, willing the storm to die out.

"I think I will spend the night at the ranch house. The basement sounds much safer than my cabin on the hill. Maybe we should all stay there," Jete suggested.

"Oh man, I was really looking forward to sleeping in my own bed. If the storm gets bad we can run across the street and into the basement if we need to. Or dive into the creepy spider infested storm cellar if we have to." Shiloh shuddered at the thought.

"Suit yourselves. I'll see you in the morning." Jete waved as he headed for the ranch house.

Klu looked at the weather app on his phone. He checked the storm cellar and the batteries in his flashlights. He filled the chain saw with gas. Something told him it was going to be a bad night. Queenie and the pups were huddled in the dog house. They sensed something in the air as well.

Henry sat on the couch staring at the television. Klu noticed his brother had been unusually quiet. "What's wrong Henry? You seem like you lost your best friend." Klu punched his brother's arm as he sat next to him on the couch.

"Well, she ain't my best friend that's for sure. But last time I saw Becky she told me not to come out to the campground anymore. Said she didn't want to see me. She had a regular boyfriend now and I couldn't be coming around anymore."

"If you ask me, she's no great loss. I didn't realize you had been out there that much."

"Yeah, I know. It's not that I miss her. I just enjoyed the beer, the campfire and the free sex. She sure does have a thing for you though little brother. She asks about you every time I'm out there. She has pictures of you on her phone. When I asked about them she told me she just likes tattoo art. She took a picture of mine too."

"That's a bit creepy if you ask me." Klu shook his head.

"Becky says Shiloh Lawson is the one who made the anonymous call that turned us in. Do you think she did it?"

"How in the hell would Becky know who made the call. It was anonymous."

"Good point. I sure would like to know who did it so I can punch their face. Girl or no girl!"

"I hope you never do find out. Punching someone in the face, especially a girl sounds too much like Dad. And you are not like him, thankfully, neither of us are. It's good you are staying home tonight anyway. There's a storm coming. Several tornadoes in southern Illinois have torn things up. It's moving in our direction."

"It's mighty late for tornadoes."

"Yes it is. I don't have a good feeling about this one." Klu checked the weather app again. They were still directly in the projected path of the storm.

Shiloh fell asleep on the couch. Dorothy covered her with a blanket. No sense sending her upstairs with a powerful storm on its way. She could hear the wind pick up. Rain began to fall.

Hazard walked nervously to the door and back to the couch several times. He didn't want out, but he didn't want to be in either. Dixie sat unusually still, watching Hazard and Dorothy for any sudden movement. She was like a tightly coiled spring ready to release energy at any moment.

Dorothy smiled as she watched Hazard. The dog was pacing like a worried person, back and forth, back and forth. Suddenly both dogs jumped. Hazard started barking. Dixie howled.

Dorothy's cell phone buzzed with weather warning texts. Shiloh's phone vibrated on the table. A weather warning text announcing a tornado showed on the screen. Then Dorothy heard the faint sound of a train engine.

"Shiloh!" she screamed, running to her daughter. "Get up! Come on! We have to get in the storm cellar! Hurry!" Dorothy nearly dragged Shiloh off the bed in a panic.

"I'm up Mom, I'm up, let's go! Come on Hazard!"

They ran to the kitchen and opened the door to the back yard. Lightning flashed. Dorothy could see the tornado on the west horizon. It looked massive. The rotating column of ominous air stretched from clouds to land and was at least a mile wide. Lightning flashed again and thunder rattled the windows.

Shiloh briefly stood still, mesmerized by the funnel cloud. Dorothy shoved her from behind and shouted, "Get to the shelter!"

Shiloh jerked the storm shelter doors open and scrambled down the steps. Dorothy followed. Hazard and Dixie raced past their legs and into the cellar. Shiloh turned to reach up and help her mom pull the doors closed. They nearly lost their grip but managed to secure the latch and step back. It was dark until lightning flashed again. Shiloh grabbed a flashlight and turned it on. They were both wide eyed and trembling.

"That was too close for comfort," Shiloh shouted. "That twister was really moving fast. Gosh we only had to run a few yards but we are all soaking wet. I never saw it rain so hard in all my life."

Hail began to pound on the door. The noise was deafening making it impossible to carry on a conversation.

Dorothy opened a big plastic tub and took out four blankets. She wrapped Shiloh in one and herself in the other. She sat down on a small bench and called to Dixie who was shaking in a corner.

The hail stopped but the rain fell in torrents fueled by strong gusts of wind. "Come here girl. That's it. Come on. It's all going to be okay." Dixie trotted to Dorothy and snuggled into the blanket on the floor at her feet. Shiloh put the folded blanket on the floor for Hazard, but he wanted no part of it. He stood with hackles up growling at the door.

Dorothy began to pray out loud, "Dear God, just as your disciples who were caught in a mighty storm in a small boat, we too are fearful of this terrible storm around us. Please protect our homes and family. Please protect our friends and those who may be in the path of this storm. Please lessen its fury and be with us in this time of danger. Amen."

Shiloh couldn't hear her mom but knew she was praying. She clasped her hands and prayed that Jete had made it to the basement of the ranch house.

After ten minutes the roaring sound of the tornado died down. Rain slowly subsided. They waited another ten minutes before opening the cellar doors. It was still too dark to survey any damage. They could see pea sized hail in the yard in the beams of the flashlight. They went back into the house. "The lights are out," Shiloh reported. "I'll get some candles lit."

Dorothy opened the front door and stepped onto the front porch. "I can see your Uncle Jete over at the ranch house. He's carrying a lantern. Here he comes."

Jete drove his truck across the street and up to the farm house. "Are you guys alright?" he yelled from the truck as he got out.

"We are fine. The lights are out, but that's all we know for right now," Dorothy answered. "Did you see the tornado? It was to the west and moving fast to the north."

Jete stopped in his tracks. "How far west?"

"I couldn't tell but it looked to be beyond your cabin, but I didn't exactly stand around puzzling on it."

"Let's take a quick look around here then we will go check the cabin." Jete relit the lantern and walked to the barn. Shiloh joined him with a spotlight. They didn't see any big issues, just a few limbs down and some shingles blown off.

"The sun will be coming up in about thirty minutes. Should we wait until we can see better before we go check the cabin?" Shiloh asked.

"I'm going now, I can't wait. The suspense is too much." Jete headed for his truck.

"I'm coming with you. Give me a minute to get dressed," Shiloh said as she ran to change clothes. Moments later she was back and out of breath.

"Be careful. The main phone line is down, there's no dial tone. Are your cell phones working?" Dorothy asked.

"Mine is," Shiloh replied as she jumped into Jete's truck.

"Mine too," Jete called over the sound of the engine revving up. "We'll call you as soon as we know anything."

The Dugans emerged from their storm cellar. Klu shined his flashlight on the house and shed. He checked the garage. "No damage. I cannot believe it. Mom, your prayers worked. I can't believe we don't have any damage. That tornado sounded like it was on top of us for a minute or two."

Henry helped his mom into the house. Their lights were also out. Charlene brought candles from the bathroom closet. She set two of them on the kitchen counter and lit them. She carried two more into the living room, lit them and placed them on the coffee table. Then she collapsed on the couch. "I hope everyone is safe."

Klu started searching his cell phone for information on the tornado's path. "Oh my gosh. There were two tornados. One was on the ground for about a mile and went through just west of us. The other one went right over our heads but didn't touch down. It hit the bluff just north of us and lost momentum." Klu sat down next to his mom. "We really dodged a bullet."

Dorothy put her hand on Klu's knee. "Klu, how far west of us? How far west of us did the tornado touch down?"

Klu abruptly stood up. "Shiloh." He tried to refresh the search to get more specific information. "It's too soon, nobody has a good handle on it." He paused to read posts on social media. "Oh my God. There was another tornado. It hit the southeast side of Findlay. Dozens of homes are damaged."

"Oh no." Charlene put her hands together and whispered a prayer.

"I'm going to check on Shiloh, uh, I mean the Lawson place. If they are okay I'm heading to Findlay. I'll grab my chainsaw and tool box. Don't worry I'll call you."

"I'll come with you Klu," Henry said as he grabbed a camo rain jacket, a pair of gloves, and followed Klu out the door. They jumped in Klu's truck and quickly raced to the Lawson farm. Klu was relieved to see the house and outbuildings still standing. The ranch house was in good shape too. He cruised past the house slowly and then continued west toward Findlay. When he got to Jete's driveway he could see dozens of trees blown over in the yard. He turned in and drove toward the cabin. Jete was working to remove a big tree limb from the drive with his chain saw so they could get closer to the cabin. The building was intact, but trees were down in many places.

Shiloh saw the headlights and stopped picking up limbs. She was surprised to see Henry and Klu get out of the truck and walk up to Jete. She tossed the limbs off to the side and joined them. She heard Klu's voice first. "Hello Jete. Are you guys all okay?"

"Yes. Everybody is fine. No one got hurt. Our homes are okay. We just have a lot of big limbs and busted up trees here at the cabin. It's like it tore up the trees in the yard and then jumped right over the cabin. How about your place? Is Charlene alright?"

"She is pretty shaken up, but otherwise just fine, thanks. We didn't have any damage to speak of." Klu walked closer to Jete and stuck out his hand. "If you could use some help, I brought my chainsaw."

Jete returned the strong grasp of Klu's handshake. "I would welcome your help." He extended his hand to Henry. Henry shook it and nodded his head but didn't say anything. Shiloh stood next to Jete, surprised by Klu's offer.

"Hey Shiloh, I'm glad you're okay."

"Thanks Klu, you too." Shiloh shook his hand.

Henry cleared his throat. "What about Findlay? Klu says there is major damage in Findlay. If people are in trouble maybe we should be going there to help."

Klu didn't know if his brother was trying to avoid helping a Lawson or if he really felt concern for the people of Findlay.

Jete nodded his head in agreement. "If that's the case, you are exactly right Henry. These trees can wait. Let's head west to town and see what we can do to help." He carried his chainsaw to his truck and got in. Shiloh quickly joined him without saying a word. Klu backed his truck down the lane and pulled back far enough on the main road for Jete to get his truck out of the driveway then they all headed toward Findlay.

Two miles down the road they were surprised to see the old Hammond place completely flattened.

"Oh my gosh! I hope Carter and Rose were not staying there last night!" Shiloh said in a panic.

Jete pulled the truck as close to the house as he could. Klu did the same. They all got out and began calling for Carter and Rose.

Shiloh tried calling Rose on her cell phone. "It's going straight to voice mail." They split up and continued shouting. By now the sun was up and they could see the path of the tornado clearly. Suddenly Shiloh heard a voice from under the piles of twisted wood. "Carter!" She yelled again. "Carter!"

Klu joined her. "Did you hear someone?"

"I thought so. Listen." From under the rubble Shiloh could hear someone yelling for help. "Do you hear that? It sounds like Carter!"

"Are you sure? I don't hear anything. But I can't hear as well as I used to. Too many rounds of ammo shot through too many guns and no hearing protection." He gave her a quick apologetic look.

Shiloh began digging through the rubble, pulling up debris that used to be a house. She stopped and listened again. "There! I can hear someone for sure. Help me move this stuff." They worked to drag away wood and pieces of the house. "Jete come here. I think they are under here!"

Together they dug through debris to the cellar door below. Henry and Klu pried it open. Carter and Rose stood looking up at them. "I've never been so happy to see another human being in all my life!" Carter shouted. Rose was crying and laughing at the same time.

They helped them out of the cellar. When they finished hugging everyone they looked around. Both were in shock at all the damage. Finally Rose spoke. "We were planning to remodel the place but this is a bit much."

"Oh Rose. I'm so sorry. We will help you rebuild," Shiloh promised.

Carter put his arm around Rose. "We have insurance honey, we will be fine, don't worry."

"You can stay in the ranch house for the rest of the summer. And you can move in with me and Mom when hunting season starts."

"You guys didn't have any damage?"

"Nothing substantial. Mostly trees, a few shingles and such. But I hear there may be significant damage in Findlay. We were headed that way when we came upon your house."

"Look at that." Rose pointed at a big oak tree in the yard. "There is a giant three foot long wooden splinter driven right into that tree. We parked our truck right next to it and there is not a scratch on it. That is bizarre."

"Holy cow," Jete said. "Look at that. I've heard stories

about weird things happening in a tornado but sure never saw anything like that."

"And the big tobacco barn is gone. It is in shambles." Carter scratched his head and looked at the pile of rubble.

Jete put his hand on Carter's shoulder. "Well Carter, it's not a complete loss. We talked about tearing down that barn and salvaging as much as we could. We can make some mighty good picture frames from any wood we can salvage. Barn wood frames bring good money."

"He's right about that Carter. Uncle Jete can make some amazing things from wood. And barn siding wood is in demand. Why don't I take Rose back to our house? You guys can go on in to Findlay. There is probably a massive rescue mission underway now. What we have here can wait. I don't mean to diminish your loss, but we are all lucky to be alive and unhurt, others may be in need of your help right this minute."

"You're right Shiloh," Klu said. "Let's go guys." Klu and Henry got back in Klu's truck. Jete and Carter followed in Jete's truck. Shiloh watched them drive out of sight.

"It's a good thing we left the keys in the truck," Rose said. "I have no idea where they would be in all this mess."

Shiloh put her arm around Rose's shoulder. "Let's go get mom. We can come back here with some tools and see what can be salvaged."

FIFTEEN

Becky and Ricky were admiring the buds of a new subspecies of marijuana from a plant Ricky cultivated in the ditches behind the campground. The gallon sized plastic baggy was packed full. Ricky pulled enough weed from the baggy to smoke in a bong and returned the bag to his refrigerator. He packed the bowl and offered Becky first toke. She accepted.

Ricky packed the bowl again and took a long drag and held his breath before releasing a stream of smoke into the air above his head. "Did you hear about the tornado in Findlay? A bunch of people were hurt. Houses on the southeast side of town were flattened." He flicked his lighter and fired up another hit from the bong. "It's all over the news this morning."

"No I hadn't heard. I know it rained like hell last night but everything seems fine here."

"One went through Findlay on the ground. An F-four. A second touched down about thirty miles east of town. There were a couple more twisters that didn't touch down. Four of them in all. Weird time of year for tornadoes."

Becky wasn't sure of the mileage but thought Klu's house was about thirty miles east of Findlay. Her mind started racing. She stood up and said, "I gotta run some errands and, uh, do a little shopping. Will you run me back to my place?"

"Sure." Ricky opened the door for Becky and closed it behind them. He drove her to the new motorhome in the electric golf cart. "See ya later." He waved as he drove off.

Becky scrambled around in her new motorhome looking for the bag of dog collars and soft, canned dog food. She changed from flip-flops to tennis shoes, grabbed her purse and went out the door. She got in the new SUV and drove west through Cedarwood toward Klu's house. Even though she told Henry not to come to the campground anymore, she reasoned it would not seem strange for her to pay a visit to him. She could say she heard about the tornado and wanted to check on him. Secretly she was worried that Klu may have been injured in the storm if the tornado had gone through his property.

If no one was home, she could snatch the pit bulls.

Charlene called Dorothy on her cell phone. "Hi Dorothy, is everything alright at your place?" she asked with genuine concern.

"Yes, we are fine. Klu said your place is okay too, I'm relieved to hear it."

"The old Hammond place was destroyed. Carter and Rose are fine, just a few cuts and bruises. The men all went to Findlay to see how they could help with rescue efforts. Rose, Shiloh and I are here at the farmhouse. We are going to go over to Rose's place and see if anything is salvageable. We will start the cleanup in whatever way we can. I think it is harder for her to sit here doing nothing."

"Would you mind if I joined you?"

"You would be most welcome and I know Rose will appreciate it. We're leaving now, come whenever you can."

"I'll see you in a few minutes." Charlene wasn't sure what to do next. She changed into her gardening clothes, went to her kitchen, made sandwiches, put them in a cooler, grabbed some gardening tools from the back porch and left. When she arrived, the other women were picking up limbs. She parked and joined them.

"We are a bit overwhelmed by the destruction," Dorothy said to Charlene. "I think the men are going to need to bring some big trucks and heavy equipment in here to deal with this. We just decided to clear as many limbs out of the yard as possible so they could still mow. No sense letting the grass get out of control. Sounds kind of silly but we just wanted to be doing something."

Rose joined them with a pile of sticks in her hands. "I really appreciate what you gals are doing. I know it doesn't seem like much but it does mean so much to me."

"Of course, we want to help in any way we can," Dorothy responded.

"Rose, if you don't mind my asking. I heard you sold the hardware business and the building. Had you already moved into this house?" Charlene asked.

"Not yet. We had a few items in there that Shiloh brought down for us. But there was nothing that can't be replaced. It was mostly kitchen supplies, new curtains, blankets and things like that. Nothing major, nothing sentimental. We were lucky. We moved all of our belongings into the storage facility on the north east side of town while we worked to get this place ready to move into. Thank God the tornado missed that or we would be in a world of hurt. Last night was our first night in the house. We were going to start painting today. But we have insurance. And we still have all of our possessions, so we will be fine." Rose looked at the ground and shook her head. "I can't say as much for some of those poor folks in town. It's a sad situation."

Becky slowed the SUV to turn into the Dugan farm. She noted almost no tornado damage and prepared herself mentally to pretend to check on the family if Henry and Klu were home. She parked and went to the front door. She peered in the window before knocking. No answer. Becky opened the door. She called Henry's name. No answer. She called for Klu. No answer. She walked through the house to the back door.

A sense of urgency came over her as she became certain the house was empty. She hoped Queenie and the pups were still in the back yard.

When she opened the back door and called for Queenie the pit bull emerged from the dog box and ran to her. Queenie was glad to see Becky. The pups followed, but were unsure why their mother was so excited. Becky patted Queenie on the head and gently shoved the pups out of the way. She went to the SUV to retrieve the bag of collars. Queenie followed.

When Becky opened the door Queenie jumped in. Becky was shocked. "Good girl Queenie. Now how do we get the pups inside?" Queenie jumped to the front passenger seat and barked. The pups were running around all over the yard by now. "Stay Queenie. Stay there. Good girl."

She closed the door and took three cans of dog food from the bag. She opened the cans and dumped the food on the ground. "Here puppies, come here. Come get this nice food. Come on." The puppies responded to her gentle coaxing. One came forward and found a pile of food. It began to gulp the food and the other puppies noticed. They came to get their own piles. Becky put a collar on the first puppy and lifted it under her arm. She opened the back door and tossed the dog inside. It started barking.

Queenie jumped into the back seat.

"Oh crap," Becky said as she quickly closed the door, trapping the first puppy and Queenie inside. The other two puppies had finished all the food and were jumping on Becky looking for more. She placed a collar on the second puppy and picked it up. The puppy squirmed as Becky struggled to shove it inside with Queenie and the first puppy without letting all the dogs out.

Puppy number three took off running around the SUV barking wildly. Queenie and the two puppies already inside went nuts. They jumped from seat to seat, window to window, barking wildly. Becky realized the puppies had probably never been inside a vehicle and their reaction was also scaring Queenie. Puppy number three was losing momentum. It ran to the dog house and crawled inside looking for her litter mates and mother.

Becky followed and called to the dog. It growled. "Don't growl at me you little shit," Becky muttered through clenched teeth. Becky cooed at the puppy and made kissing noises with her lips. The puppy refused to budge. Queenie had calmed down and the other pups were silent now. Becky sat on the ground and called to the puppy in a soft nurturing tone. "Come here you little troublemaker."

After five minutes of listening to baby talk the puppy finally emerged from the dog house and sniffed Becky's hands. It could smell food and started licking her fingers. "That's it. Good puppy." Becky put the collar on the pup and picked it up. It continued licking her fingers as she carried it to the SUV. "Don't they feed you around here? Probably too busy with tornado business and forgot to give you breakfast. Lucky me."

Becky opened the back driver's side door of the SUV and shoved the puppy inside. Then she cracked open the driver side front door and told Queenie to get back. All the puppies were in the back seat. Queenie jumped to the passenger front seat. Becky got in and looked around. The inside of the new SUV was filthy with dirty dog paw marks and slobber. "I clearly didn't think this through," Becky said to herself and Queenie. "Oh well. At least I got all you little fuckers. Now to get out of here before someone sees me," she said looking at Queenie.

Becky turned the SUV around and drove down the lane to the hard road. She turned toward the campground and took off. Queenie settled into the passenger seat and watched Becky. "You're really not such a bad dog, ya know." Becky reached over and patted Queenie on the head. "You all smell like crap though."

When she got to the campground she stopped at Ricky's trailer. He wasn't home so Becky continued on to her new motor home. The goons and Ricky were sitting around the camp fire. Becky parked in her usual spot and got out. She let Queenie out of the vehicle. Queenie stayed by her side as she approached the men. "Hi guys. I have something for you. Well, for Eddy."

Ricky got up and walked toward Becky. Queenie moved to the opposite side of Becky and shied away from being petted by Ricky. "Not very friendly is she?" Ricky commented.

"She only likes girls," Becky lied. "I have three puppies in the SUV. Will you see that Eddy knows I got him the dogs for a gift?"

Ricky raised his eyebrows and looked at the goons. They looked at each other but said nothing. "Uh, yeah sure Becky. I'll tell him. What do you want me to do with them? I mean do you want me to take all of them or just the puppies?"

Queenie moved close to Becky's leg and stood still. "Just take the puppies. I think I will keep Queenie for a while."

"Okay." Ricky looked inside the SUV at the puppies. "Hey guys, do you have some rope?" One of the goons moved and Queenie growled.

Becky smiled. "Yep, I'm keeping Queenie for sure. Get the rest of them out of here, I'll take Queenie inside the motor home while you do it."

Klu, Henry, Carter and Jete worked all day helping tornado victims. The tornado devastated a residential area. Many victims were still asleep in their beds when the fast moving twister tore through town. The impact of the tornado was immense. Cars were hanging in trees. Twisted metal wrapped around tree trunks. Roofs of houses were torn off. Jagged walls held the contents of rooms that were visible from the street. Electric lines were down and tangled.

They joined an effort by two other men to remove rubble from a house where a child was trapped. The mother was beside herself, crying and rocking back and forth, as the men worked together to find the child. The roof of the house was gone. They focused on the bedroom area. After several minutes Henry shouted that he could see the child's arm under a mattress. Henry used brute force and adrenaline to carefully remove the debris on top of the exposed arm. They found the little girl in her crib, which had been partially crushed by the weight of the king size mattress. A pillow smothered her head. She wasn't breathing.

Jete began CPR. A hush fell over the small crowd of workers as they watched helplessly. After several chest compressions she started breathing, then crying. Everyone celebrated the sound of her cries.

Jete handed the girl to her mother. "Get her to the hospital. She has several cuts and bruises." The mother hugged Jete and quickly disappeared with family members helping her navigate the debris that was once their home.

Henry and Carter teamed up to work tirelessly together to dig through the rubble to find trapped people and animals. Henry was profoundly impacted by the experience. At one point he stopped digging and stood frozen, overwhelmed by the enormity of the devastation. Carter put his hand on his shoulder and asked if he was alright.

Henry responded, "Why do bad things happen to good people? If there is a God, why does he let this sort of thing happen?" He looked at Carter while fighting back tears. "All this seems pointless."

"Come over here son and sit down," Carter said, pointing to a curb. Henry sat down and slumped over with his head in his hands. Carter sat beside him and put his arm around his back.

"I don't have all the answers Henry, but I do know that the bad things help us to see and appreciate the good things. God can use bad things to work toward good outcomes. Bad things have been happening since Eve first gave Adam a taste of the forbidden apple. So you could say we invited evil into this world. We sometimes feel like victims. But you must remember that Jesus was also a victim of the circumstances that led to his crucifixion. God used the resurrection of Jesus to give us hope and the promise of life after death. The symbol of the cross, which used to be associated with a horrendous method of punishment and death, is now a symbol of everlasting life. Only God could make that horribly bad thing result in something so amazingly good."

Henry raised his head up and thought about Carter's words for a few minutes. He looked around and straightened his back. "A lot of people need help. We can't be sitting here on the curb feeling sorry for ourselves." Henry subconsciously rubbed his bad knee. "Let's get back to work." Henry stood up and reached out his hand to help Carter get up from the curb.

"Thanks for the talk." Before the day was over he and Carter had formed a bond that became the seed of a new friendship.

Klu focused on using his skills with a chain saw to remove tree limbs and cut paths for rescue vehicles. Jete assisted emergency responders with first aid. His military training enabled him to save more lives. All four were exhausted by the end of the day.

Charlene had food prepared and waiting when Henry and Klu arrived home just after dark. They showered and changed clothes then sat down to eat. No one noticed that Queenie and the pups were gone.

After supper Klu remembered to feed the dogs. He went outside and filled their dog bowls. He was so tired he wasn't thinking straight. He assumed Queenie and the pups were in the dog house. They would come out to eat any minute as usual. He turned and nearly stumbled walking back to the house. He walked through the kitchen into his bedroom and fell on his bed. He was asleep seconds after his head hit the pillow.

Henry offered to help his mom clean up the kitchen but she refused, sending him to bed too. As she put things away she smiled and shook her head because she couldn't remember Henry ever making such an offer before.

Over the next few weeks they assisted with the ongoing recovery efforts. Klu helped Jete cut up the salvaged barn wood into usable pieces. Jete began to teach Klu how to make picture frames from the barn wood. They were all so busy, no one spent time looking for Queenie and the pups. After a while they didn't think about them anymore.

Henry and Carter also worked to clear rubble and debris

from Carter's demolished house. Carter and Rose decided to purchase a double wide modular home instead of rebuilding a frame house from the ground up. They stayed at the ranch house until it could be delivered and set up.

Henry worked at his mechanic job then went to Carter's in the evenings. Over time they became such close friends that Carter offered to back Henry in a new business venture when he completed the terms of his parole.

The mechanic shop in Cedarwood would soon have new owners.

SIXTEEN

Shiloh met Maxine at the coffee shop in Cedarwood. They needed to discuss wedding plans. All Shiloh knew was that Maxine wanted a small wedding but she didn't know if she wanted a bachelorette party and a bridal shower or what else might be on her mind. They slipped into a booth and faced each other. Shiloh noticed Maxine's unusually beautiful glow.

"So, Maxine, how have you been? You look amazing."

"Fabulous!" Maxine's smile was bright. She started to speak again but the waitress interrupted them. Shiloh watched Maxine converse with the waitress over menu choices. She noticed Maxine's beautifully manicured fingernails. They were polished to a high sheen and brilliant red. Shiloh looked at her own nails. No polish, cut short. She noticed Maxine's makeup. Her foundation looked airbrushed and flawless. Maxine's pale blue outfit looked tailor made. When they finished ordering Shiloh complimented Maxine on her designer look. "You look like you stepped off the cover of a fashion magazine."

"Oh, thanks. But look at you. Not a drop of makeup,

perfect complexion, and those eyelashes. Honey, what I wouldn't give for those long brown eyelashes. Putting mascara on and taking it off every day is a pain."

"I suppose it is. I wouldn't know, but thanks. Seriously Maxine what's your secret? You look amazing."

Maxine blurted out, "I'm pregnant!" She giggled and dug into her purse looking for her favorite package of sweetener. "Ah here it is. The restaurants don't carry it," she said, holding up the packet and grinning.

"What! Oh my gosh, Maxine, that's wonderful! Congratulations! Wow, two kids!"

"I know." Maxine leaned forward. "Delmar's online car dealership is doing great. He got a new partner. Some guy named Eddy. He made enough money last month that we're going to Jamaica for our honeymoon. Can you believe it?" She leaned back as the waitress delivered their appetizer of nachos and dipping sauces.

"So. I never knew people bought so many cars online."

"I don't know much about it. Eddy has a used car lot in Findlay. They sell to corporations, move fleets of rental cars, I don't know. All I know is I don't have to work, I can stay home with my kids and Delmar is not gambling anymore. All is good. I know you and Delmar had a big falling out over politics when we were in college, but that was a long time ago. Delmar thought it was a fine idea that you be my maid of honor, considering our life-long history together and all."

Shiloh regretted not telling her best friend that the disagreement with Delmar had nothing to do with politics. She had caught him stealing money from the cashier's box at the annual fundraiser. Delmar had begged Shiloh not to tell

Maxine. Not long after, Maxine quit school, moved to Vegas with Delmar and had a kid. They had had almost no contact in the years since.

"Speaking of being your maid of honor, I was wondering if you wanted a bachelorette party or a bridal shower or what?" Shiloh held her breath waiting for an answer.

"I don't want to put you to any trouble. Me and Delmar have been living together a long time and we have a kid so it's not like I need the traditional stuff. I wouldn't mind some kind of small party though. But I can help pay for it, we have plenty of dough."

Shiloh breathed a sigh of relief. "I was thinking about this and wondered if you would want to have a combination sleepover bridal shower at our ranch house. No one would have to drive after having a few drinks. We could play cards, watch movies, whatever."

"You mean your grandparent's old place? I thought you had a tenant farmer living there?"

"Well, we did. But he retired. We have it all fixed up for our new business. Jete, Mom and I are starting an outfitting business."

"What's that?" Maxine looked perplexed.

"Outfitting for deer and turkey hunts. We offer guided hunts. Hunters stay at the ranch house, we feed them, take them hunting and they pay us."

"Sweet. You always were such a tomboy. I never did quite understand the whole hunting thing. Don't get me wrong I like meat just as much as anybody but I couldn't kill an animal."

Shiloh decided not to start an argument as Maxine's cheeseburger was placed on the table by the waitress. "Okay so text me the list of gals you want invited to the party and I will take care of everything. You just show up and enjoy the fun."

Over the next hour they discussed wedding plans, the upcoming festival in Cedarwood and generally got caught up on their friendship.

After the luncheon Maxine told Delmar all about Shiloh's plans to start an outfitting business. Delmar told Eddy. Eddy told Ricky. Ricky mentioned it to Becky, who didn't seem to be paying attention at the time.

Two weeks later Shiloh held Maxine's party at the ranch house. Maxine, her sister, mother and three friends had a fabulous time with Shiloh, Dorothy, Charlene and Rose, staying up until the wee hours of the morning.

Jete worked on salvaging wood from the downed trees for his woodworking business. Klu worked out a deal with Jete to help remove the damaged and unwanted trees from Jete's place. Klu wore out one chain saw and had to buy another when Henry could no longer keep the old motor running. Klu sold cords of firewood at the gas station, kept up with his online courses and agreed to several writing assignments. Money was good. He didn't need to deliver pizzas anymore.

Klu had looked for Queenie and the pups for a couple of weeks but finally gave up. He wasn't that fond of the dog anyway. He was glad his mom and Shiloh's mom were spending more time together. Henry seemed to have buried the idea that Shiloh was the anonymous caller. Klu wondered if he believed it and forgave her, or whether he didn't really believe it and just decided to forget it. Klu was relieved that Carter was having such a positive influence on Henry's life. He secretly wished their father would never get out of prison.

Dorothy, Charlene and Rose worked together on a handmade quilt for the upcoming fundraiser. Every year Cedarwood held a big festival. Proceeds supported the children's home in Canyon, Kentucky.

Shiloh painted a scene of a trophy whitetail buck tending a bedded doe in a cut cornfield. She also painted a dozen kindness rocks with wildlife themes to hide at the festival. She had purchased the smooth, flat, river rocks, called skippers, from a landscaping shop. They fit in the palm of her hand. On the back of each rock she wrote, *Have a blessed day*, and signed her name. Her favorite was a silhouette of a whitetail buck with double drop tines against a yellow and blue sunset.

Jete made a frame from barn siding for Shiloh's painting. He also carved a large owl with his chain saw to donate to the fundraiser.

Shiloh, Jete and Carter worked on getting additional treestands and ground blinds in place. They cut shooting lanes and repaired elevated box blinds. They fertilized food plots, mowed grass, checked trail cameras, answered phone calls and booked hunters. The web site and social media ads that Shiloh developed were bringing in additional bookings. The work was never ending.

Shiloh lost track of the days and scrambled to buy Maxine and Delmar a wedding gift on the day before the wedding. She settled on a fifteen piece set of stainless steel steak knives in a wooden block and matching wooden block cutting board. The rehearsal went well. Delmar's best man, Eddy, was pleasant. Shiloh was relieved that Eddy was taller than her when she wore heels. She didn't want to look like a giant walking down the aisle next to him. And she figured a dance or two would be required.

The next day as she and Maxine dressed for the ceremony she secretly loathed the peach colored bridesmaid dresses. They were covered in pale blue flowers, and more flowery than Shiloh would have chosen. Her maid-of-honor dress was similar in color, peach with blue trim but didn't have the blue flowers. It was almost tolerable.

Maxine looked beautiful in her white wedding dress. The bodice was covered in elaborate beadwork. The train was long and flowing. She looked in the mirror to adjust the veil. "I know I'm not a virgin but I'm wearing white anyway. A girl dreams of a white dress and flowers and all that stuff. Delmar said to go for it. Spare no expense. So I bought the most expensive dress in the store. Not that there was much to choose from, but I do love this." Maxine gazed lovingly at the dress in the mirror.

"It is absolutely breathtaking Maxine. You look gorgeous. Really."

Maxine whispered, "And I bet you will be getting a white dress for sure if you ever get married someday because I know you are still a virgin, girlfriend."

"Maxine! You're being catty, stop!"

"Well my gosh, do you even have a boyfriend? How do you stand it? A girl needs sex too ya know. We have urges too. Virginity is overrated."

"I think the Lord and every Godly man I know would disagree with you on that point." Shiloh thought she saw a hurtful look in Maxine's eyes. "For now we are just going have to agree to disagree."

"Maybe so. Delmar was the first guy I ever had sex with. So being a virgin and marrying the guy you lost your virginity to is sort of okay with God don't you think?" Maxine sat down.

"Don't sit down you will wrinkle your dress. What's wrong? All of a sudden I get the feeling you are having second thoughts about getting married. You love Delmar don't you?"

"Oh, no I'm not having second thoughts about marrying Delmar. It's nothing." Maxine sighed and seemed to come out of her worried mood. "He's a good man. He makes a good living and provides for us. He gave up gambling and drinking. He's home at night and on the weekends. He's good to our daughter. Of course I want to get married. We're going to Jamaica for a honeymoon for crying out loud." Maxine quickly changed the subject. "If you and Eddy hooked up then we could do stuff together as couples, that would be awesome."

"Maxine, stop. I hardly know the guy and here you are making couple plans."

"I know, I'm just nervous. Words are coming out of my mouth. Sorry. Okay, here we go." Maxine walked out of the dressing room and waited outside in the hall. Shiloh went to the chapel door and waited for her cue. She realized Maxine never said anything about loving Delmar. The music changed and she slipped her hand under Eddy's arm and smiled politely at him.

"You look beautiful," Eddy whispered.

"Thanks. Nice suit," Shiloh responded nervously.

Becky was seated in the middle of the chapel on the groom's side next to her date, Ricky. She had accepted his invitation to attend the wedding because he told her Eddy was the best man and she didn't have anything better to do.

Eddy liked having some of his minions around at all times. Ricky would do whatever his uncle asked.

Becky planned to dance with Eddy at the reception and make sure she stayed on his mind because driving for Eddy paid very well. Henry was out of the picture so there was no reason she and Eddy couldn't hook up. She wanted to know if he liked the pit bull puppies she got him. It had been quite a while since she had talked with him in private. Maybe he would drive her home tonight. Becky adjusted the front of her bra. She bought the low cut, dark red, designer dress just for the event. It showed her cleavage well.

Shiloh and Eddy began their walk down the aisle to join Delmar at the altar. Becky looked at Eddy and then at Shiloh. She nearly shrieked when she saw her, but whispered to Ricky, "What the fuck is Shiloh Lawson doing here?"

"She's the maid of honor. Maxine and her are best friends." Ricky noticed that Becky's face was turning red. "What's the matter with you?"

"Nothing. Shut up." Becky seethed with jealousy as she watched Shiloh walk down the aisle on Eddy's arm.

After the wedding ceremony everyone departed for the reception. Becky went straight to the bar. Drinks were free. She ordered a beer but suddenly changed her mind. "Give me whiskey and coke." Ricky joined her. She held up the drink and asked, "Are you the designated driver tonight?"

"I am indeed. Knock yourself out, well, not literally." He was hoping to get lucky tonight. Eddy had given him permission. "Bartender, whiskey and coke please. Becky, shall we find a table?" He carried her second drink to an empty table and sat down. Becky followed. The wedding party was preoccupied back at the church with the traditional photo session. By the time the wedding party arrived thirty minutes later Ricky was bringing Becky her third whiskey and coke.

Becky watched as Shiloh and Eddy were seated together at the head table. She glared as they danced. She drank more whiskey. When Ricky went to the bathroom, Becky downed another shot of whiskey and walked across the room to Eddy. She pulled on his sleeve. He turned to face her without saying a word. Becky smiled and asked Eddy to dance with her. "Come on baby, it's been a long time. How about dancing with me?" She watched his eyes look at her breasts and hover for a moment. Encouraged by his look, Becky moved closer.

Eddy looked over her shoulder, then asked, "Where's Ricky?"

"Ricky is in the bathroom. He doesn't dance. Come on Eddy, let's have some fun." Becky reached to put her arms around Eddy's neck.

Eddy knew people were watching. Becky's low cut, red dress was drawing attention. Eddy let her embrace him and he guided her to the dance floor. As he danced he looked around the room for Ricky.

Becky was not a good dancer. The band was playing a waltz and she had no idea how to do it. Eddy guided her farther away from the wedding party. He spotted Ricky at the bar. When their eyes met, Eddy motioned for Ricky to come to him. Ricky quickly did as instructed.

"Ricky, I want you to take Becky home. Becky, you are stumbling. You've had too much to drink." Becky started to argue but Eddy grabbed her by the arms and squeezed. He growled into her ear, "Go home you dumbass bitch. You're drunk. If you don't leave now you'll be sorry." He shoved her into Ricky. "Take her home."

"Sure Eddy, no problem," Ricky said, wide eyed.

Becky stood and watched Eddy walk away. She saw him touch Shiloh on the shoulder and she took his arm. She watched them dance.

Ricky pulled on Becky's elbow. "We better go." He followed Becky to the car, got in and started the engine. He looked at Becky and thought she was unusually calm. "You okay?"

"Ricky? Have you ever killed anyone?" Becky asked quietly, staring straight ahead at the dash board.

"What kind of question is that, Becky?" Ricky pulled out of the parking lot and began driving back to the campground.

"I need to know." She started to slur her words, "I juss wanna know thas all."

"Well, no. I personally have never killed anyone. But I saw a guy kill somebody once."

Becky's words came slowly. "If I wanna hire someone to kill somebody would this guy be for hire?" Her head fell back against the seat.

"You ain't talking about hiring somebody to kill Eddy are you?" Ricky watched her closely for a response.

"No. No. Course not. I loves Eddy. I was juss wondering." Becky passed out before giving any more details.

"Damn it Becky. You can sure drink beer but you cannot hold your whiskey. Just rest while I drive home. Maybe you will feel better when we get there."

Becky did not feel better when they got to the campground. He tried to wake her, but she was nearly unresponsive. He attempted to carry her into the motor home but couldn't lift her weight off of the passenger seat. Ricky decided to throw a pan of cold water in her face to wake her enough to get her out of the car. He dug through her purse for the motor home keys and went inside to get a pan of cold water. He tried one more time to rouse her. When she didn't respond he stood there contemplating whether to just leave her in the vehicle or throw the water on her. With the tiniest of hope that he might still get lucky, mixed with frustration that he might not get lucky, he decided to throw the water in her face.

The shock of the cold water had the desired effect. Becky shrieked and fell out of the car, landed on her hands and knees and cussed his actions. He helped her up the steps into the motorhome. Once inside, she pushed him away, fell on the bed and passed out again.

He thought about lifting her dress, but decided against it. If she came out of her stupor he didn't know how she would react. He didn't like drugging girls the way Ivan and Eddy did, but he wasn't opposed to getting them completely drunk with alcohol despite the hypocrisy of the thought.

Ricky dejectedly closed the door and left her to sleep off the alcohol.

SEVENTEEN

When the annual festival rolled around, everyone was ready for a break. Dorothy, Charlene and Rose finished the quilt and took it to the public square to be displayed for the auction. The quilt pattern was called Kentucky crossroads. It was big enough to fit a queen sized bed. The combination of colors made it the perfect fall blend of gold, light and dark browns and a touch of cobalt blue.

Shiloh wandered around the festival checking things out and hiding her supply of painted kindness rocks. She almost kept her favorite one but decided to place it on a park bench for someone to find.

Her painting of the buck tending the doe was displayed on an easel next to the quilt. Several people admired her work.

She received a commission offer to paint a man's buck in a clover field with fall colors in the background. He showed her pictures of the mounted deer and asked if she could recreate the scene he had in mind. Shiloh accepted the offer but told him she could not work on it until after the hunting season. He asked if she could come to his home in Findlay and look at the mounted head and additional photos he had of the animal. She politely declined, explaining how busy she would be with the upcoming hunters. He finally agreed to her timeline. They shook hands and exchanged information.

Jete's carved owl stood four feet tall and was elaborately detailed for a chain saw carving. He had stained it with light and dark browns and covered it with weather resistant sealer.

Several other items donated by townspeople were displayed, waiting to be bid on to raise money for the children's home. It was a beautiful August day with temperatures in the seventies and attendance on the rise.

Charlene's homemade chocolate wonder cake won first prize in the cake baking contest. Her cookies won first place in the general baking contest. Charlene pinned the blue ribbons on her purse strap and blushed throughout all the congratulations and hand shaking.

Over the summer Klu's wood cutting business earned him twice as much as in previous years. He decided to attend the auction and bid on something to help the kids. When he saw Shiloh's painting he knew he had to have it.

The auction was scheduled for five o'clock Saturday afternoon. Everyone gathered with their festival food at the dozens of picnic tables set up on the square. Spotters roamed the crowd and the auctioneer began talking. Big speakers were strategically placed so everyone could hear.

Bidders spent money freely and everyone cheered when the quilt brought a winning bid of two thousand dollars. Jete's carved owl brought seven hundred dollars.

The auctioneers entertained the crowd and cajoled reluctant bidders. Nearly thirty large ticket items had been donated for the live auction along with several silent auction prizes.

Becky found Klu in the crowd and slipped up behind him. She threw her arms around him and hugged him tightly. "Hi Klu, I haven't seen you in such a long time. How have you been?" she asked as he pried her arms away. He turned to face her. Her perfume was overwhelming.

"Hi Becky. I'm good. Thanks for asking. How have you been?" He asked out of politeness, not really caring to hear the answer.

"Good. Real good. I got a new motor home. You should come check it out. What are you doing later?"

Klu didn't answer because he heard the auctioneer announce the next item up for bid. Shiloh's painting was next.

Becky noticed a painted rock on the park bench and picked it up. "Hey Klu, look at this. It was just sitting there on the bench." Klu glanced at her and nodded then returned his attention to the auction. The auctioneer asked for two hundred dollars and received an immediate response. The bidding kept going up by increments of twenty-five dollars. When it seemed to pause around four hundred Klu raised his hand. The spotter yelled. The auctioneer asked for higher bids but when none came, he declared Klu the winner. A spotter brought him a sheet of paper to sign.

Shiloh was watching as the bids went higher and higher. She was shocked to see Klu Dugan declared the winner. She turned to Jete and said hesitantly, "Did you see that? Klu Dugan just won my painting. He had the highest bid."

Jete noticed that Shiloh seemed uncertain about Klu as the winning bidder. "Shiloh, I want you to know that Klu is a good guy. I've been wrong about him. Wrong about him and his brother Henry too. Their dad might be the meanest prick around but he's been out of the picture for a long time now. With him gone, I think they have their lives together. You need to go over and thank him for the winning bid. That's pretty cool."

Shiloh relaxed. "You're right Jete. And thanks for telling me all that. I feel better about this now." Shiloh maneuvered through the crowd to stand near the table where winning bidders paid and claimed their prizes.

Klu looked at Becky and said, "Excuse me, but I need to go pay for my winning bid." He turned to go.

"I'll go with you. What did you win?" She tried to take his arm but he pulled away.

"Suit yourself," Klu said without breaking stride. He smiled as he saw Shiloh standing next to the table.

Shiloh extended her hand to Klu. "Thank you for bidding on my painting. And congratulations on winning. The funds will really help the children's home." Klu reached out to grasp Shiloh's hand. The helper at the table interrupted them and gave Klu some paperwork.

Becky took a few steps back and stood beside a food truck. She glared at Shiloh as she talked and laughed with Klu. Her jealousy grew as they walked together to Shiloh's painting and stood talking about it. They had their backs to Becky and did not feel the anger radiating from her body.

Shiloh wrapped the painting in an old blanket. They walked together to Klu's truck where he placed the painting carefully inside. He locked the door and asked Shiloh if she wanted to go get a drink.

"Oh, I don't drink," she replied.

"I meant get a soda or tea or something, not alcohol. I don't drink anymore either. Do you want to go to the coffee shop with me for a few minutes?"

"Oh." Shiloh laughed, suddenly feeling like a nervous school girl. "Well yes, since you did just place the winning bid on my painting how can I refuse?"

Becky followed them at a distance and watched as they entered the coffee shop, slid into a booth and laughed over something Klu said. She fumed as they seemed to be enjoying each other's company. Becky stormed away in a jealous rage unsure what to do next. When she got to her car she realized she was still carrying the painted rock. As she turned it over she read the words, *Have a blessed day,* and saw Shiloh Lawson's signature.

Becky's rage boiled to the surface as if the Lord had just whispered blessings in the devil's ear. She growled Shiloh's name and threw the rock with all her might. It landed on the pavement, skipped and rolled for another thirty feet and ended up under a dumpster. Becky drove east out of town, got on the interstate and went to Canyon, Kentucky. It had been awhile since she visited the Jacklight Bar.

The bar had a big dance floor, a band and three bull-riding machines. The parking lot was well lit by neon signs and flashing strobe balls. Becky parked and went inside to the first seat she saw open at the bar. She ordered a beer and a shot of whiskey. She downed the whiskey and followed it up with a long drink from the beer bottle. She thought about Shiloh and Klu together and gripped the bottle tightly. Moments later she felt a presence beside her and a deep voice broke her concentration.

"What's a pretty woman like you doing here all by yourself on a Saturday night?" said the voice.

Becky turned her head to see muscular arms covered in tattoos. She studied the artwork from top to bottom before looking at the man's face.

He smiled and tipped his cowboy hat. "Mind if I sit down?"

"Suit yourself," Becky replied, taking a second long drink of beer.

"My name is John."

"Nice to meet you John." Becky continued to stare at her beer bottle.

"What brings you out tonight, you meeting someone?"

"No. I just hadn't been here in a while. I was tired of the same old crap bars in Cedarwood."

"I know what you mean. After I got off work I asked around and folks recommended this place. I work for the carnival. It's a temporary gig. After we get done with the festival in Cedarwood I may head up to New York to visit my cousins. Unless I find something better to do."

"What kind of work do you do?" Becky turned to face him. She watched his eyes look at her breasts then rise to meet her gaze.

"All kinds. You could say I'm a man of many talents. I especially like rescuing damsels in distress. And if you don't mind my saying so, you seemed pretty distressed when you came in here. You having trouble with your boyfriend? I could knock him around a bit for you."

"You get paid to do that kind of thing?" Becky leaned

forward.

"Can I buy you another beer?"

Becky looked John up and down and smiled. "Make it a whiskey and coke."

"Bartender! Bring the lady a whiskey and coke. Make it two." John finished the rest of his drink and smiled at Becky. "Want to move to a table where we can talk more privately?"

"Sure John. Is that your real name?"

"I'll answer to whatever you want to call me tonight honey." John handed Becky her drink and led the way through the crowd. He chose a booth with two young men seated next to each other. John glared at them without saying a word. They tried to ignore John, but his presence was overwhelming. Becky watched in amusement. Finally the two men grabbed their drinks and reluctantly gave up the booth without saying a word.

Klu and Shiloh ordered drinks and sandwiches. Klu led the conversation, discussing the weather, festival and tornado. Shiloh was easy to talk to. He was working up the courage to tell her the truth about his pen name. "Shiloh, I have been meaning to talk to you for quite some time. I know you are planning to start an outfitting business and I think that is great. I just wanted to let you know that for quite a few years I have been writing stories and articles and blogs under a pen name, an assumed name."

"Well I didn't know that. That's impressive, being a writer and all. Why the pen name? Why not your own name?"

"I was young when I started writing. I told my dad that's what I wanted to do for a living. He wasn't impressed. It's a long story. So, I kept it a secret from him and wrote under the name of K. D. Oakley."

Shiloh spit some of her drink. "What?" She stared at him with her mouth open.

Klu laughed. "Yes, you heard right. My pen name is K. D. Oakley. K is for Klu which is actually Klumont. My middle name is Oakley. My mother was into genealogy when I was born. She named me after surnames of some great, great grandmothers or aunts or something. So I have three surnames Klumont Oakley Dugan. I just used initials and switched up the order and came up with K. D. Oakley."

"You have got to be kidding me?" Shiloh sat back. "I invited K. D. Oakley to hunt with us the first weekend of the season. I got an email back accepting the invitation."

"I know. That was me. *Hunter's Honor*!" Klu reached into his wallet to get his driver's license. "Here, I'll prove it to you. Here's my driver's license." He held it out for her to see, but paused when he saw the look on her face. "You're upset. I'm sorry. I meant to tell you sooner. Things just got so busy. I was going to tell you seriously. I'm sorry. I don't have to come if you don't want me to."

"What did you say?" Shiloh's eyes were wide as she stared at Klu.

"I said I don't have to come if you are uncomfortable with the whole situation. But I will write an article for you. I have plenty of good places to get it published."

"No, it's not that. You said, *Hunter's Honor*."

"Oh, yeah, that. I uh, can explain."

"I thought only Syder, Jete and I, used that saying. Since my dad and grandparents died I haven't heard anyone else say it." Shiloh was bewildered.

"Your dad told me about it. When we were little. He made me promise not to tell anyone. I just let it slip."

"My dad told you? When did my dad tell you?"

"When we were little, maybe six or seven years old. We were in line for one of those big rides at the festival. You, Syder and your dad were ahead of me. Syder was teasing you, telling you that you were too small to ride this one and if you got on, it would fling you out into the parking lot, where you would land on the concrete and break into pieces. Your dad kept telling him to cut it out, to stop scaring you."

"I remember that." Shiloh's mind wandered back.

"So, Syder kept telling you how scary the ride was and you were starting to cry, because you wanted to ride it with all the other kids but you were getting scared. Your dad whispered in your ear and then you challenged Syder with *Hunter's Honor* to see if he was telling the truth. Your dad said Syder would never kill another big buck if he lied under the challenge of *Hunter's Honor*. Syder confessed that he was lying about the ride. After that you were all happy and got on the ride."

"I do remember all that. I don't remember you being there."

"I was in line behind you. You and Syder went on the ride and your dad stood there watching you. I tugged on his sleeve and asked him all about *Hunter's Honor*. He got down on one knee and looked me right in the eyes and told me what it meant, how important it was to tell the truth, to keep your word, to never lie; that there was honor in your word. He explained that there was honor in being a hunter; respecting the land, and the wild game, and the other animals, and each other. He said it was a promise and a vow of truth stronger than a pinkie swear, or swearing on my mother's grave, or cross my heart and hope to die. It was quite the speech and made a big impression on me as a little kid. I never forgot it." Klu blushed and rubbed his face. "I never had a father figure talk to me like that before." He looked down at his food, unsure what to say next.

Shiloh had to fight back tears. She reached out, extending her hands across the table. Klu quickly reacted, gently taking her hands in his. "Thank you for telling me that story. I know he told you never to tell anyone but I'm glad you told me. It makes me feel so much closer to him, knowing that he had such a positive impact on your life. He was a wonderful man and I really miss him a lot."

"I wish I could have known him better." Klu squeezed her hands and held her gaze. He felt a connection like none other. They held hands for several more seconds.

Shiloh wondered why she had never noticed his piercing blue eyes before today. Another wave of nervousness caused her to shiver. She pulled her hands back and broke the spell. "It's really weird how people can live so close to each other but not really even know each other."

Klu nodded in agreement. "It sure is." He took a drink, cleared his throat and grinned mischievously. Leaning closer he said, "Well, I guess we need to have a real conversation about this outdoor writer you invited to hunt."

"I guess we do." Shiloh smiled and held Klu's gaze again.

The twinkle in his eyes looked familiar, reminding her of the jovial nature of the men in her family. "I haven't really had time to absorb the shock. I'm not sure if I should be mad, glad or relieved."

Klu puffed out his chest. "I've heard this K. D. Oakley guy is an excellent writer, and a great hunter, fine figure of a man and all that. You should say yes, that's all you need to know."

"Oh so now you're imitating Jeremiah Johnson." Shiloh giggled. "I loved the movie they made about him."

"Me too, one of my favorites."

"Okay, it's settled. He can come. K. D. Oakley I mean. I'm still not sure about Klu Dugan."

They laughed throughout the evening, reciting favorite movie lines and talking about hunting, life, their families and their future.

Shiloh suddenly realized she had checked off an item on her bucket list. "Hey, I just realized you helped me check off one of the items on my bucket list. To create an oil painting someone will actually pay money for." She raised her glass in a toast.

Klu raised his glass and touched hers. His eyes were twinkling with mischief again. "Well, it was a donation for charity so somebody had to do it."

"Oh gee thanks. That's real comforting."

"I'm just teasing. It was a beautiful painting. You are very talented. You should do more, maybe open a gallery."

"Now I know you are making fun of me. I have no desire to be a starving artist. Hopefully this new outfitting business will be profitable and I can retire in style and paint all I want when I become eccentric in my old age."

"Well, if the outfitting business is any good I'll see what I can do about writing an article or two to help you out. But only if the hunting is good and my guide is pretty."

"Hmm, you drive a hard bargain. I'll have to see what I can do about that." Shiloh sat back and sighed, wondering how she could have misjudged this man for so many years. She had never felt so comfortable with anyone other than family. He was easy to talk to, funny, and shared many of her interests and ideas. And he was incredibly handsome. She blushed at the thought.

They were shocked when the coffee shop manager interrupted them to announce it was closing time.

Shiloh checked her phone to verify the time. "Holy cow! Time sure does fly when you're having fun."

"It does indeed. I had a great time Shiloh. Can we go out sometime?" Klu held his breath.

"Yes, I would love to."

"Awesome! I'll walk you to your truck. It's late."

They walked arm in arm to Shiloh's truck. She kissed him on the cheek and said goodnight.

As she drove away, she felt like she was floating in peaceful bliss. Shiloh thought about the times she heard people talk about the moment they fell in love. She wondered if it was possible to fall in love in a single moment.

EIGHTEEN

Shiloh and Jete scrambled to finish everything in time for the opening weekend of the Kentucky whitetail bow season. They purchased archery targets that resembled deer and others that were block shaped and placed them in the back yard at twenty, thirty and forty yards. Lanes were mowed, trail cameras were checked and food was stocked.

Shiloh and Dorothy had decorated the three rooms that housed the hunters with a different theme for each. Room one was labeled the Wolf Den. It had a framed topographical map on the wall that showed the length of the Yellow Wolf River in Kentucky. Two double beds had bedspreads with wolf themes. Nightstands beside each bed had a lamp with silhouettes of running wolves on the shades. Each hunter had a dresser and plenty of closet space.

Room two was designated the Whitetail Room and decorated accordingly. It had framed prints featuring big bucks and antler themed décor. Room three, was posted as the Turkey Roost, and decorated with a wild turkey theme. Each hunter was provided with a small locker inside their half of the closet for valuables.

Over the summer Jete built a screened in room off the back deck and put up tables for the hunters to stash their outdoor gear. He hung hooks from the ceiling and side walls for them to hang bows or clothing.

Carter and Jete put up another elevated box blind. It was a name brand blind with sliding glass windows and indoor/outdoor carpet on the floor and walls. Carter looked it over carefully and said to Jete, "You know we could probably make more of these blinds ourselves for next year." Jete agreed.

They double checked every stand to see if limbs needed additional trimming and that lifelines were in place. Dorothy made sure the ranch house was ready for its first group of hunters. She stocked the hallway closet with toilet paper, boxes of tissue, paper towels, rags, first aid kits, batteries and cleaning supplies.

Shiloh and Klu talked to each other every day on their cell phones. They met for lunch several times and went to supper and the movies one evening when it was raining and Shiloh finally agreed to take a break.

"I can't remember the last time I went to the movies," Shiloh said. "They can do most anything with animation these days."

Klu held the door open as they exited the theatre. "I haven't been to a movie in about five years," he confessed, then laughed. "I love movies though. I would like to write a book that would be made into a movie. Wouldn't that be awesome?"

"It would. I bet you could do it if you set your mind to it."

"Thanks. Maybe someday. Right now there isn't time for that, those pesky bills keep coming each month."

"I can relate to that. This outfitting business is a dream, but I am making it up as I go along."

As they walked down the sidewalk toward Klu's truck a young couple came up behind them. The boy said something to the girl but Klu couldn't quite understand what he said.

Klu and Shiloh stopped and turned around to face the teenage couple. Shiloh thought they looked as if they hadn't had a good meal in months. The boy was dressed in skin tight jeans that had several holes in them. He wore a pink, short sleeved T-shirt and a brown stocking cap. Klu thought the combination seemed odd. The girl had on white leggings under jean shorts and a layering of shirts in tie-dyed bright colors. Her shoulder length hair was as multi-colored as her shirt choices. Klu had no idea what her true hair color might be. He instantly went on guard when the couple approached unusually close for strangers on a street corner.

"Are you Shiloh Lawson?" the girl asked.

"Yes," Shiloh responded politely, facing the girl.

"You're the one doing that hunting thing?"

"If you mean the outfitting business, then yes. Why do you ask?"

"How can you kill animals? That's barbaric."

Shiloh clenched her fists, expecting a fight as the girl moved closer. "I doubt anything I can say right here and now will change your mind about hunting."

"What's the attraction? What exactly do you feel when you shoot an animal?"

"Recoil." The word came out of Shiloh's mouth before

she could stop herself.

Klu suppressed a smile as he kept his eyes on the boy.

"I hope you get what's coming to you someday." The girl glared at Shiloh for an awkward moment before stepping back. "Come on, let's go," she said to the boy who had remained frozen throughout the confrontation, his eyes wide with fear.

Klu and Shiloh watched the couple walk twenty yards away down the sidewalk. The girl had her hand behind her back giving them the finger as she walked. When they disappeared around the corner Klu looked at Shiloh and shrugged. "That was weird."

Shiloh shook her head. "I get a few snarky remarks online but that's the first time anyone has ever walked right up and said anything to my face. I will never understand anti-hunters."

"Seriously? What kind of remarks do you get?"

"Oh, things like, how can you kill helpless defenseless animals or; I hope you die a horrible death; or I hope your children are skinned alive and hung upside down."

"Are you kidding me? Have you told the police? Those are some serious threats." Klu held the door open for her when they got to his truck.

"No. I keep a screen capture of them. Then I just block and delete them."

Shiloh got into Klu's truck. He closed the door and went around to the other side and got in. Before he started the engine he looked at Shiloh and said, "I hope I never run into one of those chicken shit online bullies in person. It would be a very long time before they could use their fingers to post messages like that ever again."

"Oh now that's not very nice." She smiled, secretly feeling protected and safe.

Klu started laughing. "I can't believe you said – recoil!"

"Oh my gosh, it just came out of my mouth without thinking. That was bad wasn't it? Sorry-not-sorry."

"No, that was perfect. She already had her mind made up anyway."

On the drive home they talked about the upcoming hunting season, ultimately agreeing to tell the other hunters in camp that Klu was there as the outdoor writer K. D. Oakley.

On the Friday before opening day, Klu arrived with his hunting gear and a big box of homemade cookies from Charlene. "Mom sent these for good luck. She makes the best chocolate chip cookies ever." He offered the cookies to Dorothy. "Except for yours, I'm sure yours are much, much better!" He ducked as if hiding from an expected blow and quickly exited the kitchen. He chose a bedroom and piled his gear at the foot of the bed, then went to find Shiloh.

"I see you made it. How was the trip?" Shiloh greeted him with a hug.

"Oh, it was a long drive but I didn't have any trouble finding the place. Your directions were spot on," Klu joked. "I brought some of Mom's homemade cookies. She insisted. If I didn't bring them she would have just followed me over here and blown my cover."

"Mom told me. She says to tell you they are truly delicious. Now, I want you to get the full experience of what it is like to hunt with Lawson's Hunting Adventures. So no, you cannot go home and sleep in your own bed. We are probably hunting some of the same deer you have on your farm. I'm sure they move back and forth all the time."

"I don't have any trail cameras out. I'll have to get some put up one of these days. It's just that we have hunted the place for so many years we kind of already know where the best places are. Once in a while you do get surprised by some big buck that comes out of nowhere, especially during the rut."

Jete interrupted their conversation. "It must be the unofficial start of autumn. I just saw a starling murmuration and two of the hunters are here. They are pulling up to the house now."

Shiloh took a deep breath. "Okay, here we go, Lawson's Hunting Adventures is about to get real." She and Jete went to greet the hunters on the front porch. Klu went to the back yard range to shoot a few arrows before supper and look up the definition of murmuration on his cell phone. It wasn't the first time he had to look up something Jete said. He chuckled to himself. He was supplementing his college education by just hanging out with the guy.

The first two hunters were from Florida. They were dressed in jeans, long sleeve shirts and jackets. They exchanged greetings and followed Shiloh into the ranch house to see the accommodations. She showed them their room and left them to carry in their gear.

The second twosome of hunters arrived soon after. They were from Wisconsin. They arrived wearing shorts, short sleeved shirts and flip flops.

Jete whispered to Shiloh, "Okay that's weird, the guys from Wisconsin look like they have been at the beach and the guys from Florida look like they have been ice fishing."

Shiloh nodded in agreement and laughed. She showed them to a room and gave them time to get settled. When everyone was unpacked and had their gear placed where they wanted it she invited them to shoot a few arrows in the back yard range before supper.

Klu greeted the other four hunters. Everyone exchanged handshakes and introduced themselves. Jete, Carter and Shiloh watched while the hunters got in a few practice shots. Everyone did reasonably well, hitting within a paper plate at forty yards.

Jete nudged Shiloh and nodded toward the targets. "That's a relief. At least they can all shoot."

"Well I should think so. Why on earth would they go on an expensive out of state deer hunt and arrive not being able to shoot their bows?"

Jete snorted sarcastically and raised his eyebrows. "We shall see missy, mark my words, the season is just getting started."

"Oh you're being silly." Shiloh punched Jete playfully in the arm. She checked the time. "I'm going to see how Mom and Rose are coming along with supper."

After supper Shiloh, Jete and Carter stepped in to the office to have a discussion. Shiloh began, "Do either of you have any preference as to which two hunters you will be guiding?"

"Not really," they said in unison.

Jete reached in his pocket and pulled out a quarter. How about we flip for it?" Shiloh and Carter looked at each other and shook their heads in agreement. "Okay, heads I take the

Wisconsin guys, tails I take the Florida guys. I know there is no reason to flip for who gets to guide Klu. Our fearless leader has already called first dibs." Shiloh's face turned red. She couldn't think of a comeback.

Jete pretended to be about ready to flip the coin. "Are you sure you didn't purposely *not* book a sixth hunter this week just so you and K. D. Oakley can be alone in the wilderness?" Jete raised his eyebrows and winked at Carter. They both started laughing and nodding their heads up and down at Shiloh.

"Gosh it is hard to get good help nowadays. Flip already!" Shiloh waved her hand at Jete and tried to conceal a grin.

"Okay, here goes." The coin landed and rolled a couple feet, coming to rest with tails up. "Florida guys it is. Carter, you get the Wisconsin guys." Carter nodded in agreement.

"Okay let's go do the orientation."

Shiloh called all of the hunters into the great room for the meeting. While she waited for everyone to arrive she gazed around the room. Jete had done a wonderful job with the renovation. The stone fireplace went from floor to ceiling. Her biggest buck was hanging half way between the mantle and the peak of the ceiling. Four more of her biggest mounts were on the south wall. Her dad's, and some of Syder's bucks, were there too. It was an impressive display.

When everyone was settled she began. "I would like to welcome everyone to Lawson's Hunting Adventures. We are excited for all of you to hunt with us for the opening of the Kentucky bow season. For this first hunt we have five in camp. You have all met Jete and Carter. They will be guiding you. Carter will be taking Charles and Jerry," she called the

Wisconsin hunters by name. "And Jete will be guiding Bob and Sal." She waited while they all nodded to each other in agreement.

"I will be guiding Mr. Oakley," she added quietly. "Okay, moving right along. Let's talk about when you will be hunting. During this time of year we usually only hunt afternoons. If we don't disturb the deer in the mornings they are pretty regular about coming out to the green fields in the last hour. But that is something you can talk to your guide about. If it drives you crazy to only hunt the afternoons we can accommodate you."

"Excuse me," Dorothy said as she entered the room holding a big plate of cookies. "I am going to leave these on the kitchen counter if any of you would like some, help yourselves. Rose and I are going home now. My phone number is on the fridge if you need anything food related. We will put the continental breakfast out tonight for you early birds. Brunch will be served at 10:30." She waved goodbye as the group said thank you and goodnight.

Shiloh continued with instructions, "Your guide will take you directly to and from the stand or blind. We ask that you not wander around. We have hunted this farm for generations so we have a pretty good idea where the best spots are. Every treestand has a lifeline rope, you are required to use it and wear a safety harness. If you don't have one, we can let you borrow one."

Charles interrupted, "I have a safety belt. It's what I always wear, had if for years, never had a problem."

"We require every hunter wear a harness type fall restraint system. If you fall with just a belt it could suffocate you."

"Hog wash!"

Jete entered the discussion. "Charles, if you fall wearing only a safety belt it can asphyxiate you by tightening around your chest because of your own weight. It can become so tight you cannot breath. Or you can easily be flipped upside down, or it can cause serious internal injuries. It's not just a hunting thing, check the OSHA rules, even construction workers don't wear belts anymore."

"Jete is right Charles. Everyone needs a full-body harness. It gives you the best chance of surviving a fall." Shiloh demonstrated the use of the harness strap on the lifeline. "Connect the strap to the rope with the carabiners. The harness strap is connected to the lifeline rope at all times when you go up or down the tree. The prusik knot moves up and down easily but will restrict you from falling when heavy pressure is put on it in a downward fashion."

Jete pulled a strap from his back pocket. "We also require that you have a suspension relief strap with your full body harness."

Charles interrupted again, "What good is that little thing?"

"I'll show you." Jete put on a safety harness. "This strap needs to be easily accessible at all times. If you fall and are suspended in your harness you can hang there for a short period of time. But over time the circulation gets cut off in your legs, like a tourniquet effect. This can be dangerous. It's called suspension trauma, or harness hang syndrome. It could become fatal in as little as thirty minutes. With this little strap you can hook it on either side of the harness, put your foot in it and use it to take weight off your groin area periodically allowing blood to circulate through your legs and body in a normal fashion. Without it, you could be in big trouble even though the harness kept you from falling."

Charles mumbled words that no one understood.

Shiloh looked at Charles wondering if he was going to speak up. "I'm sorry Charles, I didn't understand you. Do you need to borrow one of our rigs?"

Charles grumbled again but nodded his head in confirmation.

"Okay, no problem. If anyone else needs one just let us know. Moving along then. There is no smoking in the ranch house or on stand. If you shoot a deer please do not get down and go after it. Please text or call your guide to come get you to aid in retrieval. We field dress them where they lay. Coyotes will take care of the gut pile pretty much overnight. If you see a coyote you can shoot it. There is no extra charge for that. We have a lot of them."

"What about dogs? Do you have a problem with them running deer?" Charles asked. "What's your policy on shooting a dog?"

"We have never had a problem with it. I'm not sure what the law says. But I would advise you to call your guide and let them know if you see one and we will take care of it for you."

"What about your dog? I see it running loose around here. Is it going to be a problem?"

Shiloh pointed at Charles and said, "Don't shoot my dog. I can say that for sure. Hazard won't be running loose in the woods so there won't be any problems there. Hazard does not chase deer. He does, however come in real handy if we need him to track a wounded deer. Hopefully none of you will need his services with that."

"What about snakes, you got poisonous snakes here?" Charles asked. "We don't encounter too many of those in Wisconsin. Maybe a rattlesnake now and then."

Jete explained, "We have thirty-three species of snakes in Kentucky; four of them are venomous. Copperheads, Western Cottonmouth or water moccasins, Timber Rattlesnakes and Pigmy Rattlesnakes." When Jete noticed Charles' wide eyed expression he added, "That's why we don't want you to wander around and you should let us drive you right to the stand."

Shiloh laughed and quickly added, "We won't have a problem with snakes Charles. It is fairly cool now, should be in the forties all week."

"Forties during deer season! Heck in Wisconsin we call that a warm front," Charles bellowed.

Bob countered with, "Forties is freezing where I come from! Do you have heaters in those blinds?" He looked at Shiloh for the answer. "I'm serious."

"Uh, well, sure we can get you a heater Bob, no problem."

"I want a corn pile so big you can see it from a satellite," Charles said.

"Not me, that's not fair chase. I don't want to shoot a buck with an ear of corn in his mouth!" Bob scoffed.

"What the hell is the difference between hunting next to a corn field or a food plot and hunting next to a corn pile?" Charles argued.

Shiloh could tell things were about to get out of hand. "We can accommodate whichever way you want to hunt. Corn or no corn, it's totally your choice."

She quickly changed the subject. "As for antler

restrictions, as you know we don't have any set limits. We want you to shoot a buck that will make you happy. We hope you don't kill a young buck, but if that is your wish, it is your trophy. This is our first year of guiding on the Lawson properties and if it becomes a problem we may institute restrictions in the future, but for now we will just see how it goes. Any questions?" There were none.

She continued. "One more thing. And it's not a pleasant subject but if you wound a deer we will make every effort to recover it. If we cannot find your deer you can keep hunting, however if you wound a second deer you are done. With Hazard's help we shouldn't have a problem finding lethally hit deer, but if you make a bad shot and the deer doesn't die right away or is going to survive, that's a different story. No exceptions. I suggest you meet with your guides to discuss your morning plans. If you need anything during the night we are just across the street in the big white farmhouse. You have our phone numbers. I will be in the office so each of you can take time to come in individually and settle up. We also like to make sure you have the correct licenses and permits. After that, we will see you in the morning."

When the hunters had finished meeting with Shiloh, Klu stood up and followed her to the front door. "I'll walk you home."

"Thanks. How do you think that went?"

"Everything sounded reasonable to me. But could you get me a heater too? I might get cold." Klu pretended to shiver. "Oh by the way can I shoot your dog if he runs by my treestand? And don't let the big scary snakes bite me, ooooohhhh." Klu waved his fingers and laughed.

Shiloh giggled and put her hand over her mouth. "Oh my gosh, I didn't anticipate some of those questions."

"Gee whiz, tomorrow half the guys in camp are gonna freeze and the other half are gonna sweat. Can't you do something about the weather, outfitter lady?" Klu put his arm around Shiloh.

"Oh boy, what have I gotten us in to?" she sighed, shaking her head.

"Ah, it's not so bad, I'm just teasing. I'm sure there will be much worse problems as the season rolls along." Klu could barely finish the sentence without laughing as Shiloh gently punched him in the stomach.

"Alright Mr. Oakley I have just the right stand in mind for you tomorrow. Just downwind of that big hog farm on the far north side. Yes that should be a fine location for you to spend the afternoon, perhaps you want to take a sandwich and sit all day? I could leave you out there, no problem."

They laughed together as they approached the farmhouse. When they stopped at the side door, Klu pulled her close. Before she knew what was happening he leaned down and kissed her. He whispered in her ear. "I just had to do that."

"I'm glad you did." They kissed longer and held each other until they saw Carter and Jete exit the ranch house. "You better get going. I assume you are not hunting in the morning." It was more statement than question.

"Absolutely not. I don't guide the guide. Besides, I know better than to hunt mornings this time of year," he said with a smile and turned to walk back to the ranch house.

As Carter passed him they exchanged good nights. Klu asked, "You guys hunting in the morning?"

Carter sighed and shook his head. "What do you think?"

"Oh, I see. Well, be real quiet in the morning, don't wake me. I need my beauty sleep."

"Ha, ha. I'll try not to wake you. See ya tomorrow."

Klu walked through the front door of the ranch house in time to see Charles and Jerry standing in the kitchen.

Charles had four donuts in his left hand. He lifted his hand to show Klu every finger of his left hand stuck through a donut hole. He lifted the glass of milk in his right hand in a toast. "I'm on two diets now because I wasn't getting enough food on just one. Nothing wrong with a snack before bedtime."

"Not at all," Klu responded, then laughed and shook his head. "See you in the morning." The last thing he heard as he walked away was Jerry asking Charles to pour him a glass of milk too, to go with his cookies. He thought about texting Shiloh but decided he couldn't wait to see the lady's faces in the morning when he told them they might need more food.

Becky and John met regularly at the Jacklight Bar. She refused to let him come out to the campground, knowing Eddy didn't want anyone coming around that wasn't invited by him personally. She did, however agree to pay for a hotel room where he could stay for several days and she visited him there often. John seldom had money, but Becky didn't mind. She had plenty.

Eddy gave her three more runs to Indiana, which meant

three more backpacks. By now she estimated her wealth at close to a quarter million dollars.

The goons brought two more campers to the back section of the campground. That made six all together in the cul-de-sac. Their section was separated from the main campground by a winding gravel road that had a *no trespassing* sign at the start of it. Only one group from the main campground had strayed back there and the goons had run them off.

One evening Becky watched the goons transfer several large black plastic garbage bags from their SUV into the campers. Becky guessed they were full of money. She had tested the doors and found them locked up tight. The windows were covered. She couldn't see inside. "What else could it be?" she wondered aloud to Queenie.

It reminded her of her great uncle's spare room. It too had been filled with large black plastic bags. When she was a teenager she had been curious and looked inside the bags one afternoon when he was gone. Each one was filled with cash. There had been a few hundreds, but most of the bills were in small denominations. He used to give her some of the cash when he was in the mood. He also bought her many gifts, including jewelry, clothes, shoes and her first car.

She grew to like having nice things.

NINETEEN

None of the hunters saw deer during their first morning hunt. After the afternoon hunt everyone had seen shooter bucks except Charles. None of the bucks were close enough for a shot, but spirits were high. They all decided to take Shiloh's advice and not hunt in the morning.

Shiloh's outfit of choice for the hunting season became black or brown jeans with a black or brown long sleeved undershirt made of silk or polyester. She layered her tops with long sleeve camo T-shirts and pullovers. If it was really cold she slipped on a wool sweater with wind stopping technology. She had a camo rain coat that didn't make noise when she moved and shed stick-tight burs as well as rain. She wore a camo ball cap with Lawson's Hunting Adventures embroidered over the image of a big buck. She gave a similar hat to each hunter when they came in to her office to settle their bill on the night before their first hunt.

The next day dawned bright and sunny. It was in the low forties with a slight southwest wind. Since all the hunters, except Bob wanted to hunt over corn piles, which were legal in Kentucky, Jete and Carter left in the Polaris side by side UTV to refresh corn piles and check trail cameras. Shiloh helped Dorothy and Rose in the kitchen while Klu did some online course work. The day passed quickly for everyone except Charles and Jerry, who seemed bored to death when Shiloh checked on them throughout the day. Bob and Sal had gone to the antique store in Cedarwood to get gifts for their wives. They returned in time to hunt the afternoon.

When all the hunters had been taken to the stand, Shiloh, Jete and Carter went to put up new ground blinds. An east wind was expected the following week and they didn't have enough spots for six hunters to hunt east winds. They cleared three more ground blind locations and hung another treestand. As the sun dropped below the horizon they returned to the ranch house to wait so they would be within range to quickly pick up their hunters a few moments after legal quitting time, which was thirty minutes after sunset.

Jete's cell phone buzzed. He checked the text message. "Bob has a buck down. Saw him go down. He can see him from the stand."

Shiloh and Carter high-fived Jete.

"Does he say anything about what he shot?" Shiloh asked.

I'll text him." Jete held his phone up waiting for the response. A few seconds later it buzzed. "A big wide ten pointer."

"Awesome! We will go get our hunters and then come help you if you need it."

After they retrieved their hunters and returned them to the ranch house, Shiloh and Carter started to get in her truck to go help Jete when her phone buzzed. "It's from Jete. He says he is on his way back."

"That was quick," Carter said.

"Well, Jete has killed a lot of deer, so he's had a fair amount of practice in field dressing and dragging them out. Sounds like they could drive right to this one though."

Within moments they could see headlights coming from the woods. Jete pulled up to the barn where they had a light pole and the walk-in cooler. He positioned the head and rack of the buck so everyone could get a good look at it propped up on the side of the bed. The hunters gathered around the buck and admired its head gear, congratulated Bob and listened to the telling and retelling of what happened during his hunt. Jete and Carter carried the buck into the walk-in cooler and positioned the buck on the floor with its head and antlers propped up so it would be kept cold overnight and ready for photos in the morning.

The mood at supper was jovial. Afterward they retired to the great room to tell hunting stories and watch television. Everyone seemed to be having a great time. Shiloh was relieved.

Jete entertained the group with the story of his first elk hunt. "I had never seen an elk in my life. I was just a kid. I practiced all summer with my bow. It was a fifty pound recurve. This was long before compound bows became popular. We were hunting in New Mexico on public land. Dad and my cousins and I drove to the top of a mountain in the dark one morning and didn't realize we had busted a herd of elk over the top. They didn't go far but there was a heavy fog up there. We split up. Dad and I went left and my cousins went right."

Jete's story was punctuated with all sorts of hand and arm movements. "One of my cousins shot a cow elk. Shot right through her and hit her calf in the hip."

The hunters groaned in unison.

"Well the cow rolled down the mountain and came to rest on the side of a cliff. The only thing that kept it from rolling clear down into the valley was a single pine tree. That cow was wedged upside down at the base of the tree. We decided to go down and quarter it to get her out of that spot. They told me to go cut some eight foot trees about as big around as your arm. They were going to put the quarters on those poles and two men could carry out a quarter pretty easily with one on each end of the pole." Jete paused to take a drink.

"How old were you Jete?" Shiloh asked even though she had heard the story before.

"I'm glad you asked. I guess I was about fourteen years old. Never killed anything other than a squirrel with my bow mind you. So here I am off by myself cutting trees for the carry poles when I see something in the fog. It's the cow elk calf. The thing is bigger than a full grown deer you know. So I grab my bow and go to stalking it. It starts walking down hill away from my dad and cousins on the hillside. So I follow it."

Jete was posing with a make believe bow in his hands. "I follow it, and it has long legs you know. It gets to about fifty yards from me and stops. I take a step and it takes a step. Remember, it's wounded, going slow with its head down. I'm in full hunt mode."

Jete crouched even lower with the make believe bow. "I decided I better try to shoot this elk before it gets too far off in the fog. So I pull the bow back and launch one. My arrow sails clear over its back. The elk starts walking and I follow again. It goes another twenty yards and stops. So I give him another one. This time my arrow hits it in the ear."

The hunters groaned in unison again.

"I know it, it was terrible, right? So I only have two arrows left. The elk starts walking again. It's getting farther and farther away from the guys with the cow elk. Remember it's foggy and I have no idea where I am going. The elk goes another fifty yards and stops again. I panic and launch another arrow. This time I hit the poor thing in the spine."

The hunters groaned even louder.

"Now I'm down to one arrow. The elk is alive but down. I am lost in the fog and no one knows where I am, including me. Thankfully my dad and cousins have been wondering what is taking me so long with the carry poles so they come to look for me. I can hear them calling my name about two hundred yards back up the mountain. I made my way toward their voices in the fog. Told them all about what happened. We walked back down the mountain to the elk and I finished it off with my last arrow. It took us most of the day to get those two elk off the mountain. Some of the hardest work I ever did as a kid, but what great memories."

"I hope you have learned to hunt better since then," Carter shouted. Everyone laughed.

"Indeed I have. In fact, I have become so proficient at the art of spot and stalk I could sneak up on myself!" Jete boasted.

More stories flowed late into the evening.

The next morning Shiloh helped Jete get Bob's deer set up for photos. They positioned it against the barn siding under the outfitting sign Shiloh painted. Within an hour after posting the photo to social media Shiloh had three phone calls inquiring about hunts. Klu went to help Carter work on his house for a while before the afternoon hunt.

In the afternoon Sal shot a buck just ten minutes after getting in his stand. Jete tracked it for one hundred yards and recovered the buck. It was a big eleven pointer, still in velvet, with a small drop tine off the bottom of its left antler.

Sal was ecstatic. "This is the biggest buck I have ever seen in the wild. They just don't grow them like this in Florida." Sal helped Jete load the buck into the bed of the Polaris side by side. "Thanks for everything Jete. I hoped for a buck like this but never dreamed I would get him this early in the afternoon. And on the second day."

"We have plenty of time to take pictures before supper that's for sure," Jete replied.

When the remaining hunters returned to camp they admired Sal's buck and went into the ranch house for supper.

More stories flowed that night.

Again Jete entertained the group with his tale of his first bowkill. "I was hunting a buck that I saw walk down the peninsula toward the river. The river was flowing pretty strong so I figured when he got down to the point, I would have him trapped. I stalked after the buck, being real quiet. Had my recurve bow all ready to shoot at a moment's notice. But this dang squirrel keeps following me and chattering like crazy. It runs up a tree about five feet away and looks me square in the eye and goes berserk. It's five feet up the tree and acting like it's gonna kick my butt."

Charles interrupted, "I read in the news last week about some guy who kept an attack squirrel for a pet, fed it meth to keep it mean. They arrested the guy and released his squirrel into the wild, maybe that was the same squirrel!" Charles laughed at his own joke but no one else did.

"Don't you know he's telling a story that happened back when he was a kid, not last week you knucklehead!" Bob chided and threw his hands up in the air. Everyone laughed.

Jete continued, "So, here I am trying to ignore the *attack squirrel* and keep on stalking. I go about ten yards and here it comes again. Runs up a tree near me, to eye level, and goes berserk again. This goes on all the way down the peninsula. When I get to the end the buck is not there. I don't know if it swam the river or slipped past me when I was looking at that doggone squirrel, or what. The squirrel is actually laughing at me by now. He's three feet up a tree flipping his tail all around and chattering like crazy. I pulled back and shot instinctive-like. That was my first bowkill and it sure tasted good fried up with gravy the next day."

The story inspired the others to share stories of their first kills with bow and gun. They talked well into the night. Jete thought it odd that Charles had not contributed a story. He did, however like to stir things up.

"I heard the supercenter in town is no longer selling ammunition," Charles said loudly. "It seems they caved to the pressure and no longer support us hunters and shooters. It's now a gun free zone. You can't carry concealed weapons there. I guess they think that will deter shootings. Maybe they should follow that same train of thought and declare the whole store a theft free zone, then that will stop all the shoplifting. I hope you aren't shopping there anymore."

"Haven't shopped there since they opened," Carter said.

"Damn place ran me completely out of business."

Charles shouted, "Good!"

Carter responded, "Dude!"

"Oh crap, I don't mean good they ran you out of business, I mean good you don't shop there anymore. They don't have a problem selling alcohol, but people keep getting killed in drunk driving accidents. They don't have a problem selling tobacco, but people keep getting lung cancer. They don't have a problem selling sugary foods but people keep getting diabetes. Bunch of damn hypocrites."

Carter and Charles bantered politics for another hour as the rest of the hunters drifted off to bed.

On day three, Charles wanted to move to a new location. Carter took him to an elevated box blind overlooking an alfalfa field. The blind was about nine feet high. Carter handed Charles his gear after he climbed up the ladder into the blind. He refreshed the corn pile before driving away. The bucks did not make it to the pile until after legal shooting time. Charles was disgruntled and complained about the location of the blind. "It should be farther to the north near that corner."

Carter promised to move him to a new location for the next hunt.

Klu saw a huge non-typical from his stand on the third afternoon's hunt. He told Shiloh what happened when she came to pick him up. "I was standing there looking down at the break in the fence. Had my bow hung up and didn't expect to see anything until closer to dark. Deer started moving early. Every single deer that jumped the fence walked right past my stand at twenty yards and went out into the field. Then this monster non-typical just appeared like an apparition. He jumped the break in the fence and made a scrape at seventy yards. I expected him to come past me on his way out to the field like all the other deer, bucks and does, but he turned and went back in the timber and disappeared. It's like those big bucks have a sixth sense."

"We have a non-typical buck like that on trail camera coming through there three or four times a week. You'll get him tomorrow, for sure. I hope."

"I hope so too. I may not sleep a wink tonight trying to hurry up time."

At supper Jerry told about seeing several small bucks and one shooter, but it would not come to the corn pile with the rest of the deer. "Those big old does kept running everything off that corn pile. Those velvet bucks don't want to get kicked. Can you take me to a spot where there are not so many does?" Cater told him he would move him for day four.

Charles asked Klu, "You see anything? You've been mighty quiet."

Klu told the story of the big non-typical encounter.

"Hmm, I see how it is. You put the big shot outdoor writer in the best spot to kill a giant non-typical and the rest of us don't see shit." Charles shoved a big bite of potatoes in his mouth.

"That's not how it is," Klu said angrily.

"Oh really?" Charles mumbled with his mouth full.

Klu shoved his plate away. "Well if you're gonna make an issue of it you can hunt my stand tomorrow. I'll move to another place. You can have a crack at that buck. They have him on camera coming through there a lot."

"I'll take you up on that." Charles reached for another

helping of potatoes. "Mighty nice of you."

Everyone paused their eating, surprised that Charles would take Klu's stand. Klu was starting to get mad and decided to just walk away. He didn't want to cause problems for Shiloh. They talked later that night and agreed to a new game plan.

In the afternoon of day four, Carter took Charles to the stand where Klu saw the non-typical. The lock-on stand was twenty feet up in a big, old, white oak tree. They had had to use an extra piece of logging chain to go completely around the tree before they could get the stand in place. He put Jerry in another spot on the opposite side of the field.

Jerry killed a beautiful, high-racked, narrow, fourteen point, velvet buck an hour before dark. He texted a picture of it to Charles.

Charles sat in his stand fuming. Several does and small bucks jumped the break in the fence seventy yards from his stand but, for whatever reason, chose to go in the opposite direction.

After supper Charles complained to Carter about the stand location. "Those deer are jumping the fence seventy yards from that stand. You need to move that stand down there next to the break in that fence."

Carter tried to explain to Charles that normally the deer come right past his stand at twenty yards, but Charles insisted the stand needed moving.

Klu motioned to Charles, "If you don't like that spot I'll be happy to take it back, and they can leave that stand right where it is. Give me a chance to show you that big non-typical up close."

Shiloh joined in, "Charles, we can move you to a new location, but we are not moving that stand. It's been good for a big buck every season right where it is in that big oak tree. We've killed a lot of deer out of that treestand."

"Fine," Charles grumbled. "I ain't giving up that spot. But I'm telling you it needs to be moved closer to that fence break. You would kill a lot more deer if you moved it there, I'm just saying."

Jete whispered to Carter, "Looks like your hunter is a real vertical turd."

Carter nodded in agreement. "You got that right."

On the final morning of his early season velvet bowhunt Klu helped Shiloh and Jete check trail cameras, put up a couple more stands and scout the creek for new deer crossings. He wanted to stay busy and away from Charles. "Charles is a butthead," Klu said. Jete agreed.

Shiloh added, "Oh my gosh, how can someone who has only seen the place a few hours, think they know so much more than the people who have hunted here their whole lives?"

Jete said, "We will kill that non-typical out of that tree. My guess is those deer didn't come past the oak last night because one of those old does got a look at big fat Charles up in the stand and took all the deer out the back side to the other field. How much you want to bet?"

"That is probably true. I will be surprised if he sees anything tonight. They have him pegged. We may have to let that stand go un-hunted for a few weeks until they decide to walk past it again." Shiloh shoved her gloves into her back pocket. "That sucks."

"It does indeed." Jete winked at Klu then turned to Shiloh. "So, you made a rule that if a hunter wounds a second deer they cannot come back. Can we make another rule that if a hunter is a complete dickhead they cannot come back? I would love the pleasure of looking right in his unprepossessing face and telling Sir Charles to hit the highway."

"Yes we can make that rule and yes you may have the pleasure of telling him, if the time comes." Shiloh grinned and adjusted her cap. "Mom got the second installment of the cash rent for the crop fields south of the house so we can turn down dickhead money now. Let's just hope there are not too many of them."

"We better go put dickhead in his stand. Everybody else is killed out. Klu, why don't you tag a monster tonight just to completely piss him off." Jete patted Klu on the back.

"I'll see what I can do."

"I told Carter he didn't need to stop working on his house just to carry Charles to the tree. I'll do it. You two go find a big buck to kill."

"Okay, thanks Jete. You're the best. See ya later."

They returned to the house so Klu could get ready for the hunt and Jete could pick up Charles.

Charles was waiting on the porch when Jete drove up. "Did you move that stand like I told you?" Charles asked Jete as they loaded his gear.

"No, we left it in place. If you don't want to go there Klu said he would hunt it. I can take you somewhere else."

Charles made a disgusted huffing noise and cleared his throat, "No, I'll go there."

They rode to the stand in silence.

Shiloh took Klu to one of her favorite spots. It was a crossing with a sand bar on Lost Baby Creek that had a heavily used deer trail passing thirty yards away from a big Silver Maple tree. The tree was ancient with multiple trunks. The stand was only fifteen feet high on one side but nearly thirty feet high on the side next to the creek.

"This is one of my favorite stand locations. I killed my first deer here. It's fun to watch them cross through the creek and splash in the water. In the winter if the creek is frozen the deer have quite a time slipping across on the ice. Dad put me in here because there are so many trunks, he must have figured I could do a tap dance in here and not be seen."

"Why don't you sit on stand with me tonight? There's an extra lock on and a safety harness in the back of the side by side. It would only take a second to hang it. You could go park off in the brush and I can put the stand in real quick. How about it?"

"Are you sure? I don't want to mess up your hunt."

"Of course I'm sure. You won't mess up anything. The wind is right. The leaves are still on the tree so we will be hidden in there. If a big buck comes through the creek I want you with me when I shoot my first deer at Lawson's Hunting Adventures. You will bring me luck."

"Sweet. It's a deal. I'll go hide this and be right back." Shiloh handed Klu the lock on stand and went to ditch the vehicle in some brush. She grabbed the safety harness from the bed and slipped it on. By the time she got back Klu had hung the second stand and had his gear in place. He helped Shiloh step up into the second stand.

She secured her safety harness to the tree with the tree

strap and sat down, slightly above Klu. "Too bad I don't have a video camera, the view would be perfect. Oh wait. I could film this with my cellphone. It would be great for the social media site. Okay, now you really have to shoot a buck."

"Oh, thanks, no pressure," he said as he checked the wind with a wind puffer.

"Wait. Do that again, let me film it." Shiloh held up her phone.

"I'm beginning to rethink my decision." Klu grinned at her.

"Okay, you're right, I was getting carried away. Just shoot something would ya?"

"Stop talking and I'll try. Quiet. I need to listen. Oh wait. One more thing." Klu stood up and turned toward Shiloh. When he was standing, his head was even with hers while she was seated. "Notice how I put this stand in just the right spot," he said as he leaned in to kiss her. He loved that she smelled of soap instead of heavy perfumes.

Shiloh whispered in his ear, "A world record could walk right up to this tree and we wouldn't see it if we keep this up."

"That's okay. It's worth it." They kissed for a while longer until a squirrel noticed them. It began to chatter and jump around above their heads.

"Oh great, we're doomed."

"There's only one thing we can do then." Klu kissed her for several minutes, until the squirrel finally moved on, chattering all the way. "I guess I better get serious. About buck hunting I mean. It's getting close to prime time."

He turned in the stand to face toward the creek crossing. He had a perfect shot through a well-trimmed shooting lane.

He sat down to watch and held his compound bow in his hands, braced between his knees.

Shiloh hadn't wanted him to stop kissing her. She kept her hand on his shoulder for a while then grabbed her binoculars.

"Klu, look across the creek, about one hundred yards out. It's a buck. He's coming this way." Klu stood up and positioned himself for the shot, if it would be presented. "He's coming. Seventy five yards," Shiloh whispered. "He's by himself."

"I see him."

For the next few moments they were silent as they watched the buck. It had begun to shed its velvet. Strips hung from its antlers making it look like it had several drop tines. It stopped briefly to rub its antlers in a small bush. Some of the velvet stayed behind on the bush. The buck's body was thick and heavy. Its main beams were as big as soda cans at the bases. It wouldn't score much but it was impressive nonetheless.

"I know that buck. He is ancient," Shiloh whispered. "He might be seven years old. Here he comes." Shiloh lowered her binoculars and let them hang from the strap around her neck. She slowly pulled out her cell phone and swiped the screen to activate the camera. When the buck closed the distance to fifty yards she began filming with her phone.

Klu's muscles tensed as the buck dropped down the bank on the opposite side of the creek. It stopped to get a drink and look around. It tested the wind. It took three steps across the creek and stopped. When the buck turned to look up the creek, Klu quickly pulled his bow back. Two more steps and the deer would move into the shooting lane at thirty yards. Klu held at full draw. The buck stood staring up the creek away from the hunters. Klu began to worry that he might have to let the bow down. He willed himself to stay at full draw. Finally the buck took a step, then another, and another. It stomped its foot, still looking upstream. Klu steadied himself and touched the release.

Traveling at three hundred and eighteen feet per second, the arrow sliced through the buck's chest and buried in the mud on the opposite side. Shiloh saw the buck drop to gather momentum and bolt away. She tried to keep the camera on the deer as it ran up the creek and fell over in the water less than fifty yards away. When they were sure it was down for good, Klu and Shiloh hugged and laughed and celebrated, shaking the tree limbs with their antics.

The squirrel resumed its chatter, but they didn't care.

They lowered their gear from the tree with the pull-up ropes, climbed down quietly and walked up to the deer. Klu bent down and lifted its head. "Wow, he's better than I thought. Most of the time you have ground shrinkage but not with this one. A heavy six-by-six typical. He's got a few little stickers here and there but otherwise he is really symmetrical. And the bases are huge. His tines aren't that long but I bet in his prime he was king of the woods."

"He is a stud." Shiloh looked at the buck's teeth. "Gosh, he barely has any teeth left, they are worn down so much."

Shiloh went to get the side by side while Klu tended to permit harvest requirements. Klu pulled the arrow from the ground and looked at the fixed blade broadhead. All three blades, the shaft and fletching were covered in blood. He carefully secured the arrow back into his quiver.

Shiloh pulled the UTV as close to the deer as possible, careful not to bury the vehicle in the muddy banks of the creek bed. They hooked the deer up to the winch and pulled it up the side of the bank and onto flatter ground out of the creek water. When they finished field dressing the buck they struggled to lift its dead weight into the bed.

"This deer has to be just shy of two hundred and seventy pounds. He is a brute. He must have been over three hundred pounds before we field dressed him. I called Jete when I went to get the UTV. He will be here in five minutes to help us get him loaded."

They watched the footage over and over as they waited for Jete to come help lift the buck into the bed. When he arrived, and finished admiring the buck and hearing the story, they struggled to get the massive buck loaded, then gathered up all the gear and headed for the ranch house. There was still an hour of legal hunting time left.

A mile down the bluff Charles was standing in the treestand with his arms crossed. His bow was hung on a hook on his right side. His back was to the bow as he leaned against the tree with his left shoulder and watched the fence-break crossing. He hadn't yet seen a deer. He was planning to give them an earful when he got back to camp. As he waited he heard a shuffling noise below the tree. He slowly looked down, directly below his bow, and just under the stand was the massive non-typical making a scrape under a small tree.

Charles didn't dare make a move. The buck was rubbing

the glands of its eye against a branch above its head, which positioned it to look directly up at Charles. When the buck stopped rubbing its eye and forehead in the tree branches it began to paw the ground. Charles tried to make a move. He shifted his weight and turned to reach for his bow. The buck looked out at the field and stopped what it was doing. Charles froze. He was afraid to move. Soon his leg began to cramp. He began to sweat. He decided to try to lift his bow off its hook. He took a breath and gently moved the bow, bringing it to his chest without spooking the buck.

Charles took a deep breath and held still, willing his heart to stop pounding. The buck took two steps away from the scrape tree, still looking out at the field, away from Charles. Charles slowly shifted his weight, easing his feet into position on the stand platform. He raised his bow and drew back. He needed to bend at the waist and shoot dramatically downward at the buck just seven yards below the stand. Charles tried to find an opening in the limbs of the scrape tree that he could slip an arrow through. He told himself – top pin, hold it low. The buck needed to take two more steps to be clear of the small tree below. Charles held at full draw, hoping the buck would move.

Seconds passed. Charles held at full draw. The buck didn't move a muscle.

More seconds passed. The buck's left ear moved, flicking away a fly.

Charles began to tremble. The buck didn't move. Charles' eyes watered, his nose ran. He couldn't take it anymore and let the bow down.

The buck turned its head, looking back the way he had

come. It was the biggest set of antlers Charles had ever seen in the wild. Long, heavy main beams sprouted massive tines with points and stickers in all directions. Charles was in awe of the buck.

Suddenly the buck lowered its head and took several quick steps forward, clearing the tree. Charles panicked and jerked the bow back, banged his elbow into the trunk of the tree and punched the release. His arrow sailed limply through the air, landing in a bush.

Miraculously the buck ran thirty yards and stopped. It went on high alert, every muscle flexed, ears pricked, uncertain of the source of the noise in the brush. Charles scrambled to pull another arrow from his quiver and knock it in place. He glanced at the buck. It was still there, but facing directly away. No ethical shot. Charles contemplated shooting the buck in the spine. He drew back carefully, trying not to smack his elbow into the tree trunk again, and settled his top pin on the buck.

The massive non-typical slowly took a step. The hair on its back was bristled up. When it was broadside, Charles looked through his peep site and saw that all the pins in his sight were aiming at brown hide. In the same instant the buck looked up, spotting Charles in the tree. With no more thought to which pin to use, Charles touched the release.

In a phenomenon of speed the buck ducked the arrow.

Unscathed, the non-typical spun on a dime, took off running back the way it had come, jumped the fence and disappeared into the forest. Charles clung to the tree, leaning around the trunk to watch his prize run away. Behind Charles, at the fence break, an old doe spotted his movement. She stomped and blew in protest then took off running back in the direction from which she had come.

Charles' heart sank. His legs became weak. He had to steady himself against the tree to sit down; afraid he might fall at any moment. It was several minutes before he could stand up.

When Jete came to pick him up he drove right to the base of the tree. Charles was still sitting in the stand, in the dark, with his head in his hands.

"Charles, are you alright?" Jete whispered.

"No, I'm not alright," Charles answered in a loud voice.

"We're gonna have to leave this stand un-hunted for a month," Jete mumbled to himself.

Charles lowered his bow with the rope attached to the stand. He dropped his pack on the ground and began to climb down. Jete gathered his things and put them in the vehicle. He hopped into the driver seat and waited for Charles to get in. When Charles walked over to a spot twenty yards from the tree and bent over, Jete got out and joined him. Charles found his arrow and pulled it from the ground. He looked at it, hoping against hope to see it covered in blood, knowing it wasn't. It was a clean miss. He could see the miss in his mind's eye, replaying in slow motion.

Jete followed him to a bush, wondering what the heck he was doing. When he pulled another arrow out of the bush, Jete asked again, "Are you okay? What happened here?"

"You are not going to believe this. If you don't mind, I will wait until we get to the ranch house so I only have to tell it once." Charles' head hung low as he walked club-footed to the vehicle.

"Oh, no. What happened?"

Charles looked at him with glassy eyes, almost like he had been crying. He lurched into the passenger seat like a drunkard. "Just drive," he said quietly.

Everyone was admiring Klu's buck when Jete and Charles drove up. Much to their surprise Charles congratulated Klu on his buck and listened to the story, asking questions and laughing. Jete watched him with suspicion and concern. He couldn't figure out the odd swings in behavior.

Charles called everyone to attention. "I'm a changed man. I've had a supernatural experience and I will never be the same. It was so profound I actually cried."

"What the heck Charles?" Jerry asked, putting his hand on Charles' shoulder.

"Come inside I have one heck of a story to tell. Craziest experience of my deer hunting life." They followed Charles inside. He told them every detail of what happened. "I thought for quite a while about not telling anyone what happened. But the buck and the whole experience was so amazing I had to share it. And there was no excuse for not killing that buck other than my own thick headed stubbornness for not listening to my guide. I was up there in that tree pouting like a baby when the buck of a lifetime walked right into my lap. God sent me a lesson to change my ways."

"Did you ever hear such a story?" Jete whispered to Shiloh.

"Nope, but the Lord sure works in mysterious ways."

TWENTY

On the north side of the farm a gray squirrel scolded the reckless invaders that were trespassing on Lawson land. Their approach had been quiet as the canoe slowly glided through the waters of Lost Baby Creek. Water dripping from the paddles was the only noise the two canoers made as they worked their way east.

The squirrel followed their progress, jumping from tree to tree as they navigated the creek waters surrounded by forest. Hardwoods of elm, maple, oak, walnut, hickory and sycamore were still partially dressed. Brilliant reds, yellows, golds and greens typical of fall in western Kentucky shimmered in the breeze. Soon they would lose their glorious colors as trees began a process similar to hibernation. The annual dormancy would suspend growth and slow their metabolism.

The trespassers glided to a sand bar and beached the silver canoe. It was scratched and battered, but sturdy and stable. They listened to the squirrel, wondering if its chaotic chatter and tail flipping would ruin their plans. A second squirrel became upset, joining its furry cousin in bringing attention to the disturbance on Lost Baby Creek.

Uncertain of the trespassing laws, they moved cautiously. They had been told floating on any free flowing waters of a stream, creek, or river was not technically trespassing. Stepping on the banks of this creek would be criminal. Emboldened by misguided passion they stepped out of the canoe. They were willing to go to jail for this.

The sun peeked over the horizon, sending rays of yellow light into the cloudless sky. Shiloh stomped around the tree. She made no attempt to be quiet. She kicked at random sticks, sending them flying. She walked in small circles looking under bushes and checking behind logs. With clenched teeth she pulled her phone out and called Jete.

On the third ring he said, "Hello."

"Someone stole the steps and treestand out of the big old hickory tree on the west end near Lost Baby Creek!" she blurted out.

"What? Are you sure?" Jete sounded confused.

"Of course I'm sure. Nobody has hunted it yet this year. I brought my hunter to it before daylight this morning. While he was getting his stuff out of the Polaris I went to switch out the SD card from the trail camera on the little oak off to the left of the stand. At first I thought I was losing my mind because I couldn't find a camera on that little tree. My hunter complained that there was no pull-up rope, said he couldn't see the stand. I walked over to point them out to him and shined my flashlight up in the treetop and sure enough, they were gone. We have trespassers. I'm going to call the game warden."

"What did you do with your hunter?"

"I put him in that box blind on the east pasture. He was not very happy, but he didn't say much. I came back to the hickory tree to look around now that the sun is up."

"Damn!"

"There's more. Someone spray painted the hickory tree."

"What?"

"Yeah, it looks like they tried to write the word 'murderer' up the trunk but couldn't reach the last letter, it's just a faint blur."

"I'll call the game warden. I'll be shocked if he's around though, he's about ready to retire. Last time I talked to him he told me he had a bunch of vacation and sick days to use up before the official retirement date so he's probably out west on a fishing trip about now."

"Well that's just great."

"I'll be there in a few minutes and we can look around for clues."

Shiloh sat down at the base of the tree to wait for Jete. She didn't want to disturb the area any more than she already had.

The pawn shop owner greeted his first customer of the day. A young man wearing a brown stocking cap stepped up to the counter with a shoe box in his hand. He gently placed the box on the glass case and pried off the lid. He didn't make eye contact with the owner as he pointed to the box and asked, "How much can I get for this?"

The owner took the trail camera from the shoe box and looked it over carefully. He noticed the young man's hands were trembling. "Does it work?"

"Uhm, yes, yes it works. There are six batteries in it."

"That doesn't mean it works."

"It's new. You can see that."

"That doesn't mean it works either. Where did you get this?"

"My girlfriend gave it to me for my birthday."

"So you're a hunter huh?"

"No!" The young man took a step back. "I, uh, I mean not anymore. I used to, but my girlfriend doesn't like it, so I uh, just gave it up and now I want to sell some of my gear."

"Your girlfriend doesn't like hunting but she gave you a trail camera for your birthday? Kid, I think you are full of B S. You're as nervous as a dog shittin' peach seeds." The owner shoved the shoe box back across the counter. "You better take this and get out."

The young man grabbed the box and ran out of the pawn shop.

Shiloh fumed as Jete surveyed the area near the tree. He walked slowly, looking for tracks or any other clues. He made ever widening circles and stopped near the creek bank.

"Do you see something?" Shiloh asked.

"Yes, there are boot prints here in the mud. Come look. Did you walk over this far?"

"No, I didn't go near the creek bank."

"Someone crawled up the bank and slid a couple time." Jete pointed at the marks in the mud. "Let's go down and follow the boot prints."

Shiloh followed Jete down the bank, careful to stay directly behind him. "Do you see any more tracks?"

"You can see two sets of boots in the sand leading to and from the sand bar. I'm guessing they came in by canoe and beached it on the sand bar. Let's walk further down the creek bed."

Shiloh and Jete walked quietly in the shallow creek water wearing knee high rubber boots. Jete led the way. After fifty yards he stopped abruptly.

"What?" Shiloh said as she nearly ran into him. "Do you see something?"

Jete pointed at a bush on the left side of the creek. "Look there."

"I don't see anything."

"Come on." Jete started walking quickly, splashing through the water toward the bush. He lifted a few low hanging branches and pointed underneath. "Looks like they stashed the stand and steps here."

"Is it all there? Is the trail camera there?"

"Just the stand and steps, I don't see the camera."

"Maybe they plan to come back for this. We aren't far from the road. Why didn't they take it all?"

"If someone wanted to steal the stands to keep for their own or sell them, they wouldn't go to the trouble to spray paint the tree like that. This doesn't feel like an out and out theft, it feels more like a case of hunter harassment. The trail camera was just a bonus." Jete began pulling the gear from under the bush.

Shiloh helped gather the equipment and carry it back to their vehicles. "Let's put some trail cameras on the creek and conceal them really well. Maybe we can catch them coming back for the gear or trying to get more."

"Good idea. Let's go pull two from the field and move them right now. We will keep quiet about this. Maybe the jerks will think they got away with something and be more apt to try again."

Shiloh nodded in agreement. "It's not easy to navigate Lost Baby Creek. There are many more popular creeks for people just out for a fun canoe trip. I think you are right, this was a deliberate venture. They had to portage more than once to get from this bush to the tree with the stands in it. But we have other stands that would be much easier to reach by just walking across the land, why go to all the trouble to paddle a canoe up here?"

"Maybe they think if they are on the water they won't be charged with trespassing. I think this was an exploratory trip. They just lucked into that set and decided to grab it. Quick grab and go. If they got caught walking around on our land how would they explain it? But if they get caught canoeing they can argue the water is public domain."

"I guess that make sense."

Jete carried the stands back to the Polaris and put them in the bed of the UTV. "I'm not putting these back up until we get some chains and locks."

"This is too good of a spot not to hunt it, that's for sure. But I agree we need to lock the stands to the tree. And bring some brown or black paint back and cover up the word murderer. I don't think our hunters would feel too great about sitting in a tree with that painted on its truck." Shiloh took pictures of the tree trunk with her cell phone. "Might need this as evidence if we catch them."

The young man opened his laptop and logged into his social media account. He searched for Lawson's Hunting Adventures. He looked through the photos and read a few comments.

His girlfriend sat next to him. "Have they posted anything about the tree or the missing equipment?"

"Not yet. I doubt they even know about it yet. We just did it."

"Look at their disgusting smiling faces posing over those poor dead animals." She reached over to touch the laptop screen and scrolled through the photos. "All the same. Look at all the beautiful deer they killed just so they can have their heads and antlers displayed on their walls. How creepy is that? It's disgusting and wrong. They think it is cool to shoot them for fun."

The young man removed his brown stocking cap and rubbed his head. "She's kind of hot." He pointed at a picture of Shiloh.

"Bull shit! She is a merciless trophy hunter. She's clearly seeking approval and admiration from like-minded sick men.

You should be ashamed." The girl jerked the laptop from his hands. "Let's just see what they have to say about this," she said while typing a flurry of words on Lawson's Hunting Adventure's social media page.

"What are you typing? Stop!" He grabbed the laptop and jerked it back, quickly deleting the post. "I logged in under my real name. We need to create fake pages if we are going to start posting on her site."

"Fine. Let's do it."

Klu and Shiloh finished eating supper at the diner. They walked to his truck arm in arm.

"I needed this break, thanks," Shiloh said.

"My pleasure. I don't get you all to myself very often."

Shiloh felt her phone buzz in her pocket. She looked at it and sighed.

"What's wrong?" Klu asked.

"I'm not sure. A text from Jete says look at our social media page."

They got into the truck and Shiloh called up the page on her cell phone. After a few moments she groaned.

"What?' Klu leaned over to look at her phone more closely.

"Two knuckleheaded anti-hunters have been posting for the last three hours. Now some other hunters have entered into the conversation and a big argument has ensued."

Klu took his phone out and logged on to Shiloh's social media page. He started reading. "What a bunch of jerks, they have no clue. And are you kidding me with these names? Nosmo King and Win Denergy. Obviously fake accounts."

"How can you tell they are fake?"

Klu started laughing. "Okay, who names their kid Nosmo King? Move a couple letters and you get No Smoking."

Shiloh started laughing too. "Oh my gosh I see what you mean. Move a letter in Win Denergy and you get Wind Energy. Pretty clever."

"These jokers created fake accounts to get on here and harass you, your business, and your hunters."

"You're right. Gosh the hunters are really going back at them. This is turning ugly. I think I need to delete this whole thread and block Nosmo and Win. I don't want to give them a platform to spew this crap all over my page."

"Or you could let it run for a few hours. It's cheap advertising and you are getting lots of attention and new likes."

"Wow, our followers have tripled since this started a few hours ago."

"Something to think about."

"Oh my gosh, listen to this one. *Shiloh Lawson targets defenseless unarmed creatures for sport in her blood lust. If you care about animals in the wild and don't think they should be killed by every psycho like her who can wield a gun then go over to our new KILL SHILOH LAWSON page and sign our petition to get her business closed down.*"

"What? They actually have a page with that name!" Klu searched for the page. "It has a thousand followers already."

"Okay, that's it. I'm deleting this crap and blocking them from my page. They get no more time in the spotlight on my page."

"I'm going to report the new page. That's inciting violence, not free speech. It's disgraceful they allow things like this."

It took most of the ride home for Shiloh to delete every anti-hunting comment and block the posters. She kept at it throughout the night and finally managed to shut down the attacks on her page by morning. She was used to operating on very little sleep but felt especially ragged as she went downstairs for coffee.

The young man and his girlfriend tried to post more comments on Shiloh's social media page but were not successful. Without the hunters to argue with the new site was slowing down as well. In spite of the pause, the two were invigorated by the activity.

"We need to go back in there and tear down more of their killing towers. Maybe we should set fire to the woods," the girl suggested.

"You would be setting fire to the animal's homes."

"They can run from the fire." She shrugged when she saw the look on his face. "Why don't we just slip back in there and grab more of their stuff. We can park on the road and walk in at night. Then we don't have to load and unload that damn canoe."

"What about trespassing? If we use the creek we have a right to be on the water."

"It's only trespassing if you get caught and charged. It's

just a slap on the wrist anyway."

The young man thought about this for a few moments. "I guess. When do you want to go?"

"Tonight."

Shiloh received a call from the local radio station inviting her to come talk to the morning show host about the social media incident. She accepted.

Jete entered the kitchen as she hung up the phone. "We don't get many calls on the land line anymore. Who was that?" he asked.

"The radio station. They want me to come to the studio in the morning to talk about the social media stuff that went on yesterday."

"Ah the morning show has a good audience, should be mostly farmers and people that would understand your side of the thing."

"That's what I thought. Can you take my hunter out in the morning?"

"Sure, no problem."

"I will probably be preaching to the choir but at least I will get a chance to speak about the positive aspects of hunting."

"Maybe so." Jete held up a plastic bag containing a cardboard box. "Guess what I have here."

"I have no idea."

"It's one of those newfangled trail cameras that sends pictures to your cell phone and alerts you if the camera is moved. It has a GPS device in it so you can track it if someone steals it."

"Wow! How much did that cost?" Shiloh whistled.

"You can afford it," Jete said with a laugh.

They spent the next few minutes getting familiar with the new trail camera and left to put it in place.

The young man and his girlfriend argued about whether to take the canoe or just walk on to Lawson land. After a great deal of persuasion the young man convinced his girlfriend to go in by canoe.

"We already know we can do it. It's gonna be dark and we would not know where to go on land. Even if we don't find anything else we can at least grab the stuff we stashed. We can take it somewhere and sell it."

The young man looked at himself in the mirror. He pulled the stocking cap down over his face and adjusted the eye and mouth holes. "You should get something to cover your face. We already know they have trail cameras up. We got lucky last time."

"We could take the stuff to the pawn shop. How much do you think we could get for it?" she asked, rummaging through her dresser for something to cover her face.

"I already tried the local one. He wouldn't give me anything for it."

"Why not?"

"He sort of acted like he thought it might be stolen. He started asking questions and I didn't expect that. So I wasn't real sure what to say."

"I know a guy who can help us. One of the bartenders at Eddy's Tavern is my second cousin. He'll know what to do. We might have to give him a cut, but that's okay. It's mostly about stopping the hunting anyway."

"Yeah, but a little extra cash would be nice."

Shiloh and Jete walked down the creek to the bush where the treestand had been stashed. Jete looked around for a suitable place to put the trail camera. "If we hide this high enough in that tree on the opposite side of the creek they won't see it. We can get photos if they come back for the stands. And if they don't find them maybe they will try going farther up the creek to look for another set."

"I can climb up to that first big limb on that cottonwood. It looks to be about the right height and direction. And it angles down a bit so that will work."

"Good choice. I'll give you a boost." Jete leaned over and cupped Shiloh's boot in his hand and lifted her up. She scrambled up the tree and scooted out on the limb. Jete tossed her the trail camera. "I might need a twig or two to shim it into just the right place so it points right at the creek and the bush."

Jete found a couple of limbs and handed them to Shiloh after she strapped the camera in place. "Let me go over by the bush and look back at the camera before you tighten it down for good."

Shiloh waited while Jete crossed the creek and stood next to the bush. He looked back and gave Shiloh a thumbs-up sign. "I think you got it."

She tightened the strap, locked the trail camera in place, turned it on then crawled out of the tree and dropped to the ground. They ran a couple tests to make sure the camera was working and sending photos of themselves to Jete's cell phone before heading back to the house.

Later that night as the Lawson family slept, the young anti-hunters slipped their canoe into the waters of Lost Baby Creek. They covered their faces and turned on headlamps.

"Everything looks different in the dark," said the young man.

"It does. I can't remember how far the bush is from the road. Can you?"

"It's not far. Come on."

After ten minutes of floating the creek they began to argue.

"I can't tell how far we've come. These bushes all look the same," complained the girl.

"We haven't gone far enough. Keep paddling."

"But the first portage is right in front of us. We went past the bush."

"Well, which bush is it?"

"I have no idea. Let's get out of here. This is too creepy out here in the dark."

"What are you afraid of?"

Before she could answer a pack of coyotes began to howl. Something splashed heavily in the water just beyond the beam of their headlamps.

"Oh crap. Let's get out of here!"

They didn't worry about making noise as they turned the canoe around and headed for the road. As quickly as possible they pulled the canoe from the water and tied it to the top of their car.

They had no idea a trail camera had sent a photo of them to Jete's phone.

TWENTY-ONE

Shiloh kissed Jete on the check as she headed for the door. "Thanks for taking my hunter out this morning."

"No problem."

"I hope somebody is actually awake at this hour and listening to the radio."

"Good luck."

Shiloh drove to the radio station. The parking lot was well lit and several cars were in the lot. She walked through the front door and was greeted by a receptionist.

"Good morning Miss Lawson. Let me show you to the studio. Frank is already there."

Shiloh followed her through the halls to the back of the building. Inside a small studio she saw the morning radio show host talking into a microphone. He looked up and waved her in without missing a word. He was talking about the price of pork bellies and its impact on the global economy as Shiloh took a seat across the table from him. The receptionist pushed a second microphone closer to where Shiloh was seated and quietly stepped out of the room and closed the door.

Seconds later the host tossed to a commercial, flipped a switch and took off his earphones. "Welcome Miss Lawson, thanks for coming. Can we get you a cup of coffee?"

"Oh, no thanks, I've already had my limit."

"Okay then. I'm just going to ask you a few questions. The microphone will pick up your answers so you don't need to lean into it or anything, just talk normally to me across the table like we were having a casual conversation over coffee. Which is actually what we are doing," he said with a big smile and a wink.

The host flipped another switch and began talking to the audience. "Folks, I would like to welcome Miss Shiloh Lawson to our studio. She and her uncle Jete Lawson are running an outfitting business on their farm and I know several of you have been wondering how that venture is going. Shiloh, why don't you tell us how this all got started."

"Oh, uh, okay, well I decided that after college I wanted to try to make a living on the family farm. My dad passed away a few years ago and my uncle has been like a father to me. He's got a few head of cattle. And we cash rent out the crops, but I felt like we could do more. We have always had great deer and turkey hunting on our property, so it seemed like a good way to supplement our income."

"Several of our listeners are landowners like you and I'm sure they are wondering if this is something they could do on their land. Do you have any advice for them as they look into the idea?"

Shiloh laughed. "Well, it has its good points and bad points like most any job I guess. There are lots of expenses for equipment, ground blinds, treestands, lifelines and safety harnesses and such. Not to mention the gear you need to cut shooting lanes and carry hunters to and from the stands. We have a walk-in freezer for the deer to be kept as fresh as possible since we don't want to lose any meat."

"Let's talk about that. Some folks think you are running a trophy hunting operation and don't care about the meat. What do you have to say about that?"

"Of course we care about the meat. And as far as trophy hunting, that's not an accurate description. Yes, any wild game animal taken legally is a trophy. So, you could say we are trophy hunting, but we don't hunt just for a trophy. There are lots of reasons why people hunt that have nothing to do with trophies."

The host leaned back, crossed his arms and smiled. "Would you like to elaborate on that?" He nodded and pointed at the microphone. When she hesitated he gave her a thumbs-up. "I've been hunting my whole life and understand what you are saying. But for those listening who may not be hunters, can you explain the allure of hunting?"

Shiloh took a deep breath. "It's a very personal thing. Hunting means different things to different people. My grandmother first took me hunting. I was about six years old. I walked along beside her in a big white oak timber. She was carrying a twenty-two caliber rifle and was dressed in camouflage. I looked up at her and thought she was the most beautiful woman and I wanted to be just like her. We snuck through the woods and she showed me how to sneak along and spot and stalk. Of course my attention span was very short. I lost interest in the squirrels when I found a box turtle," Shiloh said with a laugh. "But she was very patient with me and made it a big adventure. Them my dad took me on my first turkey hunt and I was hooked. For me hunting is about family ties, tradition, and heritage. My uncle Jete taught me about conservation and how important sound management practices are to the health of the wildlife and the ecosystem."

"Some folks might disagree with you. I understand you experienced some backlash on your social media page here recently. Did any of their comments change your mind?"

"Of course not. I make no apology for being a hunter. Hunters contribute to the economy and to the health of the game populations through sound management. Hunters care deeply about the wild game they pursue. It's hard to explain how you can love the species you are hunting but we do. Not to mention how satisfying it is to bring home your own food, to provide for your family and know where your food comes from. It comes from the woods and fields and waters and not only from the grocery store in a sterile plastic wrapped package."

"What about the people who do not agree with eating animals. I see where some of the comments you got on the social media site had a lot to say about not eating meat."

"That's a personal choice. I don't try to force meat down the throat of a vegetarian so they shouldn't try to force their food choices onto me. And the Bible has a lot to say about eating meat and hunting. In Genesis for instance, take thy weapons, thy quiver and thy bow and go out to the field and take some venison; or every moving thing that liveth shall be meat for you. There are other verses in Proverbs and Jeremiah and Acts. I can't remember them all word for word, but it's no sin to be a hunter. There are rules of course. To be an honorable hunter you must care about the game you pursue, you must understand it, you must do what is best for the long term health of the wild game populations and the habitat."

The host stopped her. "I can see you are very passionate about this subject. We are just about out of time. Tell the folks how to get in touch with you, your web address and so on."

Shiloh gave the audience her phone number, web address and social media information. When she was done talking the host sent the broadcast into a commercial.

"Thank you for coming Miss Shiloh. You did a great job. If you will excuse me I'm going to grab another cup of coffee before the break ends. I will walk you toward the reception area."

The interview had gone much more quickly than Shiloh anticipated. She was just getting started on the virtues of hunting and describing what *Hunter's Honor* was all about when she was cut short. She turned on the radio and listened to the host talk about the road commissioner and plans to repair a bridge in the next county. "I wonder if anyone was listening to my interview," she said aloud. "The sun has only been up for forty-five minutes."

She started her truck and was about to drive out of the parking lot when her cell phone rang. She put the truck back in park and answered the phone.

Jete's voice came over the speaker, but the call was full of static. She checked her signal. Good. "Jete, I can't understand you." The call disconnected. She sat for a moment waiting for him to try again. When her cell phone buzzed she opened the text from Jete. It was a picture of a piebald buck with her hunter smiling from ear to ear posing behind the massive set of antlers. Shiloh nearly dropped the phone.

"Oh my gosh!" She tried calling Jete again but the call went straight to his voice mail. She tossed her phone in the passenger seat, put the truck in gear and tried not to spin her tires as she took off out of the parking lot headed for home.

TWENTY-TWO

Klu and Jete were just about finished taking pictures of the piebald buck when Shiloh pulled into the drive at the ranch house. Klu waved and ran to meet her.

"I can't believe it!" Shiloh said as she hugged Klu. "Have you ever seen this buck on your farm?"

"No, never. I've never even heard anyone talk about seeing a piebald buck in this area."

Shiloh walked to her hunter, shook his hand and congratulated him on the beautiful buck. "You sure have something special here Mike. Tell me what happened."

"I still can't believe it myself. I was in the stand and just started getting enough light to see. I noticed a doe moving through the timber then spotted a buck behind her. Actually three bucks followed her, each one bigger than the first. They were not shooters. I hung my bow up and then here she came back again. So I grabbed my bow and waited. She went right by me and stopped at thirty yards. She looked back, so I did too. That's when I spotted a giant rack. It was so wide, I just knew it was a shooter immediately. He was coming after the

245

doe on the same trail so I pulled my bow back and made a grunt noise when he stepped into the shooting lane. I hit him perfect, but he took off running back the way he came. I saw a few flashes of white but didn't really know he looked like this until we found him."

Jete gave Shiloh a hug. "Isn't this deer incredible?"

"What stand did you put him in?"

"The acorn flat up on the north end. It was a real acorn buffet up there. We don't hunt it much since it is so close to the north boundary. I had to call old man Swale and get permission to go in from his side of the cliff because the buck fell off the cliff right into his property. We drove the truck around and went right to him. Amazingly he never broke a single tine. His left hip is broken, but the rack is perfect."

Shiloh was speechless. She couldn't stop staring at the buck. The hide was mottled with brown, cream and white colored hairs in a beautiful pattern. The ten point rack was almost twenty-four inches wide with sweeping main beams over thirty inches long. The tines were symmetrical and long.

Jete, Klu, Shiloh and Mike stared at the buck for a few moments more.

Klu shook his head and put his arm around Shiloh. "I took about a hundred pictures. I have his story recorded on my cell phone. I called my editor and sold him the story. He wanted me to try to get a photo worth putting on the cover of the magazine. So we have been working on that while the morning light is so good. I think I have several that will work. I'm going to go home and work on the story. The editor wants it immediately. They are working to rearrange some copy so it can go in next month's issue."

"Okay that sounds great. Thanks. I'll see you later."

Klu shook hands with Mike and congratulated him again. "What are you planning to do with him?"

Mike grinned. "I'm planning to get a full-body mount done. Miss Shiloh, you said you have a good taxidermist here, right?"

"Oh, yes, Mulch is one of the best. He won so many awards at the annual taxidermy convention that he finally just quit going. I think the other competitors were glad he did. Anyway, I can give him a call if you want to take the buck there now."

"Please do. After we load this buck back into the truck I'm going to go take a shower and change clothes."

Shiloh called Mulch to make sure he would be open when they brought the buck to him. She helped Jete and Mike load the buck into Jete's truck and went inside to get something to eat.

Jete followed her inside and sat down across from her at the kitchen table. "How was the interview at the radio station? I didn't get a chance to listen with all the activity this morning."

"It went pretty well I guess. I didn't get to talk very long, but I guess that's a good thing," she said with a grin.

"I have something to show you." Jete pulled his cell phone from his pocket and opened the gallery. He pushed it across the table to Shiloh. "We had some visitors last night."

"What?" Shiloh grabbed the phone and looked carefully at the photo. "Well those trespassing little jerks. They have their faces covered but they look like kids. Was anything else stolen?"

"I don't think so. We got them coming in and going out and it was only a few minutes between pictures. And they don't seem to have anything in the canoe that I can see in the photos anyway."

"Hmm, that's weird. Why go to the trouble to canoe into our land after dark and then don't steal anything?"

"Well, they may not be thieves. Maybe they are anti-hunters determined to undermine our operation somehow. After we get done with Mike's deer let's go take a look around on the creek again. I got some cables and locks, we can rehang the stand they took down and lock it in."

"Okay, sounds good." Shiloh yawned. "I could use a good long nap; at least ten hours would be nice."

"You can sleep again when hunting season is over."

Mike entered the kitchen and grabbed a donut. "I'm ready whenever you are."

"Your buck is loaded, and Mulch is waiting. Let's go," Shiloh said. "Do you mind if I let people know about the buck? Mulch would love the excitement."

"Go right ahead," Mike said proudly.

Shiloh posted a picture of the piebald buck on her social media page and told people to come take a look at it at Mulch's taxidermy shop. By the time they arrived a small crowd had gathered.

"Gee whiz, some people must live on social media. I'm lucky if I get my page checked once or twice a day," Shiloh said.

Mulch greeted them in the parking lot. "Jete told me you were bringing in one of those luna mystic bucks. Let's see this beauty."

"I told you it was a buck with partial leucism. It's leucistic, not luna mystic," Jete scoffed.

"Well that's what I said," Mulch retorted, letting the tailgate down to expose the buck in the bed of Jete's truck. "Holy cow! Look at that." Mulch let out a long wolf whistle. The crowd surrounded him and began talking about the buck. Mulch asked loudly, "Has anybody seen this buck before?"

Everyone answered no.

Jete, Mike and Mulch slid the buck out of the truck bed and into the receiving area of Mulch's shop. The crowd followed and stood admiring the deer. Mulch took Mike inside to discuss how he wanted the deer mounted.

Mulch mumbled to himself, "Let's see now, I've been trying to do everything on the computer instead of paper. But I can never remember my password. It's protected by CRS. Can't remember sh….,uh, stuff. Oh to heck with it." Mulch grabbed his old notebook and began writing notes on what Mike wanted. They settled on a price for a full body mount with a base and some habitat.

When they returned to the crowd a few more people had arrived. Several were taking pictures. Mike didn't seem to mind. A reporter from the local newspaper showed up. He interviewed Mike and took photos. Mulch was enjoying the attention and publicity.

After half an hour Mulch told everyone he needed to get to work on the buck and they all needed to get out. The crowd left and Shiloh and Jete took Mike back to the ranch then went on to reinstall the treestand and explore the creek for any more sign of the trespassers.

The young man received a text on his cell phone. It was a link to an online newspaper article that had just been posted. The story was about a piebald buck that had been killed at Lawson's Hunting Adventures. He texted the link to his girlfriend knowing she would react negatively to the story.

The girl emerged from the bedroom in a rage. "Oh my God, can you believe someone would kill such a beautiful creature?" She ranted and raved for another ten minutes before sitting down next to him. She was seething with anger but had finally stopped talking.

"What are we going to do about this?" he asked, not sure he wanted to hear her answer.

"We are going to set that hell hole of a taxidermy shop on fire."

"We can't do that. That's arson. Somebody could get hurt, or killed!"

"We will do it tonight. That way they won't get to stuff that poor deer's body and put it on display in a trophy room somewhere. Sick bastards."

"I don't want any part of that. You've lost your mind if you think arson is the way to handle this. Count me out!" The young man grabbed his coat and left.

"Fine, you little chicken shit. I'll take care of it myself."

As the sun traveled across the sky, Shiloh and Jete busied themselves with chores on the farm. Mulch worked on the buck. Klu wrote the story and sent it off to his editor. They agreed to meet Mulch at his shop after hours and celebrate the harvest of the buck.

Shiloh invited Carter and Rose to the party. She called Klu and told him to bring his mom and brother. Mulch invited his poker buddies. It was going to be quite the celebration.

The girl stopped at the convenience store and bought lighter fluid and shop rags. She told the clerk she had some oil spots on her car to work off. She also grabbed a bag of baked potato chips, a fifth of vodka and a small carton of orange juice; paid for the items and returned to her car.

She called the young man, but he didn't answer. "Fine, I'll do it myself," she muttered.

The girl reached into her glove box and took out a small metal container. She looked around the parking lot. Too many people. She put the container back, started the car and drove to the park. The sign said the park would close at ten. She drove to a back section to wait and smoke her joint. After she smoked half a joint she drank some of the orange juice then poured vodka into the carton with the remaining juice. After she ate her chips she finished the drink, put her seat back and fell asleep.

Shiloh ordered pizzas to be delivered to the taxidermy shop. Everyone brought their own drinks.

Jete and Mulch began their usual routine of bantering with

each other   .

"Mulch, why do you have a bandage around your wrist?" Jete asked.

"Slammed my wrist in the freezer yesterday, dropped the lid of that old clunker right on top of it trying to get that elk hide out, dang near chopped my arm off."

"Probably because you are getting so near-sighted you can't see past the brim of your hat. Only a baby would need a bandage. Heck, I wouldn't even have felt that little bump on the wrist."

"Huh, a normal man would be in the hospital right now."

"We all question whether or not you are a normal man."

"I just wrapped this up myself and went right on working even though the doctor showed me on the x-ray that there was a hairline crack in my crapall bones."

"Don't you mean the carpal bones?"

"That's what I said. Just because you know all that military medicine doesn't make you some kind of doctor."

"Well sure it does."

"Ha! What kind of surgery have you ever done?"

"Well, I did my own vasectomy!"

Everyone exploded into laughter with Jete's comment.

Mulch waved his arms. "Well, that ain't nothin' to brag about. When I was six years old I died once and my old man made me walk it off."

Jete laughed and waved a napkin in surrender. "I can't beat that."

The pizzas arrived and everyone grabbed a paper plate and helped themselves.

Jete asked Shiloh if she had received any response to her

radio interview.

Shiloh laughed. "Oh yes. I had four messages. One was an invitation to join the chamber of commerce. The second was from the high school asking me to do a presentation at career day. The third was a salesman from the newspaper with a special deal on advertising. And the last one was from the radio, another salesman with a deal."

"Oh well, at least you didn't get any negative calls."

"Have you looked at our social media page lately?"

"No. Why?"

"There is quite a lively argument going on over whether Mike should have shot the deer at all. Some say it's not legal, some say they would let it go, others say they are full of beans. Hunters can be their own worst enemies sometimes."

"Are you going to block and delete them?"

"No, let them have at it. The deer is legal. Our hunter is happy. He doesn't seem to care about the negative comments because I already asked him if he was okay with it. Mulch is happy. I'm happy. It's all good."

Klu added, "When Shiloh is happy, I'm happy." He raised his soda can in a toast.

Jete quickly agreed, raising his coffee cup to meet the toast. "Here, here, I agree, when our fearless leader is happy we are all happy."

"How can you drink coffee at night and then still get to sleep? I'm sure there's a doctor somewhere that would order you not to do that."

"All cowboys drink coffee at night. You watch westerns on TV, you should know this. Besides, cowboys don't take orders, we barely take suggestions."

Mulch and his poker buddies were arguing loudly about politics on the opposite side of the room. "You know what is wrong with California?" Mulch asked. "All those politicians forced everyone to put solar panels on every building. And they got all those wind turbines all over that place. Solar panels and wind turbines are drying up the whole state that's why they have so many wildfires!"

"I'm so sleep deprived that Mulch almost made sense for a split second there," Shiloh said with a laugh. "I'm going home."

Most of the guests followed her lead, helping Mulch clean up and close the shop.

At midnight the girl woke up. She had a headache and was in a foul mood. She called her boyfriend again. He didn't answer. This made her angrier. She checked online for more info about the piebald buck. Pictures of it were being shared all around social media. The smiling face of the hunter posing with the dead deer sent her into a deeper rage. It was the hottest story in the region.

She started the engine of her car, and drove slowly out of the park. Within ten minutes she pulled into the parking lot of Mulch's taxidermy shop. A lone streetlamp lit up the lot. She shut off the engine and waited, watching for any sign of life.

Thinking about the dead deer inside the building made her sick to her stomach. Imagining the deer's body being cut and shaped made her even more upset. She didn't know anything about how taxidermy worked but it seemed morbid to her.

After ten minutes had passed with no sign of life she opened the brown bag containing the shop rags and lighter fluid. She carried them to the side of the building and soaked a rag with fluid. She tucked it into a crevice at the base of a window and poured fluid on the sill. There were only two more windows so she put a fluid soaked rag on each window sill. She poured some lighter fluid at the base of the door.

There wasn't much that would burn. The building was metal with a metal roof. The windows and door were the only place she could find that might burn. She stood back and looked at the building. It would have to do. She lit a match and tossed it at the base of the door. The fluid ignited in flame. Three more matches set the window frames on fire.

She stood back and watched the flames begin to grow. It wasn't the spectacle she was hoping for.

Suddenly the door burst open and Mulch jumped through with a shotgun in his hands. He fired a round of buckshot in the air over her head. "Hold it right there! Don't move!"

The girl ran for her car but Mulch cut her off. "Stop! Don't move! I called the cops. You can already hear the siren. You're caught red handed!"

The girl screamed at Mulch, "You piece of shit! You have that beautiful deer in there! You are desecrating the body! You deserve to go down in flames!" She made a move toward her car.

"Not so fast you crazy nut! You are not going anywhere!" Mulch shot her front left tire.

The girl ran to the other side of the car. She tried to hide behind the car, while looking for a way to escape.

Two police cars raced into the lot, followed by a fire

truck. A second fire truck arrived a minute later.

The girl began running away from the scene.

Mulch yelled at the officers, "She's getting away! She's running!" He pointed at the girl who was stumbling through the empty lot next to Mulch's shop. She tripped over a piece of concrete and fell on her face just as the police caught up with her. They handcuffed her and dragged her kicking and screaming back to Mulch's shop.

Mulch identified her as the one who set the fire. "I have her on security camera. She set off my silent alarm when she walked next to the door."

The footage on Mulch's security camera confirmed the girl with rainbow colored hair was indeed the person who set the fires around his windows and door.

In the morning a photo of the girl appeared in the local newspaper. Shiloh recognized her from the confrontation at the movie theatre. She called the police.

After several hours of interrogation she confessed to stealing the treestand, trail camera and painting the tree with the word murderer. She also confessed to the fake social media page, Win Denergy.

She refused to tell them the name of her boyfriend. The young man was wanted for questioning but he disappeared along with Shiloh's trail camera.

TWENTY-THREE

Earlier in the year Shiloh had donated a youth hunt to the Pheasants Forever organization to use as a fundraiser. They auctioned off the hunt at their annual banquet and a man from Findlay bought the hunt for his twelve year old daughter. Shiloh had the perfect spot picked out for the girl's hunt and felt optimistic that she would get her first deer.

The father-daughter team arrived at noon on Friday. Shiloh greeted them in the front yard. "Hi, did you have any trouble finding this place?" she asked the father.

"No problem. Hi, I'm Curt, this is my daughter Gina."

Shiloh shook hands with each. "I'm Shiloh. Nice to meet you both. Come on in, I will show you around, and then you can unload your gear. After that we will go to the range and make sure the gun is shooting okay after the trip."

"That would be good. We shot it last weekend. She did really well. But it doesn't hurt to get a little more practice in," Curt said.

Shiloh said to Gina, "You are the only hunter in camp this weekend. So you have the run of the place. I do have an excellent spot picked out for us to hunt in the morning. Are you going to shoot a doe or hold out for a big buck?"

Gina looked at her dad then said to Shiloh, "I would like a big buck. But it is my first deer hunt so I'm not going to be picky. I would shoot a doe."

Shiloh smiled and said, "That sounds like an excellent plan."

Curt said, "The decision is completely up to her. I told her if she shot a nice buck we would get it mounted. Do you know a good taxidermist?"

"I sure do. His name is Pete Moss, but everyone calls him Mulch. He plays poker with a bunch of lifelong buddies and none of them go by their real names. One guy is called Quincy, he's a retired doctor. There's another one called Cheese, he's from Wisconsin, of course. And Rocket. I have no idea why they call him that. And my Uncle Jete. Jete is his real name. Grandma said she named him after a dance-jump-move because she could feel him kicking in the womb, a lot. I guess the guys thought his real name was unusual enough that he didn't need a nickname." Everyone laughed.

In the morning Shiloh took Gina and her father to a ground blind near the Yellow Wolf River. She explained their set up while they were inside the blind waiting for sunrise. "There is a big bend in the river right here and the deer cut this curve going from the big crop fields back to a bedding area in the morning. With the river behind us it makes a natural funnel. Whenever we get a straight south wind this blind is good for morning and evening hunts. They come right back through here from the bedding area out to the fields in the afternoon. Tree plantings are what make this spot so good. It's a good pinch point. Hopefully they will be within one hundred yards of us as they walk through here."

Shiloh helped Gina adjust the tripod gun rest and use her rangefinder to mark yardages. "You see that big cedar tree out there? It's one hundred yards exactly. Everything on this side of the tree is fair game. Legal shooting time is thirty minutes before sunrise, which is in just a few minutes so keep your eyes open."

"There's a deer Miss Shiloh." Gina pointed cautiously.

"Well that was quick. Good job girl. Ah, to have young eyes again, I can barely see her without binoculars." Shiloh scanned the tree plantings with her binoculars. She spotted a glimpse of white antler near the cedar tree. "I see a buck Gina, but he's a hundred yards out by the tree. I can't tell exactly what he has on his head. He's behind the cedar tree." Shiloh watched the buck for several minutes. It appeared to be made of stone. An occasional twitch of its ear was the only indication it was a real animal. "Gee whiz that buck is nervous about something, he hasn't moved in minutes."

Suddenly three coyotes ran through the tree plantings. Shiloh lowered her binoculars to watch them. One of them was the black coyote with yellow eyes. A doe snorted and stomped her right front hoof, then took off running with her white tail flagging through the trees. Three other deer followed her. Shiloh moved her binoculars back up to her eyes to look for the buck. "He's gone. I don't see him." She lowered the binoculars and spotted a glimpse of the white antlers moving toward them. "Oh Gina, here he comes. He's coming right at us with his head down. See him?"

"Yes, I see him. He's a nice one!" Gina's breathing began

to speed up. Shiloh could almost hear her heart pounding.

"Get your gun ready. Put the crosshairs on him, but don't shoot until he turns broadside. He's going to have to turn if he wants to get past us." Shiloh glanced at Gina. She had the gun up and ready and was following the buck through the scope on her gun.

The buck stopped, took two more steps and looked back. When he did, his body angled broadside to Gina.

Shiloh asked, "Are you on him?"

"Yes."

"Okay, take the shot, nice and easy."

The gun roared. Shiloh saw the buck do a mule kick with his back legs and take off running directly away from them. He ran past the cedar tree and disappeared.

Gina was squealing with delight. She high-fived Shiloh and her dad. Her dad nearly knocked them all over as he gave Gina a big hug. "Okay tell me how you felt about the shot. Were you steady on him? Did you squeeze the trigger real easy?" he asked. Gina shook her head yes.

"Here, give me your gun," Shiloh said. She took the gun from Gina and flipped the safety to on. Let's just wait twenty minutes before we get out of the blind. I did not see the buck go down, but I think you made a good hit. I saw him do the classic mule kick."

"I'm going to call my mom. Wait until she hears this."

Gina whispered excitedly to her mom over the cell phone then the parents talked to each other.

Shiloh let twenty-five minutes go by before she stepped out of the ground blind. She motioned to Gina and whispered, "Bring your gun and follow me. Let's be as quiet as we can and just slip over there to the cedar tree. Hopefully he is just lying over there behind it."

When they got to the tree the buck was not there but Shiloh found a good blood trail. They followed it for another hundred yards then found a place in the timber where the leaves and dirt had been stirred up. Blood was visible in several places on the leaves.

"What happened here?" Curt asked. "Why is the blood trail all over the place?"

"Coyotes," Shiloh said grimly. "Remember the three coyotes we saw earlier? I'm afraid they are on the buck's trail too. Looks like the buck tried to fight them off right here."

Gina's eyes were wide. "That's not cool."

"I agree completely. Stay where you are. I'm going to walk in ever widening circles and see if I can find his blood trail again."

Within seconds Shiloh had the trail. "Here it is. Come on, follow me. He's bleeding a lot. He's circling toward the river. Looks like he is following this trail. There is a good crossing up ahead where it is shallow. He's probably heading right for it." They followed the blood trail for another fifty yards to the bank of the river. "Here he is! He tried to cross but the coyotes pulled him down. They ate a small part of his back hip already! Dang coyotes!"

Curt and Shiloh waded into the water up to their knees and drug the buck back onto the bank. "Well, you guys, we are going to have to do a little bit of creative cropping for this grip and grin session. He's a beautiful buck Gina. A real symmetrical eight pointer. I'll bet he scores about one-hundred-forty. Congratulations."

After calling the telecheck system and taking photos they took the buck back to camp. Everyone congratulated Gina and listened to the retelling of the story. Jete caped the buck and salvaged most of the meat.

Curt asked, "Do we have time to take this to the taxidermist now?"

Shiloh checked the time. "Sure. I'll give him a call and let him know we are on the way."

When they arrived at the taxidermy shop Mulch was putting the finishing touches on the nostrils of a big non-typical pedestal mount. "Hey Shiloh, come on in. So your message said you have a first ever deer for a fine young gal. Bring it right on in here let's have a look at it."

Gina was beaming as she helped her dad place the head and cape on the work table.

"Ah, this is a real dandy buck my dear," he winked at Gina.

"I got to get out of school early on Friday to come on this hunt."

"Oh you did? Well, you know what they say? Education is important, but hunting is importanter. Let me just get some particulars written down. Now where is my record book?" Mulch limped to his desk and rummaged through papers. "Ah, here we go."

"What's with the limp Mulch? Did you hurt your leg?" Shiloh asked.

"Some dang kids riding their four wheelers on our back forty again. Cut the fence and did donuts in my field. I tried to catch them running that counterband a few weeks ago, banged my knee into a fence post."

"Counterband?" Shiloh and Gina shrugged at each other

"You know, smuggled black market stuff."

"You mean contraband?"

"That's what I said ain't it? Anyway I wrenched my knee. I've had to feeble my way around a bit but it's fine. I just get flustrated with those dang renegades. Our game warden is close to retiring so he doesn't want to do much but drive around in his truck looking for good places to hunt after he quits for good."

Shiloh laughed and said, "Well I don't know about that, but it sure will feel strange when he retires. He's been the game warden in this area for most of my life."

"Mulch, will you take a personal check for the deposit on the mount?" Curt asked.

"Yes, of course. The only person I won't take a check from is Jete Lawson."

"Why won't you take a check from him?" Shiloh asked.

"Because the last time he wrote me a check he signed it Dill Pickle."

Everyone laughed, including Mulch.

"That's a fact. Now young lady let's talk about how you want this fine first buck mounted?"

Klu talked Jete into an informal partnership. In their spare time, which wasn't much, they worked on building custom box blinds. They designed a better window system so they could be opened and closed silently. They included shelving and hooks for hanging bows and a rack to hold a gun securely but still quickly accessible. They carpeted the floor with indoor-outdoor carpet. Every crack and crevice was sealed to prevent mice and bugs from getting inside. They painted some of them green with a leafy template camo pattern that Shiloh designed. In an experiment they painted one a pale sky blue.

Jete joked, "We can market this as a back yard playhouse that doubles as a hunting blind."

Klu made arrangements with the gas station in Cedarwood that sold his wood to let them put the blinds on the edge of their parking lot. Much to everyone's surprise the blue one sold in the first week. After that they averaged selling one blind per week.

The next few weeks flew by for Shiloh. With each group of hunters came new challenges. As they worked through the highs and lows a pattern emerged. Jete took the two most serious, hard core, experienced hunters of each group. Shiloh would guide the odd ball, difficult and inexperienced hunters. Carter took the remaining two hunters.

They all agreed Shiloh had the better temperament to handle the unusual, plus she was the head guide so, as Jete said, "The knuckleheads were defaulted to her."

She experienced two father-son duos. In one group, the father wore a red plaid jacket and smoked. He insisted on hunting only in a ladder stand. Every time she went to the tree to get him, several of his items were on the ground. She knew he was smoking in the tree but didn't scold him.

"The guy must be close to ninety years old. I'm worried about whether he can actually pee off the treestand," Jete joked.

She knew the old guy was just enjoying the whole

experience so much she didn't want to spoil it for him.

His son, on the other hand was a scent control freak. He kept all his clothing, including underwear and socks, in scent safe bags. Each time she took him to the tree he stepped behind the truck and stripped completely naked while she covered her eyes. He changed clothes and got into the treestand. When he came down from the stand he reversed the dressing procedure. He showered three times a day, once in the morning before hunting, again in the afternoon before hunting, then at night before bed. In spite of all his preparations he never got a deer. Not because he didn't have an opportunity, he just wanted to hold out for an older trophy class buck.

In spite of not tagging a deer the twosomes had tremendous fun together. Shiloh realized she was mostly babysitting the father so the son could hunt, which was fine with her, they were a loving team.

The other father-son duo seemed to be at war with each other. The forty-something father seemed to delight in driving his twenty-something son, nuts. They dressed in similar camouflage outfits, shot similar bows, wore similar boots and seemed to like the same foods, sports teams and politics. Shiloh couldn't figure out why the son was always mad at his dad.

When he wasn't hunting, the dad wore a fishing cap with at least fifty pins stuck all over it. She asked him about the collection. He showed her each pin and told her the significance of every one. When they got to pin number twenty-five Shiloh began to wish she hadn't asked. They were nice stories but didn't really matter as much to her as they did to the hat's owner.

When it was time to hunt she took them to stand locations about half a mile apart. She walked the dad into his stand location and showed him where the stand was in a hickory tree near a corn field. She took the son another half mile down the road, told him to follow the hedge row to the end and the stand would be in a gnarly hedge apple tree overlooking a food plot.

She ran a few errands in town and returned early to pick up her hunters. As she pulled up to the drop off point she noticed the dad sitting along the path. He told her the hunt did not go well. Some dogs were barking in the distance, a farmer started combining in the next field. He didn't see any deer. Shiloh apologized for the bad luck and promised him a new stand location in the morning. They drove on down the road to pick up the son. They waited until dark and soon he appeared. He had seen a few does and one shooter buck in the distance. He put his gear away and got in the truck.

As she started to drive back to the ranch house the dad said, "Hey, wait a minute, I forgot my release. I left it where I was sitting when you picked me up."

"Okay, I'll drive back down there and you can grab it." Shiloh pulled the truck to the side of the road and the dad got out. After the dad looked for his release for several minutes the son joined his search. Shiloh watched and decided she should go help.

Before she could get out of the truck the son jerked the passenger door open and said, "Well guess what? He shot a doe. And he buried her under leaves and now he cannot find her. He wanted to surprise us all when we came to help look for his supposedly lost release. He was going to unveil her, but now he cannot find her."

Shiloh just looked at him in the darkness trying to process the story and finally said, "I'll get my flashlight."

After several minutes of looking near where the dad was sitting when she picked him up, she asked him to retell the story of shooting the doe. His description of events didn't make sense. She asked him to follow her to the treestand and retell the story, this time pointing in the direction the deer had gone after the shot. When they got to the tree, the dad pointed in the opposite direction of the spot where he had been sitting. Shiloh found a blood trail and followed it, finding the doe one hundred yards in the other direction.

They debated for five minutes over who was going to field dress the doe. The dad said, "I ain't never had no girl field dress my deer before."

"Well, I could have had it done in the amount of time we have been standing here debating this. I'm you're guide, it's my duty. It's part of the service we offer here at Lawson's Hunting Adventures."

"Fine," the dad relented. "If you insist. I shall not stand in your way. But do not tell any of my friends I let a girl field dress my deer."

"It's a deal. Now move aside. Please." Shiloh was struggling to keep her composure as she put on her plastic field dressing gloves, pulled her knife from its sheath and quickly took care of the deer. When they got back to the ranch house the other hunters were done with supper and watching television in the great room. Dorothy served the duo a late supper and sent Shiloh home with a plate of food and instructions to get some sleep.

The next week Shiloh was paired with two hunters that couldn't be more opposite. One was from Texas, the other Missouri. The Texas hunter was about twenty, and more than six feet tall. He told Shiloh if she guided him to a trophy book buck he would give her a one-thousand dollar tip. She looked at him in disbelief. "What did you just say?"

"If I get a buck that will make the bow hunting record book I will give you a thousand dollar tip." He adjusted his cowboy hat.

"Okay then," Shiloh said with doubt.

The Missouri hunter stayed on stand all day, every day. He hunted hard and got a big buck on the last day of his hunt. The Texas hunter had done just the opposite.

After lunch on the second day he told her he wanted to hunt in a stand where no one else had been. She brought the truck around and told him she could do that, but they would need to travel on the hard road for about twenty minutes because she did not want to drive through the farm, instead she wanted to come in from the top side. A bridge was being repaired so they would have to take the long way around. She waited while he went to get his gear. When he jumped in the passenger seat she asked if he was ready to go. "You got everything you need? This is kind of far away."

"Yep, I'm good to go."

But he wasn't.

When they arrived, Shiloh jumped out of the truck, opened the tail gate and waited for him to get his gear so he could follow her to the stand.

"Uh, I forgot my bow," he said, looking sheepish.

"You're kidding?"

"No. I thought it was in here from this morning's hunt but I forgot that I took it out to do some shooting and didn't put it back in. It's hanging at the range."

"Get in. I'll put you in a spot behind the ranch house, so at least you can hunt for an hour or so."

"That's okay. I'm good. I don't need to hunt today."

Shiloh started to think the kid was afraid he might actually get a deer and didn't have the money to pay for his boasting offer of a big tip.

The following morning when Shiloh went to get him from the treestand she got to within one-hundred yards of the stand and stopped. Her hunter was walking in her direction but the smell of skunk was overwhelming.

When he got to the vehicle he said, "Do you like my cover scent? I used my own rope to lower my bow from the stand before I started to get down. I didn't see the skunk at the base of the tree. I hit him square on the head."

He never got a deer, nor did he leave a tip, for the cooks, or Shiloh.

During the third week Shiloh guided two men from the east coast. She began to think they were incapable of speaking in anything other than the loudest volume possible. Neither one could hit the paper plate at twenty yards. She wondered what the heck they were doing on an expensive guided hunt.

"Guys, today I am taking you to a spot where the deer come out of the fields, walk past these stands and bed on the bluff just a couple hundred yards from where I will be dropping you off and picking you up. If you don't get a deer in the morning just slip out real quiet and we will ease out of there. You can go back to the same stands in the afternoon and if we don't disturb the deer on the bluff they will come right back down past those stands on their way to the fields this afternoon. The wind is right for both set ups. Got it?"

They assured her they understood.

When they closed their doors quietly and whispered to each other in the morning darkness she thought there might be hope. Later that morning she went back to pick them up for brunch. Hunter number one opened the passenger side door and yelled, "Squirrels! All we saw were dozens of squirrels!"

Hunter number two dropped the tailgate of her truck with a loud bang and tossed his bow in with a clunk. They both slammed the truck doors when they got in. They seemed happy as could be with all the deer they saw in the morning. Shiloh put her head in her hands atop the steering wheel and sighed. She didn't have the heart to tell them they would not be seeing deer that afternoon.

Not all of Shiloh's hunters were knuckleheads. Their season was going really well. Most hunters had an opportunity at a buck. Several nice ones were killed. The days were running together. By the third week all the hunters wanted to hunt morning and evening. This meant Shiloh and Jete were up well before dawn, worked all day adjusting stands, checking cameras, refreshing corn piles, mowing yards or doing anything else that needed fixing or moving. They were running on too little sleep when the rain started.

It rained all day and into the night of the first muzzleloader season. All the hunters opted for ground blinds or elevated box blinds in the morning. After they got all the hunters out the rain stopped. Jete told Shiloh he was going to check a stand that a hunter had complained about the previous week, saying it was loose and squeaked when he shifted his weight.

"I'll go with you, let me grab a few things first," Shiloh said. Jete pulled the side by side up to the back door and waited. Shiloh came out with SD cards in a baggie and stuffed them in her pocket. "Might as well switch out a few cards on the way."

When they got to the stand Shiloh walked thirty yards to the small tree with the trail camera on it and proceeded to change out the SD card. Jete looked in the back of the side by side and cursed under his breath. He looked at Shiloh, then up at the stand. He knew not to climb the stand without his safety harness, but didn't want to go back to his truck to get it. He decided to climb the ladder anyway. He would be careful.

Shiloh closed the trail camera case and turned just in time to see the treestand swing dangerously as Jete lost his footing and fell from the top rung of the ladder. "Jete!" she screamed.

Jete landed in a heap at the base of the tree. "Oh shit! That was stupid," he groaned, holding his left arm.

Shiloh rushed to his side. "Are you okay?"

"I think I broke my arm. And my foot."

"My God, you're lucky you didn't break your neck. Don't move." Shiloh called 911. Then she called her mom and Carter, then Klu.

Within minutes Klu was by her side. He checked Jete carefully. "Stay still," he instructed Jete. "Carter is at the house and he is going to guide the paramedics to this spot. Then we will all carry you out of here on a board. We need to be sure you didn't break your back or your neck. Lie still."

"Does it hurt?" Shiloh asked.

"It hurts enough to make a glass eye cry," Jete grimaced. Shiloh and Klu burst into laughter. So did Jete. "Stop laughing, you're making it worse," he said. "I'm alright. Just banged up."

"Bullshit. You have a big knot on your forehead. You might have a concussion," Klu said.

"I hear the ambulance. Hold on Jete. They will be here to get you any minute."

"This is just damned embarrassing. I know better."

Shiloh nodded in agreement. "Well, you can be the poster boy for enforcing the rule to always wear a safety harness and use the lifelines. We have had some guys bitch about it. They won't stand a chance of winning the argument now."

Carter arrived with the paramedics in tow. They carried Jete to the ambulance and headed to the hospital in Findlay. Shiloh and Dorothy followed the ambulance in her truck. Klu and Carter stayed behind to pick up the hunters later that evening.

After the doctor examined Jete he came to see Shiloh and Dorothy in the family waiting room. "Well, Jete is very lucky. He does not have any injuries to his spine. He did break his forearm, cracked two ribs and has a hairline fracture in his foot. His arm will be in cast for a while. He will need to keep that foot elevated for a few days until the swelling decreases. Once the pain subsides in the next two weeks he can gradually reintroduce weight bearing activities. The ribs should heal on their own in about six weeks. He will need to restrict his activities for a while. We are going to keep him overnight for observation because of the bump on his forehead. You can go in to see him now, but don't stay long. If he does well overnight he can go home in the morning."

When the doctor left they went to Jete's room to see him. They gathered around Jete's hospital bed and joked about his hard headedness. Shiloh said, "I hope that fall knocked some sense into you so you won't climb trees without your safety harness anymore."

"My mind is so sharp even my thoughts have splinters," Jete responded groggily.

Shiloh and Dorothy laughed. "I think your mind is in serious need of some sleep." Shiloh adjusted his pillow and kissed him on the forehead. "We will see you later."

Dorothy prayed, "Dear Lord, thank you for saving Jete's life in the fall from the treestand. Please help him heal quickly. Amen"

Seconds later Mulch arrived at the door to Jete's hospital room. He took off his hat and stepped into the room, looking sheepish. "I hope I'm not intertruding. They said only family could come visit, so I fibbed a bit and told them I was your cousin although I think we may be related since my mom's maiden name was Lawson and your mom's maiden name was Moss. I'll bet if we did one of those ancestorator searches we would find out we are related for sure."

"Come in Mulch, you are not intruding at all and you are family, of course," Dorothy said.

Mulch walked to the side of Jete's bed and shook his hand gently. "How ya doin' old buddy?"

"Oh I'm just laying here with my toes pointed at the sky but thank God it's not permanent."

"Your face looks like you kissed an airbag."

"Really? I haven't looked in the mirror yet."

"I'll bet it hurt when you hit the ground."

Jete rubbed his head. "Well, to tell you the truth I remember the fall but don't remember the actual landing."

"Heck, my memory is so bad I went and bought a pair of those shoes with memory foam so I can remember where I'm going." Mulch continued when everyone started laughing. "Damn things don't work. I still forget why I went into the kitchen or where I parked the truck."

"How did you know I was in the hospital?"

"Heard it on the police scanner. I called your phone, then Shiloh's but no answer. So I called Klu. He told me what happened."

Shiloh looked at her phone. "I'm sorry Mulch, I see the missed call, but I missed it."

"That's alright honey. Klu filled me in. So, you and Klu are becoming an item."

Shiloh blushed.

"Has he kissed you yet? You know the biggest event in a relationship is not the first kiss. It's the first fart."

Jete began laughing as Shiloh protested Mulch's teasing.

"Mulch! Seriously?" Shiloh said, trying to suppress her amusement.

"It's not that big of a deal Shiloh. Farts are just the screams of trapped turds and everybody has turds," Mulch said with a wink.

Jete tried not to laugh but couldn't help it. "Oh that hurts," he said holding his arm.

Dorothy raised her hand. "That's enough nonsense you three. Jete needs to get some rest, we need to go."

Shiloh's cell phone buzzed. She read the brief text. "Both

of my hunters shot deer. I'll text Klu and see if he and Carter can go take care of them before we get back."

"Go on. Go on back to the ranch and take care of things. I'm fine. Go." Jete waved them all out the door.

When Shiloh arrived at the ranch she texted Klu to see if they had found the deer yet. He replied that one was recovered but the other one didn't leave a blood trail and asked that she bring Hazard to the east pasture. Shiloh loaded Hazard in the side by side and left to go help track the deer. When she arrived, Klu, Carter and the two hunters were standing next to the other side by side. A nice buck was already loaded into the bed.

Shiloh congratulated Ralph and asked about his hunt. "Wow, great buck Ralph! Congratulations. Tell me what happened."

Ralph explained the encounter with exciting detail. When he had completed his story Shiloh congratulated him again and turned to her other hunter and asked, "So, Ben, let's hear about your buck."

Ben explained the shot and pointed to the direction the buck ran. Both hunters relayed the increase of midday buck movement. Shiloh listened intently then said, "Sounds like the young bucks are really out cruising in the middle of the day. Seems early for that much activity but this has been a strange year, late tornadoes and all."

Klu agreed the activity seemed out of the ordinary for the time. "Maybe we aren't going to have that October lull like in years past. I don't expect to see the big boys out for at least another week or two. Both these guys shot decent bucks, but nothing like what will come out of the woodwork pretty soon.

Anyway, we looked for one hundred yards. We couldn't find a drop of blood. Ben is sure he made a good shot though. That's why we called for Hazard."

Shiloh turned to Ben and patted him on the shoulder. "Don't worry, Hazard will find your buck. He hasn't lost one yet. It's a big help that you marked where you last saw the buck. That will save us some time and energy." She pulled a leash from the glove box and clipped it to Hazard's collar. They walked to the big pine tree where the hunter had last seen the deer. "Come on boy, let's see if we can find the buck. Hunt 'em up boy. Here boy, find the buck, hunt' em up." She pointed at the ground. Hazard put his nose to the ground and began searching. He circled the tree twice then headed east.

Klu followed Shiloh and Hazard while Carter took Ralph and his buck back to the barn. Ben followed along behind Klu. He was having trouble keeping up.

Klu noticed it first, and asked, "Do you want to wait at the vehicle while we do this? I can come back to get you when we find your deer." Ben seemed relieved and limped back to the side by side to wait. By now Shiloh was trotting along behind Hazard who seemed to have the wounded deer's scent trail figured out, at least for now.

Klu caught up with Shiloh and Hazard. He followed along behind, careful not to interfere with the dog's tracking ability. Hazard tracked the buck all the way around the pasture to the dry creek bed that separated the Lawson and Dugan properties.

"You okay with us going over on your land?" Shiloh asked. "It sure looks like that's where Hazard wants to go."

"Absolutely. Keep going." Klu pushed down the top

strand of fence and crawled over. Hazard jumped the fence and Shiloh followed across.

"Here boy, keep going. Hunt 'em up. Find the deer." Shiloh followed Hazard as he found the place where the deer jumped the fence. "Look! Blood!" Shiloh pointed to the spot where the deer landed. "I can see a blood trail now. Good boy Hazard, find the deer."

Hazard put his nose on the blood trail and kept going. Shiloh had trouble keeping up with him. They followed the blood trail for one-hundred yards before it began to get fainter. Shiloh could not see any drops of blood but Hazard kept on the trail.

"This buck is going uphill. This is not looking good. He's gone a long ways and now he is going up the hill. We may not find this one," Shiloh said with a worried face. "It's getting unusually warm today too."

Klu pointed to the top of the hill, "Look," he said quietly. "There's a buck up there."

Shiloh followed his gaze. She grabbed her binoculars and looked at the buck. "He's got his head down. I can't see his antlers. Ben said he shot a ten point typical right?"

"Yes, with a double left brow tine."

"We better not go any farther if that's him. I don't want to jump him. Let's just wait." She watched the buck through her binoculars. "I can see the double left brow tines. That's Ben's buck. He's going to lay down. That hill must have been too much for him. I think we pushed him up there and got him bleeding again."

"Let's back out of here and go up to the house. We can let the buck stiffen up. Maybe it will die right there if we don't push it."

"You're right. How far is your house from here? Is it closer to go there or should we retrace our steps and go back to the east pasture that way?"

"My house is just a hundred yards east. Let's go there. I can borrow Mom's car and we can drive back down the dead end road to get Ben and the side by side. "

"Okay, sounds good. Plus I will get a chance to see if you hung my painting on your wall." Shiloh looked at Klu, who grinned back at her. They slipped quietly away from the buck and snuck past a grove of pine trees and started walking toward Klu's house.

Suddenly Shiloh stopped. "Oh gosh, I just realized I am going to need another guide. Jete may be out of commission for a while. You interested in helping us out?"

"Work for you?" Klu screwed up his nose in mock disgust then started laughing when he saw the look on her face. "I'm kidding! Of course I will help you out."

"I don't know, I might change my mind. I need some character references."

"My mom is home, she will vouch for me."

"Well then, I guess you are hired."

TWENTY-FOUR

Becky was bored. The headache from her night out with John was finally gone. She had upgraded him to a suite at the extended stay hotel in Canyon. She still wouldn't let him come to the campground. He didn't have a vehicle so she didn't worry about him showing up unexpectedly.

Ricky knocked on the door of her motor home. She opened the door and let him in. He handed her one of two cardboard boxes he carried. "I brought you a package. It came in the mail yesterday. I wanted to deliver it personally."

"Thanks." Becky sat down at the table with the package in front of her. Ricky stayed as if he wanted to see her open the box. "It's some spices and dog treats I ordered online. It's nothing." Ricky looked disappointed. She pointed to the box in his hands. "What's in the other box? Is that one for me too?"

"Oh, uh, no, it's stuff for the, uh, dog fighting thing." Ricky held the box tighter.

"Really? How's that coming along? Are the pups I got you guys in training now?"

"Yes. Yes they are doing fine. I need to start them on a bait dog any day now."

"What's a bait dog?"

"Don't you remember? I told you how they need a small dog to train on since the pups are young. We don't want them to get their asses kicked in their early training or they will be afraid to fight."

"Oh yeah, I forgot. That makes sense. Why don't you take one of those little yapping dogs in the main campground?"

"Can't do that. Then the campers would be walking all around the campground looking for it. They might search out in the woods and end up finding the box canyon. We don't want that."

"Hmm, I suppose not. Well, thanks for bringing my box. I'll see ya later." Becky opened the door and let Ricky out. She watched him walk past the multi-flora rose bush and disappear down the trail toward the box canyon. Then she ripped open her package. Inside was a large purse. It was gray and black with a double strap and a zipper that closed the bag securely. She set it aside and took out the remaining contents.

The first item was a stun gun wrapped in plastic which she had some difficulty cutting open. Becky read the instructions and description in the paperwork that came with the stun gun. *Simply touching an attacker with the stun gun will disrupt the brain signals to the voluntary muscles. It will deliver a high voltage shock. This will cause loss of balance and muscle control, confusion and disorientation. It will bring your attacker to his knees and stop aggressive activity.* Becky smiled.

The other items were various sex toys. She looked each

one over carefully, thinking about how surprised John was going to be tonight.

Becky decided to try one of the toys. She looked through the drawers in her motor home for batteries but did not have the right size. "Son-of-a-bitch, there is never the right size battery in here when you need it." She put the items in her new, big purse and grabbed a flask of whisky from the cupboard. She took a drink and placed the flask in her purse, then transferred the handcuffs she had taken from the box near the canvas tent in the box canyon, from her purse to her new bag.

She went into the bedroom and opened her jewelry box and slipped several bracelets on her wrists to cover the bruises the handcuffs had made the previous night. John was getting a little rougher with each visit, but she liked it.

She grabbed the keys to the convertible and a backpack full of money and went outside. "Queenie, you stay here. Mama is gonna take a ride in the convertible. We won't have many more nice days like this one."

Queenie crawled back under the motor home to lay down again.

Becky put the big purse and back pack in the small trunk, put the top down and drove away toward Cedarwood to get batteries. It would give her a chance to pick up her prescription for birth control pills and go shopping. She also wanted a new outfit.

As she drove toward Cedarwood she checked her phone for messages. When she looked up, a doe darted in front of her. She swerved and saw a buck hot on the doe's trail. She slammed on her brakes just as the buck jumped over the hood of her car. He didn't quite make it all the way over, lost his balance when his back hoof hit the hood, and fell against her windshield. It rolled over the top of her car, landing on the road behind.

Two men in a dark blue sedan were traveling in the opposite direction and saw the accident. They turned around and came back to park behind Becky who was sitting in stunned silence. They ran up to her and asked if she was alright. "Holy crap, we saw the whole thing. That buck went airborne when he hit your windshield. He just rolled right on over the top!"

Becky looked up at the men and shook her head. "Where did that thing come from? Is it dead?" Becky looked in her rear view mirror.

"No, it's getting up and limping off now. Too bad we don't have that on video it would get a million views," said one of the men. "Looks like all you have is a busted windshield. It can be fixed up. It's kind of weird that your air bag did not go off." He walked around the front of the car. "There is no damage to your car, just the busted windshield. If that buck could have jumped just a little higher he would have missed you all together. But you are one lucky lady, anyway."

"Thanks. I guess." Becky put the car in drive and waved as she slowly moved forward. "Thanks for stopping. I'm going to the mechanic shop now." She drove the rest of the way to Cedarwood very carefully. She had trouble seeing through the hundreds of spidery cracks in the windshield. It looked like it was about to fall in her lap at any moment.

She made it to the mechanic shop with no incident. She went inside to find Henry. She waved through the glass window when she saw him. He came out to the front desk to talk to her. Becky showed him her car and explained what happened.

"We can fix this Becky. We will need to order the windshield. Might take a few days." He picked a few brown hairs out of a crack.

"Oh. Hmm. I guess I hadn't thought of that."

"Do you need a ride home?"

Becky thought for a moment. "I'm not sure. Can I sit down? It's been a crazy trip into town."

"Sure, have a seat in the front area by the desk. I'll need to take down your information and fill out the forms so we can get this repair started. "

Becky watched Henry write on some forms. He asked her a few questions. While she waited for him to finish writing down her answers she asked about Klu. "So, how is your brother? I haven't seen him in a while."

"He's doing really great. He's working for Shiloh Lawson in her outfitting business. In fact, I talked to Mom a little while ago and she told me Klu's out helping her track a deer now."

If Henry had been looking up from his paper work while he talked he would have seen Becky's face turn red and her disposition change. He didn't notice. By the time he completed the forms Becky had diluted her jealous rage with a sip from her flask of whiskey.

"You said Klu is working for Shiloh? What's he doing?"

"Yeah, her uncle Jete got hurt bad last night so Klu is going to help out for a while. He's guiding deer hunters."

"How long will he be doing that?"

"Well, Jete should get out of the hospital in Findlay today. Not sure how long he will be laid up though. He broke his arm and his foot. Fell out of a treestand. Lucky he isn't paralyzed."

Becky sat and stared at the wall for several moments. "You okay?" Henry looked down at her as he walked around the counter.

"I would like to see Klu. Do you think he would see me?" Becky asked as if in a trance.

"What the hell do you want to see Klu for? He's dating Shiloh now. I don't think he wants any part of seeing you romantically Becky."

"But if I could just talk to him. If he could understand how I feel."

"Seriously Becky, are you sure you didn't hit your head in the accident? You're talking crazy."

"That Lawson bitch is the problem." Becky looked up at Henry. "I know she has been the problem all along."

"Becky, you're nuts. Go home. Do you need a ride?" Henry reached to help her up from the chair. Becky stood up slowly. "Have you been drinking?"

"No, just a little sip from my flask now and then when my head hurts. But I'm not drunk or anything if that's what you mean. I can get my own ride. Thanks." She started to walk out.

"I'll have your car done in a few days." Henry held the door open for her.

"I just need to get a couple of things out of the trunk."

"Do you need some help?"

"No. I got this." She waved her hand as if to fling him away.

Henry watched her retrieve a big purse-like bag and a backpack from the trunk of the damaged convertible and then walk across the street to the drug store. He went back to work when she disappeared through the door.

Becky picked up her prescription and bought a fifth of whiskey. A display of cut flowers was near the exit. She pulled a bouquet of yellow, red and white flowers from the display and returned to the register to pay. Before leaving the drug store she slipped the whiskey from the paper bag and put it in her purse. She crumpled up the bag and tossed it into the trash can outside the door. Then she walked the five blocks to the used car dealership. There, she bought the cheapest car in the lot for three-thousand dollars in cash. It was a silver, four door, Mazda sedan with one hundred-ninety-three thousand miles on it. It needed new tires and a new muffler but the engine ran surprisingly well. When she was done with it she would just give it to John. But first she had something to do before giving John his new ride. She drove it off the lot and went to the mall.

She rushed inside to buy a new outfit. She wanted to look her best when she found Klu. After making a selection she took the items to the dressing room to try on. She admired herself in the dressing room mirror. The pants she had chosen were made of black spandex and fit tightly from waist to heel. She also chose a long sleeved sweater of red cashmere that buttoned up the front with tiny white buttons. She left the top six buttons undone. She pulled the tags off the items and went to the shoe department where she chose a pair of black heels. She liked the look of the red sweater so much that she grabbed a black one from the shelf and added it to her purchase. She handed the tags from the clothes she was wearing to the clerk and paid with cash. Then she went to the parking lot, got in the car, started the engine and drove toward Klu's house.

When Becky pulled into the driveway of the Dugan farm she wasn't sure of her plan. She just knew she wanted to talk to Klu. Her nights with John had done nothing to quell her lust for Klu. She had become fixated on the idea of making Klu her own but didn't know how to make him feel the same way. Everything she had tried so far had failed. She didn't want to accept that he might be serious about Shiloh. She had to know. She couldn't accept the thought he might actually be dating her, spending time with her, laughing with her and more. The jealousy drove Becky nearly insane. She was having trouble processing it. She drove the car up to the house and stopped.

Klu came out the front door. "Becky, what are you doing here?" He thought her outfit looked ridiculous.

Becky grabbed the bouquet of flowers and got out of the car. She walked toward Klu. "I heard about Jete Lawson. I heard he was hurt real bad. Henry told me. I don't know him or the family very well but I just wanted to express my concern. I brought flowers." Becky handed Klu the flowers.

"Becky, I thought you hated the Lawsons. And if not, you could have sent flowers to the hospital."

"Well I don't have any problem with Jete Lawson. It's that, uh, Shiloh and her brother Syder. You remember Syder, the one who killed poor Al. Henry told me Jete was probably getting out today and I just now found out about it so of course these flowers would have missed him. I thought it would be easier if I just gave them to you, since I know you and all and you could give them to him."

"Your story is just down right strange Becky. As long as I have known you, you have always been a liar. Something about your story doesn't add up. What are you really doing here?"

"I wanted to see you. Okay so, there. You caught me. I needed an excuse and I brought the flowers. Okay so you caught me." Becky moved closer to Klu. "I wanted to see how you are. It's been such a long time."

Shiloh opened the front door and came out of Klu's house. She walked up to them and smiled politely. "Hi Becky. What's going on?"

"I just came to talk to Klu that's all." Becky's face and neck turned red. "I saw you at Delmar's wedding. You were dancing with Eddy." She looked at Klu hoping it would bother him.

Klu realized what she was trying to do. He slipped his arm around Shiloh and looked at Becky. "I'm helping Shiloh with her outfitting business while Jete is laid up. It was real nice of you to bring the flowers for him." He handed them to Shiloh. "Shiloh will see that he gets them."

"Oh, yes," Shiloh said in surprise as she took the flowers. "That's very thoughtful of you. Unusual, but thoughtful."

Klu responded before Becky could say anything. "We need to get going. The guys are waiting for us. See ya later Becky." Klu glared at Becky when Shiloh turned to go back in the house.

Becky watched them walk hand-in-hand back into the house. She jerked the car door open and got in. Blinded with jealousy and rage, she started the engine, spun gravel as she punched the gas and accidently turned the wrong way when she got to the hard road. She had driven this road to Findlay so many times to go to Eddy's Tavern that she turned west without thinking. She drove past the Lawson ranch house and farmhouse before realizing she needed to turn around. She did a U-turn, squealing the worn out tires on the pavement, and headed back toward Cedarwood.

When she passed the Lawson farmhouse a greyhound dog came racing out of the ditch. She hadn't noticed it chase her car on the way by the first time. Dixie was running hard to beat her car to the end of the yard. Becky saw the dog and slowed down. Dixie slowed, keeping pace beside her. When Becky drove past the end of the yard Dixie stopped. Becky stopped. She backed up and stopped again. Tall stalks of corn hid her car from the farmhouse. She got out of the car. The dog watched her. Becky opened the trunk of the car and called to the dog. Dixie ran to her and started wiggling. Becky picked up Dixie and stuffed her in the trunk of the car. She looked around to see if anyone had seen what she had done. Satisfied that no one had, she got back in the car and drove to the campground.

Ricky came out of his camper when he saw the strange car pull in. "Becky? What are you doing in this piece of shit car? Where's the convertible?"

"I hit a deer. It busted the windshield. So I got this as a temporary ride. I have something for you." She opened the trunk and grabbed Dixie before the dog knew what was happening. Dixie squirmed. "Here. I found this dog out in the country by itself. No one saw me take it."

Ricky looked confused. "So?"

"It's a bait dog, dipshit. Duh. You said you needed a small

dog to train the pups. Here," she said, pointing at Dixie. "Small dog. I think it is still a puppy. Come take it. I have to get to Canyon."

"Uh, yeah that's about the right size, thanks." Ricky took the dog.

"I may be gone a couple days. Will you feed Queenie?"

"Sure." Ricky struggled to control Dixie.

"I'm going shopping. I got people to see, things I need to arrange. Thanks. Good luck with the bait dog. Let me know how the pups do." Becky drove away and didn't look back.

After waiting four hours, Shiloh and Klu took Ben back to the spot where they had seen the buck go down. They used flashlights to light their way, whispering and walking slowly. Shiloh held Hazard back while Klu and Ben moved toward the buck's bed. Suddenly Klu turned toward Ben and shouted, "He's down! He's down for good. There he lays, right where we left him." Everyone celebrated finding the buck.

After they recovered the deer Klu said good night to Shiloh. "I will see you bright and early in the morning." He kissed her goodnight and turned to go home."

"Klu, can I ask you something?"

"Sure."

"That thing with Becky from earlier today. That was kind of uncomfortable. Why on earth would she bring anyone in my family flowers?"

"She's crazy. And to be honest she has a thing for me. One step below stalker level. She used the flowers as some pathetic excuse to come see me."

"Really? I didn't know that. I thought she was Al's old girlfriend."

"She was. She lived with us for a while after Al died."

Shiloh gave Klu a quizzical look. "She lived with you? And she sorta has a thing for you. And she's pretending to give a crap about Jete by bringing flowers to you, so you can give them to Jete." Shiloh wrinkled her nose and crossed her arms.

"What can I say? I guess I'm just irresistible." He opened his arms wide and grinned. "Look, we both know she lies. She insists that you are the one who made the anonymous phone call to turn in my dad and Henry."

"What! That's preposterous! I did no such thing."

"Of course you didn't. Nobody believes her. Well, I think Henry wonders about it. But I never once believed you did it. Like I said, Becky lies, a lot. I have no idea what she's really up to. And do not care. See you tomorrow." He kissed her and left to go home, cursing Becky under his breath.

TWENTY-FIVE

Shiloh checked her cell phone and noticed she had a voice mail. The caller said, "Hi Shiloh, this is Tucker Wynne, the outfitter from New Mexico that had a booth next to yours at the Pennsylvania sport show. I have a client that killed his bull today on opening morning of his hunt. He's looking for a place to hunt for the next few days before he goes to Canada for his next hunt. I told him I would give you a call and find out if you have an opening. His name is Gene Tottch. He has his own hunting TV show on one of the outdoor networks. He would want to trade exposure on his show for the hunt at your place. If you are interested call me back, I can tell you more about him. Hope your season is going well."

Shiloh texted Tucker and told him to give Gene Tottch her cell number. She knew who he was and she was a fan. She would be glad to comp him a hunt in exchange for the exposure on his show. Within an hour Gene called. They made arrangements for him to arrive in two days.

Gene and his cameraman rolled into camp at noon in a rented SUV loaded with gear. They were quite a pair. The cameraman was about six feet tall, thin, wiry and strong. Gene was five feet, eight inches tall, of medium build and had grown a new beard. It was white, and if allowed to grow out, it would make him look like Santa Claus. Shiloh and Jete were waiting for them on the front porch.

After greetings and introductions Shiloh showed Gene to his room. He thanked her and began unloading his gear. The cameraman carried his suitcase of clothes to the bedroom. "Miss Shiloh, is there someplace I can put all my camera gear where I can plug in rechargeable batteries and be out of the way?"

"Sure. Over here in the corner of the great room we can put up a card table and a fold out chair. There are two wall sockets right here."

"That will work fine, thanks." He returned to the SUV to get three more hard cases. One contained two video cameras, the other held a tripod. The third contained microphones, batteries and all sorts of technical items. He put his briefcase on the table and pulled out a laptop. "Miss Shiloh, may I do some laundry? As you can see I carry more gear than clothes."

"Absolutely." She guided him to the laundry room. When she finished showing him where the detergent was stored she walked back to the kitchen.

Gene and his cameraman were soon settled and joined them. She gave them a brief rundown of the rules and asked Gene what he was expecting.

"I'm looking for a good mature buck. It doesn't have to be a trophy class buck; it just needs to look good on film, a camera deer. We usually prefer to set our own stands but I do understand we are in a bit of a time crunch so will need to rely on you for the best stand choice."

"Do you want to hunt from a ground blind or an elevated box blind or a treestand?"

"Well, of course the fans prefer the treestand set up. Do you have a place where we can slip a second hang-on stand above the hunter stand without too much trouble?"

Shiloh thought about all their stand locations for a few moments. "We are expecting east winds for the next couple days. So that really limits our stand choices since we don't get those very often."

"I understand." Gene waited patiently while Shiloh looked at the big property map on the wall. Jete joined her to look over possible locations. Gene hadn't yet commented on Jete's cast but took the opportunity to speak up. "Looks like you've been in a bit of a dust up. Were you the loser or the winner in that fight?"

"I was the loser for sure. Fell trying to fix a squeaky treestand. It had been raining and I didn't wear my safety harness. It's so stupid I hate to even say the words out loud."

"Ah, an occupational hazard. I know a couple guys who fell and it didn't turn out so well. One is paralyzed, the other is dead. Looks like you are getting around pretty well."

"Oh yes, I can limp my way around. I was lucky that's for sure."

Shiloh touched Jete on the arm, "What about the ground blind on that food plot behind your house? Nobody has hunted it yet."

"That's a good spot for east wind. A big blind too, plenty of room for two guys and all your gear. We put it out a month ago. It hasn't had any corn put out in front of it but you may not need it. The field is only fifty yards across. If they come in they will be right in your lap."

Gene nodded to his cameraman who gave a thumbs up. "Sounds like that is our spot."

"You will need to take chairs in with you when you go," Jete reminded Shiloh.

"Yes, I'll grab a couple more from the barn, thanks Jete. Gene, we will be ready to go whenever you are."

"You about ready?" Gene said to his cameraman.

"I'll be good to go in five minutes," he replied.

Shiloh went to the barn to get two foldable chairs. She tossed them into the side by side and checked the gas level. Full. She smiled as she said a silent prayer thanking God for her Uncle Jete. He may not be ready to guide hunters again, but he wasn't letting any task go untended if he could manage it.

The cameraman came out first with his video camera rolling. Gene emerged from the back door, talking to the lens of the camera. "We're hunting with Lawson's Hunting Adventures in western Kentucky. Miss Shiloh Lawson will be taking us to a ground blind they have set up on a food plot. It's perfect for the east winds we are experiencing today. Let's hope the deer are coming to the food plot tonight and a big buck is among the first to show up." He walked toward Shiloh and smiled. "We're ready."

The cameraman circled them, holding his camera low, about waist high. Shiloh froze and watched him move around. Gene laughed. "Just forget he is here and don't look at the camera, just do what you would normally do."

"Okay, easier said than done," she said nervously. "Uh,

are you ready?"

"I am indeed."

Shiloh drove them to the ground blind, stopping just shy of the food plot to look at several deer already out in the small field. "They really like this food plot, it's pretty secluded. Looks like all does and two small bucks. I'm just going to ease in here and let you out at the blind. It's early. If we keep it quiet and quick they should come back out after things calm down," she whispered. Shiloh drove right up to the blind and slipped out to put the chairs inside. The hunters carried their gear into the blind and got settled. "Is everything okay?"

Gene poked his head out of a window and smiled. "All good."

"Good luck." She smiled back but turned red-faced when she noticed the camera pointed at her from three feet away. She scrambled back to the vehicle and drove away.

When she got back to the ranch house she went inside to thank Jete for filling the gas tank and to grab a late lunch. On her way into the office her cell phone buzzed. "Holy cow, Gene has a buck down already!" She shouted to Jete, "Want to come along?"

They drove separate side by sides back out to the food plot. The cameraman was running toward them. He put his hand up to stop their progress. "I need to mic you up Shiloh."

"What? I don't need to be on camera."

"Miss Shiloh, trust me. You are going to want to be on camera for this one." He was smiling so big Shiloh just sat in the driver's seat as the cameraman put the mic on her. When he seemed satisfied he put the earphones on. "Say something."

"What should I say?" Shiloh asked, feeling silly.

"Okay I hear you fine. Wait until I give you the okay before you start driving the rest of the way to the blind." He ran all the way back to the blind, turned and waved. Shiloh began driving as instructed.

Gene crawled out of the low ground blind door and walked to greet Shiloh as she pulled up. "You sure picked the right spot for us," he said shaking his head. "I wanted you to be here when we recover this deer. And Jete, if you can limp your way along with us you had better come too. The buck is down. He only went seventy-five yards."

Gene told them how the deer came back into the field less than ten minutes after she drove off. He talked to Shiloh and Jete, and the camera, as if it was a third person. "They began feeding right away. A shooter buck came out of the timber into the food plot. It stood broadside at thirty yards staring at the blind for a full two minutes. We didn't move a muscle. He finally lowered his head to feed and I drew my bow. He looked up at us again for several seconds before turning his head away to look at a second buck that entered the field. My cameraman called me off of the shot. He told me the second buck was way bigger. So I let down and looked at the new buck entering the field. I nearly fell off my chair. It was a huge buck. That second buck just walked right up to the other one and ran him off. He was standing broadside so I drew my bow and took the shot. Perfect double lung hit. He only ran seventy five yards or so and went down on camera. He is dead, right over there." Gene pointed at the buck then turned to speak directly to the camera lens, "Let's go take a look at him."

As they walked toward the buck Shiloh could see antlers sticking up out of the grass at the edge of the plot. "Oh my gosh! Is that the buck I think it is?" she asked Jete, who nodded yes.

Gene placed his bow on the buck's body, lifted the head and antlers and knelt behind them. He turned the head toward the camera and started talking. "Folks, look at this. This is a giant non-typical. Let me count the points for you." Gene touched each tine and sticker with his finger and counted them. "Twenty-four points ladies and gentlemen! A big twelve pointer with double brow tines and a bunch of stickers all over. This deer is massive. Miss Shiloh, come over here and get down here next to this buck with me."

Shiloh bent down on her knees and touched the deer's rack. She put her hands around the bases and main beams, marveling at their thickness.

"Miss Shiloh have you ever seen this deer before?"

"Yes we have. We have him on trail camera this summer and early in the season. One of our hunters had a chance at him but couldn't pull it off. Then he disappeared. We didn't know if he was still around. This buck is amazing! Congratulations!"

Gene called for Jete to join them. "Folks, this is Jete Lawson, Shiloh's uncle. Tell me what you're thinking Jete."

Jete shook his head in awe of the buck. "If the Lord made a more magnificent animal he sure must have kept it for himself. I've never seen anything else like it."

"Amen to that." Gene gently put the head and antlers back down in the grass and stood up. Shiloh stood up too and forgot all about the cameraman who was catching every second on film. They started cheering and jumping and high fiving. Gene nearly knocked Jete over in the celebration. After calling the deer in to the telecheck service they took several pictures in the field and loaded it into the bed of Jete's side by side.

"We have a few cutaways to finish up back over at the blind. It won't take long. Do you want to wait?" Gene asked Shiloh.

"Sure. We will try to get a quick measurement on this buck while you do it." On cue, Jete grabbed a tape measure from the glove box. When they finished measuring the antlers they estimated the buck to score a gross two-hundred and eleven inches. The cameraman filmed them repeating some of the measuring and talking about the antlers and the score. Then they loaded up all the gear and headed for the ranch house.

Shiloh called Klu on the drive in. "Can you tear yourself away from your studies or whatever you are doing? You are going to want to see the buck we are bringing in. He might look familiar to you."

"Somebody shot the big non-typical!"

"Yes! How did you know?"

"I could tell by your voice."

"We are bringing him in now. Gene has it all on camera. Can you believe it?"

"I will be right there."

Klu arrived soon after to admire the buck and join in the evening's celebration. Shiloh called Tucker Wynne to tell him what happened. Within minutes of posting photos of the buck on social media, neighbors from across Helix County arrived to admire the buck and share in the camaraderie.

Becky checked Shiloh's social media page, as she often did. She saw several photos of a guy with a big buck. In the background of one of the pictures she could see Klu with his arm around Shiloh. Becky threw her phone across the room.

John asked, "What was that all about? Come here baby. What's wrong?"

Becky picked up the phone and tossed it in her purse. "John, I want you to do something for me."

"Sure baby. Take off those clothes and I will do anything you ask."

"I have a back pack of money set aside for you if you do it right."

"I'll do my best. What else do I get?"

"What else do you want?"

Tiny little pearl buttons scattered around the room when he tore open Becky's new black sweater.

TWENTY-SIX

As the season progressed Shiloh became accustomed to the quirks and diversity of the hunters who came to Lawson's Hunting Adventures. When the first group of rifle hunters arrived in November, Shiloh was not surprised by the two hunters who didn't really seem to know much about deer hunting.

One hunter from Chicago, named Calvin, arrived with a new rifle, still in the box. Klu had to help him put the scope on and bore sight it to get it shooting well enough to sight it in more accurately. The hunter watched You Tube videos on his phone about sighting in a rifle while Klu worked on his gun. They went to the rifle range in the field west of the ranch house and shot at paper targets until Klu was satisfied the guy could hit the target.

The hunter from New York, named Chris, talked a lot about hunting. It sounded like he came by everything he knew from reading magazines. He had no hunting stories of his own. Shiloh's suspicions were confirmed when he walked into the kitchen of the ranch house on the first morning in a brand new outfit, with crease marks that looked like it had just been taken out of the package.

Jete whispered to Shiloh, "Looks like you got yourself a real cheechawker. I think the tags may still be on his clothes. Good luck with this one."

Shiloh rolled her eyes and sighed, "Thankfully the other four hunters are experienced guys and seem to be good hunters. I talked to them several times on the phone before they finally booked. Klu seems to have the guy from Chicago all lined out. It's weird that he and this guy from New York just called last week to book their hunts. You know, New York paid his balance with a shoebox full of small bills, hundreds or less, all cash. Said he had been saving for a long time for this hunt. It's weird, because his clothes all look brand new, straight out of the package, but his rifle is old and worn, with several scratches on the stock and forearm."

"Something doesn't add up with this guy. Just be careful," Jete warned. "Oh, and your mom was asking about Dixie. None of us have seen her for a while. She's worried a coyote got her. She said that black coyote with the yellow eyes cruised through the back yard the other day. Ruby took off running and made it into the barn just in time. I'm gonna need to set some traps after the season is over."

"I haven't seen Dixie. I hope that coyote didn't get her. We have been seeing a lot more coyote sign though, so a few traps sounds like a good idea. I'll talk to you later. I need to get these guys going." Shiloh refilled her coffee cup. "Come on guys we need to get going. The sun will be up soon."

Shiloh waited in the truck for her hunters. She planned to drive them to the east pasture and place them on opposite ends of the field. One would be overlooking the field while the other would be overlooking a draw watching a travel corridor. She took the Chicago hunter to an elevated box blind. He climbed inside. She brought his gun and other gear up the wooden ladder and placed them inside the blind. "You all set?" she whispered.

"I'm good, thanks," he replied hesitantly.

Shiloh continued across the pasture, drove over the hill and pulled as close to the draw as she thought possible without getting her truck stuck. She pointed toward a patch of timber and spoke softly, "Just follow the bright eyes along the trail they will lead you right to the stand."

"No problem," Chris from New York replied, getting out of the truck. She watched him pull his rifle from the case, shoulder his pack and walk into the woods. He didn't use a flashlight. When he had taken a few steps into the timber he stopped, turned around and came back to open the passenger door. "I forgot my flashlight. I thought maybe you would be walking me to the stand."

"Here, I have an extra one in the glove box." She shined the light into the timber. "There, see the glowing tacks? They will lead you right to the tree about forty yards in. You will break out into an opening and be able to see up and down the draw. The deer go through here all the time. I'll be back to get you at eleven unless you text me earlier."

"Okay," said Chris, from New York, as he took the flashlight, turned and walked slowly in the direction she pointed.

Shiloh drove back to the ranch house to finish some chores before picking up both hunters at eleven. Shiloh, Klu,

Carter and Jete worked in the barn assembling a new supply of treestands Shiloh got with her new outfitter's discount from a treestand maker. All the publicity from the non-typical and the success of the season so far, were earning her points across the hunting industry. When eleven o'clock rolled around, everyone went to pick up their hunters.

Shiloh stopped at the box blind to get Calvin from Chicago, before driving across the field to get Chris from New York. She didn't know why she kept thinking of them in terms of where they were from instead of just their names alone. She just thought it was odd to have two greenhorns, from the biggest cities in the country, in her hunting camp at the same time.

When they got back to the ranch house Shiloh parked her truck in the drive and followed Chris inside for lunch. Calvin stayed at the truck to arrange some of his gear. While everyone was busy with lunch Shiloh decided to take her truck to Cedarwood to fill up with gas and grab some supplies from the grocery store. Klu offered to ride with her and she said yes. They walked to her truck and noticed the left front tire was low.

"That's weird. I just drove in here a few minutes ago and if that tire was low it surely would have flashed a notice in the dashboard."

"I can run it in town to Henry's place and have it plugged for you."

"Thanks, but I need to get supplies for Mom and a few groceries too."

"I don't mind."

"I appreciate it, but I know you are not buying maxi-pads." She laughed when she saw the look of horror on his face.

"Nope, nada, not buying those. I will take your hunters back out for you if you don't get back in time. You go right ahead and run your girl errands." Klu held his hands up in the air as if surrendering as he walked back to the house.

Shiloh whistled for Hazard to get in the truck. As she drove away and turned on the hard road toward Cedarwood, Calvin from Chicago made a phone call. "She just left for Cedarwood. She's alone." When it was time to go back out to hunt he told Klu that he wasn't feeling well. When they were all gone from the house he packed up all his clothing and gear and left.

Shiloh drove slowly to Cedarwood. The indicator light on her dashboard warned of a low tire. When she pulled into Henry's shop the tire was on the verge of being flat.

"You just about did not make it in here," Henry said.

"I was pretty worried. Can you fix it, maybe plug it or something?"

"Let me drive it in the garage and put it on the lift." It didn't take Henry long to find the nail in her tire. "Here's your problem. I'll just put a plug in it and you'll be good as new."

"Before you do, can I talk to you for a moment? In private."

"Sure, what's up?" Henry followed her outside.

"This is awkward but I'm just going to say it. Klu told me you had some suspicion that I might be the person who made the anonymous phone call to turn you and your dad in. Henry I want to tell you straight to your face, it was not me. I did not do that. I hope you believe me."

Henry shifted his weight. He looked at Shiloh for a few moments before speaking. "I did wonder. And I appreciate you telling me this face to face. I guess we will never know who really did it."

"Well, I hope you believe me." She paused, uncertain whether to go on or just drop the subject. "Klu said Becky told you. Is that right?"

"Yes."

"You know Becky hates my brother and me. She didn't tell the truth about what happened the night Al died. I'm so sorry that happened. If I could do anything to change what happened I would."

"Yeah, Becky hates you more than your brother now." Henry chuckled a bit.

"What do you mean?"

"After Al died, Becky stayed on at the house. She got real infatuated with Klu. She really has a thing for him. Borderline obsessed with him. Now that Klu is with you, Becky is not happy about it."

"Well, that could explain why she would lie to you about me making that call, don't you think?"

"It could. She does lie a lot too. No doubt about that. Has a real problem with telling the truth. Okay, I'll stop wondering if the caller was you." Henry stuck his hand out.

Shiloh shook his hand and gave him a hug. "Thanks, I'm glad to hear you say that."

"I'll get that tire fixed and you can be on your way." Henry held the door open for her as they went inside.

Across the street a man watched from a blue passenger van. He checked his watch and looked around. The street was busy. Several cars drove down the main street. No one paid attention to him or his van.

When Shiloh emerged from the shop in her truck with the newly plugged tire, the man in the van started the engine. He followed her to the grocery store. When she parked and went inside the man eased the van into the parking spot next to the driver's side of her truck. Shiloh had a habit of parking far from the door in spots where she had the least chance of a door ding.

The man smiled as he shut off the engine. He opened the sliding door on his passenger side, leaving it propped open an inch. Then he hid in the back of the van.

Hazard jumped into the driver seat, which he knew he was not supposed to do. He growled at the van.

A few minutes later Shiloh walked back to her truck with her arms full of groceries. She opened the back driver side door and piled the bags onto the seat. Then she closed that door and opened her driver side door and scolded Hazard for being in her seat. "Get over on your side, you know better than that."

Hazard nearly lunged over her shoulder but she caught him and shoved him back. Then he started barking. Shiloh shouted over his barks. "What is the matter with you? Get back over in your seat."

The door to the van swept open and the man jumped out, grabbing Shiloh from behind. He put his right arm around her neck and used his left hand to slam her truck door shut, hitting Hazard in the nose and knocking him backward, trapping him inside. In fluid motion enhanced by adrenaline he stepped backward into the truck dragging Shiloh in after him. She managed to shriek the first notes of a scream before he increased the pressure on her neck, choking her voice into a gurgled snarl. Shiloh felt herself being dragged into the back of the van.

She put her right hand on the pistol hidden under her shirt, secured by the holster under the waistband of her pants. She pulled the gun from its soft holster in disciplined motion, honed by hours of practice, twisted left and moved the gun in position to kill. She estimated center mass and fired twice, striking him in the stomach.

The man let go of her and grabbed his stomach, stumbling forward, smashing his weight against her. He groaned and fell to his knees. She struggled to maintain her footing as his bulk fell against her, nearly knocking her down. She scrambled out of the van. Then she started screaming for help.

Hazard barked wildly inside her truck. Shiloh ran into the lane behind her truck just as people in the parking lot started running toward her.

A teacher from high school recognized Shiloh and put his arm around her. "Honey, are you alright? Good God what just happened?" She didn't answer, just pointed at the van. "Somebody call the police!" the teacher shouted. A crowd gathered around Shiloh. Some looked in the van. None of them knew what to do for a man with a gunshot wound to the stomach.

Hazard continued barking at the chaos.

Two police cars arrived with sirens blaring. One of the officers took Shiloh from the arms of the teacher and led her to the back seat of his patrol car. The teacher called Dorothy.

An ambulance arrived as Shiloh sat in the back of the

police car talking to the officers. She retold the story. The ambulance took the man to the hospital in Canyon. He was unconscious, unable to answer any questions.

She was surprised to see Klu, Jete and her Mom drive up in Klu's truck. She dragged herself out of the police car and ran to them. Dorothy wrapped her arms around Shiloh. Klu and Jet took turns giving her a hug then went to get information from the police officer.

The police officer told them the van was stolen. A driver's license in his wallet identified the man. They learned he was a bouncer at Eddy's Tavern in Findlay. They asked if she knew him. They asked many more questions before letting her go. She refused medical attention. "It's just a few scratches and bruises. I'm fine. I just want to go home. It will be time to pick up our hunters from the stands," she said hollowly.

"I think you are in shock. Let me drive," Klu said as he held her.

Jete added, "Don't worry about the hunters, Carter and I can take care of them. You just go home and rest."

"But your foot and your arm?" Shiloh muttered.

Klu gently guided her to the truck. "Don't think about that Shiloh, get in the truck. Jete is doing just fine. Hazard is about to come unglued."

Shiloh got into her truck on the passenger side and Klu drove her to the farmhouse. Klu and Carter went to take care of the deer their hunters had shot while all the action took place in Cedarwood. Everyone was exhausted by nightfall. Shiloh took the medication Jete gave her and slept throughout the night.

TWENTY-SEVEN

Shiloh woke the next morning at nine o'clock. "Oh dang it, I overslept," she complained to her mom when she came downstairs.

"Klu took your hunter out this morning. He says that guy from New York is afraid of the dark," Dorothy said with a snicker.

"I think he might be right. He didn't want to walk into the woods in the dark yesterday either. I'm starved."

Dorothy gave Shiloh a surprised look. "I'll fix you some breakfast. How are you feeling?"

"Actually I feel surprisingly good for a girl who just about got abducted and then shot someone in the gut. That was the craziest thing I have ever experienced. You know what's even crazier? I didn't really get a good look at the guy, but last night I kept thinking, if I have to describe him I could say that his breath was bad enough to knock a buzzard off an outhouse."

"Oh my gosh, Shiloh! The medicine Jete gave you to make you sleep must have made you slaphappy."

"No doubt about it. Knocked me out, that's for sure. Did they tell me the guy was a bouncer at Eddy's Tavern?"

"Yes. Apparently he's going to live, but he's not talking. I hate to think what could have happened." Dorothy tried not to cry.

"I'm alright Mom. Don't cry. This morning when I opened my bible and Isaiah forty-one, verse ten jumped right at me. *Fear thou not; for I am with thee: be not dismayed; for I am thy God: I will strengthen thee; yea, I will help thee; yea I will uphold thee with the right hand of my righteousness.* And my daily devotional text said the same thing. So I'm pretty much at peace."

"Well praise God for that. And thank God for concealed carry. I'm just glad you had it on your person instead of in your purse."

"Uncle Jete was right about carrying a round in the chamber. I was always a little leery of doing that. But he finally convinced me when he explained that thinking you would have time to jack in a round before you needed it would be about the same as thinking you would have time to buckle your seat belt before you crashed."

"That makes sense."

"I'm going to tell Klu that if he hadn't refused to pick up your maxi-pads this never would have happened."

"Oh my, that's mean. He is worried enough as it is. You better text him and let him know you're up. He's called every fifteen minutes to check on you."

"Okay, I'll get cleaned up after I eat and go over to the ranch house."

When Shiloh arrived at the ranch house everyone gave her

hugs and fussed over her. "I'm alright really. Thanks all of you, but I'm fine. The best therapy for me is to get back to work. A little fresh air and deer camp is all I need. Except some of these chocolate chip cookies. Did your Mom bring these Klu?"

Klu laughed, relieved that Shiloh seemed in good spirits. "She did. How did you guess?"

"Her cookies are getting famous. She should sell them. I'm sure she would make a killing."

Jete yelled from across the room, "Speaking of that, it's unfortunate that you didn't kill that prick yesterday. But he is going to be in the hospital for a long time, then in prison much longer. Unless Klu and I can figure out a way to get to him first."

"That's a true statement," Klu agreed.

"Okay tough guys. How about we go pick up our hunters. I bet they were surprised to find out how crazy it can get out here in small town Kentucky."

Klu held up a hand. "Wait. Everybody chose to stay on stand all day. Except New York Chris. He wants to come in for lunch. I'll go get him."

"Okay thanks." Shiloh sat down. She suddenly felt tired. "Hey, where's Calvin from Chicago?"

"We have no idea," Jete said. "He just took off without a word. His stuff is all gone. No one knows why."

"That is weird. Maybe I'll give him a call this afternoon, see if I can find something out."

The rest of the day was uneventful. Deer movement was slow. They talked about doing some deer drives in the morning but only Chris wanted them to do it.

The next day Shiloh took Chris to the stand in the draw well before daylight. He seemed fond of the location now. They agreed he would keep an eye to the west end of the draw at ten o'clock and she would do a small push before she came to pick him up just to see if she could move some deer past his stand.

Both of Klu's hunters opted to stay on stand all day. "I'm free this morning, would you like me to help you with the deer drive?" Klu asked Shiloh.

"Yes, that would be great, thanks. We can leave in a few minutes. I thought we could just walk through the west end of the draw real slow toward his stand and hopefully push a buck out of there toward him. It's pretty thick in there. It would be a perfect place for a buck to bed down and stay out of sight all day. Hopefully he can shoot that old rifle."

"Hmm, city slickers with long range weapons make me nervous. I'm serious. We should wear extra orange clothing when we go in to do this drive."

"We have on a hat and a vest. What more do you want?"

"I don't know. I just have a bad feeling about this guy."

"We'll be careful. I'll text him before we get within rifle range and let him know not to shoot to the west. We better get going. If we drive down the dead end gravel road we can slip around the pasture, enter the draw and do a short push to see if anything comes out of that thicket. It won't take long." Shiloh drove her truck slowly down the gravel road and parked in the same spot near the fence where she had run into Klu earlier in the year while turkey hunting. "Things sure have changed a lot in just a few months."

"They sure have." Klu smiled and leaned over to kiss her.

"I remember a time when you would barely talk to me. And now." He kissed her again.

Shiloh didn't want the moment to end. She sighed, "Let's go, it's ten o'clock."

They slipped quietly through the woods to the west end of the pasture and down into the draw. Shiloh texted Chris, *"We're in place to begin the drive. Keep your eyes open to the west."*

New York Chris looked through the scope of his gun. He had trouble keeping the crosshairs steady past one hundred yards. He decreased the power on the scope from ten to three and watched through the scope for any movement. Five minutes went by. In another minute he saw a flash of brown. A doe came running past his stand. Chris cranked the scope back up to ten and resumed searching for movement. Another doe ran past him. Suddenly a big wide eight pointer burst from the thicket and ran past Chris. He barely noticed it.

Shiloh whispered to Klu, "Did you see that buck? He's a good one. Why isn't he shooting?"

"I don't know, maybe he didn't see it."

"No way, it had to run right past his stand. It never came out either side of the draw so it had to go right by him. Let's wait a couple more minutes."

When they didn't hear a shot, Shiloh texted Chris, *"Did you see that buck?"* She waited a few seconds for an answer.

Chris ignored the text.

Shiloh texted him again, *"We are coming in range. Do not shoot to the west."*

Chris ignored that text.

Klu looked at Shiloh and shrugged. "What do you think?

We are about three hundred and fifty yards away from him."

"Let's walk another fifty yards and climb up out of the draw. I'll let him know it's over. He will see us and know it is quitting time. Then we can walk back to the truck and drive over and pick him up."

Chris looked through the scope and found Shiloh in the brush. He tried to hold the crosshairs steady on Shiloh's head. His heartbeat and the breeze swaying the tree prevented him from keeping it steady. He lowered the crosshairs to her chest.

An experienced marksman would have a solid rest for his gun. He would make sure the line of sight was clear to his target. He would exhale slowly or hold his breath and gently squeeze the trigger, watching through the scope for the impact in spite of the recoil. Chris was not an experienced rifle shooter. He punched the trigger. The bullet ricocheted off a branch and struck Klu in the chest just below his left collarbone.

Klu was knocked to the ground by the impact. Shiloh screamed. She ducked to the ground out of fear of another shot and concern for Klu. "Oh my God, Klu, he shot you! Oh my God. Look at me. Oh shit." Shiloh grabbed her cell phone and dialed Jete's phone number.

"Hey Shiloh, do you have a buck down?" Jete asked.

"Jete, listen! Klu's been shot! Chris shot him! Call nine-one-one!"

"What the!"

"Get the ambulance to come down the dead end road. We are in the draw on the west side of the pasture. Can you come help us? You will get here long before they do. There's a first aid kit in my truck. It's parked by the gate. Tell Carter to go get Chris out of the stand. I don't know if he knows what he has done."

"I'm on my way!"

Shiloh cradled Klu in her arms and prayed for his life.

Chris replayed the action in his mind. He saw an orange body fall to the ground. He thought it was Shiloh but he wasn't' sure. He rehearsed his story. He saw a buck and shot at it running through the thicket. He hadn't seen any orange. It was a hunting accident. He and Becky had rehearsed the story many times. If it worked out just as she promised a lot of money waited for him back at the hotel.

TWENTY-EIGHT

Becky screamed and slammed her fist on the table. She held the phone back up to her face and screamed into it. "You fucking idiot! How could you screw this up? How could you miss? How could you shoot Klu? I got you the fake identification. I got you the fake hunting license and permits. I got you hunting clothes. I got you a rifle. I got you ammunition. All you had to do was pull the fucking trigger! Fuck!"

John, who had fake identification as Chris Smith from New York, started making excuses. "Becky, it's not that easy."

"Shut up! I need to think. Just go to the hotel and wait for me!" Becky hung up the phone and stared at her dog for several minutes. Her next words were uttered with a coating of black ice, "If you want something done right, you have to do it yourself."

Queenie crawled under the table sensing Becky's foul mood.

Shiloh sat by Klu's bedside holding his hand as he woke up from surgery. Charlene leaned close to his face and softly said, "Hi sweetheart. You just came out of surgery. The doctor said everything looks good. You will be sore for a while and need a fair amount of rehab but you are going to be okay." She stroked his hair.

Shiloh added, "You sure had a close call. Chris is beside himself. The cops say it sounds like a legit hunting accident. He packed up his stuff and left."

Klu tried to talk but his throat was sore from the tubes that had been down his throat during surgery.

"Don't talk now honey," Charlene said. "You rest. We are going to the cafeteria to get some supper and we will be back up to say good night."

Charlene, Henry, Jete, Dorothy, Carter and Rose left to get some supper. Shiloh stayed with Klu. She couldn't leave his side. She just sat holding his hand and thanking God that his life had been spared. The room was quiet. She listened to the sounds of machines and people in the hallway and the nurse's station. Klu whispered something she couldn't understand.

"Don't talk, just rest." She followed the direction of his eyes. He was looking at the doorway. Shiloh's mouth dropped open.

Becky was standing in the doorway.

Shiloh stood up and asked, "What are you doing here?"

"I came to see Klu. I heard he was almost killed. My God Klu honey, I'm so relieved that you are alright." Becky walked to the side of Klu's bed and stroked his arm. She ran her hands over the tattoo of the buck.

"You need to leave. You have no business here Becky."

Klu tried to speak, "Becky."

"Yes Klu." She leaned close to his face and kissed his cheek.

"Get out," Klu whispered.

"Oh honey I missed you too," Becky said, smiling slyly at Shiloh. "There you see. It's you that has no business here. Klu and I have been together for a long time."

"Becky you are delusional," Shiloh replied.

"Oh really? Here take a look." She held up her cell phone so Shiloh could see the photo of Klu, shirtless, with his tattoo plainly visible. Becky had cropped the photo, cutting it off at the waist to make it appear Klu could possibly be fully undressed. "I have more revealing photos if you want to see them. But this one pretty much shows you that he had no problem being naked with me."

Klu looked at Shiloh and whispered, "She's lying."

Henry and Charlene walked into the room. Charlene put her arm through Shiloh's. Henry stood behind them. Charlene spoke directly to Becky with a stern voice, "Becky, you need to get out. You are not welcome here." Henry and Klu were surprised by their mom's strict order. She had never spoken up for them before.

Becky looked at Klu and said, "Klu honey, when you get out of this hospital bed I will be glad to take care of you in my bed. Just like it used to be." She gave Shiloh the finger as she walked out of the room.

Charlene sensed that Henry was about to explode. She put her hand on his arm. "Don't pay any attention to her." She turned to Shiloh and said, "She's under the mistaken impression that Klu cares about her. Trust me, he does not.

There is nothing between them, never has been and never will be. I should have kicked her out of the house years ago. If I had maybe Al would be alive. She's either been the victim of some very bad circumstances or has made a million bad decisions in her life, probably both. She has become filled with evil. Just stay away from her."

Klu whispered, "Thanks Mom."

"Geez Mom, I never heard you talk like that before. She sure had you riled up," Henry said. "Go Mom."

"Boys, I need to talk to you and this is as good a time as any. Sit down you two." She pointed at Shiloh and Henry. "Shiloh you need to hear this too. You boys know that your father and I have had our troubles. In the beginning when he would get drunk and mean I would call the police, but he begged for forgiveness and I always took him back. I couldn't leave him, I had three sons. I'm sorry to say this about your own dad, but he is a terrible man. He is the one who poisoned Syder's dog. He told me. Thought it was funny. Thank God you two boys didn't inherit your father's temper. Your brother Al was most like him. Al was involved in a lot of your father's illegal business. After Al got killed, Hank started dragging Henry into his terrible world of drugs, gambling, prostitution and Lord knows what else." Charlene paused and took a deep breath. "So, I made the anonymous call that got him arrested and sent to prison."

Henry stood up and declared, "Mom!"

"I'm sorry son. Sit down, please. I had hoped you would only get a fine or some time at the local jail. I never knew how involved you were until the trial and then it was too late. I'm sorry you got sent to prison, but I had to stop him. I had to stop you from following in his footsteps. So there it is. Now you know. I hope you can forgive me. I was not strong enough to stop him on my own. I didn't know what else to do."

Henry sat with his head in his hands for a few moments. Then he stood up and hugged his mom. "I understand. There is nothing to forgive. You did what you thought was right. I love you."

Charlene hugged Henry then brushed back tears before kissing Klu on the forehead. "I'm going home now. Shiloh, Henry, let's go. The doctor says he needs to rest. We all need to rest. It's been a terrible week. You can come back first thing in the morning." Charlene hugged Shiloh. "Say good night. I will wait for you in the hall." She kissed Klu on the cheek and smiled at Shiloh as she left. Henry followed her out the door.

Shiloh kissed Klu. "I'll be back in the morning after we take the hunters out. I have to take Hazard to the vet at eleven so I will stop in to see you before that. You get some sleep." He nodded his head and closed his eyes. She walked out of the room and embraced Charlene. "Thanks for getting rid of Becky. She has been a thorn in my side, for years."

Charlene smiled and nodded. "Jete gave me your keys, he rode home with Dorothy. Are you sure you're alright to drive home? You could ride with me and I will bring you back in the morning."

"I'm fine. Thanks. Besides I have a message on my cellphone from earlier that the vet had a cancellation and I can bring Hazard back with me tomorrow to get his shots. I'll just call them in the morning before I leave for the hospital and let them know I am bringing him in at eleven. I can see Klu before going to the vet and then come back afterward."

"Okay, that sounds good."

Later that night Shiloh went to bed and stared at the ceiling. She talked to God, prayed for Klu's safe recovery and thanked Him for sparing his life. When she fell asleep it was well past midnight.

Becky spent a sleepless night in the motor home. She drank whiskey and cried over Klu getting shot and almost killed. Guilt consumed her, but evil influences soon twisted her heart into an even deeper rage toward Shiloh. She paced the floor, scheming. Like a mad scientist, Becky obsessed over her plan, thinking it through, envisioning the outcome. She put on a pair of blue jeans, boots, T-shirt and heavy sweater; got in the cargo van and drove to the hospital at dawn, to wait.

The sun was shining through scattered clouds when Becky watched Shiloh walk into the hospital. She moved the cargo van to within three spaces of Shiloh's truck, shut off the engine and got out. She wanted to be close enough to make her move but not close enough to bring attention to the big vehicle. She tucked a dog leash under her arm, pried open the pop-top on a can of moist dog food and tossed the lid on the ground.

She walked to Shiloh's truck, opened the door, spoke to Hazard in her sweetest baby-talk and used her fingers to scoop out a glob of soft dog food which she placed on the seat. Hazard smelled the food and took a few bites. Becky attached a leash to his collar. She gave him another glob of dog food.

Hazard gulped it down. Becky pulled on the leash and called for Hazard to get out of the truck. He gladly obliged, happy to get out of the truck and follow the aroma of canned beef and chicken. She walked him to the cargo van and coaxed him inside with more dog food. When he was done eating she placed a muzzle on him and tied him in the back of the van. She wiped her fingers on her jeans and got back in the driver's seat.

While she watched the hospital door, patiently waiting for Shiloh to emerge, she cut lengths of rope with her pocketknife.

Klu improved greatly overnight. By morning he could talk and sit up in bed, and his voice was much stronger. "Good morning sunshine," he said when Shiloh entered the room. "Mom and Henry just left."

"Wow, you look so much better! How are you feeling?"

"I feel a lot better than yesterday, that's for sure. Hopefully the doctor will let me go home in a couple days."

"I'm glad to hear your voice. You could only whisper last night. Can you believe that Becky? What's with the naked photo of you on her phone?"

"Are you jealous?"

Shiloh blushed and shook her index finger at Klu, scolding him. "No, of course not. I was just concerned about your sanity. I wanted to make sure you two weren't an item back in the day." She sat on the edge of his bed and took his hand. "And your Mom. Wow that was quite the confession. How do you feel about all that?"

"I feel good. I'm glad to know it wasn't you who turned my dad in. I was really beginning to wonder."

"Klu Dugan if you weren't a patient in the hospital I would box your ears."

A nurse interrupted their playful banter with a routine check of vitals. When she left Shiloh continued, "I can't stay long, I have to run Hazard to the vet but I will stop in again before I go home." She spent a few more minutes with him then left to take Hazard to the vet, promising to return soon after the appointment.

Shiloh walked to her truck. At first, she didn't notice that Hazard was not sitting in the passenger seat, because she was thinking about Klu and how well he was doing. She opened the driver side door, hopped into the driver seat and was momentarily preoccupied looking in the back seat for Hazard as she reached to pull the door closed behind her.

Becky was hiding behind the cargo van when Shiloh opened the door. As Shiloh got into the truck Becky started running right at her. She reached the side of the truck while Shiloh's arm was still extended to pull the door closed. Becky jammed the stun gun into Shiloh's neck.

The voltage rendered Shiloh helpless to fight Becky off or pull the door shut. She felt Becky pull her from the truck seat. A second later she hit her head on the pavement.

Becky attacked her with the stun gun again.

Shiloh couldn't control her own body or think straight.

Becky jerked Shiloh's shirt up and took the concealed carry gun out of her waistband. She shoved it into the back of her pants. Before Shiloh could regain control of her body Becky pulled her arms behind her and slapped handcuffs on her wrists. Then she dragged Shiloh through the parking lot to the back of the cargo van. Becky was in such a rage she didn't look around to see if anyone noticed. She shocked Shiloh again then opened the back doors. Becky struggled to get Shiloh into the van but finally dragged her in. She closed the doors and kicked Shiloh in the stomach.

Shiloh nearly threw up. She felt Becky roll her on her stomach and tie her feet with rope. Then her wrists and ankles were hog tied and a hood was pulled over her head. She was vaguely aware of Hazard lunging to the end of the leash.

Becky got in the driver's seat and started the van. Before she pulled out of her parking spot she ran back over to Shiloh's truck and shut the driver's side door. Becky smiled to herself because no one had noticed the struggle, but they might see the truck door standing open and get suspicious.

The black SUV was back at the campground, packed with all the backpacks of money and three suitcases stuffed full of clothes. When she was done with Shiloh, she would disappear for a while. She planned to come back for Klu once he got over Shiloh's death.

Becky drove to the campground relieved to discover Ricky was not at his camper. The goons were gone too. She pulled the cargo van up to her motorhome and got out. Queenie crawled out from under the motor home, pleased to see Becky.

"Hello girl. Where are all the dickheads? Are they back

there at the dog fighting ring? Well guess what, I have a surprise for them. You need to stay here. I don't want you to get caught up in a dog fight. When we get done, you, me and John the idiot will go to California. We'll just keep him around until it is time to come back for Klu. How does that sound?" Becky chained Queenie to her dog house. "I know this sucks. I almost never tie you up, but this is for your own safety."

Becky opened the back doors of the cargo van, untied Hazard's leash, led him to a picnic table and retied him. Then she went back for Shiloh. She pulled the pocket knife out of her pocket and cut the ropes that tied her, but left the handcuffs on her wrists. She pulled the hood off and told Shiloh to get out of the van. When she didn't move Becky put Shiloh's gun up to her face and hissed out a command, "If you don't get out of the van I'm going to shoot you with your own gun."

Shiloh struggled to get up. "Where's Hazard?"

"Your dog is outside. If you don't do as I say I'm going to shoot him too." Becky shoved Shiloh out the door. Unable to catch herself with her hands behind her back, she landed face down in the grass and gravel near the picnic table. Hazard strained against the leash.

"Get up." Becky kicked Shiloh's leg.

Shiloh struggled to her feet and looked around. "Where are we?"

"Walk over and get your dog. Then walk toward that bush." Becky kept the gun on Shiloh and pointed at the bush with her free hand.

Shiloh sat on the picnic table seat and turned backwards.

She fumbled with the piece of rope that kept Hazard's leash secured to the picnic table leg. "You need to take these off I can't do this with my hands behind my back."

Becky took the handcuff keys out of her pocket and walked toward Shiloh. "Stand up and turn around. If you make one wrong move I will shoot you right here." She used the key to unlock the cuffs and stood back. "Now take them off and put them back on with your hands in front. Do it!" Becky waggled the gun and pointed it at Shiloh's chest.

Shiloh hesitated. She thought about rushing Becky or dodging and trying to run.

Becky seemed to read her mind. She raised the gun and pointed it at Shiloh's face. "Go ahead and try."

Shiloh hesitated. Becky centered the gun on Shiloh's chest. Abandoning the thought of ducking and rushing her captor, Shiloh moved the cuffs and hooked them back on her wrists with her hands in front. Becky waved the gun at Hazard. "Now get your dog and walk toward that bush." She pointed at the multi-flora rose bush. "You see that trail on the other side of the bush? Follow it."

Shiloh started walking down the trail with Hazard beside her on the leash. Becky kept the gun pointed at Shiloh's back as they walked, shoving her with it every few feet to remind her of the threat of the gun.

"Becky, what's going on here? Where are you taking us? Why are you doing this?"

"You want to know how I ended up having to do this? Because I sent John to kill you. Yeah that's right. My boyfriend John, who you know as Chris from New York, was supposed to make it look like a hunting accident. He was supposed to kill you. But he shot Klu by accident, the dumb son-of-a-bitch. So I figured if you want something done right, ya gotta do it yourself. And it works out better this way anyway because I get to see you suffer before I kill you. When you are gone and a little time has passed, Klu will come to his senses and see how much I love him."

Shiloh stopped walking and turned to face Becky. "Are you insane? Klu doesn't want anything to do with you. And you won't get away with this Becky. Someone will hear the shot."

"You're wrong. Klu is just confused. Why would he choose your skinny ass over me? We've been living together a long time. You're the one who fucked things up. Now get moving."

Shiloh didn't move. Becky took the knife out of her pocket and fumbled to open it while still holding the gun in her right hand. Shiloh nearly made a move but Becky took a step to the left. She pointed the gun at Shiloh as she walked up to Hazard and stabbed him in the hip then jumped back and pushed the gun toward Shiloh. Hazard yelped and tried to get away from Becky.

"Move or I will cut your dog again."

"Okay, my God, don't hurt my dog!" She pulled Hazard close and bent down to put her arms around him. Hazard was trembling and confused.

Becky kicked Shiloh, knocking her down. "Stop stalling. Get up and walk."

Shiloh slowly stood up, calculating whether she could grab the gun and overpower Becky. Her boldness was making Becky angrier.

"Move, bitch!" Becky screamed and jabbed the gun toward Shiloh.

Shiloh looked at the barrel of the gun then did as she was told.

When they came to the clearing Shiloh abruptly stopped. She could see three men in the opening working on one of three, white canvas, outfitter-type tents. They were almost done putting up a third tent. Shiloh began to panic. Any hope that she might get a chance to outsmart or overpower Becky faded like mist dispersed by a gust of wind. With three men in the equation she felt doomed. As she walked toward the tents her feet became heavy; her movements were labored, like moving through quicksand. She struggled to breath.

Ricky and the goons stopped working when they noticed Shiloh and Becky walking toward them across the small grassy field. When they got to the fireplace ring Becky told Shiloh to stop. She kept the gun on Shiloh. The men noticed the gun and didn't move. They appeared confused.

Becky realized the men seemed afraid of her since she had a gun in her hand. She smiled and pointed it at them for a few seconds before putting it back on Shiloh. "Come and get this dog from her."

Ricky slowly took his eyes off the gun, walked up to Shiloh and suddenly recognized her. His mouth dropped open before he reached for Hazard's leash. He lifted the picnic table and sat the leg down on the leash handle, then turned to face Becky. "What's this all about?"

"I want you to use her dog, as a bait dog, in a fight. I want you to let Queenie's pups tear her dog to shreds right before her eyes. I put a muzzle on it, so it shouldn't be too much trouble for the pups to kill it. After she watches something she loves get ripped away from her, I'm going to kill her with her own gun. I want her gone and out of the way. Becky looked at Shiloh and seethed, "Maybe I'll throw your body into the dumpster where I threw your stupid rock."

"What? What rock?' Shiloh asked.

"Shut up!" Becky turned to the goons. "You guys are going to arrange it all. Then I'm taking my money and John and I are leaving."

Ricky raised his hands. "Okay Becky. We can make that happen."

Becky waved the gun. "Where are the dogs?"

Ricky exchanged a glance with the goons and slowly stepped closer to Becky while lowering his hands. The goons followed. "The pups have been coming along real nice. We will set all that up for you." Ricky pointed at the gun. "Why don't you put that gun away? She can't get away from these guys now." Ricky nodded to the goons. One of them grabbed Shiloh by the arm. The other walked to a position between Shiloh and Becky. "There now, you see, she's not going anywhere."

"I guess you're right," Becky said as she lowered the gun.

Goon two punched Becky in the side of her head with a closed fist just hard enough to knock her down but not out. He wrenched the gun from her hand and stood back. Becky was on the ground holding her face. She looked up and screamed, "What the fuck was that for?" She kicked at the goon. "You prick! Give me back my gun!" She struggled to stand up.

Shiloh noticed the smell of marijuana and sweat as Ricky pulled her by the arm a couple steps away from the goons. He whispered in her ear, "Don't move. Just do as I say." Then he said to Becky, "You dumb bitch. There is no dog fighting going on here."

"What? Bullshit! You told me all about it. You took the pups to train them."

"Yes, I took the pups. I got them all placed in good homes. I gave that cute little greyhound to one of the campers."

Becky waved her arm toward the tents. "What the fuck is this all about then?"

Ricky pointed at the closest tent. "Go see for yourself."

Becky stood up and walked to the tent, opened the flap and peered inside. Two mattresses lay on the floor of the tent. On each mattress sat a teenage girl, each with a plain blue-green blanket wrapped tightly around them. Both wore a handcuff on one wrist which was chained to stakes in the ground. They cowered on the mattresses with blank stares as if all hope had been stolen from them. Becky looked at their bare feet for a few seconds, processing what she was seeing. There were bruised needle marks in their arms and they had dark circles under their eyes. She turned to Ricky. "What is this? Why do you have these girls chained up like that?"

"Well Becky, we take care of these girls for Eddy. The guys bring them here until Delmar has a chance to auction them online. We specialize in selling virgins on the dark web. Sometimes the customer comes and samples them here. Sometimes the customer wants them delivered. We try to accommodate their desires. We ship all over the world if the price is right. It's a lucrative business. Eddy only sells virgins. The guys catch them, bring them here. We photograph them in various poses, send the pictures to Delmar and he auctions them and collects the money online. It's all pretty slick, if we can catch enough virgins."

In a rare moment of compassion, Becky said, "These two can't be more than fourteen or fifteen years old."

"Tell me about it. It's getting harder and harder to find a virgin. We keep having to catch them younger and younger. But the younger ones are easier to catch because they post everything they do on social media. Makes it easier to locate them."

"So what are we going to do now?" Becky pointed at Hazard. "I will pay you to kill her dog, then her."

"Becky you don't realize what you've done. You brought us Eddy's number one catch." Ricky smiled while nodding at Shiloh.

"What do you mean?" Shiloh blurted. Her heart was pounding and her stomach was churning, threatening to get sick at any moment.

Ricky spoke directly to Shiloh. "Eddy saw you at Maxine and Delmar's wedding. Delmar asked Maxine if you were still a virgin. Maxine told him you two had a talk about that very subject right there in the dressing room. She vouched for you being a virgin. Delmar auctioned you off online from the wedding photos. The customer only has to pay if you are certified pure. It's my job to make sure all the girls they catch are certified."

Shiloh noticed that the goons were slowly positioning themselves on either side of Becky while Ricky talked. "We have been trying to catch you for months but you don't come off that ranch by yourself very often. We sent a guy to the festival to try and commission you to paint a buck for him. He tried to lure you out to talk about the commission but you were too busy, said you couldn't do it until after the hunting season."

"I remember that guy. He works for you?"

"Yeah. Sorry honey, no commission. After that, Eddy said the customer was getting impatient so he sent a guy in from Chicago to hunt with you. The guy didn't know jack about hunting and he couldn't figure out how to get you out of there. Until finally one day you went to town all by yourself. Calvin called one of Eddy's bouncers to grab you off the street. But you shot the dumbass in the gut. Now he's in a hospital in a coma. But it doesn't matter if he comes out of it because he knows not to talk."

Becky started laughing. "Oh this is too good to be true. It's even better than what I had in mind. I wanted her to suffer before she died by watching her dog get torn to pieces in a dog fight. But now she is going to suffer as a sex slave. This is priceless. Where is she being sent?"

"Somewhere overseas. I don't know exactly. Somebody else handles that end of things. But she won't be going home ever again." He nodded at the goons. "Now boys I'm going to take Shiloh into this other tent and make sure she is a virgin. You two can have Becky."

"What?" Becky screamed as the goons lunged at her. One of them pulled her arms behind her back. She kicked at the second goon and he punched her in the stomach. They dragged her toward the third tent and threw her on a mattress on the ground just outside the tent. Becky screamed again as the goons began tearing at her clothes.

Ricky laughed. "No one can hear you scream Becky. This box canyon is too far from the rest of the campground."

Shiloh tried to run but Ricky had her by the hair on the back of her head and made her watch as Becky tried to fight off the goons.

Becky shouted at Ricky and the goons, "Eddy is going to have your ass for this. You won't get away with this!"

Ricky laughed again. "Becky, you have been wagging your tail in our faces for months now. Me and the guys have been talking and planning. We will just have to tell Eddy you got in your SUV and disappeared with all that money. Ran off with that dickhead you been seeing in town. We can send you along with Shiloh when the pick-up guy comes. We'll use your SUV and some of your money to bribe him to keep quiet about you. Me and the guys will split up all your backpacks full of money and no one will be the wiser. You'll never be seen or heard from again." He turned and shoved Shiloh into the tent.

Ricky did not know that dogs can hear four times better than humans, especially the higher pitched sounds. Queenie heard Becky scream and began lunging at the end of her chain. When Becky screamed the second time Queenie turned around and pulled against the chain, letting the collar slip backwards off her head. Then she took off running for the box canyon in the direction of Becky's screams.

Shiloh backed away from Ricky. "You sicko. How can you do this? How can you have compassion for dogs, find them good homes, but chain up young girls and sell them for sex? And Becky is no saint but this is all wrong."

He stepped closer to Shiloh and held his hands up, "What

can I say? Dogs love you no matter what you do. Girls call you sicko and tell you to fuck off." Ricky shoved Shiloh, tripping her onto the mattress. She fell to her knees then turned to face toward Ricky. "Now we can make this easy or we can make this hard. I just need to conduct the examination to make sure you are a virgin. If you are, we can get on with the sale. If not, we will call Eddy and tell him a big made up tale about how you didn't cooperate. Either way, you are gonna disappear."

"You maniac, you cannot tell if a woman is a virgin by conducting an examination." Shiloh's mind was racing, trying to figure a way out of the danger.

"Well maybe so, but those two idiots out there don't know that. I examine all the girls. They think I'm some kind of a gynecologist when I tell them I am checking to see if the hymen is still intact. Of course this time I'm willing to settle for just a blow job. If you do a good job I will tell the guys you are a virgin and they should leave you alone. But if not, I will tell them they can have their way with you. It's our little pact. Eddy just thinks he runs things here, but me and the boys have a few things going on the side. What Eddy and the customers don't know won't hurt them."

"Those young girls, they will tell somebody."

"Nobody believes what the girls say. Most of them don't talk much. We have ways of making sure of that. So stay on your knees and do your very best and I won't let the boys get at you. We only have a couple hours before you are scheduled for transport. You can spend that time relaxing here in the tent after we are done, or you can spend that time entertaining the boys. It's all up to you."

Ricky started to unbuckle his belt. Shiloh forgot about her own safety, consumed with a sudden desire to protect the two innocent girls. Adrenaline raced through her veins. In an instant her fear turned to anger. When Ricky moved his hands out of the way to expose himself Shiloh punched him in the balls with all her might. He doubled over and she quickly stood up. Before he could rise up straight again, she kicked him in the throat as hard as she could.

Ricky fell wheezing to the mattress. The pain from his crushed windpipe was paralyzing. He writhed on the floor making gurgling groans and wheezing noises. He was so used to dealing with scared little girls he hadn't expected a fight.

Shiloh could hear Becky screaming and the goons laughing. They weren't paying attention to what was going on inside the tent. She crawled under the back wall of the tent and ran, not knowing she would be trapped at the end of the box canyon in a matter of moments.

Queenie ran at full speed across the grassy opening and hurled herself at the goon on top of Becky. Queenie bit down hard on his forearm and started growling, shaking her head and body with all her might. The goon began screaming. The only thing that kept his arm from being destroyed by her mighty jaws was the sleeve of his denim jacket. He couldn't escape from her grip.

The other goon, who had been holding Becky's arms, stood up and grabbed the gun from the back of his pants. He lowered himself to get an angle on the dog and not shoot the man. He pulled the trigger at point blank range, sending a bullet into Queenie's brain, killing her instantly.

Becky clawed at the goon, screaming, "You shot my dog,

you asshole!" She tried to get the gun away from him. "You have no idea who you are dealing with you fucking piece of shit."

Without thinking of the consequences the goon shot her in the chest. She instantly fell to the ground, and died next to her dog.

Shiloh flinched when she heard the gunshot. She looked desperately at the walls of the canyon trying to find a way up. When she heard the second shot she crouched in the bushes to hide. Anger subsided and fear returned. She trembled uncontrollably.

Dixie danced around her new owner. She ran five circles around her before the food bowl was completely filled. The owner laughed and said, "No wonder you eat so much food, you run it off in a matter of minutes."

The owner heard a shot. She stopped and listened. Moments later a second shot sounded. "That's weird. Who would be shooting in the back of the campground? They don't even allow guns on site. You don't suppose we have some poaching going on back there do you?" Dixie tipped her head and listened a moment. When no other words were spoken she began eating her food.

Off-duty Kentucky Game Warden Parker went into her camper and retrieved her service revolver and duty belt. She grabbed her cell phone and told the puppy to stay. "I know it's my first weekend off in months but it could be poachers. Could be kids. I'm just going to take a walk back there. You stay here girl."

Dixie didn't follow orders; instead she followed her new owner at a distance until she disappeared behind a multi-flora rose bush. Then Dixie became preoccupied with Queenie's food bowl.

Officer Parker walked briskly to the back section of the campground. She twisted her waist length, straight blonde hair into a quick bun and shoved it under her ball cap. Naturally athletic, she seldom missed her daily exercise routine because her job often required rigorous back country excursions. At five foot, ten inches, she had no trouble presenting a confident, intimidating air when the situation required. She was no stranger to the woods and waters and silently wished she had sprayed for mosquitos and ticks in case she had to get into the brush.

The goon who had been attacked by Queenie stood up and ripped off his coat. The sleeve was shredded. His arm was bruising badly, changing color by the second but the skin was not broken. The goons looked at Becky's body. They called to Ricky but he didn't answer. They looked in the tent and found him on the mattress. Ricky couldn't speak. He pointed at the wall of the tent. The goons understood and went after Shiloh. It only took them two minutes to find her hidden in the brush. They dragged her out, took her back to the tent and threw her inside.

Ricky was able to utter a raspy whisper. "I checked her out. She's ain't no virgin. You guys can have her." The goons grinned at each other and shoved Shiloh to the mattress. She screamed and tried to fight them off. Ricky enjoyed watching as she kicked and screamed while they held her down and tried to remove her clothes.

None of them noticed Officer Parker until she burst into the tent and yelled, "Hold it right there, nobody move! Get your hands up!"

One of the goons pulled the gun from his pants.

Shiloh screamed, "Gun!" She kicked him in the knee.

The officer reacted and shot him in the chest. The goon fell in a crumpled heap, dead before he hit the ground. Ricky and the other goon put their hands up. Shiloh grabbed the gun and pointed it at Ricky.

"Easy now," said the officer to Shiloh. The officer cautiously walked Ricky and the goon out of the tent at gunpoint. Shiloh followed. When the officer had the goon and Ricky handcuffed and on their stomachs, Shiloh relaxed and started crying.

"It's okay, you're safe now. I'm Officer Parker with the Kentucky Department of Fish and Wildlife. I'm the new Game Warden for this area. I was camped out in the main area and heard the shots so I decided to investigate. Are you hurt?"

"No, just some cuts and bruises." Shiloh tugged her disheveled clothes back into place.

The officer reached for the gun in Shiloh's hand. "Give me the gun," she said gently.

"It's my gun," Shiloh said, looking at it to be sure.

"Right now it's evidence in a crime. I will see that you get it back." She took the gun from Shiloh and unlocked the handcuffs on her wrists. "Here, take this key and go unchain those two girls in the other tent."

Shiloh dried her tears and stepped back into the tent for a blanket. She covered Becky's body then went to free the girls. She held them both in her arms. They emerged from the tent holding onto each other.

Officer Parker said to Shiloh, "I don't have a cell signal back here in this canyon. Can you walk back out to the main campground and call the police? Here take my cell."

Shiloh's hands were shaking but she pocketed the cell phone and went to Hazard. She removed the muzzle, took Hazard off the leash and hugged him. "Come on boy, let's go get help."

The teenage girls followed zombielike as Shiloh walked down the trail to the main campground area. She wanted to run but the girls were barefoot and had trouble walking. Shiloh kept going until she acquired a signal and called the police.

Dixie came running up to Hazard and raced around him before jumping into Shiloh's arms. Shiloh laughed and hugged the excited puppy. "Dixie! How in the heck did you end up here?" Then she looked at the girls and asked, "Actually how in the heck did any of us end up here?" She wasn't looking for an answer, right now.

The teenage girls struggled to keep the blankets wrapped around themselves as they hugged Dixie who trembled in delight. Moments later sirens could be heard in the distance.

Two state police cars and a Cedarwood police car pulled into the campground with sirens blaring.

Dixie squirmed out of the girl's arms and took off running away from all the noise and chaos.

A sheriff's car arrived. Shiloh told them all, six officers in total, what had happened and pointed them toward the trail. The sheriff and his deputy, and two of the state policemen, ran down the trail to assist Officer Parker. The Cedarwood police officer put the two young girls in the back of his patrol car. He talked to Shiloh about what happened until he saw the other officers bringing the goon and Ricky to the campsite. He put Shiloh in the front of his car so she would feel safer.

They shoved the goon into the state police car and the Sheriff took Ricky. Shiloh didn't know exactly where they were going, but she was relieved they were both in custody and she and the young girls were safe. She lost track of time as they asked her more questions. The coroner arrived, followed by someone that Shiloh thought might be a reporter.

The Cedarwood police officer took the girls to child protective services.

Officer Parker took Shiloh and Hazard home.

Klu was waiting when she arrived at the farm house. Shiloh thanked Officer Parker and said goodbye then ran into Klu's arms. Hazard jumped out of the truck to follow Shiloh. Dorothy and Jete had followed Klu outside and Shiloh hugged them too. Shiloh asked Jete to look after Hazard's knife wound. "Becky stabbed him with a pocket knife. I don't think it's too bad but would you take a look at it and see if he needs stitches?"

"Sure thing. Don't you worry about Hazard I will take care of him. You just get inside and rest now." Jete treated Hazard's wound in the kitchen and put a couple stitches in it. Hazard held still after the shock of the first prick of the needle. He seemed to know the treatment was for his own good.

Shiloh went upstairs to take a shower and change clothes.

She cried in the shower for several minutes, not wanting everyone to think she was weak. She asked God to strengthen her. When she came downstairs she told them all about what she had endured. "I'm lucky to be alive. Becky didn't deserve to die. She was filled with jealousy and hate, but she didn't deserve what she got."

"Well, I might have to disagree with you on that," Jete said.

Klu added, "Becky was always full of lies."

"The devil targets your heart and lies are his weapons," Dorothy said.

Jete changed the subject. "Was that Officer Parker who brought you home? None of us even said a word to her. I guess that was kind of rude."

"She said she would come back at another time to fill us in on the investigation," Shiloh said with a yawn. "I'm kind of tired. I guess the adrenaline is wearing off. But I don't think I could actually go to sleep yet." She didn't really want to be by herself.

Dorothy got a blanket and pillow from Shiloh's bed and came back into the living room. "Here, just rest on the couch."

Shiloh snuggled under the blanket in Klu's arms. His warmth and the familiar softness of the blanket helped her relax. She began to feel safe again.

He whispered in her ear, "I can't believe I almost lost you," and held her close.

She kissed him and said, "The whole thing seems surreal. One minute you are surrounded by goodness expecting to live well into your old age; the next minute you are suddenly faced with so much evil that it threatens your life. It's a hard thing to come face to face with your own mortality. It's quite an eye opener."

"I know the Lord says we are supposed to forgive those who sin against us as he forgave us our sins." He paused a few moments then said, "I think I'm going to need some time to fully embrace that concept."

"I have to agree with you, that is a tough one. After all, the woman stabbed my dog!" Moments later she drifted off to sleep.

TWENTY-NINE

A few days later Shiloh looked out the kitchen window of the ranch house and saw a Kentucky Department of Fish and Wildlife truck pull into the driveway. She went to the front door to greet Officer Parker and gave her a hug. "It's good to see you again, especially under better circumstances. And congratulations on your Meritorious Service Award. You deserve it. If you hadn't come all the way into that back section of the campground to check things out I shudder to think what might have happened."

"Thanks Shiloh. I'm sorry we had to meet under such difficult circumstances. How is Hazard?"

"Oh he's good. He just needed a few stitches for the knife wound. Jete patched him up right there in the kitchen. He's ex-military. He knows a lot about battlefield first aid."

"And how are you? You've been through a pretty traumatic event."

Shiloh stepped out onto the front porch and closed the door behind her. She motioned to the chairs and they sat down. "I'm doing okay. I've prayed about it a lot. At first I

343

felt bewildered, and scared, then angry. I feel like the best way for me to cope is to get back to work. My family is very supportive. They understand how spending time in the woods is the best medicine for me. After the season I'm going to do some trapping and go hunting myself. Being twenty feet up in a tree is where I need to be for a while."

"I can relate to that. Treestand therapy restores the soul."

"To tell you the truth, you inspire me. I find strength in your example. You must face dangerous situations and threats to your life more often than people know but you go back to work every day. How do you deal with the danger?"

"For me, it was a calling. A sense that I should serve the greater good. Our world needs guardians to protect the innocent, both human and animal. The stress can be overwhelming if you let it. A strong spiritual life is important, lots of exercise helps, I'm sort of a health nut. And being an adrenaline junkie helps."

"What makes some people turn into victims and others turn into warriors?"

"That's a deep question, for which I have no good answer. Let me tell you a story. When I was little, maybe in fourth grade, I was standing on the playground after school talking to a girlfriend. A boy I did not know walked up to me and punched me right in the face, knocking me down for no reason that I know. I was so shocked. Nothing like that had ever happened to me before. I got up and ran home. I sat on the couch pouting over what had happened to me, wondering why it happened. After two or three minutes of feeling sorry for myself I started to get mad. I got off the couch, opened the door and marched right back up to the school. The boy was still there, talking to my girlfriend. I started running at him. When he spotted me he took off running away. I chased him all across the playground until he disappeared into the woods. I couldn't catch him, he had too much of a head start. But from that day forward, I vowed no bully would ever have power over me again, mentally or physically. I guess I have been chasing bad guys ever since."

"It's pretty amazing how God can make something good happen from a bad situation. I feel like I just made a new best friend."

"I feel the same way. Every test in our lives can change us. It can make us better or bitter. It can make us or break us. It's up to us to choose how we respond. We can choose to be a victim or a victor."

"That's the truth. Come inside, I want you to meet my family."

"I know it's Thanksgiving Day so I won't take too much of your time, I just came by to give you an update and ask a favor."

"Please come in." Shiloh held the door open for Officer Parker. The Lawson and Dugan families were gathered together so Shiloh walked Officer Parker through the house and introduced her to everyone.

Klu extended his hand to Officer Parker and thanked her for saving Shiloh. "She means the world to us. I don't know what we would have done if, well, just thank you." Klu hugged Shiloh and gave her a kiss.

"We also have two hunters in camp," Shiloh whispered to Officer Parker. "A husband and wife. Apparently they like to go on a hunt somewhere every year during the Thanksgiving holiday. They let the ex-wife have this day with all the kids and grandkids. I guess it's easier that way. They hunted this morning. My uncle Jete went to pick them up. They should be back any minute. Why don't you join us for lunch? Mom and Charlene have fixed enough food to feed a small army."

"Thank you, that's very kind but I don't want to intrude. And I'm on duty today."

"Are you kidding me? If it weren't for you this would be a very different day. You can make it official business by checking the permits of the two hunters we have in camp. Besides, you're allowed to take a lunch break right?"

"Alright, I accept. Is there somewhere we can talk first?"

"Sure, in my office." Shiloh led Officer Parker to the office. Klu joined them and closed the door. "So, I guess you have some news about the case?" Shiloh asked, suddenly nervous. She sat down behind the desk surprised by the sudden weakness in her knees.

"Yes, I wanted to let you know they don't know for certain if Maxine knew anything about Delmar and Eddy's illicit business dealings. There doesn't seem to be any evidence that shows Maxine was part of it or had any knowledge of it. She's insisting she didn't know about it. I understand you two were good friends so I thought you would want to know that."

"I have been wondering about that. I'm sure she is pretty upset. I wonder what she is going to do with a kid, and another one on the way, and her husband going to prison. I guess she's a victim too."

"Yes, that's true. Delmar, Eddy, Ivan and the others involved in this case will be facing long prison sentences

346

thanks to the evidence we have gathered and your testimony. Ricky is cooperating with the police. He's given us a lot of valuable information. One thing Ricky did not know is that Eddy had a silent partner in the tavern and the sex trafficking. Some guy named Mote Woodsen. It seems he likes young girls and not in a good way. He is Becky's great uncle. She lived with him when she was a teenager. Ricky is terrified of Mote Woodsen so he is singing in exchange for protection.

"Oh my. I can only imagine what it might have been like for her," Shiloh sighed.

Klu added, "That sort of explains some of why she was the way she was. Having an older male role model like that in her life certainly influenced her ability to relate to men. And not in a good way."

"That's most likely true," Officer Parker agreed. "She drove a cargo van for Eddy and her great uncle. Whenever they needed to move money or drugs she ran part of the route. They had a string of businesses used to hide money; some carwashes, an arcade in the mall in Findlay, the campground, so they are also facing money laundering charges. The police discovered bags of money hidden in campers at the campground."

"Wow, sounds like a huge investigation," Klu said.

"It is. Several agencies are involved. Just this morning they apprehended the man you know as Chris from New York. His name is John Smith. He will be charged with attempted murder among other things. He goes by several aliases and was wanted for a number of crimes. He'll be going to prison for a long time too."

"That's wonderful news. We have a lot to be thankful for.

What about that hunter from Chicago? Calvin. He took off without a word. Ricky said they sent him into our camp to try to kidnap me. Apparently he called the bouncer who tried to grab me, the one I shot."

"You'll be glad to know that Mote Woodsen and Calvin have been apprehended. Apparently some obscure relative claimed Becky's body and had it sent to Chicago. The FBI nabbed them both at Becky's funeral."

"And what about the guy who supposedly bought me through the online sex trafficking auction?"

"That's a long shot I'm afraid. Way out of my jurisdiction. Maybe one for the CIA to investigate."

"Makes me sick to think about it."

"Hopefully he will get what's coming to him in the end," Klu said.

"I suppose it is no coincidence that my daily devotional text this morning was from Deuteronomy. I don't remember the exact verse but it was something like, in due time their foot will slip; their day of disaster is near and their doom rushes upon them."

"God did say vengeance is mine," Klu said.

Dorothy knocked on the door of the office and came in. "Sorry to interrupt, but Shiloh, there is a coyote out by the barn. It chased Ruby and three kittens up a tree. It's still out there. It's that black one with the yellow eyes you have been seeing."

Shiloh bolted from behind the desk then stopped and turned to Officer Parker. "Can you excuse me for just a minute? I have an old score to settle."

"Of course, go right ahead."

"Mom, where is Hazard?"

"Asleep in the great room on the floor where the sun shines in."

"Okay good. Klu will you grab Hazard? He's going to go nuts when he sees me get the gun."

"Sure thing. Good luck." Klu walked into the great room and started petting Hazard and held tightly to his collar. He nodded at Shiloh.

Shiloh opened the gun safe, pulled her rifle out, loaded it quickly, went out the front door and slipped around the west side of the house. She stayed close to the house, snuck up to the northwest corner and peered around to the barn. She saw the coyote jump up twice trying to snag a kitten from the lowest limb. Shiloh eased the gun up and used the corner of the house to steady the gun for a shot. She pulled the hammer back and quickly settled the scope crosshairs on the coyote's shoulder. When it stopped circling the tree and sat down she gently squeezed the trigger. The bullet pierced the coyote's right shoulder and both lungs. It jumped and spun in a circle, snarled and bit at the entry wound then fell dead at the base of the tree. She could hear Hazard barking inside the house.

Klu and the others had watched the coyote from the back window. They heard the gun and saw the impact. Klu let go of Hazard and headed for the back door. Everyone joined Shiloh at the tree where she was trying to coax a kitten down. The kitten wasn't cooperating.

"Nice shot, Shiloh," Klu said, watching Hazard tug on the dead coyote. "He's a beautiful coyote. Are you going to get him mounted?"

"I think I will. You don't see many all black coyotes and

this one has been showing up all fall. I'm going to put it in the walk-in cooler and we can take it to the taxidermy shop tomorrow."

"I'll carry it in for you," Klu said.

"Okay, thanks. I'll see if the kittens will come down out of the tree now. Hey Officer Parker, would you like a kitten? Well, I guess they are not really kittens anymore they are about six months old. They are good mousers. Dixie used to chase them and run around them in circles when they were little so it seems she inadvertently taught them how to evade coyotes."

"No. Thanks. No cats for me. Actually Dixie is the other subject I wanted to talk to you about. I need to ask you a favor."

"Name it."

"The father of one of the young girls we rescued made a rather large donation to the department. As a result I'm getting a service dog. It's a German Shepherd named Max. He will be finished with his training in a few days and be coming to live and work with me. I'm staying in my camper at the campground until I figure out where I am going to live. They have assigned me a pretty big area. Anyway, it's about the little greyhound, Dixie. I cannot keep her. I just can't have a second dog with Max coming. So I wondered if you could take her back. She really belongs with you folks."

"Well of course, we will take her. It creeps me out to think Becky may have been stalking us and snatched Dixie off the road. That's the only explanation I can think of for how she ended up at the campground."

"Ricky is the one who brought her to me. He just walked

up to my camp and asked me if I wanted her. She didn't have a collar but he called her Dixie. He told me somebody dumped her."

"Hmm, that's weird because she did have a collar with dog tags and her name on it."

"If Becky was the person who took Dixie one of them must have removed the identification. I know he had no idea I was a game warden or he wouldn't have given her to me."

"Didn't he see your department truck at the campground?"

"I still had my personal truck at the campground. The former game warden hit a deer on his last day so it was in the shop getting fixed. I just picked it up the other day."

"I guess that all makes sense then."

"Making arrangements for Dixie was one of the main things I wanted to talk to you about. She's in a dog box in the back of my truck. Is it alright to let her out to run around?"

"Absolutely. Let's go do that now."

They walked to the back of the Department truck and let Dixie out of the kennel. She leaped off the tailgate and went racing around the yard, found Hazard and ran circles around him.

Shiloh waved to Mulch as he drove up in his old Chevy step-side truck. He waved back and parked the truck.

"Glad you could join us Mulch, Happy Thanksgiving. I would like you to meet Officer Parker. This is Pete Moss, but everyone calls him Mulch."

Mulch tipped his hat and said, "A pleasure. I hear you are the new game warden. I expect I will be seeing you at the shop before too long."

"Yes sir. I'll be making the rounds after the holiday. Nice

to meet you."

Shiloh pointed and said, "Here comes Jete and the two hunters."

"Here comes a big ball of ugly," Mulch said and winked at Officer Parker.

Jete pulled his truck up next to Mulch's and got out. "Hello you old troglodyte. I see you showed up just in time for a free meal."

"I can't believe you greet me with such an insultment. You invited me to dinner."

"I did? Now why would I do that?"

"Well, if your memory was any worse you could plan your own surprise party. You invited me several days ago."

"Don't pooch up like an old toad. I remember."

"Don't pay any attention to them. They bicker like this all the time, I call them the Bicker Brothers," Shiloh said to Officer Parker.

"They seem to have a good time," she responded.

"Uncle Jete I want you to meet Officer Parker."

Jete removed his hat. "Nice to meet you. I've heard a lot about you. We are very grateful for what you did for Shiloh." They shook hands. Shiloh noticed they seemed to hold the grasp longer than necessary. "Are you staying for lunch? It's Thanksgiving you know?"

"I am indeed staying for lunch. Please call me Clara."

"Well, thank you Clara. Let's go inside and see if we can find you a place to sit, right next to me of course." He put his hat back on his head and motioned for them to walk to the door. Jete winked at Shiloh as he held the door open for them.

"Did your hunters see anything?" Shiloh asked.

"What hunters?" Jete grinned. "Oh yes, them. They saw a nice buck. They can't wait to eat lunch and get back out there."

Dorothy called everyone to the table. She asked Jete to say the blessing and then cut the turkey. Throughout the meal Shiloh kept noticing that Jete was enjoying Clara's company and vice versa. Shiloh nudged Klu and slyly pointed at Jete. She leaned over and whispered in his ear, "I think Jete is quite taken with our new game warden."

"I've noticed. I think the feeling is mutual."

After lunch Clara received a call about suspected poaching on the other side of the county. She thanked everyone for the hospitality and said her goodbyes. Jete walked her to her truck. Shiloh and Klu watched secretly from the window and giggled like school children.

When Clara drove away Jete walked back in the house and noticed the two staring at him. "What?" he said with a wide grin. "It's a good idea to be friendly with the local law enforcement. And we are going out to dinner on her first day off thank you very much." He laughed when their mouths dropped open. "Can't talk now, I have hunters to take out."

Shiloh asked Klu, "Did I just hear him right?"

"You sure did. That's pretty cool. I'm happy for him."

"Speaking of happiness, I was wondering what you thought of us giving Dixie to your mom? I talked to my mom about it when we were putting things away after lunch. She thought it was a great idea. If Hazard could talk he would agree. I think all the running and racing around in circles drives him nuts. Your mom's little dachshund got taken by that owl and she doesn't have a dog now. So what do you think?"

"I think she would love that little dog. It's a great idea."

"Oh good. Let's go get Mom and Charlene and tell her now."

"I will go grab Dixie. You bring our moms out back and we will do it there okay?"

Charlene protested leaving some of the dishes undone but Dorothy knew what was taking place. "Let's just go outside for a few minutes. The kids want to show us something. Those dishes aren't going anywhere."

Shiloh went through the door first and stood next to Klu, who was holding a wriggling Dixie against his chest. Dorothy stood next to Shiloh. They all looked at Charlene.

"What?" Charlene asked. "Why are you three staring at me like that?"

Shiloh said, "Charlene we all talked it over and we want Dixie to go home with you and be your dog from now on." Everyone smiled and shook their heads in unison. Dixie stopped wriggling and looked at Charlene as if she knew what had just been said and was also waiting for an answer.

Charlene started to cry and laugh at the same time. She sat down on the steps and held out her arms. Klu placed Dixie in her lap. Dixie licked her face and snuggled quietly while Charlene hugged and petted her. "This is a wonderful gift, thank you. I really missed not having a dog but just couldn't bring myself to get another one. I will love this puppy and I love all of you for giving her to me."

Later that evening Klu and Shiloh snuggled together on the couch while their families and the two hunters were watching football in the great room.

Klu whispered to Shiloh, "This has been a pretty amazing day. It wasn't so long ago that lies and misconceptions kept our families at odds with each other and now look at us, all together on Thanksgiving Day."

"I think Jete experienced love at first sight when he met Officer Parker today. Do you suppose it is possible for someone to actually know the very moment they fall in love with someone?"

"Yes. I know I've been in love with you since that day at the festival when we were little kids. I've loved you ever since. Maybe I was too young to know it then, but I know it now. I love you Shiloh Lawson. I really do."

Shiloh snuggled closer and whispered, "I love you too."

Klu hugged her and smiled, then whispered in her ear, "*Hunter's Honor*? You know if you tell a lie when challenged with *Hunter's Honor* you will never kill a big buck as long as you live. It's a more powerful vow than saying I cross my heart."

Shiloh giggled and kissed him. "I do love you too. *Hunter's Honor.*"

ABOUT THE AUTHOR

BRENDA POTTS is a lifelong hunter, artist, author, outdoor writer and marketing consultant. She is a member of the Association of Great Lakes Outdoor Writers. Her work has been published in several magazines.

She has a Bachelor of Science degree in Biology from Millikin University.

Brenda served as Executive Director of the IL Federation for Outdoor Resources and was co-founder and Executive Director of the Kids Gone Hunting Foundation. She was appointed to a six year term on the IL Natural Resources Advisory Board by Governor Jim Edgar and served as Constituency Liaison for the IL Department of Natural Resources for seven years.

Brenda has written several other books in addition to creating coloring books with outdoor themes.

She owns Midwest Legacy Marketing and works on production of outdoor television shows with her husband, Stan Potts.

www.BooksByPotts.com

www.ingramcontent.com/pod-product-compliance
Lightning Source LLC
Chambersburg PA
CBHW030553180626
46816CB00005B/1523

9 7 8 0 9 9 9 1 0 0 3 2 5